Annie Clark Cole

GHOST OF
PANTHER HOLLER

A Sequel to Legend of Panther Holler

GHOST OF PANTHER HOLLER

"*Ghost of Panther Holler*" is a novel based purely on fictional characters and story. No actual person or event is portrayed in this book.

Printed by CreateSpace

Cover Design by Sanjay N. Patel
www.sanjaynpatel.com
Cover Model — Rope Spinks

Interior Design by CreateSpace

A Dream on Production Publication
Annieclarkcole.com

ISBN: 1514238608

Printed in the United States of America
ISBN 13: 9781514238608
Library of Congress Control Number: 2015909114
CreateSpace Independent Publishing Platform
North Charleston, South Carolina

ACCLAIM

Annie Clark Cole does it again! Just when I thought she couldn't top "Legend of Panther Holler", she comes out with "Ghost of Panther Holler" and blows me away! Want to read an amazing western? Well, just continue turning the pages. This book is yet another brilliant writing partly in her folksy dialect captured from the 1800's. She is an amazingly beautiful, warmhearted person I am proud to call my friend! Annie Clark Cole, you're the best!

Tino Luciano
Executive Producer/Director
Law Dog Productions, LLC

I have worked with writer Annie Clark Cole on a few feature film projects. One day she mentioned she would like me to create art for her upcoming book Legend of Panther Holler. Since then, I have created another book cover for her called Ghost of Panther Holler, which is the sequel to Legend of Panther Holler.

When I finally presented the image, I smiled. The picture I had imagined was now a reality. I will always be thankful for the opportunity Annie gave me to create these two book covers for her stories, Legend of Panther Holler and Ghost of Panther Holler that are so close to her heart.

Sanjay N. Patel.
Photographer

Acknowledgements

Special Thanks To:

James Carpenter—Editor

Bea Rouse, Lori Mixson, Kathleen Rottweiler, John Castellanos and Ralph Holliday. Your experience and encouragement was greatly appreciated.

Ghost of
Panther Holler

A masterful tale of the old west

To Sam & Becky

Great friends!

Annie Clark Cole

Dedication

To my loving husband Jim Cole who has provided encouragement to me and made it possible to have time to write. His ideas, suggestions, sacrifice, and love have been paramount in this process. For this I am grateful.

Foreword

The melodies of the wind are the ghosts of our ancestor's singing lullabies to comfort the living. In time the unspoken creed will be understood and those of the original people will know how mighty and great they are.

Ghost of
Panther Holler

ANNIE CLARK COLE

Chapter 1

THERE COMES A TIME TO LOVE AND A TIME TO HATE, THEN THERE COMES **a time to die— and Buck Dupree met his death on a hot summer day in Panther Holler.** It wasn't by the hand of Vick Porter or by his son Cain that he died, but rather, in the jaws of a hungry panther, a vengeful predator that ravaged Buck's body as he screamed in horror.

Vick felt vindication for the first time since he was a young man, especially since the world had cleansed itself of a man who had killed more than his share, then cowardly accused Vick of his crimes. These accusations cost Vick half his lifetime locked away in the New Orleans Prison. Finally, Buck was dead and Vick's nightmare of terror was over—or so it seemed.

That fateful day, the men left the luscious green landscape of Panther Holler that lay tucked away in the backwoods of Arkansas, travelling through miles of rugged terrain, while Vick's life hung by a thread. Cain knew his Pa was dying when he heard him rambling incoherently. Struggling to hold on, Vick kept asking, "Do you hear the drums?"

Orson recognized the signs of death too, and knew if things didn't change, and quickly, his friend would not be long for this world. As they rode Vick became consumed with the hypnotic melody of drums while seeing visions of Indians dancing around a fire.

"We need to stop right now," Vick pleaded. "Pa, just a little further. We have to make camp before nightfall. Water was essential for Vick's care, and they still had a way to go before they reached the stream that Johnny James had been pulled from only one day before. Cain marveled at how Vick kept clinging to life. This only proved to him how brave and resilient his Pa really was. Vick was once again at the mercy of a higher power that might intervene and save him.

At that moment, Orson saw the waterfall. Pointing ahead he said, "Look Vick—we're here, and now you can rest." The trickling water was soothing to Vick's troubled soul. *Now we can finally stop*, he thought.

While helping Vick from the saddle, Orson had flashbacks of Johnny. *Jest yesterday we pulled his cold clammy body from this very stream. The boy didn't have to die*, Orson thought, remorsefully. Orson was still carrying a tremendous amount of guilt for tricking Johnny, since the kid was young and naïve, yet to reach the age of twenty.

While waiting for the bullet to be retrieved, Vick kept seeing visions as he listened to the sounds of the comforting waterfall.

Orson was examining Vick's wound when; again, he had a momentary flashback of Johnny with his throat cut. For a time, the appalling image of the murder preempted the urgency of Vick's care. *It was Buck Dupree's claiming to be Carl Rhodes that killed Johnny*, Orson reflected. The kid believed the made-up story about a treasure, and became consumed with Carl whom he thought was his friend. Orson and Vick used the story of a hidden treasure to set Johnny up to lure Buck, alias Carl Rhodes, back to the holler. True, there was an old debt to settle for framing Vick, and then killing Cain's pregnant wife and unborn child, but they never meant for Johnny's life to become collateral damage.

Orson felt culpable using the kid like that; *but a man has to do what he has to do for justice*, he kept telling himself.

Seeing Vick lie there in agony caused Orson to snap back to reality.

His wounds needed immediate attention. *I gotta git that bullet out, and fast, if Vick's gonna live*, Orson said to Cain.

Hallucinating, Vick had already lapsed into unconsciousness while once again experiencing his spirit being whisked away. Precipitously, he was standing atop a mountain, beholding Indians chanting around a fire. Somehow, he knew it was a ceremonial dance.

Being caught in the rapture of his vision he looked up, and in the midst of a white cloud, a panther and a beautiful hawk descended. It was the same hawk that had appeared to him at Panther Holler when he thought he had died. The hawk flew down, and in a moment's time, like it had done before, metamorphosed his shimmering feathers into Chaytan; the Indian boy called Hawk, who was Vick's closest childhood friend and protector. Once again Hawk reminded him that he would fulfill his promise of his guardianship. Vick thought the significance of the panther was a reminder that Vick saved Hawk from the predator when they were young boys.

"Hawk, you've come back!" Vick muttered. Again, there was no need for words for Hawk and Vick communed as if sharing the same soul. While they exchanged thoughts silently the panther moved toward Vick. There was something regal about the large cat that was not aggressive and meant no harm.

"Why am I here?" Vick asked. Hawk transmitted his thoughts to Vick, "Now is not the time, but one day soon you will understand." Again, Vick saw the metamorphous of Hawk, as he and the panther disappeared.

While Orson was preparing to recover the bullet from his friend's chest, Vick was being celebrated by a royal host of Indian souls who had died many decades before him.

Shortly afterwards, Vick awoke fully alert and coherent. Upon opening his eyes he was looking directly into the anguished face of Orson. There was no worry on Vick's part. As he lay pondering over what he had seen, he reluctantly accepted the vision as a figment of his imagination precipitated by his injury.

"Don't ya' worry 'bout me using this knife. I've done this before," Orson reassured him just before he slipped the knife into the wound.

As Vick felt the blade make one last thrust to retrieve the bullet, the pain he felt was reserved only for the living. No doubt he was still alive.

He grimaced but never uttered a word. Afterwards, the worst came when Orson placed the glowing hot blade of the knife onto his wound to cauterize it. He passed out from the combination of pain and the overwhelming smell of burning flesh.

Concerned, Cain turned to Orson, "I think Pa stood as much as he could."

"Son, everybody has his limits—let's jest hope yer Pa wakes up. Ya' might need to prepare yerself, 'cause when a man starts talking to the spirits he ain't long fer this world."

"Do you think he's going to die?"

"Only God Almighty knows, but I'll say this about yer Pa—he's a fighter."

The grey night had finally turned into blackness except for the small glowing fire that was intended to keep away wild animals hungry for the taste of blood. Cain kept watch over Vick as he slept. *I hope he makes it through the night*, he prayed.

When Vick awoke early the next morning he smelled the aroma of fresh coffee, and found Cain standing over him.

"Pa, don't try to get up! I'll pour you some coffee."

Vick grimaced, trying to speak. "Maybe half a cup? I need something to get me moving ... Ahhh," Vick groaned as he tried to lift himself onto his elbows.

"Pa, we got time! Stay put until you feel better. No need trying to rush things."

Vick could hardly identify with Cain's fussing over him; however, it felt good hearing his son call him "Pa."

It took a while for Vick to recount the night before, and the strange dreams he had. "All those Indians and drumbeats I saw seemed real, but they can't be." He reasoned it would be best to keep what happened to himself. *It's likely the visions were nothing*

4

more than an overactive imagination caused by the stress, he thought. Vick quickly projected himself back to the present. Morning light had a way of solving the mysteries of a dream.

"Orson, you could have been a little gentler with that knife," Vick mumbled to his old friend.

"Oh, ya' talkin' 'bout my Arkansas toothpick, eh! It's somepin' else, ain't it? Don'tcha go whinin' 'bout me doin' what needed done to save that skin of yer's."

Vick tried to laugh but the pain was too great.

They had decided to give Vick more recovery time but by midday they were surprised by his readiness to make the journey back to Jonesboro. Although they took it slow and easy, he showed remarkable improvement with the resiliency of his body.

"Let's ride," Vick said. Once again Cain saw a trait in his father that he himself did not possess. *How can I ever live up to a man like that?* He imagined.

Vick looked young enough to be his brother. When his Pa flashed that same huckleberry smile Cain had inherited, hearts melted, his included. *He may have been in prison, but it didn't affect his looks*, Cain observed.

It was rough going all that day and up into the night, but in the afternoon of the following day the horses stepped out of the thicket onto the main road to Jonesboro. Cain had the last of the rations resting in a large saddlebag on the back of his horse when they came face to face with Johnny's half brothers, Lonnie and Dudley James. The two men were visibly shaken to see Orson and the Porters appear rather than their brother, Johnny, and the man called Carl Rhodes who they planned to ambush and rob for the treasure. Orson was not aware that Johnny had gotten his two brothers involved, and now the unsavory characters' plan to kill Carl Rhodes had backfired on them. The James boys trusted their brother when he told them that he and Carl would have the treasure when they came back from Panther Holler. Neither had any idea that their brother's sole purpose was to lure "Carl" to Panther Holler for a showdown. All they knew was what Johnny had told them to be waiting to bushwhack Carl for a treasure that Vick Porter had hidden at Panther Holler.

Seeing the Porters instead of Johnny and Carl threw them completely off guard. The confused brothers, having already been seen, now had no place to run.

They were afraid of the Sheriff, and quickly recalled that Orson was no fool, so they waited for him to make the first move.

Orson did not know why these two men were waiting on the main road, but he had an idea. Although a bit uneasy, he rode over to them, and delivered the news about Johnny with their horses standing nose-to-nose.

"Sorry, but we got some bad news fer ya'. We found yer' brother in a stream with his throat cut. There weren't nothin' nobody could do for the boy so we buried 'em the best we could," the Sheriff explained.

Lonnie and Dudley kept chewing their tobacco and just looked at each other without showing much expression, seeming to be pondering over what Orson had just told them.

"Ya' sayin' Johnny's dead?"

"We're sorry 'bout yer brother, but we marked the grave fer ya'. We knew at some time y'all might want to go and pay yer respects. Vick and Cain looked on while Orson filled them in with the details.

"It was that new feller in town who called himself Carl Rhodes that killed yer brother. We suspect Johnny was a friend of his. The man's real name is Buck Dupree. I hate Johnny got mixed up with him 'cause Buck had a list of murders as long as my arm. And jest in case ya' didn't hear, he's the one that killed Cain's new wife and her daddy." At first the men looked at Cain, and then their eyes focused on the bulging saddlebag that was on the back of Cain's horse, imagining it could be the treasure.

"Ya' ain't tryin' to tell us ya' thank Johnny had somepin' to do with that rich man and his daughter's murder, 'cause Johnny wouldn't hurt a flea."

"No, we ain't sayin' nothing of the sort. All I'm sayin' is Buck killed yer brother, Johnny."

The James boys kept eyeing the sack tied down on the back of Cain's horse, still assuming it too, was the treasure.

"Now that we know what happened to our brother, what about that Carl Rhodes? Where is he?"

Vick and Orson looked at each other, but before Vick could give Orson 'the eye,' he told them exactly what happened.

"We were in a showdown with Buck when a panther came out of nowher' and grabbed ol' Buck fer his supper."

Cain looked at his Pa, and cringed at hearing the Sheriff spill his guts of what seemed to be a made-up story. Cain could tell the brothers thought Orson was lying.

Lonnie's mind was running wild seeing the saddlebags on Cain's horse, and then hearing a crazy story about a panther. He was sure Johnny was killed because of what was in the saddlebags. "Yeah, they probably killed both of 'em and kept the loot for themselves." They were now sure the Sheriff and the Porters had the treasure with them, or had left it back at Panther Holler. They didn't know what to think, since Vick had been shot and needed medical attention. Lonnie imagined the bulk of the treasure was 'hid out' somewhere back at Panther Holler or in the saddlebags. *That saddlebag of Cain's can't be all of the treasure*, Lonnie thought.

Vick looked at the tall, skinny, uneducated country boys with their filthy long stringy black hair, and surmised they were two misfits waiting to rob Buck when he rode out of the thicket with Johnny.

Cain remembered how the brothers had been nothing but trouble while working with their Pa in the bootlegging business. When their old man died, Lonnie and Dudley continued on with their illegal business; locking horns with the Sheriff on many occasions.

The James' were young boys when Vick went to prison, and didn't remember him. They first heard of Vick when the Jonesboro paper announced his wedding to Elizabeth Barkin. Soon after the wedding announcement, rumors began circulating about Cain finding Vick in prison. No one in town believed Vick committed all those murders, but the James' didn't know what to believe. They just assumed that any man who had spent all those years in jail had to be guilty and figured that it was money that got Vick out of prison. Like some others who had their doubts of his innocence, the James', too, thought Vick might be capable of killing, especially if there was a treasure involved.

After Lonnie and Dudley left them, the Sheriff pondered their suspicious behavior and questioned their motives. *What would bring them boys out to a place like this if they hadn't been up to no good?*

"Orson, what are you thinking?" asked Cain.

"I spec' them boys knew about the treasure, and were waiting to waylay ol' Buck. Johnny probably told 'em about a treasure, and they planned to ambush Buck and take it for themselves. You saw that look on their faces … they were surprised. I could tell they didn't know a thang' 'bout us showing up when we did. Yep, Johnny spilled the beans, and they went 'n made a little plan of their own. I spec' Buck knew Johnny wouldn't be able to keep his mouth shut, and that's why the boy ended up dead. Why else would them boys be way out here by themselves miles away from home unless they wanted to get the drop on Buck and rob him? Them boys are bad news … ain't nobody I know that's ever trusted 'em."

Vick, who was tired, listened, but the James brothers were the least of his worries. All he wanted was to get home to Elizabeth, and let her take care of his wounds. Buck's death had ended Vick's retribution. *It's finally over, and we can get on with our lives,* he now thought.

It took most of the day for the trio to reach the manor, but when it was finally in Vick's sight with Elizabeth standing out front waiting for him, his heart melted.

Sensing that Vick was hurt, she hurried to his side to see how serious his injuries were. He slid out of the saddle, resting against his horse until he could hold her in his arms. "You're home now," she said. Elizabeth held on tightly as if she never wanted to let him go. Although weak and barely able to stand, he returned her affection with a warm gentle kiss.

"Ohh, Vick, I'm so happy you're home! Are you all right?"

"Now I am," he said, embracing her. Slowly they walked toward the manor.

"I have to take it easy—I'm sore from that cuttin' Orson did on me."

Elizabeth took Orson's hand, and squeezed it, reminding him that he had taken care of Vick like he cared for her some months earlier when he rescued her from a burning house after Spencer tried to kill her.

"Orson, what would we ever do without you?"

He didn't know what to say when people made a fuss over him. "Now Lizzie, cut it out!" Orson smiled, showing the space between his teeth. "Well then, if you don't want me making over you, how about helping me get Vick upstairs to bed?"

"Let Orson be. I don't want that quack doctor close to me," Vick teased.

"Now jest hush yer mouth and let me help ya'. It was my training that saved yer hide," Orson spoke.

When they got Vick to bed, Elizabeth bent over and kissed him. "Thank God you came home to me," she whispered into his ear.

Orson twisted up his nose at hearing the sweet talk, and headed for the door. "I reckon that's my cue to leave. I know you love birds want ta be alone."

Orson placed his hat on his head and opened Vick's bedroom door just in time to see Lucy kissing Cain.

"Can't a man go anywher' without seeing all that kissin' and huggin'?"

Cain walked over and shook hands with Orson, who was soon to be his father-in-law.

"You need to get used to it, 'cause me and Lucy just set a date."

"A date fer what?" Orson acted as if he didn't know what Cain was talking about.

"Oh, excuse me Orson, but I just gave Lucy a ring."

Cain had surprised his fiancé with a distinctive ring: a beautiful Australian Opal that was handed down to Elizabeth from her great-grandmother.

"In case you didn't know, or forgot, I'd like to ask you again for your daughter's hand in marriage." Lucy was amused, seeing how well her daddy and Cain got along. The old Sheriff pondered a bit, then answered very seriously.

"On one condition, Cain Porter. Ya' got to promise me to always take care of my little girl, and treat her special … 'cause she's special to me, too. Understand?"

"I do indeed, sir."

"And another thang', ya' gotta promise me ta supper at least once a week."

"Now Orson, that might be hard to do, knowing how you can scour down the grub." Cain laughed, "Just kidding … you know you'll always have a place at our table."

"Then it's settled," Orson said.

Cain could see the love in Orson's eyes when he spoke of his daughter.

They watched as the old man ambled away, walking toward the railing to untie his horse. Lucy ran to her father and gave him a big hug, and then watched as he spurred his horse to ride away. She wondered how many more years he was going to carry on with that tough exterior of his. Regardless of what Orson thought, she could see the years had taken its toll on him.

Chapter 2

WHILE VICK WAS RECOVERING, CAIN AND LUCY PLANNED THEIR wedding with Elizabeth's help. She was on cloud nine, seeing the young couple happy and excited about a future together.

Everything was perfect, especially for the parents who were honored to stand with Lucy and Cain on their wedding day.

Occasionally Elizabeth would recall the gruesome death of Johnson and Eileen and how close it came to destroying Cain. But now he seemed happy again. Only a short time before, Cain had taken the bodies of his wife Eileen and her father back to San Augustine, Texas for burial, and now after several months of mouring, he planned to marry Lucy. For a time she thought Cain might not recover from the loss of Eileen and their unborn child, but then realized that he was in love with Lucy before he knew Eileen was pregnant. He was not in love with Eileen but believed he had to do "the right thing" since she was carrying his child.

The surprise came when Cain having been married only one day became the heir to the entire Petty fortune after his new wife's death. Jonathan Petty, the only other living child of his deceased father, was enraged, for Cain stood between him and the family fortune. He thought after his brother died that he could now step in and claim his inheritance that his father had denied him of.

Eileen and Cain had not even had time to consummate their marriage before Buck Dupree killed her, her father, and the baby she was in child with. At the time their sudden death left no apparent heir other than Jonathan the black sheep of the family who would only be heir should there be no others left. He had no idea that the marriage of his neice to a virtual stranger from Arkansas would become the heir to the Petty estate cutting him out. It was tragic that Eileen and her father were on the way back to San Augustine to plan a much bigger wedding for the sake of society. The initial small ceremony in the manor that united Eileen and Cain was not at all the wedding her father had pictured for his daughter, considering their standing in the town of San Augustine and throughout the state of Texas.

Months after the death of Eileen, Cain realized the tremendous responsibility associated with owning the Petty estate, but still he was undecided where to live. Should he settle in Jonesboro, or should he move to Texas with Lucy in order to take care of his inheritance? These were all proper concerns, but his loyalty rested with Lucy, who was only days away from marrying him.

Elizabeth's insistence for the wedding between her son and Lucy was to be Jonesboro's biggest affair, and she was beside herself with last minute details. She knew the men of the house could have cared less about a wedding of that magnitude, but Elizabeth wanted this for Lucy, who had been less fortunate in life. Orson didn't take to the frilly girl dresses so Lucy grew up as somewhat of a tomboy. Elizabeth wanted to make a fuss over her for once. She had no trouble envisioning Lucy as a prominent debutante, and it was Elizabeth's aim to show her off and let her get an early taste of what it will be like to be a Porter.

On the day of the wedding Elizabeth had taken the Model T into town to do some last minute shopping, leaving Lucy alone to decorate with touches of flowers throughout the manor. Cain had stayed in town in order to honor the tradition of not seeing the bride the day of the wedding, and Vick was out checking timber that had matured and was ready to be cut.

The James boys had been snooping around the manor for several days; waiting for the right moment to break in and find the treasure they assumed was hidden there. After running into Vick and the Sheriff coming from Panther Holler, they couldn't shake the idea that the saddlebags on the back of Cain's horse was the treasure their brother Johnny had told them about. When they reached the manor they saw Vick ride away on Jasper and Elizabeth leave in the Model T. They had no idea that Lucy Cargill was preparing for her wedding and was left alone in the manor.

The men were well armed when they entered the back door, which was unlocked. "That's easy," Lonnie thought as he motioned Dudley into the kitchen. Once inside, they began rummaging throughout the downstairs part of the house, thinking they were alone. Lucy, who was upstairs, did not hear the men until they began talking between themselves. She first thought it was Cain, who was supposed to be in town, but the more she listened the more insecure she became being left alone.

She walked quietly downstairs toward the voices until she ran straight into Dudley, who she knew was the town troublemaker. Seeing the mischief in his eyes, she froze. She was sure he was up to no good. Although frightened, she remained composed.

"Are you looking for Elizabeth?" she asked. Both startled, reacted by grabbing Lucy, while she screamed and fought.

"Do something to shut her up!" screamed Dudley. Lonnie felt he had no choice but to knock her unconscious. He punched her in the face just as he would a man.

That's Lucy Cargill, ol' Eagle Eye's daughter. Now what? What we gonna do now?"

"I don't know, but let's hurry and find the treasure then git the hell outta here," Lonnie shouted.

Lucy lay motionless while they rummaged throughout the house, wrecking it as they went. All the beautiful flowers that had aligned the stairway were torn down, and soon the house was in shambles. After a fruitless search, and in the heat of rage, Lonnie picked up a statue and threw it against the wall.

"There ain't no treasure nowhere!" he shouted. Dudley had never seen Lonnie so upset.

Totally unexpected, there was a loud hollow thud as the vase hit the wall. He walked over and tapped on the wall with his knuckles, then placed his ear to the wall and continued to tap.

"Ya' hear that Dudley?" This wall sounds holler."

"Well now, ain't that somepin'," Dudley replied.

Lonnie kept tapping and soon found the secret door that had at one time housed the real treasure that was taken away by the governor's courier months earlier. There was nothing but a file box of documents and a large square bookcase that almost covered the floor. They knew very little about reading, and couldn't make out what the papers were but figured they must be important.

"Whatcha' suppose this is? Reckon it could be valuable?"

"Could be, since it's hidden behind this door. Might as well leave with somepin' since there ain't no treasure."

They picked up the file and walked past Lucy, who was still unconscious.

"What about her?" Dudley asked, as he looked closer. "Jest a minute Lonnie, take a look at that ring on her finger?"

"If you want it, take it; she ain't gonna need it where she's going," Lonnie admonished. Dudley looked somewhat puzzled.

"We can't leave a witness and chance gettin' caught! Git me that oil lamp over there?" Lonnie ordered.

Dudley grabbed several oil lamps and gave them to Lonnie. He then stooped down and took the ring from Lucy's finger, while Lonnie spread the oil all over the kitchen floor.

"Do you aim to burn the whole thing down?" Dudley always twitched his nose when disturbed.

"Watch me!" Dudley, who was shocked, backed away with his hand over his mouth. Lonnie smiled as he continued to drench the floor. "Here's how it's done; watch and learn." Although alarmed Dudley smiled showing his approval.

After spreading the oil, he picked up a cloth, lit it, and then threw it into the area where the oil was spread. Within seconds there was a "woof," the sound of vapor igniting. Quickly the fire jumped from floor to ceiling. The boys stood at the back door mesmerized as the massive red and yellow flames leapt from downstairs to the upstairs balcony, fueling itself as it spread. After running with the box of papers, they hid behind the barn and watched the manor turn into a raging inferno.

"There she goes," Dudley whispered. "I don't reckon we can stay in Jonesboro and chance gettin' caught after this."

There was something exciting almost magical about seeing the wealthy property owners lose something so precious to them. It was like a payback for them being poor.

Chapter 3

THE BROTHERS REMAINED IN HIDING BEHIND THE BARN UNTIL THE **entire manor was engulfed in flames.** After the home was well on its way to rubble, they rode out through the backwoods so not to be seen. They could smell the trail of smoke as it penetrated through the tall pines, drifting towards the clouds.

Dudley and Lonnie were not the only people who saw the manor burn. A Clan of reclusive people, as elusive as wild animals, had recently settled in the woods nearby, watching. Hardly anyone knew this Clan existed, for they had come as drifters from another state. Even Elizabeth and Vick were unaware that they had settled only a stone's throw away from the manor in a densely wooded area.

Upon Vick's return to his office one of the men excitedly told him there was a big fire brewing out by the manor. Seeing the billowing smoke ahead Vick jumped up on Jasper, riding at top speed. Urging the horse on, he thought it might be the barn. When he got closer he saw it was the manor. His first thought was the wedding and how disappointed Lucy and Cain would be. *This is where Lucy and Cain planned to exchange their vows. How distressing for them,* he thought.

Suddenly he thought of Elizabeth, but then remembered that she had stopped by the office earlier that morning to tell him she had left Lucy at the manor decorating, and she would be late getting home.

"Ohhhhh my God, not Lucy!" Vick cried out. He ran around the house screaming her name, but he could only hear the sounds of burning rubble creaking as large beams began to fall. He was shocked to see how much the fire had destroyed so quickly. "How could this have happened?" Something about this didn't make sense, he thought.

When the fire had at last burned itself out there was not much left other than smoldering embers. The few areas that were intact were blackened from the smoke. Vick found a few pictures and bits of furniture, but the whole thing was basically destroyed. Vick fell to the ground in despair, thinking about Lucy and what she must have gone through.

After what seemed hours of going through as much of the remnants of the house as possible, his eyes were drawn to a large vase that had held flowers. It was there that he saw his first clue that Lucy had perished in the fire. Though badly scorched, he recognized shards of clothing and part of the beautiful ribbon Lucy had worn in her hair that morning. Shaken, he realized her body must be under all that burnt rubble. If the flames were intense enough to burn through large beams, there might not even be a trace left except this telltale bit in his sooty hands. He'd have to wait until the smoldering stopped completely before trying to find poor Lucy's remains, if there were any.

Vick couldn't imagine how he was going to break the news to Orson and Cain, not to mention Elizabeth, who had lived in the manor for as long as she could remember and loved Lucy as a daughter. Orson was like family, and Cain had already had to deal with more than anyone his age should. He tried to understand how Lucy got trapped in the fire. *There is something about this entire scene that isn't right*, he thought. "How could this have happened? He kept saying over and over. How can Orson go on, knowing his pride and joy was burned alive in this fire? How is he going to cope?" he agonized.

Leaving what was left of the manor, Vick rode Jasper to the middle of town when he spotted Elizabeth in her Model T. The backseat was filled with packages as she backed up to drive home. How he dreaded to break the news. She drove over to Vick, who had reined Jasper to a halt.

"Are you waiting for me?" she called, smiling at him. Getting closer, Elizabeth instantly knew something was wrong. "Oh no, don't tell me something has happened to Cain."

Vick got off of Jasper and went around to the driver's side of the automobile to open the door. "Elizabeth, it's not Cain, but something dreadful has happened. I find it hard to put into words."

"You're scaring me, please tell me!"

"It's Lucy... she's dead."

"What did you say?"

"She's gone! Lucy got trapped in a fire."

Elizabeth could not believe what Vick was telling her. "Lucy dead? In a fire? What fire?"

"Elizabeth, I'm so sorry."

She wasn't thinking clearly, and Vick dreaded telling her the fire had destroyed the manor.

All Elizabeth could think about was Cain and what might happen when he learns that the love of his life is dead.

"No, not again! Cain just got over one loss, and now he has to face this!" Elizabeth began crying. "No, I can't believe it!"

She stepped out of the Model T and into Vick's arms. She clung to him. "That's not all," Vick said.

"What, don't tell me Orson, too?"

"No, Lucy was in the manor when the fire broke out. There's nothing much left."

"Lucy burned in the manor? Oh my God! Please Vick, please tell me this isn't so."

There was nothing much Vick could do except hold her while she cried it out.

"Lizzie, I wish I had all the answers, but my concern right now is for Cain and Orson. I'm going to need you to be strong and help me with them. Can you do this for us?"

"You're asking a lot. You know how much Lucy meant to me."

"We all loved her, but this was Orson's baby girl. What we have to do is think about the two people closest to her. I'm going to need your help."

Elizabeth continued to wipe her eyes as she drove slowly to the Sheriff's office. Vick followed on Jasper. Before they entered the office, a man came into town shouting that the manor had burned. When he saw Elizabeth and Vick, he stopped his horse short of the mercantile where people began to gather. Soon folks were talking quietly among themselves, looking over at the Sheriff's office, and then at Cain's law office close by.

Elizabeth and Vick walked in to tell Orson the news, but before they could say anything, the Sheriff began talking about the stuffy suit they wanted him to wear to the wedding. "Y'all know this ain't me—wearing one of these dang monkey suits."

Orson noticed the look on Elizabeth's face and knew something was wrong. "Looks like y'all are fixin' to tell me something I ain't ready to hear."

"Orson, you better sit down."

The Sheriff immediately grabbed the corner of his desk to brace himself as he sat down hard, like he had already guessed it was about Lucy.

"I was just out by the manor, and I've got some tragic news. Lucy was in the manor when a fire broke out."

The Sheriff's face expressed his feelings, but he didn't say a word.

"Orson, Lucy didn't make it out of there." Vick had never seen such pain as he saw shoot into Orson's eyes.

"I hate delivering this message to you, but you have to know."

The Sheriff sat there what seemed to be an eternity before he was able to speak. "Lucy, my sweet girl?—I can't believe she's gone."

Elizabeth couldn't hold back any longer. Tears began to flow as she went over to Orson and took him into her arms. He didn't try to pull away like Vick thought he would. The tough Sheriff, at whom many had marveled, crumbled in Elizabeth's arms. He sobbed for a few minutes, and then started wiping his tears with his shirt sleeve.

"I don't reckon anybody ever seen me this way. I ain't shed a tear since Lucy's mama died. What I hate most is I weren't around when Lucy needed me. She could always count on me bein' there, but this time I let her down."

"Elizabeth, you stay here with Orson, I've got to tell our boy what happened."

Vick turned and headed over to Cain's office. He walked in and Cain called out to him to come into the small bedroom, connected to his office. It was a comfortable place for Cain to sleep and wash up when he stayed overnight.

"What are you doing here? You're supposed to be home getting ready for my big day," he said, then studied the look on Vick's face.

"Well, I got to talk to you." Vick said, quietly.

Cain was beginning to sense something was not right the way Vick was looking at the floor.

"It's kind of late if you're going to tell me about the birds and the bees, ain't it?"

"Cain, I don't know how to say what I have to tell you. So I'll say it straight out. There was a fire at the manor—and Lucy died."

Cain spun around on his feet, slightly unsteady, as he held onto the bed railing to keep from falling. "Wait just a minute! Did I hear you right? You said there was a fire, and Lucy was in it? Lucy died in a fire?"

"Yes son, that's what I'm saying. Lucy died this morning, in a fire at the manor."

Cain had just suffered through the death of Eileen and his unborn child. Now to hear about Lucy on the day he was supposed to marry her was beyond any feeling he had ever experienced. He had no tears left from the time Eileen died. Cain felt enormous grief, but it was the kind he could not express in the same manner as he did with Eileen and his baby.

"Does Orson know?"

"Yes, he knows. Your Ma's there with him now."

Vick saw something die inside Cain after he told him about Lucy. He was immediately cold and withdrawn as he sat on the bed, stunned.

"I don't know if I can see Orson now. It's my fault! If she hadn't got mixed up with me, she'd still be alive. Pa, I don't know how to ask this. Was anything left?"

"No son, nothing, not even the ring you gave her. I know you're upset but you're not to blame. It was a terrible accident and could have happened to any one of us."

"I don't care about the ring— that's not important. It's Lucy! I've lost her, but why? Oh God, I hope Orson will forgive me."

"Cain, we don't know why things happen, and it's not our place to question. It was just her time."

Cain raised his voice, "You know why it doesn't do any good to question? Because there ain't an answer that makes any sense. She died before her time! Maybe we're paying for bad blood."

"Could be son. If that's the case, I would think I've paid plenty for being born. But you could be right."

"Pa, I'm sorry. I haven't been through half of what you've been through. I didn't mean to say what I did."

"Don't ever apologize. If you thought it, you might as well say it."

"My God, I don't even know what I'm saying. Now what?"

"I reckon we're going to be planning a funeral, or maybe we should call it a remembrance service."

"Pa, I hope you and Ma understand, but I'm staying in town.

"You'll be there for Lucy, won't you?"

"I'll be there. I'm just worried about Orson and how he's taking this. Right now I need to think. I need to have some time to accept what's happened. Do you mind?"

Vick turned to walk out, but before he did, he went over to Cain to give him a quick hug. Cain stood and grabbed him, throwing his arms around his neck. Vick did not know what to do, except hold him tight. The floodgate opened, and Cain cried his eyes out. Finally, he pulled away, somewhat embarrassed for showing such emotion.

"I didn't think I had a tear left in me. Pa, Lucy meant the world to me. I don't know how I'm going to make it without her."

"Son, I imagine she knows you're hurting."

"What I don't understand is how the fire started. It doesn't make sense," Cain questioned.

Chapter 4

LUCY'S SERVICE WAS A TENDER, EMOTIONAL CEREMONY. A NUMBER OF people joined Orson and Cain as they walked to the burial ground where Orson placed a homemade cross alongside her mother. There was no need for a casket for the fire had devoured Lucy's body. This scene was too familiar to Cain, after burying his first wife, Eileen, and her father, Johnson Petty, so recently in Texas. The grief Cain shared with Orson was overwhelming to both of them, as well as to the others paying their respects to this sparky young woman who grew up in Jonesboro. Everyone loved Lucy, and marveled how this little tomboy had transformed into such a strikingly beautiful woman, and now she was gone. During the service Elizabeth noticed a group of loggers who cut and hauled timber for Porter Lumber Company. These rough looking men were chewing tobacco and spitting on the ground. They talked quietly among themselves with very solemn looks on their faces. These weren't the type of men who would normally show up at anyone's funeral, but they did for Lucy's. Elizabeth remembered being quite vocal on how she hated working with the loggers who spit their tobacco everywhere.

"Don't you worry about the loggers. I know how to handle these men," Lucy would say, and she did. She was able to accomplish things that neither Elizabeth nor any man could.

The funeral was near over when three strange men rode up on horses. These weren't loggers; these were unusual men, more like mountain men, with chiseled faces. Vick and Elizabeth had never seen them before. Vick walked over to Elizabeth as if to protect her from them. They couldn't figure out who these curious people were, or why they just sat on their horses chewing tobacco and staring at them. Elizabeth's first thought was, "They look like illiterate people, although on second thought, a better description might be— insane."

Someone said, "I wonder if they're part of the Jackson Whites?"

"I ain't never heard of Jackson Whites," someone said from the crowd.

"Should we tell them to leave?" asked Elizabeth. "I don't want Lucy's funeral desecrated by these people."

"You stay here. I'll talk to them," Vick said.

He walked over to the men, who seemed in no hurry to leave. As he approached them, one spat a wad of chewing tobacco on the ground, never taking his eyes off Elizabeth as they gave her a hollow stare. They were the damnedest people Vick had ever seen. They reminded him of Skinny, one of the Warden's men, who had relished in torturing Vick while he was in prison.

Hardly anyone from Arkansas knew of the "Jackson Whites" until an old-timer from town had shared his understanding of them. He explained they were a group of mixed breeds, all descendants of a genetic anomaly spawned from inbreeding in their families.

"These chiseled-faced people had been around for centuries, and included slaves, and escaped convicts who lived no better than animals. Through their inbreeding they became degenerate, dim-witted, and remained ignorant," he explained. "They were condemned to poverty because of the way they acted and looked." Vick noticed the slobbering and vile odor as a common thread among them, along with frightening facial characteristics. Vick thought they closely resembled the mountain men who tried to kill him as a boy. They were definitely not the neighborly type.

"What's your business here? What do you want?" Vick asked repeatedly.

He received no reply. Finally, after about five minutes of defiance and constant staring, the men spurred their horses and rode away.

Vick walked over to the loggers and asked, "Do any of you know anything about those men?"

"I hear they're from the Appalachian Mountains," someone said.

Then a lady spoke up and said, "Elizabeth, they live in the woods out your way, so you all need to be careful."

Vick remembered they had recently lost some farm equipment. Now he had a good idea where it might have gone, and how the fire might have started that killed Lucy.

Orson, emotionally drained, thanked everyone for coming then turned and walked slowly into his cabin. Elizabeth was heartbroken for him, but Vick insisted she let Orson have his time to grieve. He also cautioned Elizabeth not to suggest to Orson, for Orson's own safety, that those men had anything to do with the fire that broke out in the manor.

Cain, who was not quite ready to leave, stayed long enough to organize a few large bouquets of flowers, then walked over to visit with the loggers. He never noticed the difference in the classes of folks; if he did, no one ever knew.

He turned to see Vick and Elizabeth waiting for him. "Pa, you and Mother can go home, I'll be staying awhile longer.

"You take all the time you need son. We're in no hurry. Besides, there is no home left to go back to!"

"Right! Well anyway, if you all want to go then go. I'll get a ride with someone else."

Vick could sense that Cain was under a lot of pressure.

"Son, I can't begin to know what you're going through right now; these two losses so close together, but my feeling is we all grieve different. I was just a kid on my own when my brother Sam died, and I remember how it forced me to grow up and be a man. It took me a little time, but I soon got on with it. To this day I miss him. If I've learned only one thing about life, it's made to live. So my advice is to spend as much time as you need grieving. When you come around and realize that grieving won't bring Lucy back, that's when you'll force yourself back into living. It's up to you to make your life what you want, not me, and not your Ma."

Cain could hear what Vick was saying, but somehow it wasn't registering.

"I hope you won't mind me staying in town for the night."

"Son, do whatever you want. You know where to find us."

"Oh, by the way, I guess I will go ahead with my plan to leave for San Augustine in a few days. If you remember, I have a meeting with Jonathan Petty."

"Cain, we had not planned for you to know this until tomorrow, but we bought you a new Model T! It's parked in back of the mercantile store. It was to be a wedding gift for you and Lucy."

Cain was surprised. "I don't know what to say. Lucy would have loved it."

After Elizabeth and Vick arrived back to the manor, they salvaged what little furniture was left and used it to furnish the carriage house, a cozy little place nearby. Vick thought it was quite comfortable and more than adequate. The carriage house was once a painting studio for Elizabeth when she was a young girl. Now it would serve as their new home. While moving the pieces of furniture from the wagon into the small frame house, Vick was struck by Elizabeth's beauty, with her auburn hair and sunny complexion. Her face was like ivory, with just enough freckles and rosy glow in her cheeks to give one a glimpse of how she looked in her youth. She was stunning, with big blue eyes that were a bit larger than the usual. Vick thought she resembled a beautiful painting. During this relocation process, they would occasionally look at each other and softly smile, as if to silently agree that their love was all that mattered during this sad time. All the while, as they were completing their tasks, the hollow eyes of Clan members were spying on them from a distance.

After the house was set up, Elizabeth turned her attention to Orson, whom they had not heard from since the funeral. They had driven the Model T by his house on several occasions to bring food, but there was no sign of Orson. Elizabeth would listen at the door, but Vick had convinced her that she needed to allow Orson time to grieve alone, without being disturbed.

"I don't think Orson's eating," Elizabeth said.

"Lizzie, give him time. The man's just lost his daughter."

After she left Orson's cabin, Elizabeth ran into one of her old friends in town who stopped to inquire about how Orson was doing.

"Elizabeth, we been hearing some bad things going on 'bout that Clan bunch living out your way. They say they kidnapped a young girl from over near Trumann. They been looking fer her, but they move before she's found. Last we heard, they're still living out your way. "

"They never found the girl?"

"No, never did. We heard say they breed jest like animals. There's a woman doctor over in Trumann that has delivered some of their babies, but I hear tell they're usually stillborn."

Elizabeth recoiled, "I don't want to hear the details. That's just disgusting. As long as I've lived here, I've never heard of the Clan, those 'Jackson Whites'."

The next few days were the same, until one day Elizabeth drove to Orson's house by herself. When she arrived, there was stale food left on the porch that she had been leaving for him. She began picking up plates and jars of spoiled food. She found a dumping ground that Lucy must have used to discard garbage, and, as she walked back to the cabin, she swore she saw something in the woods watching her, probably an animal, she decided. She hurried to the porch in time to see Orson's curtain move. She was thrilled to see a sign of life.

She placed her ear to the door, but there were no sounds of movement. Hesitantly, she knocked softly on the door.

"Orson, are you there?" she asked. Elizabeth waited, but Orson did not answer. The next knock was louder than before.

"Orson, it's Lizzie, can you open the door...please?" She heard movement, and then a voice.

"Lizzie, I'm sorry, but I need ya' ta leave."

The sound of his voice broke her heart, but she wasn't about to leave without seeing him. "Orson, I'm not going anywhere until you open the door and let me speak with you."

"I ain't dressed, so ya' be on yer way."

"Well, I guess I'll be sleeping on the porch tonight."

"Oh, alright! Ya' always were so dern' stubborn. Give me a minute ta dress. Dab blame ya'... ya' crazy woman. Always gotta have yer way."

Hearing Orson's grumble was a good sign and made her the happiest she had been since before Lucy died. *He's on his way back,* she thought. After he opened the door, Elizabeth saw an old man who looked as if he had been on a weeklong drunk.

"Orson, let's take a ride."

"I ain't in no shape ta ride nowhere. Now tell me what ya' want so I kin git back in bed."

"You forget, I know you better than you know yourself. I have your favorite pie waiting for you."

Orson scratched his head and looked at Lizzie like he was thinking. Then he said, "What kind is it?"

She couldn't help but chuckle at his reply. *Yes, Orson was back.*

Chapter 5

Cᴀɪɴ ʜᴀᴅ ᴘʟᴀɴɴᴇᴅ ᴛᴏ ᴍᴀᴋᴇ ᴛʜᴇ ʟᴏɴɢ ᴛʀɪᴘ ᴛᴏ Sᴀɴ Aᴜɢᴜsᴛɪɴᴇ **alone; however, with Vick's insistence he allowed his Pa to accompany him on the journey.** Although Elizabeth wanted to be with them, she had to stay behind to run the lumber company and interview applicants to fill Lucy's vacant position.

During the long drive the two men had a chance to talk about the future and what Cain hoped to accomplish by living in San Augustine. Vick was not at all happy about the upcoming distance between him and his son, but he refused to interfere. After all, it wasn't so long ago that he found he had a son and now he was concerned about their separation and having to drive from Jonesboro to San Augustine, Texas for a visit. At one point Cain asked Vick if he and his mother would consider moving to San Augustine and help run the cotton business. It seemed the logical thing to do; after all, the manor had burned, and his parents had moved into the small carriage house.

"Mother would love the big plantation home just like she's accustomed to." Cain said.

Vick listened to his son and pondered over the idea.

"Cain, I don't know; we have the lumber company to run, and then there's Orson. We've all become close … I wouldn't want to leave him alone without his friends."

"Why don't you and mother sell the lumber company and have Orson move with you? All we need is the cotton business. Remember saying how much you liked raising cotton when you were in prison?"

"Yeah, I've thought about the cotton business, but Orson, I don't know if he's ready to retire. After losing Lucy he may never want to retire. Cain do you remember me talking about Hop Babcock the man who owned a cotton business when I was in prison? I still think about him from time to time, but don't know if he's still among us."

"Where does he live?"

"I heard he moved to Memphis, Tennessee. I asked about him before I got out of prison and one of the guards told me some big plantation bought him out."

"Too bad he's not around. He could work for us."

Vick laughed. "A plantation owner like Hop having an ex-convict for a boss? That'll be the day."

"Pa, I don't like you referring to yourself as a convict. You were framed for something you didn't do. It was Buck and his lies that sent you to prison.

"Then you tell me what a man calls himself who's spent half his life in prison? I can still hear those iron doors Clanging behind me. I wasted years of my life in that hell-hole."

"But look where you are now! You're certainly not destitute or alone. You have a family and a successful business, regardless of whether you stay in Jonesboro or come with me. I hope you and mother give moving to San Augustine some serious thought. We've got a lot of living to do."

"I reckon we do, son!"

The James brothers' small cabin was a good five miles out of town in a secluded area where their daddy's bootlegging business operated. The place was only a two-room shack with a small kitchen, a few chairs, and a tiny separate room for sleeping. The entire place was depressing, much as were their personalities.

The boys had very little schooling, but they learned to write their names and sound out a few written words. They wore dark clothing and dirty old black hats, always recognizable. One night, with the lanterns lit, they began rummaging through the papers they had stolen from the manor, hoping to find something valuable. They had no idea what to make of the papers.

"Don't look like much here 'cept a Bible and papers. Dudley, here's somepin'. Look at this! Looks like a marriage paper. Oh, and here's a letter that goes wit' it."

"Reckon it's a love letter? Open it and see what it says," Dudley suggested.

"Didn't the Sheriff say that murdered woman's name was Peaty or Petty? I can't 'member."

"Look...this here paper has a name like that on it. It says 'Petty.' I thank that's the rich man and his daughter that was murdered. Dudley, we need somebody to make sure we're makin' this out right. I 'spec we got us somepin' here. We kin git ole Ned ta read 'em ta us."

Ned Holland, who was at one time a local lawyer, had lost everything and turned to the bottle. After years of drinking he had become the town drunk who would do anything for a bottle of whiskey. Ned was the James' best customers.

"Reckon he'll read it fer a couple jugs of whiskey?" asked Dudley.

"He ain't gonna turn down some of the finest home brew in Jonesboro. Yeah, he'll read it alright, and won't 'member a thang afterwards."

Early the next morning they rode over to Ned's house. After they arrived, sure enough, he was drunk as a skunk, sitting in a rocker on his front porch.

"Come on in. I 'spec you got what I'm looking fer in that sack your carrying."

"Me and Dudley want ta make a little trade wit' ya."

"Why don't you boys come in and make yourself at home."

The men walked into Ned's dingy cabin surrounded by mounds of legal papers strung about the cabin.

"Come on in, if you can find a place to sit." The boys sat around the kitchen table.

"Now, what can I do for ya?" Ned asked.

"Me and Dudley has got some legal papers fer ya' to read."

Ned walked over to the cabinet and poured himself another drink. "Now, show me them papers you talking about."

Being intoxicated, it was incredible how Ned was able to decipher what the papers were. He looked them over closely, "Don't reckon you boys gonna tell me where these papers came from?"

Dudley looked sharply at his brother, who was now regretting having Ned read the papers. "How did y'all come across this Will of the Petty Estate?"

Lonnie got very nervous knowing Ned could expose them. *We can't walk away and leave Ned to his own thoughts. He could blackmail us if he got a mind to,* Lonnie realized. This was of great concern to both of them. The two exchanged worried looks.

The sealed letter became more interesting as they listened carefully to Ned explain all about why Jonathan Petty could not receive his dead brother's estate. As long as there is a surviving heir, Jonathan will not be entitled to any of his brother's fortune the letter revealed.

"The papers clearly states that should there be no other heirs, Jonathan would have to meet certain requirements, which are outlined in a letter Phillip Bradbury, the family lawyer has for safe keeping."

"I guess me and my brother don't rightly understand what it all means," said Lonnie.

"Well, ah, not knowing all the facts, I would say that Mr. Bradbury is holding a letter that Jonathan Petty might not want anybody to know about. The way this letter reads, there's definitely bad blood between these two brothers. Apparently Jonathan raped Aggie and killed her mother. Says here that Phillip Bradbury is holding a letter that explains in more detail a family secret.

Ned took a drink and continued to explain. "Guess them Pettys has a secret they been hiding."

"It says here that Aggie Dawson can point the finger at Jonathan Petty for raping her and murdering her mother—old man Petty's mistress. I would imagine if and when Jonathan finds Aggie he's gonna kills her. This is probably why the Will tries to protect Aggie from Jonathan."

Reading on, Ned concluded. "Now—what I think doesn't matter, but if I had to guess, I would say that Jonathan's twin brother, Johnson, had this Will drawn up to keep his brother from inheriting anything upon his death. Cain Porter became the heir to the Petty fortune when he married Eileen Petty, Johnson Petty's daughter, who you say is already dead.

What I have in my hand is a marriage license that proves Cain Porter married Eileen just before she died, making him the surviving heir to that Petty fortune."

"So ya sayin' Cain Porter hit it big when that wife of his was murdered? We heared, that Eileen Petty and her Pa were both ambushed right outside of Jonesboro.

"That's what the Will says that as long as there is a surviving heir Jonathan Petty ain't gettin' nary cent. Frankly, I wouldn't want to be in Cain's shoes. My advice to him would be to watch his back, cause he's standing in the way of a man who thinks he should be the heir to his brother's fortune."

"Noooo kidding," said Lonnie, whose wheels were turning.

The brothers' were trying to comprehend all the legal ramblings. And hearing how coherent Ned was explaining it all, further complicated what Lonnie had to do to protect himself and his brother. They were as dumb as two gourds, but they were as dangerous as two rattlesnakes.

Before they left, they led Ned to his bed, and Dudley watched as Lonnie placed a pillow over Ned's face. The old man attempted to free himself but, being inebriated, Lonnie easily overpowered him. After Ned's death, the boys looked through his belongings and found enough money to make the trip to San Augustine, Texas.

"Guess we had ta' kill him," Dudley said, who was a bit wheezy from seeing the old man die.

"Ya' ain't to worry 'bout it. We do what we gotta do. We already kilt once, so what difference does it make?"

"We gotta protect ourselves—don't we Lonnie?"

Position of power was all Lonnie had on his mind. He and Dudley knew they were holding all the cards. Now all they had to do was plan how they were going to leverage the information.

"San Augustine, Texas here we come!" exclaimed Lonnie.

After more than three weeks of travel, they were ready to find a place in San Augustine and settle in. Their first thought was money. They needed work and a place to live before they could put their blackmailing scheme in motion. After asking around for directions they rode out to Jonathan Petty's small ranch, the Circle J, to hire on. Upon arriving at the homestead they saw a couple of ranch hands baling hay.

"Let's ride over to those men and hear what they gotta say," Lonnie said.

The workers were busy, and hardly looked up to see who they were talking to.

"Y'all need to check at the house. One thang's fer sure, we could use a couple more hands," the workers encouraged.

Lonnie and Dudley tipped their hats and then headed back toward the ranch house.

Lonnie said quietly, "Now, you let me do the talking."

"Don't ya' always," Dudley smarted.

Lonnie gave his brother a smirk, and then walked up the steps to the door. The house was somewhat rambling, with large windows on both sides of the door. It was a modest ranch, clean and organized, with big flowering bushes around the wrap-around porch. Off in the distance was an oversized red barn with a few horses in the corral.

The brothers thought the Circle J looked like a mansion compared to their little shack in Jonesboro.

Before Lonnie had a chance to knock, the door opened and out walked a handsomely clad gentleman. He wasn't at all what Lonnie had imagined, and he was momentarily intimidated being in the presence of someone so poised and refined.

Maybe this ain't even Jonathan, Lonnie thought.

"What do you men want?" the man gruffly asked.

"Ah, we, ah, well, we're out here tryin' to find work, that is if ya' need workers."

"So why did you come here?"

The brothers were rendered speechless as they stared into the man's eyes. After what seemed an eternity, Jonathan spoke.

"I could use a couple more hands, but I'm not sure you're the ones. I don't need two slouches. I need ranch hands who can see what needs to be done and do it." Jonathan sized up the two dirt bags and thought, *cleaned up, they might be helpful when it comes time to do my dirty work.*

"I thank we might be who yer looking fer. We could sure use the work. We been travelin' fer over three weeks, and it would help us out if ya' can let us work fer ya'. We ain't no strangers to hard work. That is if yer hirin'," Lonnie implored. The duo had their hats off, crumpled in their hands, as they looked down at their boots instead of in the eyes of a man they were unable to impress.

For a moment Jonathan felt sorry for the two misfits. "Looks like y'all could use a bath and some clothes. I'm gonna tell you what I tell every man who comes here to work—you've got five days to prove that I can depend on you. If you can't do that, then I don't need either one of you."

"We're hard workers, sir. I didn't say, but my name is Lonnie, and this here's my brother, Dudley. We're from Jonesboro, Arkansas." Dudley cut his eyes toward Lonnie at the mention of where they were from.

"Dang it, now the man knows where we're from." Dudley thought, realizing he'd just made a big mistake.

"So you men are Arkansas boys." Jonathan seemed to be interested in that fact alone. When he heard Jonesboro, it rang a bell. "Jonesboro— *I know I've heard of that town before, and not that long ago,*" Jonathan thought.

"We have plenty of clean clothes out in the bunkhouse. It looks as though you men could use some."

"We 'preciate it, we shur' do."

"Well, I suppose I need to welcome you to the Circle J. My name is Jonathan Petty, and this is the Circle J Ranch you're working for. You men have got the job if y'all can show me you can work. You'll be sleeping out in the bunkhouse with the other men. We start your pay at twenty-five cents an hour. You'll get paid every Friday night at supper. If I find either one of you drinking on the job, you're fired—Any questions?"

"I reckon ya' told us all we need to know," said Lonnie.

"Matilda serves her meals on time at seven, eleven, and four. We'll be having supper in a couple of hours. I suggest y'all get ready for the evening meal. No hats allowed at the supper table. If you aren't bathed and your hair combed, well, you miss a good supper."

"Thank ya', Mr. Petty."

Jonathan thought the men acted rather strange, but couldn't put his finger on it.

"One other question: where did you hear about me?"

"We jest asked around town."

"Town folk talking about me?" Jonathan showed his paranoia.

"No sir, it's jest that we new in town and were askin' 'bout work. We heard ya' might be hirin'."

"You men do your job and don't let me down. Hear?"

"Yes sir, Mr. Petty; ya' can depend on us to help ya' ... whatever ya' need."

After the men had the shakedown, they went to the bunkhouse to see their new quarters. The place looked different than they expected, clean and orderly, something they weren't used to.

That night when they came to supper they looked like two different men. After seeing them all cleaned up, Jonathan thought they might work out after all. He liked that they were from out of town, and thought they might come in handy if he decided to take care of Phillip Bradbury. He had to be careful and work them awhile to see if they'd be right for the job he had in mind. By the end of the evening, the charismatic Jonathan had them completely under his spell.

"He ain't nothin' like I thought," Lonnie said, walking back to the bunkhouse.

"Are we still gonna tell him about the letter?" asked Dudley.

"Ain't no need unless he starts givin' us trouble. We got good pay comin' in, and it's a sight better than what we had before. No need to mess up a good thang! If he gives us trouble, we got plenty on 'em," Lonnie pointed out. "Besides, this is a pretty good town, and I ain't ready to be dodging the law. If we play him right, we might have it good enough to stay on right here."

∽

Cain missed Lucy more than he had imagined. It was difficult for him to think about starting over after losing the woman he loved. The one good thing that happened was convincing his family to sell the lumber company and move to San Augustine.

It was meant to be, thought Elizabeth. Just a short time after making their decision, a wealthy businessman bought out everything they owned; lock, stock, and barrel. After the shock wore off from the quick sale, she thought it was the best thing that ever happened to her. Now she was fully retired from the lumber business and could devote her time to the cotton business and her family.

Before they sold the lumber company Vick talked with Orson about moving with them. He had become like family; furthermore, Elizabeth did not want to leave Orson alone to fend for himself. He needed them now more than ever. Finally, after some persuasion, Orson decided to move with Vick and Elizabeth.

What the heck, ain't nothin' fer me here with Lucy gone, Orson thought.

Vick noticed his old friend had lost a lot of his drive since losing Lucy. Orson couldn't shake the mystery surrounding her death. It kept gnawing at him. There was something fishy about the entire scene of how the manor burned. One thing they all knew for sure: Lucy was near the staircase when she died.

Before the family made the big move, Cain went to see Jonathan Petty to see about purchasing the one item Jonathan was bequeathed in his brother's Will. The item was a five-acre plot with a small three-bedroom house adjoining the plantation property. Cain knew what he would be up against; trying to make a deal with the devil, but it was worth it to him not to have Jonathan owning property next door. He intended to sweeten the deal so Jonathan would sell to him no matter what. The meeting was less than cordial, but Cain's offer was more generous than Jonathan expected, which indeed had made it impossible for him to refuse.

Cain also had a secondary reason for purchasing the land. He planned to secure the water rights to a pond that fed into the lake they shared on the plantation property. The men shook hands over the deal. When Cain turned to walk to his Model T, Lonnie James happened to ride past on his horse. Although Lonnie looked completely different, Cain thought there was something vaguely familiar about him. Later, he wondered where he had seen the stranger.

Chapter 6

THE JOB OF RUNNING A COTTON BUSINESS AND MOVING TO SAN
Augustine turned into a bigger project than first thought.
Foremost in Cain's mind was Hop Babcock, the plantation owner
Vick knew when he was in prison. Cain's plan was to surprise Vick by
contacting Hop and asking him to come and work for them. The job
had become overwhelming for two men who could use another experienced cotton farmer to work with them.

Hop accepted the job and agreed to move to San Augustine, which
surprised Cain. He reveled at the thought of his Pa's reaction when
he found out his old friend was coming to Texas to help run Pecan
Plantation. *How ironic*, he thought, "a former prisoner who once
worked for Hop would now be Hop's boss." Cain never forgot that
Hop was the only man who treated his Pa with any degree of respect
while he was in prison. For that, he felt forever beholding to him for
creating some normalcy in Vick's life.

Cain could hardly wait to see the surprise on Hop's face when
he found out the man he would be working for was Vick Porter. He
only knew Vick as a hardened criminal under the custodial care of the
infamous New Orleans prison, where few survived. Cain was moved
by what he imagined would be a happy reunion.

Orson agreed to ride along with Cain to Memphis for a change
of scenery, since he was still grieving over the loss of Lucy. Once
Orson agreed, they went about firming up their plans. Just before

the trip, Cain planned to surprise Orson with the house and acreage he purchased from Jonathan Petty. He wanted time to make sure everything was in order for his old friend. This was important to Cain, since he would have been Orson's son-in-law, had Lucy lived. He thought a larger house would be perfect for this man who had spent his entire life in the confines of a small cabin. The other task at hand was to see Phillip Bradbury, and get copies of the legal papers that had been lost in the manor fire. Vick and Cain had searched and searched through the burned manor but couldn't find the strong box but were grateful that Bradbury would have copies.

As the weeks passed, Jonathan had rousing suspicions about Lonnie and Dudley James. He thought, *Those two are like an open book; they're hiding something.* He knew he had to devise a plan to get them away from the ranch long enough to rummage through their belongings. He had suspected from the beginning that they were sneaky bastards. Now it was time to get to the bottom of his concerns, so he invented a reason for them to go into town for supplies. After Lonnie and Dudley left, Jonathan sent Matilda to the bunkhouse to search their belongings. She wasn't gone long when she returned with the copy of Johnson's Will, Cain's Marriage License, and a copy of the same incriminating letter that Phillip Bradbury held. Of course, he had already imagined the content of the letter giving a detailed account of him raping Aggie and murdering her mother Betsy. His hands began shaking as he screamed aloud.

"Noooooo." In that moment Jonathan's mental sickness that had lain dormant for many years resurfaced. Paranoia set in and he began losing it. He destroyed many treasures of his youth leaving the mess for Matilda to clean up. All those things that Jonathan had cherished through the years were now, gone because of his rage.

Suddenly, everything began to make sense and as long as Aggie was alive he would never be able to reclaim his family fortune nor save himself if she had a mind to turn him in to the law. He worried how many people may know his secret, other than these two rascals who thought they were going to blackmail him.

Learning that Bradbury and Cain Porter had information that could cost Jonathan his freedom sent a lightning bolt of panic through him. The thought of a noose around his neck, or spending the rest of his life in prison, scared the heck out of him. He was terrified of the dire consequences, should he ever be found out.

Phillip Bradbury had been the confidant and close friend of his deceased brother, and there was no telling what Johnson told Phillip in order to cut Jonathan out of the Will. He imagined the two of them scheming and plotting against him. The good thing about his brother dying was that he could bury the ghost of the past, and no one would ever know what he had done. *Now that Phillip has a copy of this letter and knows the truth, I have no choice,* Jonathan decided.

After reading the documents the brother's had, Jonathan decided he could not afford to let the information out of his hands. Instead, since he knew the men couldn't read, he kept the real papers and substituted them with some phony but similar papers he had prepared for something else. Matilda returned to the bunkhouse and carried out the switch, leaving everything looking just as she had found it.

Jonathan was steaming mad, and began plotting against the would-be troublemakers. "Those James brothers will wish they had never been born once I get through with them!" Jonathan swore.

Under the light of a full moon, Jonathan rode into town to spy on Phillip Bradbury. When he got to Phillip's road, he veered into a grove of trees, dismounted, and tied his horse to a branch. *I'll just take a look around,* he thought. Jonathan was careful, but apparently not careful enough, for Phillip saw a shadowy figure crouched by his window when he was returning from the barn. He didn't think anything about it, since San Augustine was a safe place. There had been no rumors stirring about "peeping Toms," so it was Phillip's guess that someone had knocked on his door, and when there was no answer, peeked into his window to see if anyone was home. He walked up to the stranger, thinking nothing of it. He immediately recognized Jonathan, who was a bit startled to see Phillip approach but knew he couldn't just run away.

"Oh, it's you! You here to see me?" Phillip asked.

Jonathan was caught red-handed. Somewhat embarrassed, he felt forced into a meeting. "We got some business ... mind if I come in?"

"No, not at all. Is there a problem with your brother's Will?"

Jonathan felt the heat of intense anger welling up inside him as they entered the house. Although he was treated cordially, his paranoia rose, thinking about what Phillip might know about him. *If the contents of the letter got out it could destroy my life and possibly get me thrown into prison,* he worried.

"I'm having a drink...would you like one? It's been one of those days. I'm sure you know the kind of day I'm talkin' about."

Even Phillip's last remark about knowing what it was like to have a bad day was taken as a subtle threat by Jonathan. "Yeah, today for instance," Jonathan said.

"You never told me what's on your mind? It's kinda late to be riding around in the dark. Couldn't this have waited 'til tomorrow?"

"I suppose, but this matter couldn't wait. Phillip, I see no reason to mince words with you. It came to my attention that you have a letter that is false but rather incriminating about me. Apparently my poor dead brother is speaking from the grave, perhaps to get even. I'm sure you're aware of our history."

"This sounds very interesting, but I don't know what you're talking about. Now, if you don't mind, rather than play these games, I need to ask you to leave. I'm tired and have things to do," Phillip responded.

"I'll leave when you hand over the letter you have. You know; the one that my sorry brother was planning to use against me."

"And why would your brother want to do something like that?"

"To keep me from protesting the Will, that's why!" Jonathan's voice heightened.

"No need to shout Jonathan! Undoubtedly, you know something I'm not aware of. Everything I had, I gave to Cain Porter. He's your brother's heir, so if he has anything that you feel you should have, you can take it up with him. I'm not the one you should be talking to about this." Phillip retorted.

Jonathan disliked being talked down to. A blinding fury surged within him, and before another word was spoken, he grabbed Phillip around the neck. It happened so fast that Phillip was caught in a headlock before he had a chance to react. Jonathan flung him to the floor like a rag. He was no match for the rage-driven Jonathan, who went completely berserk. They rolled and thrashed about while Phillip tried desperately to free himself from Jonathan's powerful clutch. Suddenly, Jonathan shoved him into the large fireplace, grabbed a long heavy poker that was propped against the mantel, and began striking Phillip with it, blow after blow after blow, beating him to a pulp. Jonathan continued raising and lowering the poker on Phillip's lifeless body until he was exhausted. Finally, after regaining control, Jonathan caught a glimpse of himself in a nearby mirror, as he stood brushing the soot from his jacket. His long black hair was wildly askew, and partially covered his face. Running his fingers through his hair, he was shocked by the image of his face and blood on his clothing. A frightened and sinister beast had replaced the normally steadfastly assured man that he was.

Now that Phillip was out of the way, Jonathan set about and frantically emptied every paper out of his desk searching the entire house for the damning letter in question. But try as he might, there was no letter to be found. Now his only choice was to confront the James brothers, and hope they would tell the truth.

Meanwhile, back in Jonesboro, the town folk heard that Orson was moving with the Porters to San Augustine, Texas. They assumed it was because of Lucy's death that he was leaving and wanted to meander by to shake hands and say "thank you" and "goodbye." These heart-felt gestures of appreciation for all the years of service as Sheriff brought unwanted tears to Orson's eyes.

"Orson, I know you're going to miss your job, but you'll always be the Sheriff to us folks here in Jonesboro," one old-timer, said.

"I 'preciate the kind words but I'm happy to turn over the reins ta Pappy. He's gonna do jest fine with Charlie B's help."

Orson, leaving his beloved cabin in Jonesboro, meant he was also leaving Lucy and her mother's graves, but he knew it was time to start over with the people who had become his family. He thought of Cain as a son.

Vick and Cain helped Orson place the last bit of memories he had into the back of Elizabeth's Model T everything else he left in the cabin just in case he decided that San Augustine wasn't the place for him.

Seeing Elizabeth and Vick drive away, he suddenly faced reality that after more than twenty years of serving as Sheriff, he was actually retired. Cain thought it would be good for Orson, who loved the outdoors, to ride their horses and have a bit of time on the trail to get used to the idea of moving to Texas. Elizabeth and Vick traveled on ahead of them in the Model T.

The first day they didn't make ten miles before stopping for the night. It was a beautiful starry night that was perfectly clear, so they were able to find a good piece of grazing ground for the horses. This is what Orson liked best, riding through the countryside, then stopping to make camp.

Cain found wood to make a campfire, and began cooking a bite to eat while Orson took care of the horses.

"Well Orson, here we are again, just you and me. I sure hate that we got such a late start. We probably should have stayed and waited until morning to have more travelling time.

"Cain, 'member the last time we camped?"

He didn't give Cain a chance to respond before he began reminiscing.

"It was after our visit with the Governor of Arkansas. That was some meeting we had. Then when we got home, Lucy was there awaiting' fer me."

"The conversation always drifted back to Lucy. It's going to take Orson time, Cain thought.

"I miss her too," Cain said. "Not an hour goes by that I don't think of her."

Orson confided in Cain as he lay there wrestling with his thoughts.

"I jest can't figure out why there weren't no body. Ain't nobody I ever heared of ever burnt up like that."

"What are you trying to say?"

"It jest don't make sense that there weren't no traces of a body?"

Cain felt that Orson was in denial, but let him talk it out. They talked a long time and then he rolled over. It wasn't long before Orson was snoring, but Cain lay there tenderly reliving sweet moments with Lucy, until he was able to switch to thoughts of his new life in San Augustine.

During the night as they lay sleeping, there was a quick movement in the trees. Apparently something or someone had been watching them. Neither Cain nor Orson knew that the Clan had been following them since they left Jonesboro. As the men silently approached the camp, the leader used sign language, pointing and directing with his hands. He sent some of his thieves to the horses and then had them take whatever else was valuable.

The mountain men were like termites, devouring all the belongings in their path. Usually, by the time they got through, there was nothing left. One man looked for a sign to cut Vick's and Orson's throats, but instead of agreeing, the leader gave a hand signal to halt. They didn't like it much. Their thrill came from not only stealing, but from senseless killings. Orson and Cain never moved a muscle as they slept. The men worked mutely, never making a sound, as their leader watched over them.

These men were scourges of the earth. Stealing to them had become an art, since it was their only means of survival. Generally, they would murder and pilfer, as they went, but not in this case with Orson and Cain because their deaths could cause problems for them. Their plan was to steal and wreak havoc on property owners throughout Jonesboro and Trumann, raping women and killing whomever got in their way.

They knew in time they would cause enough trouble to cause a war with the townsfolk, but timing had everything to do with how long they could stay to steal and murder anyone that posed a threat to them. Their aim was to literally pick the towns apart. They traveled in a group of about 20 men, along with some of their women. The Clan caged several young women and held them like animals until they fulfilled their usefulness. If they attempted to escape, they would be hunted down and murdered.

The next morning, as soon as Orson awoke, he knew something was wrong. It was too quiet without the horses. He jumped to his feet as he reached for his gun, but it was gone.

"What the hell!" he shouted.

Cain rolled over and saw Orson walking around the camp in his socks kicking dirt clods.

"Cain, somebody done come in and stole everythang we got. We ain't got no horses, or a dang thang left!"

Cain immediately felt for his money belt, which was intact around his waist. "Thank goodness we slept in our clothes or they would have taken them too," Cain said.

"At least I got money. They didn't manage to steal that."

"Well, I ain't got nothin'. No saddlebags, no horse and not a dadgum nickel ta my name. Not to mention my boots that some scoundrel's gonna be wearing."

They looked around the campsite, having difficulty accepting what happened.

"How we 'spect to git ourselves outta this mess?" asked Orson.

"Guess we're going to be buying us a couple of nags, if we're lucky."

Cain was right. All they found was a couple of horses that had outlived their usefulness.

Two days later Vick saw two strangers riding up, until he recognized Cain and Orson on two horses that neither of them would otherwise own. As soon as Orson got close enough to be heard, Vick knew he would have quite a story to tell.

"Now don'tcha say a word about our fine horses here. I reckon they'll fit right in with the rest of the herd." Seeing Cain and Orson in their stocking feet, Vick burst out in laughter.

"Well, well, don't y'all look nice," Vick teased.

"Is that all ya gotta say? Me and Cain like ta ride barefoot from time to time." Orson always had to have the last word.

The move and trip took longer than expected, but when they rode up to Orson's place, it was worth it.

"Boy, I don't rightly know what ta say. I ain't never had nobody do anythang like this fer me. I'm gonna have ta git me another horse if I'm gonna be living in a place like this."

The men dismounted and walked Orson up the steps into his new home, which was more than he ever imagined.

"I didn't expect nothin' like this," he said. Orson walked outside onto his back porch and saw the lake that was within walking distance of his door. It brought tears to his eyes as he thought of Lucy, and how much she would have loved living there. After standing and looking over the property with its private lake and a small barn for his horse, he turned to Cain and Vick. "This here's too big fer me."

"What are you talking about? You're family now," said Cain. "Nothing more needs to be said."

At that moment, Vick knew his friend was not the same man he was before Lucy died. Something inside had died and he wondered if Orson would ever be the same.

Word spread rapidly that Phillip Bradbury, a reputable lawyer of San Augustine, had been brutally murdered. This was a major upset, not only for the town, but also for Cain, who had neglected to contact Phillip concerning the legal papers he had lost in the fire. The loss of the Marriage License, Will, and letter, had never even been reported to Phillip. Cain didn't know Phillip that well, but he wanted to be supportive and attend the funeral, especially since he intended to be a part of the San Augustine community.

Vick accompanied Cain to the funeral, 35 miles away from San Augustine, to a little town called, Nacogdoches. Phillip's only sister, Irene, lived there. Older and very plain, she was a gentle woman who appreciated Vick and Cain's attendance at her brother's funeral. She was visibly heartbroken over her brother's brutal murder. After Phillip was laid to rest, she invited them to stay overnight, as it would be too far to drive home on the same day.

Irene was a spinster who had taught school in Nacogdoches since she was a young woman. Her brother undoubtedly loved her very much because she had everything a woman needed, except looks. She was very homely, but her beautiful heart made up for what was lacking in her physical appearance. Since she was the only surviving member of the family, she would be inheriting her brother's entire estate.

The day after the funeral, Irene approached Cain and Vick as they were about to leave, asking to travel back to San Augustine with them in order to take care of Phillip's affairs. During the drive, Cain had a chance to tell her about the papers he had lost when the manor burned, including the mysterious letter that held the secrets of Jonathan's past.

"Now, don't you worry… if the papers are there, I'll find them," she said.

"Irene, there was a sealed letter that Johnson Petty had given Phillip. It's a duplicate letter of what Johnson gave me. Being an attorney Phillip said he never wanted to open it, as it might incriminate him."

Irene listened intently trying to remember where her brother had important papers stored.

"Well, I'm not one to meddle. The last time Phillip and I talked about his estate, he said he had a special hiding place where I could find his Will and other documents, in the event of his death. I don't know if you heard, but Sheriff Wilkes said the house was in shambles. I can't imagine who would want to kill my brother."

"Unless they were looking for something," Cain said.

Again, Cain thought about the suspicious timing of events. Who would benefit from the death of Phillip Bradbury? he pondered. The strangeness surrounding Phillip's murder, and who might profit from it, brings only one person to mind … Jonathan Petty! Could it be that he knows about the letter and killed Phillip to protect himself? A desperate man would do almost anything to keep from being hung or imprisoned. The more Cain thought of Jonathan killing Phillip, the more convinced he became that the man was capable of killing anyone because of his greed. He would be the one to profit the most if there were no more Porters?

Vick and Cain walked Irene to the door of her brother's home, making sure she was safely inside before they headed home to Elizabeth and Orson. Elizabeth was anxious to hear all the details of the funeral.

"Tell me everything! Were there many people there?" asked Elizabeth.

Cain saw the stab of sadness in Orson's eyes, and quickly changed the subject. Elizabeth caught herself and began talking about how Orson helped with the chores while Cain and Vick were out of town.

"Elizabeth, we didn't get a chance to tell you, but Phillip's sister, Irene Bradbury, made the return trip with us so she could take care of her brother's affairs. She's staying in Phillip's house. What a mess she has to clean up! I think you would enjoy meeting her, she teaches school and is a very nice lady in her late sixties," Vick said.

"Well then, why don't we ask Irene over for supper?" Elizabeth suggested. "Perhaps Friday night?" With a smile on her lips, she thought of Orson meeting a lady his own age. Orson was much to shrewd sensed what Lizzie was up to. "I'm gonna stop it 'fore it starts," he thought. He was too old and set in his ways to hook up with a woman.

The next day, at mid-afternoon, a Model T came rolling up to the plantation. Irene Bradbury, who looked to be on a mission, walked up the steps to the door and ran head-on into Orson as he was leaving.

"Oh, excuse me, I should look where I'm going." They did a little dance trying to get out of each other's way. Orson glanced at the woman, but did not draw any conclusions.

"Ain't no harm done, ma'am," said Orson, as he attempted to scurry away.

Women! he thought. *Who needs a bossy woman tellin' a man what to do?*

Fortunately, Irene's visit was not without purpose; she brought with her a large envelope she imagined was what Cain had requested. She had found her brother's safe hidden under some loose floorboards behind a chest-of-drawers. Upon opening the safe, she discovered her brother's Will and other papers as well as a large envelope with papers in it. After her warm welcome from Elizabeth she felt she had made a friend. She genuinely liked her, and accepted the invitation to have supper on Friday night.

Later that week, Orson was very quiet and unsettled. He was thinking seriously about having a talk with Elizabeth. He missed the security of his old familiar surroundings, including the comfort of his small, cozy cabin. Other than Lucy, of course, what he missed most was his independence. It was hard living so close to a woman who seemed to be taking over his life. Elizabeth meant well and truly thought of Orson as family, but she was unconsciously controlling him. The harder she tried at making him happy, the more uncomfortable she made him feel. Finally he'd had enough, and approached her with a bit of defiance. He reasoned, *I ain't gonna carry this 'round on my chest no more!*

Elizabeth had never seen Orson get his dander up.

"Now Lizzie, I didn't want ta have ta tell ya', but that Cupid's bow and airry' of yers is gonna have ta be put away. It's makin' me feel like I need ta saddle up my horse and git on back up ta Arkansas where I belong."

"Orson, what do you mean?"

"That woman ya' tryin' ta fix me up with."

"Orson, I'm so sorry, I thought you and Miss Irene might enjoy being friends. She's a nice lady, close to your age; someone you could share things with."

"I jest don't like nobody runnin' my business and I ain't lookin' ta share nothing!"

"Well then, let me apologize. I'm terribly sorry." Elizabeth was embarrassed that she had upset Orson.

About that time, Cain and Vick walked in. They immediately sensed they had interrupted a tiff between Orson and Elizabeth.

"Cain I have something for you. Miss Irene came over and brought this envelope." He imagined it was what he needed.

"Did we interrupt something?" asked Vick. Being cornered, Orson made a feeble attempt to make light of the disagreement he had with Lizzie.

"No, we was jest talkin' 'bout what we servin' fer supper on Friday night."

Cain and Vick both wanted to burst out laughing, but they knew Orson was serious.

"Are you planning on cooking?" Vick asked with a straight face.

"Well, what if I wuz? I'm downright handy in the kitchen when I want ta be."

"Just maybe you got some secret talents Cain and me don't know about."

"And jest between me and y'all, I aim to keep 'em secret. Jest so ya' know."

Cain went to his room and opened the envelope, which incriminated Jonathan for murdering Betsy Dawson. The letter also explained that Hampton Petty, Johnson and Jonathan's Pa had fathered Betsy Dawson's daughter, Aggie. It also stated that Jonathan must never know for he would kill Aggie to keep her from testifying against him.

The next morning Cain shared with Orson that Jonathan was nothing but an animal for raping Aggie and then murdering her mother. "Orson, Aggie is Jonathan's half sister."

"Ya mean he raped his half-sister! What ya planning on doin'?"

"I'm going to find her before Jonathan has a chance to kill her but this is between just me and you— confidental— understand. I don't want Ma worrying about me— you know how she is."

"I reckon you've given it some thought and know what yer doin'. I jest hope ya ain't opening a can of worms. You'll be sharing yer inheritance, ya know."

"We'll work that out when I find her," Cain said.

Chapter 7

Jonathan was a character known for his cunningness. And to his discontent, was always trying to protect the confidentiality of his transgressions.

After Jonathan had Matilda rummaged through Lonnie and Dudley's things, Jonathan eagerly awaited their return. When they did not show in a timely manner, he grew paranoid with what the brothers had on him. *They are either in trouble, or up to something,* Jonathan figured.

When Lonnie and Dudley finally returned, they put their horses away, and then walked to the house where Jonathan was sitting. By now they were accustomed to their stern boss, who always seemed to expect way more out of them than either was capable of giving. They also knew that Jonathan was probably the one who killed Phillip Bradbury. The news was all over town that Phillip was dead.

"You boys look like you're running from trouble," Jonathan said.

"Could be," said Lonnie, as he hung his head. "We jest run into Cain Porter and Sheriff Cargill, who's mean as a snake."

"Oh yeah, the one you think murdered your brother?"

"Yeah, that's him alright."

"But how do you know it was the Sheriff, when your brother was running with the likes of Buck Dupree, who murdered my brother? Buck was a known killer."

"Them Porters and the Sheriff are all in cahoots together, that's why. We jest seen 'em, and they're in town buyin' supplies, gittin' ready to go fer the treasure they took from my brother. They either took it or hid it somewher'. I suspect at that Panther Holler place."

Lonnie and Dudley knew something else was up as Jonathan stood there staring them down.

"Why is it I have a feeling there's something else you're not telling me?" Jonathan asked.

Lonnie became edgy with the question. It was as though a little voice was telling him that Jonathan knew something about their past that they were not wise to. He assumed that in order to be trusted, one has to trust. Without conferring with Dudley, Lonnie told Jonathan about burning down the manor.

Dudley had his hat off, twiddling his fingers, nervous about what Lonnie had just divulged.

"Mr. Petty, me and Dudley want ta' be yer' partners so we gotta be straight with ya'.

We aim to tell ya' everythang so there ain't no secrets betwixt us."

"Why don't you tell me what else is going on?" Jonathan asked.

"We're gonna come clean with ya. When we met up with Sheriff Cargill, the day him and them Porters were comin' from Panther Holler, we was sure they had the treasure with 'em. We planned ta' wait 'til the right time, then break into that manor house and steal it for me and Dudley, 'specially since we know they killed our brother, Johnny."

"What's the manor? What 'treasure' are you talking about?" Jonathan asked.

"It's where they all lived afore they moved here. It's a big place, almost as big as Pecan Plantation. They all rich folks, long as I can remember, 'cept the Sheriff. He jest had a little cabin with his daughter, Lucy."

"And, the treasure? What is that?" Jonathan was intrigued about this mention.

"We was told that my brother and Carl Rhodes knew the wher'bouts of a treasure, and we aimed to take it from Carl, you know ambush 'em." Jonathan's eyes lit up.

"The Porter's know where the treasure is hid? Jonathan questioned. So, the Porters are rich you say?"

"Yeah, it all came from Elizabeth Porter's Pa, Thomas Barkin. He was loaded, and after he killed hisself, Vick Porter took over the property and Elizabeth moved out. That's when she got a taste of being poor."

"Just a minute, back up a bit—you're losing me. Tell me how Vick Porter got his hands on Elizabeth's daddy's property?"

"That's a big story back home. We heared ther' was a little card game going on betwixt Elizabeth's daddy and Vick. Seems ol' man Barkin was tryin' to steal Vick's land. Ain't a soul thought Vick would win, but he surprised everybody. When it came time to pay up, Barkin took out a pistol and blew his own brains out!"

"You don't say! I still don't understand how Vick ended up with the old man's property!" Jonathan responded.

"It was in that poker game; winner take all—Vick's property up agin' Elizabeth's daddy's property. Vick won everything, hook, line and sinker, and that's when Barkin blowed his own brains out. Everybody thought it was 'cause he couldn't face Elizabeth after losing her home and all that. I guess he jest couldn't handle it. We don't know, but we suspect Elizabeth left town 'cause she didn't have no place else ta go. After she left, Vick took part of his winnings and paid back every man that lost their land to ol' man Barkin. Jonesboro considers Vick Porter a hero, but to us he ain't nothin' but a outlaw who bought his way outta' prison."

"Very interesting," Jonathan said. "This is quite a story, if it's true."

"It's true alright, 'cause why else would Elizabeth marry Vick Porter? After she found out 'bout her daddy's underhanded dealings, she despised her Pa."

So Elizabeth's father turned a gun on himself?" Jonathan asked.

"Yeah ... by then, she knew her daddy was a scoundrel. There's somethin' else ya' need to know 'bout that son of ther's—Cain.. He's Vick's real son. Cain ain't Elizabeth's flesh and blood. She took the boy after Cain's real Ma died. The way I heared it, Vick didn't even know he had a son 'til Cain and "ol' Eagle Eyes" found Vick and busted him outta prison."

"So the man that moved here with the Porter's is "ol' Eagle Eyes?"

"None other, Dudley said. "He was the Sheriff and the meanest bastard we know."

"Interesting that you tell me Vick Porter was in prison?" Why? What did he do?"

"Fer killin' eight people, even his own brother, so they say. Later they found out it was Buck Dupree who murdered them people. Yeah, and Vick weren't that pearly white either while he was in that New Orleans prison conning men in them poker games."

Jonathan's ears perked up when the puzzle finally came together that it was Vick who had conned his brother, in New Orleans. Finally all the pieces fit.

"Yeah, him and the warden had some gambling business goin' on outside of prison. I heared that Vick had ta win jest ta stay alive," Lonnie offered.

"So Vick's a professional gambler. My brother didn't stand a chance. It should have been me going up against Vick."

"Why is that?" asked Lonnie.

"Cause the man would be dead instead of here in San Augustine causing me trouble."

Jonathan had only heard bits and pieces about the Porter's, but now the new information gave him a little more insight as to who they really were.

How easy it would be to turn the town against the Porters, with all their dirty laundry, Jonathan imagined. His only concern was the Porters might expose him and things could backfire. He was smart enough to leave well enough alone until his past was safely hidden.

"Okay, enough about the Porters. What else do you have on your mind?" asked Jonathan.

"We do have somepin' else to tell ya', but like you, we had ta protect ourselves," Lonnie chimed in.

Dudley couldn't believe Lonnie was allowing Jonathan in on their secrets, but Lonnie had a mind of his own.

"We need ta come clean with ya'."

Lonnie spilling his guts would either be the most brilliant thing they've done, or the most stupid, Jonathan thought. He listened intently as Lonnie unmasked himself to him.

"Mister Jonathan, after the Porters murdered our brother, we planned to break into the manor and steal the treasure that we told ya' about. We didn't know Lucy Cargill was in the place. She recognized us right away, and before we had time to think, I knocked her out cold. We searched the place for the treasure we thought they had, but all we found was that bunch of papers, so we took 'em with us.

"I suspect I know what those papers were," said Jonathan, "but go on with your story."

"We had to make Lucy's death look like an accident."

"You mean you killed her?" Jonathan showed surprise mixed with concern that they would kill so easily. Would they kill me just as easily? Jonathan envisioned, as Lonnie continued to spill his guts.

To win Jonathan's trust Lonnie had a hunch that he should tell Jonathan the truth to ingratiate himself to the man they knew was a killer. In Lonnie's stupid way, he thought confiding in Jonathan would win his trust and show that they were no worse than he was. "We had to cover our tracks jest like you with that Bradbury feller, so we burnt down the manor with Lucy in it. We stood there and watched it go up in flames. Later we heard we killed Lucy on her wedding day. But instead of getting hitched, they got a funeral," Lonnie smirked. "Them papers we found is why we came to San Augustine." He paused, looking intently at Jonathan and continued. "The Will and the letter sayin' Phillip Bradbury had a letter that could send you to prison." Lonnie squared his body to show defiance, but he was shaking inside.

Jonathan gave them a look to kill. "So instead, you planned to blackmail me— is that right? You did realize you just accused me of killing Phillip Bradbury, when you're the ones that had more reason. You knew he had a letter, and you wanted it.

Lonnie stopped short realizing he couldn't win.

"We were scared and was waitin' till the right time to tell ya we made a mistake."

"So now, that I've caught you, you've decided it's the right time, huh?"

"Yes, but that's before we came partners. Ya' can see now that ya' can trust us, comin' clean like we done," Lonnie finished, apprehensively.

Jonathan enjoyed letting them sweat for a while before he finally spoke.

"Well boys, you did earn some points telling me about killing that girl, but you might have to take care of somebody else before I can trust you. No more secrets … you hear?"

"We yer' partners— no more secrets," the boys said in unison.

"I'm still thinking about them Porters. So this is why they all moved to San Augustine. Let me ask you another question. What do the Porters and the Sheriff have in common?"

"Them Porters and Cargill's been friends as fer' back as I can 'member, and then Cain planned ta marry Lucy Cargill "ol' Eagle Eye's" daughter."

Jonathan walked over to the whiskey decanter and poured each of them a drink, then began explaining his plan. They ceremoniously drank up, and for the first time since they left Arkansas, the James' felt safe, as if they belonged.

"Boys, those Porters are a problem that's going to get bigger if we don't get rid of 'em. They could make big trouble for us, your buddy the Sheriff included! Are you with me?" Jonathan asked.

Lonnie looked at Dudley, like they were part of a grand conspiracy. Finally, they were accepted as foremost players in Jonathan's circle of deceit. *How much closer could one be than planning something as secretive as murder?* Lonnie figured.

Jonathan was cautious, but reluctantly admitted he had to trust them. For now, anyway, he qualified to himself.

"Not one of us is safe as long as the Porters are alive. Do you understand? You boys work for me, and neither of you will ever have to worry about anything."

Dudley was focused on one thing and that was the treasure. "Vick's gonna be 'round long enough to lead us ta the treasure, ain't he?"

"Maybe Vick, but I plan to pick off the others one by one," Jonathan explained.

"If you're thinking what I'm thinking, it's Aggie Dawson they're going after, and not the treasure," Jonathan added. "Maybe I can catch three fish with one hook."

Jonathan gave them a dirty look but Lonnie asked anyway.

"Watcha' plannin' to do when ya' find 'her?" Lonnie asked.

"I'm going to kill her." Jonathan stared at them with fire in his eyes.

For the first time, Dudley and Lonnie saw an evil that frightened even them.

Chapter 8

Years earlier

FOR YEARS, AGGIE SIMMONS, THE ILLEGITIMATE DAUGHTER OF A **housemaid to the Petty family, was a well-kept secret since Hamp Petty was married with twin sons.** He owned scores of properties stretching from Texas to Tennessee, including Louisiana and Mississippi.

After Hamp learned that Betsy was carrying his child, the shocking reality not only complicated his life, but Betsy's as well. The private affair had gone on for years under everyone's noses. It wasn't until Hamp was on his deathbed that he made a detailed confession to Johnson that he had fathered Aggie and that she was his and Jonathan's half-sister.

Hearing the news, Johnson was stunned as well as being skeptical, but he loved his father. Learning of his father's infidelity enraged him for that union produced another heir who could rob him of half his inheritance.

For the first time, Johnson understood the strange moods of his father. *So this is why father was preoccupied during the time Jonathan and I were growing up, should this information be the truth.*

Concerned even further, Hamp insisted Johnson not tell Jonathan about Aggie for fear Jonathan would kill her.

"Father, have you confided in Aggie that she is your daughter?"

"No, I never had the courage to tell her, since she thinks that Barney is her Pa. She knows nothing, and that's why I'm telling you now. Furthermore, I'm cutting Jonathan out of my Will for raping Aggie and murdering her mother."

Johnson could not believe all he was hearing.

Son, I'm counting on you to share your inheritance with your sister after I'm gone and it's best to keep Aggie a secret from Jonathan. No telling what he is capable of doing once he finds out. Jonathan must never know! It's only right, since Jonathan is responsible for raping his half sister and murdering her mother, that he be denied his birthright. Johnson, can I count on you to share my estate with Aggie?"

Since Hamp was dying Johnson thought the only thing to do would be to appease his Pa.

Reluctantly he agreed. Johnson knew that it would be quite a blow to his brother when he heard that he would be cut out of his inheritance.

For most of the years while Johnson's mother was living, his father had carried on his infidelity without anyone knowing except one man, Barney Simmons. Barney was a long-time loyal employee who agreed to marry Betsy for $5,000, and claim Aggie as his child. Johnson hated that his father had used Barney as part of his Clandestine affair, and it bothered him that Barney and Aggie lived right there on the plantation.

When Aggie was a child she was hardly noticed, but when she emerged from the awkward stage into the promising image of a young woman, Jonathan fantasized about her and began his audacious flirting. She was thirteen and naive when the unthinkable happened. Aggie trusted Jonathan, who was older, and followed him as he lured her into the barn to see a newborn foal. Being lost in Aggie's hypnotic beauty and feeling safe in the confines of the foal's stall, Jonathan's desire aroused him. He ultimately played out his fantasies by abruptly attacking Aggie and throwing her onto a mound of hay, where he violently raped her.

Devastated by his aggression, Aggie screamed at the top of her lungs, alerting both her mother and Hamp. When Betsy rushed into the barn, catching Jonathan in the act, he instinctively grabbed a pitchfork and stabbed her several times. Hamp stood frozen, absorbed in shock, while Betsy was quickly slipping away. Finally stepping forward, he tried to reason with his son to calm down but was quickly backed against the barn wall by the wielded pitchfork.

Aggie screamed hysterically as she witnessed Jonathan stab his father with the fork.

Johnson, drawn by her screams, ran into the barn in time to see Jonathan stabbing their father, and quickly interceded by trying to wrench the fork away from his brother. They fought until Johnson was able to wrestle the deadly tool from Jonathan's grasp and hold him down with the pitchfork handle across Jonathan's chest to calm him down.

Johnson pleaded, "Jonathan, father is badly injured, and we need to help him. Please, we have to save him," he implored.

Slowly, Jonathan's eyes turned to his Pa lying there dying, and finally grasped what he had done. Barney ran into the barn, but his attention went immediately to Betsy, who was lying very still on the ground. Kneeling next to her, he felt for a pulse. He looked at Aggie, and the look in his eyes confirmed what she already knew.

With her clothes in disarray Aggie tried to straighten herself up. Seeing her daddy she cried as she rushed into his arms. Barney held her and let her cry it out. What Jonathan had done to Aggie was obvious, and he wanted to kill him.

"I'm here, and I'm not going to let anyone hurt you ever again," he vowed. He knew he had to protect her. It wasn't safe to be near Johnson and Jonathan, if they found out her true identity. *If they learn the truth, they'll consider her a threat to their inheritance.* The boys were that selfish and would stop at nothing to protect their wealth.

Jonathan was lucky that his father and Johnson covered for him after he had murdered Betsy. "If the law finds out, they'll kill him,"

Hamp said. "He's sick like his mother!" Hamp considered Jonathan the devil's child, but his guilt and fear of public disclosure prevented him from turning his son over to the Sheriff for murdering his mistress and raping Aggie. Hamp had lived for years with a deranged wife, raising his two sons alone. When Margaret finally passed away, it was too late for him to step in and try to be a husband to Betsy and a father to Aggie, but he loved her, and never failed to show her attention, often presenting her with things she might need as she grew into a young girl.

After he married Betsy to protect the Petty name; Barney grew to love Betsy and the daughter he agreed to raise as his own. He refused to confess his love to her for he knew her heart belonged to Hamp. Now it became more than just keeping a promise to his boss; he was so emotionally vested that he would never divulge to Aggie that her real father was Hampton Petty.

As soon as Hamp's wounds healed from the attack, Johnson was ushered off to another plantation in Memphis, Tn. where he met his wife and eventually married. After a number of years away, Johnson's wife died, prompting him and his teenage daughter, Eileen, to return to San Augustine to live. It was during this time that Hamp fell ill and summoned Johnson to his bedside.

"Son, there's not much time. I need you to send for Phillip and have him change my Will."

While Johnson was sitting at his sick father's bedside, Jonathan, who was estranged from his father, was in town drinking and gambling. It was no secret to Johnson that at some point his father would cut Jonathan out of his Will, but nothing could have prepared him for his father acting upon having Aggie share in the inheritance. He learned just before Phillip arrived, that his father was going forth with awarding half the estate to his half-sister.

Johnson was aghast when his father explained to Philip all the illicit details of his affair with Betsy. Johnson had no idea his father would admit that he had a daughter from his affair with a housemaid.

After reassuring that Johnson would be the heir to his and Jonathan's fortune, he insisted that Phillip change the will to include Aggie, who was to receive half the fortune.

Johnson caught Phillip's eye and motioned him to follow him to a private room so they could talk.

"Phillip, he doesn't know what he's saying. He's been babbling nonsense ever since I got here."

"Maybe he's telling the truth, and Aggie is your sister."

"Not a chance. I'd know if there was an ounce of truth in what he's saying. Phillip, can you imagine what this would do to our family and my daughter's good name? This would be a disgrace."

Being a family friend, Phillip did what he was told by Johnson and agreed to manipulate the revisions to his liking, making him the sole heir to the family fortune and stating that his daughter, Eileen, would be the heir if he and Jonathan passed. It further stated that should Eileen be deceased, her surviving heir would be bequeathed the fortune. The Will also stated that as long as there was a living heir, Jonathan would not receive any portion of his father's estate, except for a house on five acres of land next door to the family home at Pecan Plantation in San Augustine. In addition to the new Will there was another extremely important and potentially damaging document; a letter Johnson drew up exposing Jonathan as a rapist and murderer and the knowledge that Aggie was their half sister. That was the least he could do since he had cheated her out of her birthright.

Johnson warned Phillip to beware of Jonathan in the event he found out about the incriminating letter, explaining that it was to be used strictly as leverage to keep Jonathan in line and nothing else.

"He's not going to be happy knowing you received your Pa's entire estate."

"I know what I have to do to shield myself. The letter will be my protection."

Jonathan remembered the last words his father said to him: "Protect yourself and never let Jonathan know he has a sister. He'll kill her if he finds out she's an heir. Take care of her." These were Hamp's dying words.

Although Johnson wished Aggie dead, he wasn't a murderer. He devised a plan to keep her as far away from her inheritance as possible. She must never know she is my sister.

After Hamp's funeral, Barney and Aggie loaded their wagon and went to live on another plantation a distance away. His greatest fear was that Jonathan might find out the truth and kill Aggie. Although Johnson was bitter at having a half-sister, he had the forethought to suspect he might need her one-day to prove that Jonathan was a murderer and a rapist. Until then, his plan was to protect her. She might come in handy if Jonathan ever contests our father's Will. Johnson's greed and Aggie's importance to him in the future were the motivation behind his penning two letters with the Will. The first acknowledged that Aggie was his sister and the second to document that Jonathan had raped Aggie, murdered Betsy Dawson, and then tried to kill his father with a pitchfork. Phillip Bradford, who was forbidden to open the letters, was asked to keep them sealed until such time as they were needed.

After the Reading of the Will, Jonathan reacted just as expected; becoming angered by his father's favoritism to Johnson and storming out of the house, threatening to challenge the Will.

"Jonathan, before you go to the trouble, I have letters that can send you to prison for the rest of your life. So you need to back off," Johnson warned as he was on his way out the door.

He knew Jonathan understood what he was saying, but he could never be certain of what went on in that devious mind of his. After all, Jonathan was his mother's son, and the signs of mental illness were showing more often now.

For a few seconds, the monstrous evil of the deeds Jonathan had committed came flooding back to him and he thought, As long as Aggie is alive, I'm not safe!

Chapter 9

Barney Simmons loaded down the wagon, and left San Augustine with the intent of relocating to another plantation in order to protect Aggie. His motivation was twofold. Of paramount importance was her safety, but he also wanted to provide her with a chance at a good life, something she well deserved.

They lived and Barney worked contentedly on a small plantation near Lufkin, Texas, about 50 miles from San Augustine that Johnson had owned for several years, until Barney encouraged Aggie to move on with him farther away. She was now old enough to be on her own, but she chose to stay with her Pa, as he had become sickly.

"Aggie, we got to git outta here. I saw one of Jonathan's old friends in town, and it ain't safe here no more."

Once again, they loaded the wagon and turned it northward, traveling over the immense flat ground, heading into a world that neither of them knew much about. That's the way it seemed for the two inexperienced travelers who had turned into nomads as a means for survival. Aggie studied her Pa and wondered if even he knew where they were going.

Barney had enjoyed many years of security working for the Petty's, but now for the first time, he knew what it was like to suffer hardships. We never had much, he thought. But we had a roof over our heads and enough to sustain us.

After miles of travel, Aggie was forced to take over the reins and find a place to live, after Barney became gravely ill. Decisions had to be made, and when her Pa became too weak to sit, she discarded personal property from the wagon in order to have a place for him to lie down and rest. He sensed her determination and encouraged her that, in the event he died, to be strong and try to make it on her own.

"Aggie, I want you to listen carefully. Ain't nothin' that can wear a woman down faster than marryin' young and being strapped with a bunch of babies. Ya' got yer whole life ahead of ya'," Barney admonished.

"Daddy, don't you worry, 'cause I'm not marrying nobody. I got too much livin' to do."

"That's my girl. Ya' keep thankin' like that and yer sure to make something outta yerself."

She made her father as comfortable as possible, and then followed her instinct, traveling in the direction of the next town, not knowing what it was.

Barney's condition worsened, and just before they arrived on the outskirts of Henderson, Texas, she saw what looked like an abandoned cabin with a small barn far enough off the main road to provide the privacy they needed. It wasn't much of a home, but it would have to do since her daddy was near death. She didn't know at the time, but she was only a short distance from Henderson. Another day and he'll be gone.

She drove the wagon as close to the porch as possible to save steps, and then helped her Pa into the cabin.

The frail cabin looked as though it had been abandoned. An old bed with a dusty old mattress, a small table and a three chairs were all that remained,. There was also a small box lined with cork to keep food cool, since there was no icebox.

After helping Barney to bed, Aggie drove the wagon to the barn. She unbridled the horse settling it down and then walked around the property until she found a water well. "Gosh, I hope there's water in this well," she said out loud. It wasn't until her third try that she heard a splash.

Aggie filled her pail with water, took some to the horse, and hurried to the house to take care of her Pa.

"Thank you baby girl," Barney said, as Aggie bathed his face. "You don't deserve this happening to ya'."

"Daddy, don't worry about me. I'm fine, and you'll be better come tomorrow."

"Aggie, there's somethin' I been keepin' from ya' that can make a difference to ya'. I'm sorry I ain't told ya' this sooner, but I couldn't bring myself to tell ya' the truth."

She imagined her Pa was rambling because of his fever.

"Baby girl, ya' believe me when I tell ya' that ya' ain't safe goin' back to the plantation with them Petty boys. Johnson warned me about Jonathan coming after ya'."

She stiffened in fear. "Jonathan's coming after me? Why…when? He's already done me harm enough."

"Cause yer a witness to him murderin' yer Ma. Yer the one who can point a finger at 'em and have him hanged for what he done. Ya' understand what I'm tellin ya'? Neither one of them boys know what I'm 'bout to tell ya'. If they knew, both of 'em would want you dead, and me too for tellin' ya'. "

"What else is there to tell?" she asked in fear.

"Aggie, I couldn't leave ya' without ya' knowing—I ain't yer real Pa."

Stunned at hearing those words, she was certain Barney was talking out of his head. She chuckled, for that was the last thing she expected to hear from her dying father.

"Daddy, that's not true…you're sick and … "

Barney broke in before she had a chance to finish. "Aggie girl, Hamp Petty was yer' daddy. I got papers—they all signed and legal. Hamp is yer real daddy. Them papers will prove that Hamp Petty is yer' Pa."

By this time Barney was struggling to speak. "Aggie, I want ya' to be careful, cause there's bad blood in that family and Jonathan ain't gonna rest till he finds ya'."

She didn't know it at the time, but those were the last words she would ever hear Barney say.

Baffled with the news that Barney was not her real father, Aggie sat motionless, unable to move. Although she wanted to disregard what he said, she knew there was a possibility he was telling the truth.

She remembered, from the time she was a little girl, how special Hamp made her feel. Now that she thought about it, they did share a bond. He's my real Pa and never told me. Suddenly she understood a lot of things, like why Barney never showed his love until after her mother died. She now reasoned in light of this news that he felt like he didn't have the right. She remembered her mother and Barney were never close as husband and wife. Now she understood. It made sense. It was because of Hamp that Barney never felt he should impose his spousal, or fatherly role until after that terrible day in the barn. At the time, she had felt her father's new attention was just to help her get over that day.

Each night, Aggie stayed awake nursing Barney as he struggled for another day without ever regaining consciousness, just occasionally tossing, turning, mumbling. Inevitably, on the morning of the third day, she was faced with burying him. The man who raised her would always be her daddy, regardless of what he told her before he died. The truth did not take away the love that she had. He had cared for her all the years she was growing up, and had treated her like his own, and for this she would be forever grateful.

After she patted down the last shovel of dirt on the grave, she read a verse from the Bible and thanked God for all the years she had with him.

"He'll always be my daddy," she asserted.

That night, as she gazed into the flames of the fireplace, she relived some of her favorite memories. There were a few good times for sure, but the others troubled her, especially when, at a young age, she wondered why her mother and father never seemed to have anything in common. They shared very few laughs, which she never understood—until now.

Several days later, Aggie went through Barney's personal things, but did not find the letter that supported what Barney had told her. He must have been out of his mind, she thought, for there were no such papers. Denial won out over reasoning, and she laughed out loud at how absurd her Pa was by claiming Hamp was her real father.

After living in the cabin for almost a month, Aggie found a small garden in a grove of trees a short distance from the cabin. Someone must be living here, she concluded. The garden was well maintained, with an abundance of tomatoes and onions planted among some other vegetables. She was happy to have found the garden, but she questioned who planted it and wondered when they would come back. The least she could do was keep the vegetables weeded and cared for, since she had helped herself to the garden. Besides, working in the garden kept her busy, as the days alone seemed long, and the nights—longer.

Aggie anguished, thinking of the time she would have to leave, for the owner of the little run-down shack would surely return.

One evening, as Aggie was walking from the barn to the cabin, there sitting on the doorsteps was a big one-armed Negro man with his hat in his hand. At first she was startled, but when she saw his big friendly smile she immediately felt at ease, sensing he was harmless.

"Howdy ma'm, I see ya' done found muh place."

"Oh, I'm sorry, the cabin was empty and I assumed no one lived here. I was traveling, and when my Pa got sick and died, I didn't have a choice. I can leave now that you're home."

"Well, I'm a part-timer. I come and go in muh travels and I ain't 'bout to go pushin' nobody out of a place to stay. I noticed the work yo' done. Yo' sho' makin' it purdy 'round here."

"I tried to help out to pay for my stay. I found your garden out back and I've been trying to take care of it for you. There's some nice tomatoes and squash ready to pick."

"I come back 'cause it's 'bout time fer me to put out some good collard greens and do a little canning. Yo' like collard greens and corn pone, don'tcha?"

"I grew up eating collards and cornbread."

"Yo' say yo' daddy got sick?"

"I buried my daddy out back in the wooded area, I hope you don't mind."

"I'm sho' sorry 'bout that. Muh name is Bradley Johnson, and I don't usually stay in the house no way. I have a right cool place out in the barn if ya' don't mind me stayin here fer a while. I promise I won't make a bother of muhself. I need to get that garden goin' fo' I take off agin."

"Bradley, this is your place. I don't even know where the next town is?"

"Well missy, yo' jest a spit's landing away from Henderson."

"How far is that from San Augustine?"

"Fer enough. I don't go in that direction. I come from a little town called Carthage."

"Is that in Texas?"

"Sho' is, Carthage ain't too fer from here. I go back and forth tryin' tuh do what I kin to make a little money. Can't do some things with one arm, but I kin swing an ax and cut wood jest like the best of 'em."

"Well, it's nice to meet you Bradley. My name is Aggie Dawson." This was the first time she had thought about using Dawson, which was her mother's last name. She was glad she was thinking defensively, since Jonathan might be looking for her as Aggie Simmons.

"Nice to meet ya', Ms. Dawson."

"Please, you can call me Aggie. I'm not used to Ms. Dawson." She thought about how nice it would be to have someone living close by, and since Bradley had a milk cow tied behind his wagon, and a load of chickens, everything began looking up.

"Bradley, are you sure you want to stay in the barn. I can stay there just as well as you can."

"Ain't no purdy lady like Ms. Aggie gonna be stayin' in no barn."

"There's a mattress in the barn that belonged to my Pa, if you want to use it."

"Well, thank ya' Ms. Aggie, that's mighty nice."

Each day, Bradley and Aggie worked on improving the place, and soon they were like family. He had wonderful recipes, and with his guidance, Aggie became a wonderful cook and baker.

"Yo' sho' have a way with baking, Ms. Aggie."

The more he complimented her, the more she experimented with her baking.

Bradley would say, "Ms. Aggie, this'll make yo' slap yo' mama down."

Barney's old mattress came in handy, making the barn a very comfortable place for Bradley to stay.

Life had become much easier with Bradley living near, so Aggie began feeling like Henderson was home. One evening, as they sat reminiscing, he told Aggie about the time Henderson burned.

"You mean the whole town burned?"

"Yes'm, it was a Union man, dey thought, hired a Negro woman to burn Henderson down. Dey finally caught dat man and put a noose 'round his neck, dragging 'em through town. We Negro folk made ourself scarce durin' dem times. Sho' got mighty bad fer a while. I had to be lookin' over muh shoulder to make sho' ain't nobody got no rope. Yes'iree, dem was bad times."

"I never heard of Henderson burning. I suppose the news didn't make it to San Augustine."

"I reckon yo' was a lot younger in dem days 'cause this was jest bout Nineteen Hundred.

"I bet if yo' daddy was still livin', he'd 'member."

They sat quietly, and then Aggie began to open up about herself.

"I don't talk much about what happened to me a few years ago, but mama was trying to protect me, and was murdered by someone very close to me."

"I reckon I knew somethin' was troublin' ya'. I kin tell when yo' git real quiet and don't say much."

"Then, just before my daddy died, he told me he wasn't my real Pa. I suppose we all have our troubles, but to find out your Pa ain't your real Pa is a shock."

"My, my. I had no idée' that yo' been through somethin' like that."

"Before he died, he warned me to be careful 'cause the man that killed my mama might come looking for me, since I'm a witness."

"Yo' daddy's right, but don't go worrin' 'bout no man comin' 'round ya' as long as I'm here. Ain't nobody gonna ever hurt ya' 'cause dey'd have to git by me first."

She believed Bradley, and for the first time, she felt secure.

Time passed, and Aggie adapted to being poor, but she was hopeful that the future would bring prosperity.

"Ms. Aggie, why don't yo' sell some of yo' baking?"

Aggie thought Bradley had come up with a good plan, and with an abundance of eggs and milk on hand, she developed quite a baking business, traveling into Henderson with her wagon full of tasty deliveries. Her business grew and the money she had left over began to burn a hole in her pocket. One day she looked in the window of the Henderson Variety Store and saw a beautiful dress. I'm going to have to take a better look, and perhaps try it on for size.

Ms. Jones, the proprietor, was very smug and promptly insinuated that the dress was too expensive for her to try on, and that it was specially made for a proper lady. It incensed Aggie that the owner of the store would remind her of her class and station in life. Aggie retaliated by impulsively shelling out a ridiculous sum of money to pay down on the dress. Upon seeing the money, Ms. Jones allowed Aggie to have credit.

"And throw in the hat and shoes," Aggie added.

Ms. Jones wrapped the package with the extra purchases, while Aggie continued to fume.

On the way out she heard Ms. Jones say, "the baking business must be mighty good, and don't forget the balance is due the next time you make your delivery."

Aggie ignored her, hoping one day she would show Ms. Jones that she was every bit a proper lady as any who shopped in her store.

Aggie would not allow herself to think how impulsive she was to make such a purchase. Her concern at the moment was getting back at Ms. Jones and showing her that she was not to be spoken to in such a manner. After Aggie finally settled down, she wondered when and where she would ever wear such a dress.

Unfortunately, the worst happened; Aggie's eggs began to dwindle. She panicked when she saw how this began to affect her business.

"Bradley, I have debt, and Ms. Jones is looking for me to pay her when I make my deliveries."

"But Ms. Aggie, somethin' is happenin' wit' dem eggs, and now some of our chickens is gone missing too."

"Not the chickens!"

"Yes, ma'am…they disappearing right and left."

All Aggie could think about was Ms. Jones and the money she owed her. She began applying pressure on Bradley to find out what was happening.

"I'm gonna' find out fo' yo'. Don't yo' go worrin' yo' purdy little head."

That night, he pulled his wagon up close to the chicken yard to stake a trap; more like a wire pen with a trap door on the front of it. He hung a piece of meat in the very back of the trap to lure the varmint inside. His plan was to capture whatever was stealing the chickens, and then destroy it.

Bradley put the wagon in place, and then climbed inside to wait it out. It was the wee hours of the morning when the fog began rolling in, making the night very shadowy. There was just a hint of a moon as Bradley tossed and turned, trying to stay awake as he lay there in wait. The moon was hypnotic, and he became captivated as the fog moved upward, creating a mist over the moon glow. The glow was pulsating through the intermittently thick fog, as the air began to cool. Bradley was blinking, doing his best to stay awake. In his euphoria, he thought back to the time he was a child, when he had both arms. I reckon I was near five years old when they took my arm, he recollected. He remembered the dreadful night the doctor told his daddy that they needed to amputate his arm to keep him from dying. Jest 'cause a spider bit me they took my arm, Bradley remembered.

He relived the doctors tying him down while he was screaming in pain. They didn't give me nothin' for muh' pain, they just went to sawin'. The memory was still as vivid as it was when he was a child. I reckon I almost died, 'cause it hurt so bad.

He must have drifted off to sleep about that time, for he was startled awake by a guttural sound.

He sat straight up at hearing a growl. That sound is coming from somewhere in the fog. He strained to see what was stirring, as he crouched down, looking through slats on the side of the wagon. This is when he saw what appeared to be a dog. No, it's a wolf.

The more he observed the staggering creature coming toward him, the more convinced he was that it was sick with rabies. Bradley was stunned and terrified.

The thought of a rabid wolf scared the hell out of him, after witnessing several of his friends die from rabies, while being locked away in a smoke house. It's a horrible death, he remembered.

Bradley was convinced the hungry wolf had picked up his scent, as it continued on a direct path toward him. It's as though the wolf knew Bradley was inside the wagon.

I got to git' outta dis wagon and run fo' da' barn, he thought.

Bradley began scooting backward out of the wagon—just a few more feet and I'll hit the ground and start running, he planned.

The wolf kept wobbling on his feet as it continued toward him. The sick animal's mouth appeared to be moving uncontrollably, as froth dripped from its jowls. Bradley's feet finally hit the ground, and he quickly turned, running toward the barn. The unthinkable happened; he tripped. The rabid wolf leapt at Bradley with every ounce of energy left inside him. He latched his teeth behind Bradley's neck and would not let go. Bradley rolled onto his back and tumbled around trying to free himself. But with only one arm, there was little he could do to help himself. Finally, in desperation, he began screaming.

"Ms. Aggie, help me! Git' the gun!"

Aggie awoke to Bradley's bloodcurdling screams. She was in her nightgown when she grabbed the shotgun and ran out into the night. Her eyes locked on the animal attached to Bradley's neck. Terrified, she kept waving the gun trying to get a shot. I'm afraid I'll hit Bradley, she thought. Aggie knew what was happening, but couldn't take a chance of possibly killing Bradley, and then having the wolf turn on her.

"Shoot, Ms. Aggie." Those were the last words Bradley spoke.

Unfortunately, after several attempts to get a clean shot, Bradley stopped fighting, and surrendered quietly to the beast. Instinctively, the beast had gone for the jugular vein, which sealed Bradley's demise. The emaciated, and now weakened animal, stood glaring at Aggie as though she would be next. Her concern was for Bradley and she prayed he was still alive. After taking careful aim, she fired and hit the animal, then fired again. She expected the wolf to yelp or put up a fight, but he didn't. Instead, it made several quick movements, as if to thank her for relieving it of its misery. She ran over to Bradley, but it was too late. He was dead. What a horrible way to die, she thought.

She cried, blaming herself for not being able to save her friend.

She knelt down beside him and cradled his head in her arms. "Bradley, what will I do without you?" she cried.

Aggie looked down at her gown. The wolf must have cut Bradley's artery, she observed. "Poor man didn't have a chance!" Blood was everywhere, and most of it was on her.

Aggie moved the horse-drawn wagon inside the barn after she mustered up enough strength to pull Bradley's body up some planks and into the wagon.

She cried every step of the way as she walked back to the cabin for a blanket. I'll bury Bradley when the sun comes up.

She would miss him for he was the kindest soul she had ever known, and their time together was cut much too short.

After losing him the days that followed were difficult, for the emptiness and pain were too great.

Everyone I've loved has died, and why? she questioned. If disappointment and death are to make me stronger, then there must be something unbeknownst to me that will test my strength. Aggie had no idea how close to the truth she was, for the days ahead would test her beyond measure.

It was several months before she could enter the small room Bradley had made for himself.

Perhaps I can fix it up and rent it out, she planned.

As she walked into his cozy little room, she couldn't help but notice it was neat as a pin. Bradley didn't have much, but what he had was kept clean and organized. She looked around the room and spied a small rectangular shaped black box, much like something she had buried when she was a child. The lid was scratched and partly rusted, as she picked it up to examine. Apparently, this was his only personal property, aside from a few clothes that were folded on a makeshift table.

When she opened the box she found a few dollars he had saved, along with a small family picture of himself before his arm was amputated. Apparently, the man and woman in the picture were his Ma and Pa. She ran her hand over the picture as if to comfort the man she had cherished as a friend. The picture must have been kept to remind him that once upon a time he was normal like everyone else. I'll always keep this to remind me of you Bradley, she resigned.

Aggie was stripping Bradley's bed when something protruded from within the mattress. The protrusion was large and thick. It was apparent the mattress had been ripped open and sewn back, as if to protect the contents. She knew whatever was in the mattress had either belonged to Bradley or her daddy, since it had one time been her father's bed.

As she opened the loose stitches, she remembered what Barney had said about papers he had that would change her life. Her hands shook as she opened the large envelope. Bradley had no idea he had been laying on top of an envelope that would transform Aggie's world.

When she opened it, her eyes went directly to a large roll of money, bound tightly with string. It was more money than she had ever seen. She also found a paper which described the $5,000 Hamp had given Barney for marrying Aggie's mother. This was every bit of the money Hamp had given Barney for keeping quiet.

Such a web of deceit, she thought. The final paper she opened was a legal document drawn up by Hamp Petty claiming Aggie as his daughter.

There was nothing to indicate she was an heir to his wealth. "I have no birthright," she thought, other than this acknowledgement that I am his daughter, on paper. I could go back and challenge Hamp's Will, but why take a chance on being murdered, when my father never openly acknowledged me as his child? Aggie thought about it and resigned herself to the fact that she was excluded from a share of the inheritance left to her half-brothers. She had no idea that Johnson and her niece had been murdered and this information could entitle her to the Petty fortune.

There had been nothing said of an inheritance to Aggie when Hamp Petty passed away. I'm sure if I were to be included, that Phillip Bradbury, who read the Will, would have advised me at that time.

She now understood that Barney was right to warn her that there were clear signs her two half-brothers might want her dead in order to protect their inheritance.

As long as she remained in hiding and away from Jonathan and Johnson, she might be safe.

After reading the papers, Aggie was impressed that every cent Barney was paid for marrying her mother was kept for her. "This money could have changed my parents lives, and yet Barney kept all of it for me. These were parents who loved me, she thought.

Pride swelled within her, knowing her daddy loved her so much that he never spent a dollar that Hamp had given him. She wondered if her mother knew Barney had been paid to marry her.

He really did love us, she tenderly acknowledged.

Aggie, who was raised poor, knew what it was like to be frugal, but there was something she had to do. The next morning she hitched her wagon and drove to settle her balance at the Variety Store.

Ms. Jones was waiting to hear Aggie's excuse of why she could not pay her bill. But instead, Aggie purchased two more dresses she had been admiring.

"My, my, the baking business must really be doing well. Can I help you with anything else, Ms. Dawson?"

"Thank you, Ms. Jones. Just make sure the packages are wrapped well."

Aggie took her bundles, along with a large tote she purchased, and left Ms. Jones with her mouth open. She then climbed back into her wagon and headed to the blacksmith shop to purchase a new horse and buggy, something she needed but never thought she could afford.

After she pulled her fine buggy up to her cabin, she had an epiphany. She looked at the small cabin, and then over at the barn. There's nothing more for me here. I have to make my own way, Aggie responsibly accepted.

Chapter 10

JONATHAN, GRIPPED BY FEAR, HAD TWO THINGS ON HIS MIND: KILLING **the Porters and finding Aggie Simmons, who knew his terrible secret.**

He had already murdered two people, and would not hesitate to do it again if it meant saving his own skin.

There was no need to put it off any longer now that he had someone to do his dirty work. His main worry was the Jameses stupidity, and the baggage they brought with them, being cold-blooded killers themselves. Jonathan feared being implicated in the murder of Orson's daughter, even though he had nothing to do with it. Lonnie and Dudley's confessions caused him uneasiness, since the decent thing to do was to report the information to the law. But it's not smart for one murderer to expose another murderer.

Jonathan had no idea of Orson's vengeance, but the James' knew all too well how the Sheriff administered his justice. Their Pa had told them plenty, since more than once he had personally tangled with "ol' Eagle Eyes".

Orson was also known for his shrewdness, acute powers of observation, and intuition. If he saw Lonnie and Dudley in San Augustine, his "gut instinct" would tell him that they had something to do with his daughter's death, or they wouldn't be in San Augustine. Woe be unto them if Orson ever suspected them of killing Lucy. For if he did, Jonathan's plan would begin to unravel. *These men could end up costing me*, Jonathan thought.

Time was of the essence. Carrying the guilt of having murdered Phillip Bradbury was making Jonathan more paranoid each day. The town Sheriff was still beating the bushes, asking questions, trying to find out who murdered him.

Before Cain and Orson left for Memphis, Jonathan called Lonnie and Dudley in to give them a job to do.

"I want you boys to stake out them Porters, and see what they're up to. I think there's something big going on."

"Ya' want us followin' 'em?," the two said in chorus.

Jonathan winced at their stupidity, but stopped short of chastising them.

He shrugged, "That's right! Follow them and let me know what's going on."

After a few days of snooping, they saw the men load their pack-horse with supplies.

"They gettin' ready to move out," Lonnie said. "Yeah, the bo'-hog man's gonna like this." The men hightailed it back to the Circle J, barging in on Jonathan without knocking.

"They gittin' ready to move out!" Lonnie shouted.

At the sound of someone coming through the door unannounced, Jonathan spun around, drawing his pistol in the same motion.

"Hey, how about knocking! Walking in on a feller like that could get your head blown off."

"Sorry boss, but 'ol' Eagle Eyes,' I mean the Sheriff and Cain are gittin' ready to head out somewhere'. We saw their packhorse loaded down with supplies. Looks like they gonna be leavin' bright and early tomar' mornin'." Lonnie smiled proudly at Dudley for the remarkable way in which he delivered the message.

"How do you know they're leaving in the morning?" Jonathan asked.

"Uh, I guess 'cause they ain't gonna be loadin' no pack horse two days before they travel." Lonnie smiled again.

Jonathan scratched his head, considering what to do. He got up and poured himself a drink. "So, they're leaving. I didn't tell ya' but I'm planning on going with you."

Dudley gave Lonnie a surprised look. "You plannin' on riding with us?"

"Y'all have a problem with that?" he challenged. "You might need me for cover."

"Boss, we can use the cover," said Lonnie, nodding "yes."

"Then let's get a little shuteye, 'cause I want to be ready bright and early… and I mean early," Jonathan ordered.

Jonathan looked out the window making sure no one had followed Dudley and Lonnie to the ranch.

"I ain't waiting for you, so don't be late…you hear?" Jonathan looked at them like he meant business.

"Yessiree," they abided.

The men scrambled out of the house and left Jonathan alone.

"Why ya' suppose he's a'goin' with us?" Dudley asked his brother.

"Hell, who knows? Ain't ya' figured him out? He's a crazy sonvobitch. We could end up dead with a drunk like him coverin' us."

"What we gonna do, then?" asked Dudley.

"Jest keep an eye on which way he's a'pointin' that gun of his."

Dudley stopped walking and thought a minute, then hurried to catch up with Lonnie.

That night, before Jonathan drifted off to sleep, he thought about Aggie and where she might be hiding. *She's close…I can feel it.*

The day before Cain and Orson left for Memphis, Vick rode into town for a few supplies. Riding alone, he recalled the apparition he had seen when he left Panther Holler. The memory of that event was haunting, and the more he tried to brush it off, the more vivid it became.

That night, long after Vick and Elizabeth retired to bed, and during the early morning hours, Vick was jarred awake. At first he was alarmed, but as his eyes focused, his bedroom transformed the night into day. He looked around his room, and yes, it was his bedroom. Once comforted, there appeared before him an Indian warrior dressed in full battle array. What is this? This can't be a dream. This must be real, he thought.

Vick, who was not frightened, grew increasingly curious, as he trusted the Indian who beckoned him to follow. They were traveling through a wilderness, when suddenly; Vick was in a wooded area much like Panther Holler. "Wait, it is Panther Holler," he discerned. They continued traveling weightlessly at an incredible rate of speed he did not understand. His feet were just above the ground. It was exhilarating, something he had never imagined. Then everything slowed to normal. He followed the warrior but he did not know where. Vick had a moment to gaze over the area, and then followed the warrior in another direction. As Vick wondered of the significance, he saw a very bright stone that sprung forth from the ground. As the dream continued, he looked toward the sky, as a brilliant hawk descended to the stone. Its' gaze was penetrating as if the hawk was sending Vick a message. He understood the message but did not know what it meant. *"The road that roars," what could that mean?* He thought. Vick supposed the hawk might be Chaytan, his Indian friend who previously had appeared to him when he almost died at Panther Holler. In an instant, the strange encounter ended and Vick slipped into a dreamless state.

In the morning when he awoke, he lay there thinking of the message, "the road that roars," which did not make sense. He pondered why he was having such strange dreams and what they meant. *It seems too real to be a dream.* The road that roars kept ringing in his ears and he knew the phrase would become important to him in days to come.

Vick loved the sound of the rain peppering down on the tin roof, a sound he had forgotten about when he was locked away in prison. Elizabeth rolled over and saw Vick propped up on his pillow watching her sleep. "Have you been awake long?" She asked

"No, not long…the rain woke me. You were sleeping so soundly, I didn't have the heart to wake you," he said.

"I wish you had."

Vick kissed her and held her close.

They lay there a moment, just listening. Then Elizabeth turned to him.

"Vick, I can't believe Cain and Orson are leaving for Memphis in this kind of weather. Do you think we can talk some sense into them?"

"You know Orson, he'll tease Cain to death if he backs out just 'because of a little rain'."

"This is not exactly a little rain; this is a guzzler," Elizabeth added.

Jonathan and the boys were drenched as they hid out, nestled in a group of trees, waiting for the men to pull out. They were watching them say their goodbyes.

"Y'all, got everything ya need?" asked Vick.

"Hell, we don't know," Orson said. Rain was running off his hat like a river, their long dusters so far keeping their clothes dry, while their horses were jumping around, raring to go.

Elizabeth laughed, thinking she was glad it was not her riding off in the rain.

"Y'all have to be crazy leaving in weather like this."

"Vick Porter, I always knew ya' were a softie. Afraid ya' gonna melt, huh?" Orson mocked.

"No, I'm just a little smarter." Vick gave Orson a playful nudge.

Elizabeth knew Cain would have waited for a better day, but Orson would have perceived that as being weak. He knew he would be kidded all the way to Memphis and back if he gave Orson the upper hand.

"No, Pa, we're not afraid of a little rain."

"A little rain ain't never hurt nobody," echoed Orson.

Off in the distance Jonathan and the James' were watching, and plotting to overtake Orson and Cain. They wondered why on earth they didn't put off leaving till after the rain stopped. Vick felt an overwhelming urge to stop Cain and Orson, but he knew not to intervene.

Just as expected, the first day of travel for the men was miserable, trudging their horses through rain and mud, losing time. The conditions were such that not even Jonathan wanted to risk an ambush in that kind of weather. It was tough going, but by the afternoon of the second day, the sky cleared, and the sun began drying things out.

Traveling was slow due to the packhorse, but Orson and Cain didn't mind since they enjoyed the outdoors and spending time together.

Occasionally, when bored, Orson rode up alongside Cain to talk.

"Yer Pa's gonna be surprised as all git-out when we bring Hop Babcock back with us."

"Yeah, I can't wait to see his face."

"Are you 'bout ready ta stop fer the night?" Cain smiled inwardly; glad he wasn't the first one to mention, "stop".

"I'm ready when you are. How about we ride till we find a watering hole, and then make camp."

They rode another five miles before they came to a fork in the road near a small lake.

"This looks good. What you say we camp here so the horses can have a little grass and fresh water?"

"Suits me," Orson said.

The men took the horses to the water's edge and let them wade out for a drink.

"Looks like a good place to camp across the road in those trees to me. What do you think?" asked Cain.

"How 'bout you checkin' while I hold the horses?"

It was a perfect place, with plenty of wood left by the last drifter. Jonathan and his men kept out of sight, but in a distance they could see Cain and Orson stirring around their campfire.

"Don't let 'em see ya'," Jonathan said to the James brothers.

"Wish we were closer to the lake instead of here," Dudley complained.

"Don't you worry, we'll be there soon enough, and then, BANG!"

They smiled, imagining the outcome.

"Just remember, we got time, so let's don't go jumping the gun before they're asleep," Jonathan admonished.

Dudley pulled out his pistol and made a shooting gesture, trying to impress Jonathan.

As soon as darkness fell, the men moved cautiously toward Orson and Cain's camp.

Jonathan whispered, "Now don't go storming the camp until I say so."

Lonnie shook his head in agreement.

Before the two drifted off to sleep, Cain noticed that faraway look in Orson's eyes, and supposed he was thinking about Lucy. Seeing his sadness, he broached another subject to change his mood.

"Orson, do you think we'll ever be able to find Aggie Simmons?"

"I don't know. Yer guess is as good as mine…too many small towns 'round San Augustine."

"If Aggie's with her daddy, I would imagine they settled somewhere here in East Texas, wouldn't you think?"

"Let's hope she didn't git too fer, 'cause, if her daddy headed west, we might as well give up. She's bound to be around these parts but yer' planning on Memphis before we look fer Aggie. Ain't cha'?"

"What about that fire? Ya' want to let it burn itself out or put another log on?" Cain asked.

"I better keep it going to keep the varmints away. Lets talk about Hop in the morning."

Orson rolled over, and before the logs hit the fire, he was snoring.

When Cain settled down for the night, he lay there listening to the crackle of embers until he drifted off to sleep.

Jonathan and the James' waited before walking their horses quietly toward where Cain and Orson lay sleeping.

Jonathan whispered, "Why don't we spook their horses and then pick 'em off."

The boys, crouched down in the bushes, nodded their heads in agreement. Jonathan threw a rock at the horses, and they started running off. He then motioned the men to inch closer.

As soon Orson heard the horses, he started rolling, and tried to determine the direction of the sound. He sprung to his feet firing his gun. One of his bullets hit Dudley in the leg.

"I'm hit," Dudley yelled.

"Okay you hombres, show yerself?" Orson shouted, and began firing again.

Cain, waking in a start, fumbled with his rifle while Orson stood shooting bullets into the night.

Having the advantage of being hidden by the darkness, Jonathan began walking and firing at the same time, until he hit both Cain and Orson.

"Cain, take cover, I've been shot." As Orson fell to the ground, he saw a face that looked familiar.

Cain took a bullet, then hit the ground with a thud.

"My God, you've shot muh boy!" Orson yelled.

The last two shots were for the Sheriff, who took a bullet in the left shoulder and one in the leg. Both Orson and Cain lay still in the darkness.

Jonathan and his men examined the bodies and determined that Orson and Cain were both dead.

"We got 'em. What about their bodies?" Asked Lonnie.

"Let 'em be. We did what we came here to do. Now let's get the hell outta here in case someone heard all those shots and comes looking," Jonathan commanded.

Even Lonnie sensed Jonathan was a man without a soul. He later told Dudley, "He's a cold sonvobitch."

The next morning, Orson showed signs of life, as his eyelids began to flutter. He was weak from loss of blood, but his injuries were not life threatening.

"Cain," he whispered, "where are you? Answer me son, are you alright?"

There was no response, and although difficult to move, he knew he had to try to stand.

Using a strong stick to support himself on the injured leg, he searched the area around the campsite, but Cain was nowhere to be found. They must have killed him and hid his body. As Orson struggled to climb onto his horse, he noticed both the packhorse and Cain's horse were gone. "Maybe he's alive and rode on." Regardless, Orson was in no shape to think clearly.

Cain had awakened much earlier than Orson, and stumbled away from camp dazed and confused. He collapsed on the side of the road in an area where tall grasses hid him from view as he lost consciousness. He had only ventured a short distance from camp. He lay there, suffering from head trauma, a chest wound, and a bullet to the leg.

It was a couple hours later that Orson awoke and rode out of camp, heading back toward the Plantation. Orson's wounds were not as serious as Cain's, but being he was in his seventies, he knocked himself unconscious after falling on a bed of rocks. Riding out of camp, Orson did not see Cain lying helplessly near the fork in the road.

Hours passed, and then about dusk a young woman in a hurry to get home drove by in her horse-driven buggy. She got a glimpse of what appeared to be a piece of clothing peeking from the weeds in the ditch near the road. She stopped to get a closer look and realized it was more than just clothing. It appeared to be the body of a man, a dead man.

Her instinct was to render aid, ignoring the chance of possible danger.

If this man is still alive, he is too far gone to hurt anyone, she thought.

After briefly checking his pulse and wounds, she knew he needed care as soon as possible. *He's alive, but for how long?* Cain's face was unrecognizable, caked with dried blood from the wound on his head.

Now, to get him into my buggy, she told herself. At that moment she was sadly reminded of another man she was once forced to lift into her buggy.

Using that same technique, along with a gutsy pioneer woman's determination, she got Cain into the buggy.

Living only a short distance away, she soon arrived at her cabin, and using the bit of strength she had left, managed to get the injured man into her bed.

She removed a money belt containing a substantial amount of cash, and put it away for safekeeping. *No robbery intent here,* she thought, as she stripped him of his bloody clothing. Being as respectful as possible, she undressed him and cleaned his wounds. *I can't be bashful at seeing his nakedness. There's no one else but me to tend his wounds.* Even so, Aggie thought it only proper to keep a cloth over his privates. She was now eighteen years of age and remembered the horrible vision of Jonathan raping her, which left her traumatized at that impressionable age.

After close examination of the stranger's wounds, she knew he needed more care than she could give. In a frantic attempt to save Cain, she took enough money from the money belt to fetch the town doctor. He would later tell her that had she waited another two hours, he would have been dead.

As it turned out, the next few days were touch and go, as she continued to watch over him. Aggie kept wiping the stranger's face and wondering if he was married or had a family. *He must be well off, carrying the kind of money I found on him.* She was convinced his wounds were not the result of a robbery. Whoever did this, wanted him dead, and that concerned her.

Each day that passed she imagined she might never know who he is, should he die. Cain remained in a coma for almost a week without food. *How much longer before he wakes?* she wondered.

On the sixth night, Aggie had just bathed his face, when she saw his eyelids flutter. *He might be regaining consciousness,* she hoped. That evening, she drifted off to sleep earlier than usual, and did not wake until morning. When she awoke, the injured man was gone. She also noticed that he had eaten the leftover food from the night before. *He must have been starving*, she thought. At first she was afraid he wandered off, until she opened the door and found him sitting on the porch, looking lost and somewhat bewildered.

She normally would have been frightened, but during the short time she had cared for him, she felt there was something mysterious and special about him. She couldn't help but notice how handsome he was, and as she studied him, she wondered if he had a family or was married.

He turned toward her as she walked out the door.

"Are you okay?" she asked. The somewhat stunned stranger looked pensively at her standing before him. She knew he was still struggling, even though he was improving.

"You were sleeping, and I didn't want to wake you. I don't think I know you, do I?" the young man asked. Aggie thought it was strange that he would ask if he knew her.

"No, we've never met. My name is Aggie Dawson, and I brought you here after finding you near death from your wounds. I hope you don't mind, but I had a doctor look after you. You were badly injured, and the doctor said you would have died if I hadn't fetched him for you. I used some of the money from your money belt. Don't worry, it's safe, and all is there except what I used to pay the doctor."

"I had a money belt on me?"

"Yes, but you weren't robbed."

"Do you remember what happened?" asked Aggie.

He looked at her trying to remember. He noticed her smile and how beautiful she was, but there was no memory. "I've been trying to remember what happened, but I can't."

"Do you know your name?"

He shrugged his shoulders as if he was confused.

"How long have I been here?"

"About a week, but you're still not healed. I see you found your clothes. I hope you don't mind, but I had to wash them…they were soiled with blood from your injuries and there are no bullet holes in them."

Cain was embarrassed that a woman had to bathe him.

"You've been taking care of me?"

"I hope you don't mind, for there was no one else. When I found you, I brought you here. I couldn't leave you in the shape you were in."

"I'm grateful, but I can't stay any longer."

"Well, you're not going anywhere just yet, at least for a few more days. Don't worry, you're no bother."

"Cain sensed Aggie's sincerity. The way she talked indicated she was from a good background.

"I bet you're hungry."

Cain smiled. "Thanks, but I hate to be an imposition."

Aggie placed her hand on his shoulder to let him know he was safe with her.

"You never answered me. Do you remember your name?"

He looked at her, still puzzled. "I've tried to remember…but I can't."

"Well, don't you worry…just give it time." Aggie remembered his wounds, and imagined, It might take longer than he thinks.

~

It was a long journey returning to the plantation since Orson was injured and having to take his time. He had to make several stops to rewrap his wound with pieces from his shirt. Finally, he made it back home.

Vick was cleaning stalls in the barn when he looked up to see Orson struggling to stay in his saddle. He immediately knew something was terribly wrong since Cain was not with him. Suddenly, that old feeling crept back and he had a sinking spell, much like the one he had when his brother Sam died. "Not Cain!" Vick thought.

He saw blood on Orson and his horse and ran to help.

"Lizzie, come quick!" Vick shouted.

Elizabeth hurried out the door at the same time Vick was approaching Orson.

"Oh my God, something has happened!" she cried.

He was slumped in his saddle, barely able to hold on.

"Orson, we're here now," Vick said.

"I don't know what the hell happened," Orson mumbled. "We were ambushed,"

"Lizzie, we got to get him in the house. Do you think you can help me?"

Elizabeth supported Orson, while Vick pulled him out of the saddle. With both their efforts, they led him into a bedroom not far from the porch. They sat him on the bed and Orson fell back with no energy left in him.

Vick pulled his boots off and began unbuttoning his shirt.

"Lizzie, I got to get him out of these clothes. Why don't you get some hot water so I can wash the blood off him."

Orson was struggling to speak." Them hombres ambushed us in the night. They shot me and Cain."

"Orson...where is Cain?" Vick feared the answer.

"He ain't here?"

"No, we haven't seen him since he left with you. Do you remember what happened?" "You mean to tell me Cain ain't here? I looked around camp and couldn't find him. His horse was gone and I thought he'd be here with you."

"Take it easy, don't try and talk too much." Vick looked at Elizabeth in a panic, for he knew something bad had happened to Cain.

"Men...maybe two or three of 'em shot at us. One man was on a paint horse. I was playin' dead and saw him when he came into our camp," Orson offered.

"That's good that you saw the man's horse, but what about Cain?"

Orson tried to raise his head, but fell back onto his pillow.

"Cain's here with y'all ain't he? He left me—and thought I was dead."

"Orson, try to understand. Cain never made it home. Something must have happened to him. Try hard to remember."

"Orson kept mumbling, talking nonsense and rolling his head back and forth."

Elizabeth bent down and looked Orson in the eyes.

"Please Orson, for Cain's sake, try to remember anything! Do you know what happened to Cain?"

"Lizzie, I don't know. I came to and couldn't find him. We were both shot.

Elizabeth turned away and began to sob.

"Oh no, Cain's dead! Something tells me he's dead!"

Vick was shaken. He sat there for a moment, and then walked toward the door as if he was looking for Cain to ride up. "Lizzie, we don't know that he's dead. I'm going after him."

"I saw him shot, that's all I remember," Orson said to Elizabeth.

Vick walked out on the porch, imagining who might be responsible for ambushing his son. He couldn't bring himself to think Cain was dead. I got to keep drilling Orson to remember.

"Orson, you were lucky. I looked at your wounds and after a couple of days rest, you'll be back to normal. Those bullets grazed you bad enough to draw blood but they weren't bad injuries."

Vick thought about leaving immediately, but traveling in the night would be a waste. Little could be done in the dark, he reasoned.

That night Elizabeth wept, as she thought about her son needing their help. She wondered why they had left Arkansas, and her home, when they had everything they needed there. So many things have happened. First Lucy died, the manor burned to the ground, and now Cain, were her thoughts. Laying there remembering, she thought their trouble began when Cain found he was the heir to the Petty fortune. *We had no problems until I met Johnson Petty, and now it seems the world has been turned upside down.* Who would have thought after Johnson died that he would have a twin much worse than he was?

Her memory went back to the day Johnson and Eileen arrived at the manor with the news that Eileen was pregnant with Cain's baby. Then she remembered the horror of Johnson and Eileen being murdered by Buck Dupree. The only good thing that came from knowing Johnson Petty, was finding Vick in prison...not just any prison, but one of the most deplorable prisons ever known, where few people survive.

The next morning, after little sleep, Elizabeth packed clothes and enough food to last for Vick to search for Cain. She was sure he would not return home until he found out what happened to their son.

"How do you know where to look?" Elizabeth asked.

Orson hobbled into the room just in time to hear her question. "I know where to look and ya' ain't goin' no place without me!"

Vick and Elizabeth were surprised to see how well Orson looked, compared to the night before.

"Orson, you're in no condition to be on a horse," Vick countered.

"I had me a good night's sleep and I'm alive, so let's git movin.'"

"Why don't you take the Model T...it'll be easier on the both of you and a lot faster," Elizabeth insisted.

"Not this time Lizzie. A horse can take me where that automobile can't. But Orson, you're in no shape to be going nowhere."

"I ain't no good to myself stayin' 'round here when I know Cain might be out there a'needin' us. You don't worry about me holdin' ya' up. Let me do the worrin'."

The men were both packed within minutes and Elizabeth saw Vick and Orson disappear beyond the plantation.

With mane and tail tossed by the wind, Orson's steel gray horse streamed in front of Vick. He was amazed by the resilience of his old friend.

Chapter 11

Vᴠᴄᴋ ᴀɴᴅ Oʀsᴏɴ ʀᴏᴅᴇ ғʀᴏᴍ ᴇᴀʀʟʏ ᴍᴏʀɴɪɴɢ ᴜɴᴛɪʟ ʟᴀᴛᴇ ɴɪɢʜᴛ **before stopping to make camp.** "If it weren't for me, we'd already be there," Orson complained.

"Now, don't go worrying. I couldn't do this without you," Vick tried to reassure him.

"I guess it's safe to say we got another full day's ride a'fore we make it to where we were ambushed." Orson took it slow and easy, as he gingerly slipped out of the saddle.

"I reckon I might be jest a little bit sore here and there." It wasn't very often that anyone heard Orson Cargill complain of a physical frailty, no matter how small. When they settled in for the night, they'd hardly said goodnight before Orson was snoring. It had been a long day.

At first light they emerged from their bedrolls and rode on, following a creek that twisted and turned, until they came upon a trail. Just before sundown Orson pointed out to Vick, "Look, up there! See that lake? That's right near the camp where Cain and me was ambushed."

"Why don't you ride on and see if there's any clues, while I check around the lake." After Vick searched on horseback without any luck, they tied their horses and set out on foot, lifting bushes and scouring the countryside, trying to find any sign of Cain.

Vick sensed Orson was disturbed at being there, and might be reliving what happened to him and Cain.

"We were layin' 'round a fire right here when them hombre's started shootin' at us. Cain was quick up on his feet, but then fell to the ground jest a few feet from me. All I could do was keep shootin' in the dark. When I went down I saw one man's face that looked damn familiar. I clipped his partner 'cause I heard him yell he was shot."

"Do you remember what the man looked like?"

This was the first time Orson tried to concentrate on what he saw. He scratched his head. "Well now, since I'm thanking 'bout it, it's a little crazy, but if I put a name ta' the face, I would have ta say it was one of them James brothers from back home. Ya' remember them two men a'waitin' fer us when we came from Panther Holler? I swear that's who that man looked like, one of them boys."

"Orson, that couldn't be. Jonesboro is a hell of a long way from here. There ain't no reason a man from Jonesboro would be this far away from home ambushing you and Cain…especially them two."

"I reckon yer right. Ain't nothin' 'bout what I said that makes a dang bit of sense."

"Didn't you say you saw a paint horse?"

"I'm sorry I ain't no more help than that, but it was dark, and me and Cain had already dozed off when we woke ta' them gunshots. I do 'member that paint horse though. He had white markings on one back foot."

"You mean like a white stocking on his leg above his hoof?"

"Yep. I seen the back side of the horse and it was on the left hind leg."

"I don't know if that will help, but at least it's something," Vick admitted.

The next morning, Vick awoke to the smell of strong coffee. Orson was up, dressed, and ready to go.

Vick poured himself a cup, took a drink and spit it out. "Orson, you're killing me. Everything you make is strong. I remember the night you spiked the punch before me and Elizabeth got married. Everybody nearly passed out."

Orson smiled, knowing he lifted Vick's spirit, even if it was for only a moment.

"Strong eh? That's one reason I ain't invited ta' them shindigs."

"So this is your secret. Strong coffee and whiskey."

"The stronger the better. And I ain't talkin' 'bout no women."

Vick was much too serious, and Orson sensed the time was not right for ribbing his friend. After coffee, they stamped out the campfire then headed to Carthage, Texas. Upon arrival, they went directly to the Sheriff's Office for information.

"No sir, things are purdy tame here in Carthage—with nothin' but a bunch of farmers," said the Sheriff. "Farmers ain't fer makin' no trouble, at least not 'round here."

"Well, I hate to disappoint ya', but about five miles from here me and this man's son was ambushed in the night. We were both left fer' dead, and when I come to, his son was gone. This all happened in yer neck of the woods."

"Did ya' find a body?" the Sheriff asked.

"We went back to where the ambush happened, but didn't find my son," Vick spoke.

"That's a good sign, if ya didn't find no body. He could be holed up someplace restin'. Give 'em time to git back home."

"Appreciate it Sheriff, but if my boy's alive, we aim to find him."

"Where y'all from, in case we git a lead?"

"We're from San Augustine, about 50 miles away," answered Vick.

"Y'all might check with the blacksmith, jest in case he's seen 'somepin.'"

After they left the Sheriff, they dropped by the blacksmith shop before leaving town.

The blacksmith hardly looked up while he was working.

"I don't reckon I remember no paint horses wit 'dem markings. I'll keep an eye out fer 'em."

The weary riders left Carthage and traveled ahead until dark. Vick could see the first signs of exhaustion when Orson began slumping in his saddle. Knowing what his old friend had been through, he stopped at the first spot to make camp. Bone weary, and with few words, they ate some jerky and then rolled up in their blankets for a good night's rest.

Elizabeth couldn't shake the suspicion that Jonathan Petty had killed Phillip Bradbury. He's the only one who would profit from Phillip and Cain's death," she reasoned.

She racked her brain, and began imagining all kinds of things. "What if Jonathan is holding Cain on his ranch? He might need help, and Vick's not here to do anything about it," she worried.

She knew it would be dangerous going after him without Vick, but she couldn't afford to waste time sitting around waiting for them to return home. If Cain's still alive, he might be dead by the time they get back, she convinced herself.

By late afternoon, Elizabeth was beside herself with worry. She knew if she did what she planned, she would need a disguise. Realizing how critical it was for her to be successful in pulling off her ruse; it could mean death for Cain, and her too.

Dressed in some of Cain's clothing, Elizabeth looked into the mirror and even shocked herself at how much she resembled her son. Walking to the barn, one of the workers mistook her for Cain. "Ms. Elizabeth, I thought ya' was Mr. Cain."

Before she left, she swore him to secrecy.

"If anybody asks me…I ain't seen nobody," the man assured her.

Riding out to Jonathan's ranch, she wondered what his reaction would be when he saw a rider that looked like Cain.

Elizabeth felt confident, If he's the one that killed my son, he'll think he's seeing the dead.

She knew if Vick found out about her snooping around a dangerous man's house, he would be livid. Still, she was determined to find out what she could before Vick and Orson returned.

Elizabeth, an excellent horsewoman, turned into the Circle J from off the main road when it occurred to her that her plan could backfire, and perhaps she should turn around and go back. However, something greater than fear was driving her, as she had to make every effort to find Cain.

At the time she arrived at the cattle gap leading up to his house, Jonathan was alone, and had been drinking all afternoon. Dudley and Lonnie were busy drinking too, but they were in town whooping it up in their favorite saloon. Dudley was still nursing his wound after being shot by Orson.

Jonathan's paranoia was getting the best of him, and when his suffering was too great to bear, he tried to drown his demons in alcohol. For the moment, he was being tormented by his fear of Aggie testifying against him. For no reason in particular he walked over to the window to look out. At that time Elizabeth had not yet come into view.

Disguised as Cain, Elizabeth approached Jonathan's house at dusk, riding her horse slowly as she came into Jonathan's view. She was caught off guard when barking coon dogs met her, causing her horse to act up. They were ferociously snapping at the horse's legs causing him to rare up as if ready to run. Knowing horses as well as any man, Elizabeth regained control, turning him around in an effort to distance her from the house. She hoped she had not been recognized.

Jonathan thought he was seeing things. Blinking his eyes several times to focus, the image he saw definitely looked like Cain. Jonathan spoke aloud, "My God, the bastard's still alive!" He ran outside and began shooting at Elizabeth. Lucky for her, pistols are not so accurate from such a long distance. She hastily spurred her horse to a full gallop.

Although Jonathan feared he might not be able to catch the rider, he jumped on his horse anyway, and went after her.

Oh my God, he's coming after me! she thought.

I've got to lose him before he gains on me. She looked back and saw Jonathan trying to catch her." I can't slow down," she said, as she reached the main road. Elizabeth had never ridden so fast, and certainly never pushed her horse this hard.

She remembered her training as a kid when she went coon hunting with her father. He had trained her well. She had not lost her touch: cutting her horse right and left, running around trees, and jumping bushes of wild honeysuckle growing between the large pecan trees along each side to the entry of the Plantation.

Jonathan was also an excellent horseman, but Elizabeth was far enough ahead that she could make it into her barn before Jonathan could see where she went. He didn't need to see her turn into the Plantation though, because thinking the rider was Cain, he chose the obvious. Elizabeth whipped her horse into a special room inside the barn that housed a number of saddles and supplies. She had just enough time to quickly unsaddle her horse and put him away when she saw a rider slowly riding toward the barn. She climbed the ladder to the loft and hid among the hay bales. There she lay silently, spying on Jonathan as he looked around for the mysterious horseman. *Why doesn't he leave?* she thought.

He was now out of her sight, but she could hear him moving about the barn. Elizabeth, afraid to even breathe, was frightened that he might hear her. *He's going to find me*, she feared.

She lay motionless for a long period of time until she heard Jonathan leave.

Although relieved that he was gone, she was still too frightened to move. The adrenalin was flowing as she got up and ran to the house. *I can never tell Vick or Orson how foolish I was.*

~

The days ahead followed with good meals and generous care as Cain continued to heal. He had been with Aggie over a week when he became concerned about overstaying his welcome.

After making substantial progress, Aggie helped him get settled in the small barn where Bradley had stayed. Simultaneously, he began asking questions about how she found him.

One evening after supper they talked about his memory, and a possible plan for his recovery.

"Aggie, I can't continue to impose. It isn't fair to you."

"Please don't worry about that. I'm alone, and it's good you're here."

He wondered what she meant by that.

"Aggie, I hope you don't mind but I need to ask you something about the day you found me. Did you find any of my personal belongings?"

"Only the money belt I told you about. When you get better we can ride back to the place and look around. Perhaps we'll find a clue that can help you remember."

"How about tomorrow? I don't want to wait...we can take your buggy if you don't mind." Cain suggested.

There was something about his eagerness that bothered her. She had never been in the company of such a handsome man, and the way he carried himself was very appealing. His eyes seemed to penetrate through her. She didn't want to admit it, but she was growing very fond of this stranger whom she had saved. His presence made it easy for her to procrastinate about leaving, since she had fear of the unknown. She wanted to relocate to Beaumont, but there was an uncertainty she did not understand.

It bothered her that he was so concerned about leaving. *If it weren't for me he wouldn't be alive, and now he seems ready to get on with his life*, she thought. She was not prepared for the unpredictability of her future.

She wanted to help this young man who looked to be a few years older than her, but the words of her father kept ringing in her ears.

One evening after supper she tried to get a feel for what he was thinking.

"I hate to keep asking, but have you thought of anything that might help you remember?" she asked.

"For some reason the name Ben pops into my head," Cain answered. "I've tried to remember, but I can't."

"That may be your name…the name suits you. How about I call you Ben? You need a name."

Cain smiled, "Sure, maybe hearing it over and over will help me remember."

The next morning Aggie was eagerly awaiting their ride out to the site where she found Ben. Walking from the barn, he happened to pass by her window. He had not intended to look, but as he glanced; there she was, slipping into her skirt. He couldn't help admire her beauty, and her curvaceous body awoke a desire that surprised him. *She's beautiful*, he thought. *I'm definitely getting better.*

Ben changed his mind about knocking on her door, and instead, walked to the corral and hitched-up the horse and buggy. He would surprise her while she finished getting dressed.

When he drove the buggy around to pick her up, she took his breath away; dressed in such high fashion, which puzzled him, considering where she was living. Aggie looked pretty as a picture in the new clothing she had purchased from Ms. Jones. Cain walked to the edge of the porch and helped her as she held out her hand like a sophisticated lady. He could feel a rush of chills come over him, like it was the first time he had seen her. As a matter of fact, he felt like they were a young married couple about to enjoy a Sunday ride together.

He had assumed she was from a poor family, however, seeing her dressed so elegantly made him think he had missed something from her story. She was bright, confident and apparently well educated. She certainly was not a girl one would think had come from a very poor family.

Ben wondered the same about himself, and what his background was. *What if I have a family who thinks I'm dead? Perhaps what I know*

now is all I will ever know, he pondered. Then he looked at Aggie and thought, *This would not be bad at all, as long as she's with me.*

He popped the whip and the horses began to trot, with Aggie sitting next to him. Every now and then they would touch. *I wonder if she feels the way I feel?* Ben thought.

When they got to the fork in the road where she had found him, they got out of the buggy and looked around for anything that looked familiar. They found the place where he had camped the night of the ambush, but he remembered nothing.

"I'm sorry Ben, I thought for sure being here and walking around might help you remember what happened."

"Yeah, me too. If I could remember my name, perhaps in time everything will fall into place."

After they left and were headed back home, she helped him find a place where they could have their picnic.

"Bradley used to bring me here," she said.

Cain felt a tinge of jealousy, which surprised him. *Why should I be jealous hearing about a friend called Bradley?* he thought. *I hardly know her.*

She began explaining who Bradley was, and how he helped her after her father had died.

"You've had more than your share, haven't you?" He felt such empathy for her.

Aggie sensed his tenderness, and this made her feel special, like he cared about what's happened to her.

Perhaps this was meant to be, she thought.

When they arrived, she spread a quilt so they could sit and have their picnic.

"Now you know the story about Bradley and how he died. If only you had been here to shoot the rabid wolf and save him. It still makes me sad knowing I was unable to protect Bradley." "Aggie, I'm not certain I could have saved your friend, so don't feel badly."

"I was afraid to shoot for fear of hitting Bradley."

"Rest assured, I'm not sure I could have done any better."

"Ben, I hope you don't mind my saying, but you need to protect yourself in case those people who ambushed you return. When they shot you they thought you were dead."

"I know, I've been thinking the same thing."

Tears welled up in her eyes as she thought about Bradley.

"I should have been able to save my friend."

He reached out and took her in his arms, which seemed natural as he wiped away her tears.

"Aggie, I hate to see you in such pain."

"I'm sorry. I thought I was over Bradley's death. But I guess I'm not."

He continued to hold her until she cried it out. Afterwards when her tears had dried, he had a desire to kiss her, until she began talking about guns.

"Ben, I have two guns –my Pa's .45, and also an old rifle. You don't look like a man with enemies, but somebody out there has picked you as theirs."

This was the first time Ben felt the urgency to discover who he was.

Aggie thought of her own plight and the warning from her father that both her brothers would kill her rather than share their inheritance. For the first time, she wondered what kind of skeletons might be in Ben's past.

It pleased Aggie seeing Ben enjoy the picnic, but there was something far more important that he had to find out. She knew he would not rest until he solved the mysteries surrounding his being there.

In the following weeks, Vick and Orson traveled to many East Texas towns, asking townsfolk if they had seen anyone who fit Cain's description. Finally, after near exhaustion and no leads, Vick made a decision.

"Orson, what ya' say we head back home? There's nothing more we can do out here. I think I know who's behind the shooting, and we're not proving a thing out here."

"You mean, Jonathan Petty?"

"Yep, he's the one, and I doubt we're going to find Cain's killer riding through East Texas towns when he's no more than three miles down the road from where we live."

"It's yer call, I'm with ya'."

"I'm ready, let's get outta here."

In spite of Elizabeth's heavy heartedness, she was excited when she saw Vick and Orson ride up. She'd been without her husband for too long, especially under the circumstances of having to deal with the possible loss of Cain.

She never wanted to deceive her husband, but her attempt to spy on Jonathan would remain her secret.

She ran from the porch to meet Vick, and practically jumped into his arms. They held each other while Orson looked on.

"No luck?" she asked quietly.

He looked into her eyes and she knew the answer to her question.

"I missed you Lizzie."

The Sheriff looked at the two lovers and rode on to his house.

"See y'all later," Orson said.

"Hope you're feeling better, Orson." Elizabeth called out.

Vick and Elizabeth walked arm and arm up to the house. He was wishing he had some hope to give her. She had many questions.

"Vick, I was hoping you had news about who might have killed Cain?"

He turned and looked at her. "Lizzie, don't ever say Cain's dead!" She was startled by his demand.

"Do you understand?"

Vick did not have to explain his outburst, for Elizabeth understood. Cain would remain alive, even if it were a lie.

That night when they retired to bed, Vick began opening up about what Orson remembered.

"It's kinda crazy, but he said he got a glimpse of one man who looked like one of the James brothers."

"The James brothers? Why that's crazy, don't you think?"

"Yeah, at first, but I don't know. Do you remember us talking about Johnny's brothers waiting for us when we came out of the thicket from Panther Holler? You remember when I came home wounded?"

"Yes, but that's not possible. What would the James' be doing this far away from home?"

"I don't want to scare you, but we know the ambush was not a robbery. It took a while, but now we know someone wanted Cain dead, and Orson got caught in the crossfire. I think it was Jonathan Petty and some of his hired hands that ambushed and shot Cain and Orson. And as for the James boys, I can't see how they could possibly be mixed up in all of this. Doesn't make sense... so I think Orson saw someone that favored them boys."

Elizabeth wanted to tell her husband about riding out to Jonathan's, but she decided to keep quiet. He would think I am as crazy as Orson, who thought he saw one of the James boys, she thought to herself. I could have very well gotten myself killed, and Vick doesn't need to know.

"Do you think it's all about Cain inheriting this place?"

"I'm sure it was Jonathan who shot Cain...you wait and see. When he comes calling we'll know he's the culprit. Besides keeping hope that Cain is alive, we need to convince Jonathan that Cain is alive."

"Why is that? If he did something to Cain he needs to pay."

"No Lizzie, you don't understand. If Jonathan is waiting for a legal death announcement so he can protest his brother's Will and overturn Cain's inheritance, it might take long enough to give us the time we need. I believe that Cain got away and he's still alive. We'll know in a couple of days. Does anyone know that Cain's missing?"

"Only Ms. Irene, but she wouldn't tell anyone."

"Good. When you talk to her be sure she knows to keep quiet about Cain. One other thing, Orson said the man he saw was riding a paint horse. The horse had white markings right above the hoof on the left back leg."

"Vick, what are we going to do if Jonathan comes to take over Pecan Plantation?"

"First, he'll have to prove Cain's dead, and with no body he can't prove a thing without incriminating himself. Just you wait and see. I bet he'll be around before the weeks over, asking questions, and that's when we'll know for sure that he killed Cain. Lizzie, I want us to play along like Cain's alive and frustrate him. He can't do anything about this property until he proves Cain's dead."

"Vick, how are we going to be able to look into the eyes of a killer?"

"We do it for Cain, that's how."

Jonathan was sure his mind was playing tricks on him the day he saw who he thought was Cain. At first he was certain the image was real, but after remembering his drunken stupor and the condition he was in, he brushed it off as pure fantasy. There was no way Cain could be alive, when he saw both Orson and Cain murdered by Lonnie and Dudley James. Now, the only thing standing in his way was the official notice that Cain Porter was, in fact, dead. Once there's proof, he will set about disclosing the contents of his brother's Will and reclaim his property.

Vick and Elizabeth waited while Jonathan became more aggravated with himself at the careless way they left the bodies of Cain and Orson. "They could be ravaged by animals and possibly never found, and my hands are tied until I can prove Cain is dead," Jonathan bemoaned.

In the meantime, Vick did not want anyone knowing Orson was alive, in order to force Jonathan's hand and expose him for the attack on Cain and Orson. He knew that Jonathan would eventually come calling if he had not heard any mention of the two men's whereabouts.

Vick shared his plan with Orson.

"Orson, I don't want Jonathan knowing you're alive, not just yet. If he finds out, he'll be frothing at the bit to get us off the plantation, and I want to protect Cain's inheritance and bring Jonathan to justice for the kind of man he is."

"Well, it's likely they gonna find out if I stay here. Ther's somthin' I been aiming to tell ya' and I know ya' ain't gonna like it, but I'm going back to Jonesboro. I know y'all like this place, but it ain't fer me. I'm plannin' on leavin first thang in the morning, before sunup."

Vick knew better than argue with his old friend when he had made up his mind.

"Orson, I reckon a man's gotta' do what he has to do, but I sure hate to see you go, and I know Lizzie's not going to like it."

"Well, Lizzie will have to git over it 'cause my mind's made up."

Vick had seen that far away look in Orson's face as they traveled through the small Texas towns in hopes of finding Cain. He knew he wanted to be back where Lucy and his wife were buried. And now that Cain was gone, there was nothing left to remind him of Lucy.

Elizabeth was heartsick seeing Orson leave, but she understood. Unbeknownst to Vick, she was a bit jealous that he was leaving and she wasn't. "Home is where the heart is," she thought. And Elizabeth's heart was with Vick, who did not have the connection to Jonesboro that she and Orson had. The next morning they saw the Sheriff off. Lizzie had biscuits and bacon wrapped up in a cloth bag and enough jerky to last until he got back to Jonesboro.

"Now you be careful Orson, and when you feel the need, you come on back."

They stood watching Orson ride away.

In the following weeks, Jonathan continued to read the papers in hopes of finding an announcement about Cain's death. But there was nothing.

After a month without any notice, Jonathan was fit to be tied. "I'm not any closer to my fortune than I was before I killed Cain and that sheriff friend of his." Jonathan thought. "It's time to make something happen."

~

Ben had been a welcomed, but short-termed distraction for Aggie, as her memories of Jonathan continued to haunt her. She also remembered the promise she made to Barney that she would not marry and saddle herself with children. She had seen the way Ben looked at her, and knew it would only be a matter of time before they both would have to face the future and deal with whatever it held for each of them.

As long as Jonathan was alive, he would represent a continued threat she was forced to live with.

Oftentimes, Ben would walk from the barn and find her in tears. *If only she would confide in me*, he wished.

Aggie lived every day with the terrible image of Jonathan raping her and murdering her mother. Even after all these years, the trauma of that day still haunted her. She knew she had to get on with her life in order to maintain her sanity.

As she pondered over the circumstances of her mother's death, she wondered if her life would ever be normal. *"Not if I stay trapped here,"* she conceded.

It had been over a month since Ben's injury, and his body had healed, but not his memory. He thought about leaving, but he had developed a genuine concern for Aggie, and worried what kind of future she had without him.

It was early spring, right after the last frost, when Ben decided to tackle the garden. There was something about tilling the garden and planting crops for another harvest that excited him. *"It seems familiar to me, and maybe it's a connection to my past,"* he thought.

Observing Ben working in the fields, Aggie once again remembered what Barney had told her about marriage and children holding her back. *I've gotta make my own way*, she fretted.

As usual, when Ben worked the field, she would make a picnic lunch and carry it to him. On this particular day the atmosphere must have had an enchanting effect on them.

Working hard in the garden, Ben had just shed his shirt when he looked up to see Aggie climbing through the fence. He noticed her movement and how delicate she was as she made it through the barbed wire without snagging her clothes. She's so beautiful, he thought.

As she cheerfully approached him, she became embarrassed at seeing his naked torso. She turned her head away to give him enough time to put on his shirt.

I'm sure he knows how handsome he is, she thought.

Ben quickly grabbed his shirt and put it on, leaving it unbuttoned as he took the basket of food.

She could not deny how drawn she was to him.

What's wrong with me? She wondered, as she noticed the beads of sweat on his chest. She could feel her face flush, and it wasn't the sun that caused its redness.

Ben saw how flushed she was, but had no idea it was because of him.

Aggie, come sit under the tree, you're getting too much sun.

Oh no, he knows, she thought, He's *noticed my face and how red it is.*

Aggie tried to ignore his suggestion.

"You're going to eat with me, aren't you?"

She looked into his eyes and they seemed to be saying something else. *He really likes me*, she thought.

They sat close, enjoying their lunch and talking about the garden and what he intended to plant. Soon the conversation reached a more personal level.

Aggie, do you like living here? You haven't told me much about your past."

"Well Ben, you haven't either," Aggie laughed, making light of Cain's inability to remember.

"Let's talk about you since you know who you are. I know you have a past and there's no reason you shouldn't share some of it with me."

"Well, you know about my daddy and also about Bradley."

"Yes, but that's all I know. Do you plan on living here or do you plan on living elsewhere?"

Aggie smiled, and said, "Maybe Beaumont."

"Beaumont, eh?" Ben pretended to know about the town, but of course, his memory was blank.

After helping Aggie to her feet, Ben had an overwhelming urge to kiss her. The two stood close looking into each other eyes as she smoothed her hair back. It was a special kind of look, one of desire, and without further pause, he gave her a sweet kiss.

"Ben, what are you doing," Aggie said, pulling away from his embrace.

This was a surprise to him, for he thought she wanted the kiss. She stood quietly for a moment, and then totally unexpectedly, Aggie became the aggressor and gave Ben a long lingering kiss.

"Oh my, that was a pleasant surprise," he said. And then without further consideration, Ben took her in his arms and kissed her like she had never imagined. There was no one to answer to but themselves, and that helped clear the way for their mutual desire to make love, which was sweet and giving.

Ironically, afterwards they lay thinking of how weak they were. Ben apologized to Aggie for what he was sure was a mistake.

"Aggie, I don't know what to say. My emotions got the best of me. Please forgive me."

She was disgusted with herself for giving herself to him.

"Ben, I don't know how this happened, but I'll make sure it doesn't happen again. With that she took the empty basket and walked back to the cabin.

The days that followed were very uncomfortable, as they tried to pretend nothing happened.

I've got to get away from him, she thought. Barney had left an indelible impression on her about a future she would regret should she marry young. *There's plenty of time for marriage*, she reassured herself. She remembered her father's parting words before he died. "Take care of yourself Aggie and give yourself a chance. Make something of yourself, spread your wings…fly away and be happy." She remembered how unhappy her mother was, living a lie married to a man who was paid to marry her. Barney had been like a father to Aggie, and yet, she resented being deprived of her real father's love. She would always remember Hamp Petty who treated her like a daughter, but failed to acknowledge her as his own.

Why couldn't he have told me I was his daughter and that he loved me? Will this forever trouble me?

Chapter 12

BIRDIE CRUMB LIVED IN A SMALL TOWN IN ARKANSAS CALLED TRUMANN, **which rested halfway between Jonesboro and Memphis, Tennessee.** She had driven to Jonesboro to tend to her sister Winnie, whose sickness had recently left her bedridden.

Birdie had taken care of her sister all week when it was time for her to go back home. She wasn't too far out of Jonesboro when she made a wrong turn and was taken off the main road. She was preoccupied and had lost focus with her sister's poor health and her aching shoulders from washing on a scrub board all afternoon. She was worried Winnie would not survive. Her mind came back to the moment at hand when the narrowing road suddenly looked unfamiliar. Realizing she had made a wrong turn, she drove farther to find a place to turn around.

As she did, she was alarmed to see a woman's body just off the road in a wooded area. Birdie, who had some medical training, stopped her automobile and went to the aid of the woman, who looked like she had been badly beaten, and was also suffering from some very serious burns. She couldn't tell too much about the woman other than she was in distress and would not last much longer without proper treatment. Relieved that the woman was alive, Birdie helped her to her feet, and together they walked slowly to the Model T. After Birdie got her bearings, she found her way back to the road that led to Trumann.

Even though better treatment was available in Memphis, she felt driving there would be a mistake, since it was much farther than where she lived. *This poor woman may not last until I get home*, she thought, seeing her slump further down into her seat.

When Birdie arrived home, and examined her, she found her burns were months old and had healed, except for her hands. Her throat appeared to have had a restraint around it, and her wounds were more from rope burns than the actual burns from a fire. *Lord only knows what this woman has gone through.*

She was as gentle as possible with her patient, but infection had already set in, and there were clues that her hair loss was also from a fire, since it showed signs of growing back. She tried to comfort her.

"Please don't be afraid, I'm here to help you," Birdie said. She could see the fear in the woman's eyes as she tried to talk. Apparently the restraint around her neck had damaged her throat or vocal cords.

"Don't try to talk…you've got time."

She badly needed treatment for her. I sure wish Jason would get here soon, she said to herself.

As the days passed, she became more concerned while waiting for her brother. She could only do so much, since it appeared her patient suffered more from beatings than the actual burns that had become infected.

She bandaged her burned hands because of water seepage, and then treated the other abrasions with a salve her brother had left with her. In time she will recover, but not before she experiences a lot of pain, let alone the emotional trauma from being molested.

Birdie's medical knowledge, though limited, was enough that she recognized molestation when she saw it. And it was so severe; she doubted the woman would ever be able to bear children.

Doctor Jason Crumb, Birdie's twin, had just finished his residency in Memphis and was in route back to Trumann to set up his practice.

He planned for his sister to assist him, since she was as motivated as he. They had shared the same goals, but since women were not welcome in medical school, they decided the scrutiny she would have to go through was not worth it, especially since Jason could teach her. He began teaching her all the techniques to be a qualified medical assistant. She was brilliant and caught on fast. Soon she had the necessary knowledge to treat patients, and even operate if she had to. Each weekend he would come home and give her a cram course on what he had learned the week before. Their plan had worked, and by the time Jason had finished his internship she was ready to assume the duty of his assistant.

Jason was extremely handsome and soft spoken, but intensely focused on a career, which left no time for marriage or a social life. Her brother's one ambition was converting his wealthy family home into a hospital, which he and Birdie worked tirelessly to have ready before Jason graduated.

He was one of the most promising doctors in Memphis, and could have stayed there, but after his internship he planned to return home so he and his twin sister could practice medicine together. Poor Birdie knew she would never be a head-turner because of her masculine features. She was plain and reclusive, but otherwise available to her brother, and of course, patients she had treated. Jason's dedication to medicine, along with his wealth, made him desirable to women. This concerned Birdie, who was afraid such a relationship would interfere with their plans and goals.

There's a bond between twins that seldom can be broken, and their sister Winnie had never been close to either twin. It was as though she was never allowed in their circle, and although she was their sibling, she never felt she belonged.

Time and time again women tried to catch the eye of Jason, but their plans were defused as soon as Birdie realized what they were up to. Had he understood, Jason would not have liked Birdie's interference. All he observed was a sister's love, and of course, loyalty. Lucky for her, Jason had one love, and that was medicine.

The twins were from old money and had lived in Weona, which was renamed Trumann in 1904. At that time Trumann was thousands of acres of virgin timberland, which created a labor boom after a large company moved in to gain control of the lumber business. That company had purchased the Porter lumber company in Jonesboro to increase its' growth. Elizabeth and Vick sold the company in order to allow them to accompany their son Cain to San Augustine, Texas, where he would make use of his inheritance of the Petty fortune.

Neither Birdie nor Jason had ever heard of the Porters, since medicine was their only interest. But they were glad to see the growth of Trumann, which expanded their medical care and the future hospital of Trumann.

The thriving lumber industry attracted workers from all around; mostly hard-up folks thankful for the opportunity to get their hands on some money. And anyplace jobs were plentiful, a number of shotgun houses were built for the poor folks who worked in the sawmills. It was evident who the more influential and prosperous people were by the design and size of their houses. They purposely wanted to set themselves apart from what they considered riff-raff.

As more and more people moved in, they brought with them the same vices normally found in larger towns and cities. These "growing-pain" problems consumed the town, and murders and unscrupulous dealings soon were taking place. Trumann reached the point where it desperately needed a hospital. It was Jason's dream to provide medical care for the town his daddy helped put on the map.

The parents of Jason and Birdie were community leaders and very wealthy at the time of their death. Not long after they had purchased their first Model T, one rainy day they were drowned when their car skidded off the road and slipped into a stream of raging water. As a result, all three of the Crumb children were left very wealthy.

Jason and Birdie's home was a sprawling estate left for the three to share, but Winnie, who was married, moved away. Living away from the twins didn't bother her since she was always independent of them. However, she learned early on that the twins were different. It was like they were strangers to the rest of the family.

During the time Jason was away at medical school, Birdie converted the family home into a hospital then moved her things out of the big house into the carriage house in order to give her brother privacy. She was just being "Birdie", putting her brother before herself and convincing him they needed the extra room for patients. She was happy to inconvenience herself for the sake of her brother's benefit.

When Jason arrived home, he found the finishing touches of the hospital had been completed, and Birdie had settled into her very comfortable carriage house. "Tell me something about our patient," Jason queried.

Birdie explained how she discovered the woman who was badly burned and had no voice. "I didn't know about her hands. They were badly infected," said Birdie. "Where is our patient now?" Jason asked.

Birdie led him outside into a garden to meet the mystery woman. "She doesn't talk, so don't expect much." Jason saw a woman's figure standing near a backdrop of roses. She immediately turned to face him when she heard Birdie's voice. Through the singed and shortened hair, and the burn created scarring, he saw before him a strikingly beautiful woman. He was so taken aback that he stammered when he talked. Birdie immediately noticed. Something had triggered this change, since he was normally very confident and deliberate when speaking to his patients.

Jason examined her hands and knew it would be some time before she could write and tell them who she was.

Prior to Birdie being ready for her weekly visit to Jonesboro, they received a telegram that Winnie was near death. Jason discussed his concerns and it was agreed that he should stay and take care of their patient while Birdie went to care for Winnie. They were both shaken at hearing they were possibly losing their sister. Birdie had tried to have her sister come to Trumann when she first became ill, but Winnie would have none of that.

"What if she dies while I'm there, then what?" Birdie asked.

"Send me a telegram and I'll come, but I'll need someone to stay with our patient."

In spite of Birdie's quick response to travel, her sister died before she reached Jonesboro.

Maggie Smith, who lived on Winnie's property, met her as soon as she arrived, and gave her the news that her sister had passed. Birdie was sad, for she did not foresee the end coming so soon.

Before she walked into her sister's room, she stopped in the door-way and looked at the bed where her sister lay covered with a white sheet.

"Thank you Maggie. I appreciate you being here with Winnie."

Maggie sniffled, but Birdie held it together. Denying emotion came easily, since she had trained herself to be strong for families of her patients.

The funeral was quiet, with only a few people attending. Birdie did not bother to send a telegram to Jason, once again thinking of him and what he would have to go through to leave the hospital. *After all, Winnie was already dead, and what more could anyone do?* she thought.

After the funeral, Maggie stayed with Birdie while she went through her sister's personal things. She later discussed what needed to be done with the property. Afterwards, Birdie explained that she had found a badly burned woman on the outskirts of Jonesboro when she drove home from her last visit. "She is a pretty young woman, but cannot speak to tell us who she is."

"Can't she write her name?" Maggie asked.

"No, her hands were badly burned and we have them bandaged. She'll recover, but it's going to be a long time. Do you know of any-one lost in a fire around here?"

"I did hear of one fire. It was that big mansion owned by Elizabeth Barkin. I think her son and the sheriff's daughter Lucy Cargill were to be married the day the fire broke out. Later, I heard her daddy and the man she was supposed to marry were both murdered someplace in Texas. Seems like I heard the entire family along with the town Sheriff who lost his daughter in the fire, all moved to Texas."

"Does she have anymore family?"

"No, just the sheriff. I mean Mr. Cargill… but now he's dead."

"You think that might be the young woman, Lucy, who was to be married?"

"I don't know, but I'm gonna find out when I get back to Trumann."

"Yeah, that fire was big news. That musta' happened months ago. Lucy's daddy's cabin is still jest sittin' there. Don't know what's gonna happen to it," Maggie revealed. "Yeah, I heard when her daddy died that nobody ever found his body, or the body of the man Lucy was gonna marry. That Porter family has had a lot of tragedy."

"Maggie, thank you for sharing. At least this is something to go on. I can't imagine this woman being the one you're talking about. By the way, if you hear of anyone needing a house, you write me and I'll give 'em a good deal. Just address it to Birdie Crumb, in Trumann."

Jason was pleased with the progress his patient was making. The swelling had left her face and he could see more of the woman's beautiful features. He felt sorry for her, and noticed how confused she looked each time he tried to explain to her how his sister found her. He couldn't tell if her voice would return because he did not know how damaged her vocal cords were. He wanted to be able to reassure her, but only time would tell if she would ever speak again.

Birdie had been gone long enough for Jason to develop quite an attraction to this mystery woman.

One time he walked in on his patient while she was looking into the mirror. She was running her hand over the abrasions that had healed, but still showed discoloring that eventually would go away.

"Don't be embarrassed, you're doing fine. All the swelling has left your face and one day you'll be just like new."

The woman nodded to relay she understood and approved, but deep inside she felt she would never be whole again.

Jason was drawn to her, and wanted to find out who she was. He decided to begin questioning her.

"Today…I want to try and ask you a few questions? Do you mind? The woman shook her head for "no."

"Good. Now I want you to tell me if you remember who you are?" Again she cooperated by shaking her head "yes."

"Are you from Jonesboro?"

She hesitated, and then responded with the same "yes."

"Do you remember what happened to you?"

Tears welled up in her eyes and she started crying. Jason's heart went out to her. "She's so sweet and beautiful," a phrase he had begun to say to himself too many times each day. He had developed an undeniable affection for her, and he wondered if she felt the same.

He couldn't stand to see her cry this way, so he sat down beside her and took her in his arms. For the first time, she gave way to her emotions and let all the hurt come out.

"Now don't you cry. We're going to get to the bottom of this, and when Birdie returns I might be able to tell you who you are."

She looked into his eyes and shook her head "yes."

That evening, Jason heard the Model T drive up. Birdie was loaded down with clothing she brought for their patient to wear. Some dresses were beautiful, and others were plain housedresses, good for everyday wear. Winnie would have loved having someone get use out of the clothing she had saved.

That night, as Birdie and Jason sat around the fireplace, she told Jason who their patient might be. After she explained what happened, and that Lucy lost her life on her wedding day, it took a little time for him to absorb everything.

"What are you thinking?" asked Birdie.

"Oh, I don't know, I suppose when we tell her, she's going to want to leave and go to Jonesboro."

"Well, what's wrong with that?" she asked.

"There's a lot wrong with that. I'm concerned about the treatment she will receive. She needs to stay here and let us take care of her."

Birdie was surprised. There was something about his tone she did not like. *He's falling for her*, she thought.

She quickly dismissed herself and left the house.

It was disturbing to Birdie to think what could happen as a result of this type of relationship between Jason and this woman who might be Lucy. Birdie thought how this could spoil her future and adversely affect what role she might lose in her brother's life. The life she had envisioned for herself and her brother all these years was now threatened.

The next morning, Jason looked out the window and the woman he now believed was Lucy Cargill was walking among the flowers. What a picture of beauty she was as she strolled in and out of the camellias. He did not know but Lucy was actually reliving the day she and Cain would have been married.

Later that day Jason told Lucy about her father and Cain being murdered and that after her death the family along with her fiancé had moved to Texas to live.

All the pain and anguish was in her eyes as she fell to the floor and cried. He had never seen a woman so distraught. After he allowed her to mourn he helped her up and took her in his arms. Somehow Jason's big strong arms gave her peace.

I have no one now, not even Elizabeth and Vick, she thought.

Lucy knew it would be too painful to return to Jonesboro since Elizabeth and Vick now lived in Texas. *There's no need to have the reminders of a life that could have been*, she thought.

Chapter 13

ENOUGH TIME HAD PASSED AND JONATHAN'S PATIENCE WAS RUNNING out. His plaguing paranoia over who might know of Cain and Orson's murders was motivating his next move. Time was marching on, and no one seemed interested in Orson and Cain's deaths. His mind raced, *why haven't the Porters come forward about Cain and that Sheriff friend being dead?* Finally it hit him. *They don't want the Will overturned because they would have to move off the plantation and give up the house and land they want for themselves. They have no right to my inheritance.*

"I'm not one to wait around," he told the James'. "You boys ride to town and keep your ears open in case something is mentioned about Cain and that Sheriff being dead. All this waiting is nonsense, when I know they're dead."

"Yes sir, boss," Lonnie said.

As they turned and walked away, Matilda, who had been cleaning the bunkhouse, entered the room holding something in her hand. Jonathan, focused on reading his brother's Will, paid little attention when Matilda began her questioning. "Mr. Jonathan, what do you want me to do with thees? I found thees outside the tack house," Matilda said in her heavy Mexican accent.

She was holding a ring with a beautiful New Zealand Opal. Little did she know that this was the engagement ring Cain had given Lucy before their wedding.

Jonathan glanced up but paid no attention to the ring.

"If you found it, it's yours," he said.

Matilda was very excited that the ring was given to her. She quickly slipped it on her finger admiring its beauty.

"Oh thank you, Meester Jonathan," Matilda said, as she went about her work.

Jonathan kept reading, thinking he might have missed something important in his brother's Will. Although it clearly stated that he is not eligible for any part of the estate should there be living heirs, he now felt secure that the fortune of his brother might be overturned when it's proven that Cain is dead and himself left as the only living heir.

I've got to get this moving, since I'm no closer to my family's fortune than I was before we killed Cain.

Then there was Aggie, who was a constant thorn in his side. He was still unaware that Aggie was his half-sister. His greatest fear was her sudden appearance, pointing the finger at him for raping her and murdering her mother.

~

While in town, Lonnie caught a glimpse of Elizabeth loading a churn into the back of her Model T. "Dudley, ain't that Elizabeth Barkin from Jonesboro?"

"Eh', shore is. I recognize that fine automobile she's got ther'. Ain't it the same one she had in Jonesboro?"

"I ain't talkin' 'bout her damn automobile. I'm talkin' 'bout her seein' us."

Lonnie nudged his horse and rode off.

"Wher' we goin'?" Dudley cried out.

"Back to the ranch, you knucklehead."

Lonnie spun a lie to Jonathan that no one had reported anything about Cain Porter and Orson Cargill being dead.

"Damn, what's taking so long!" Jonathan shouted.

Dudley looked at Lonnie and rolled his eyes, which meant, "let's git outta here."

The following morning, Jonathan, who was still annoyed, decided he would ride out to Pecan Plantation and do some snooping.

Seeing the silhouette of Jonathan in his long black coat, Vick never gave him the courtesy of looking up as he and a worker loaded bales of cotton onto the flatbeds.

He waited for Jonathan to speak.

"Looks like you need a couple more hands to help you load that cotton," Jonathan said.

Vick had been waiting for the murderer to show his face, and now his suspicion was confirmed. He wanted to pull Jonathan from his saddle and beat the living hell out of him until he told him where his son was, but he knew he had to be smart and not show his hand, not just yet. Vick played along with his charade.

"Yep, been aiming to hire some more men, but time manages to get away from you,"

"Where is your son, to help you out?" Jonathan asked.

This was treading on the edge, Vick thought, as he resisted the urge in order to mask his inner feelings.

"Cain had to go out of town awhile back. You got a reason for being here?"

It suddenly hit Jonathan that as long as Vick played the cat and mouse game, very little could be settled without a couple of dead bodies.

"I suppose I can relay the message through you since you're his Pa. When your boy comes home, tell him I need to see him. I'll be protesting my brother's Will. That means you and that pretty wife of yours will be moving out— and I'll be moving in."

"Cain might not be back for awhile. Anything I can help you with?"

Vick could see guilt all over Jonathan's face when he spoke of Cain being away.

"If I don't hear from your son in a few days, start packing." Jonathan stressed.

He turned his horse to ride away and then stopped to ask a question. "You sure you don't know when your son will return?"

"Hard to say; I'll tell him you were here."

Jonathan wondered why he didn't get a rise out of Vick when he told him he and his wife would be moving out. The man's an enigma to me. Perhaps that's why he was known as such a good poker player; 'cause he's hard to read, Jonathan surmised.

That night, Vick told Elizabeth that Jonathan came by to say he was protesting the Will.

"So he's protesting the Will? Why would that surprise me? Do you realize the problems we've had because of the Petty's, and it's all my fault?" Elizabeth cried out.

"Now let's don't jump before we have to. Maybe there's another Will and letter."

You think Ms. Irene overlooked them? What good does it do to have the Will when it clearly states that Jonathan gets everything if we can't produce an heir.

"Vick I remember reading Johnson's Will, and without Cain Jonathan gets everything. The judge will award Jonathan the entire estate, our hands are tied."

"Lizzie, we can't give up on Cain. I still believe he's out there somewhere."

"Let's pray you're right but he may not make it home before Jonathan takes over the estate."

The next morning Elizabeth was ready to go see Miss Irene before they went to the County Clerk's office.

Upon arriving at her house, she invited them into the parlor and served coffee with some of her delicious homemade desserts.

"Thank you for seeing us on such short notice."

"Y'all are always welcome...come on in." Irene smiled and listened intently as they told her of their plight.

"I'm sorry Elizabeth, but I've looked, and there's not another Will or letter. What I had I gave to you the other night."

"And as you said, I gave it to Cain. That's the last I saw of it. He must have placed it somewhere for safekeeping. Cain did mention at the time, that it was an incriminating letter that he could use against Jonathan should he challenge the estate.

"I'm sorry Elizabeth, but after going through all of Phillip's papers, the only thing I came across was the letter I gave to you for Cain," Ms. Irene disclosed.

"If that's the case, we must find the letter if we want to control Jonathan," Vick stated.

"All I want is for Jonathan to pay for what he's done to my son," Elizabeth replied.

"You think he's the one, do you?" asked Irene.

"Just as I know he murdered Phillip, everything points to Jonathan, and no one else.

"My brother was such a kind man. I hope if it is Jonathan, that he's exposed for what he did."

After leaving Ms. Irene's, Elizabeth and Vick arrived at the County Clerk's office, only to find there was an old Will of Hamp Petty's that was recorded leaving the entire estate to Johnson.. It specifically stated that his son Jonathan would inherit Pecan Plantation and all other assets, should there be no other heirs.

It was explained to them that without Cain, Jonathan could receive everything.

On the way home, Elizabeth cried, knowing she may never see her son again.

"Lizzie, I don't want you worrying about moving out. If we have to move we will move right next door. Cain had the house put in Orson's name, so Jonathan can't force us out. At least we'll be close enough to keep an eye on Jonathan and be here when Cain comes home."

Elizabeth's only solace was that she had Vick and everything would work out.

~

There was not a day that passed that Aggie didn't think of Ben and the intimacy they shared. *Never again*, Aggie thought as she shamed herself for being so impulsive. There was no denying that Ben had fallen for Aggie, but he was not sure she felt the same about him. She had become obsessed with what her Pa, and of course Bradley, had told her about marriage and having a house full of kids. I'm too young and I want time to live, Aggie reminded herself.

After Ben worked all day planting more vegetables in the garden and had time to rest up, Aggie thought she should cook him a nice evening meal. This would give her a chance to wear one of her new dresses that she had kept for a special occasion. It was important for her to see Ben's reaction in her new dress. She remembered Ms. Jones' remark about being a proper lady.

That evening, Ben was speechless when Aggie opened the door in her beautiful dress. He could hardly contain himself as he handed her a small bouquet of wild flowers. Ben was totally dumbfounded by her beauty. This is only supper, and she's dressed for a dance, he thought. "Aggie, I ah, I hope I'm not too early."

Ben wanted to kick himself for his corny statement. *Couldn't I have thought of something more appropriate, like, 'Aggie, you are so beautiful'.*

She noticed his embarrassment and tried to put him at ease.

"The flowers are like a breath of fresh air...you shouldn't have."

She knew he had not walked ten feet to pick the flowers, but it was the thought that mattered to her. The fields were covered with flowers this time of year.

Ben was lost in the rapturous evening with a beautiful woman and a fantastic meal. *This is heaven*, he thought.

He kept second-guessing himself, fishing for the right things to talk about, like her dress or her hair.

She stood there and smiled, waiting for him to speak.

"Ben, I'm slightly overdressed, but this is my new dress I've had for several months, and I was dying to wear it. I hope you won't mind indulging my silliness, dressing up for such a simple occasion."

"Oh no, I mean yes. This is a simple occasion and you have…ah, every right to dress however you want. The dress is beautiful, but you, ah, well Aggie, I think regardless if you are in a new dress or not, that you are beautiful." Ben immediately began to wonder if that was the appropriate thing to say.

She smiled a bashful smile again, and then changed the subject.

"I wanted it to be special tonight. I saw how hard you worked in the garden, and you deserved a good meal."

She turned and walked to the cabinet for the dishes she needed.

"I really appreciate you going to all the trouble for me." Ben walked over to the stove and lifted a lid on a pot in an effort to act normal.

"I thought I smelled my favorite."

Aggie was impressed that he finally seemed to relax.

"Ben, I meant to ask—do you remember anything yet? Since you recalled your favorite food was snap beans, that might be a sign you're beginning to remember things."

"Snap beans?" Ben chuckled, then walked over to the cabin window and looked out as if he was still lost. He then turned and asked if he could help her with setting the table. There was only one thing on the table, and it was a large bowl for the main dish.

"If you would like," she said, while handing him two plates and two forks.

During supper the two shared polite conversation, and then Aggie got up and poured a glass of Bradley's wine.

"Would you like a glass?" she asked.

Ben held out his glass while she poured it to the brim.

"This is mulberry wine. I hope you like it."

The wine was very mild and just a tad sweet, but it succeeded in loosening them up.

"Aggie, I can't tell you how much I enjoyed your stew and green beans. And if you don't mind me saying again, you look very nice in your new dress."

Aggie finally asked the question she had been waiting to ask all evening. "Ben, do you think I look like a proper lady?"

Is she asking a loaded question, he thought. "Uh, ah, Aggie, you are most definitely a proper lady."

She loved his reassurance. Ben kept over-analyzing everything. Perhaps it's best if I give short answers and not too much information. That way I'll keep out of trouble. Amnesia didn't seem to block this common thread amongst all men.

Ben and Aggie sat in two chairs facing each other while Ben wondered if he had enough courage to take her in his arms. He remembered his promise and restrained himself from making advances toward her. I want to do this right, he reasoned.

"Ben, I've been meaning to tell you how much I have enjoyed you being here. When I found you unconscious I had no idea you would become this important to me. I mean, as a friend. I want to make this clear that you have become a very good friend, but that's all, just a friend."

Ben was taken back at how she emphasized that they were only friends. So everything I've been feeling about her was only my imagination. Stupid me, for being so wrong, he anguished.

"Aggie, I feel the same." It was like something took over him as he began telling her he would be moving on and would never forget her. "You've done so much for me, and without your help I could have died. I think I've overstepped myself around here and I'm really sorry about that."

Aggie had not anticipated how bothered she would be when Ben announced he would be leaving soon.

"Aggie, thank you for the evening. I guess I better git goin'. I want to finish replacing the windows in back of the cabin tomorrow and get that chore out of the way."

Aggie was not ready for the evening to end, and didn't anticipate that over-emphasizing their platonic friendship would have brought on his eagerness to leave.

When Ben stood and walked slowly out the door, he thought, *Boy, did I ever read her wrong. She's not at all interested in me.*

After Ben left, Aggie had a wave of loneliness come over her. Now she was afraid that he would leave, and she would be left alone again. *How am I going to handle this when he tells me he's leaving?*

Everyone I've cared for has left me, she lamented.

The more she agonized over Ben leaving, the more she thought it best to leave first, instead of facing rejection.

The following day, a wall went up between them. Neither was able to carry on a simple conversation. It was painfully uncomfortable.

After writing Ben a letter explaining her sudden departure, she packed her bags and slipped the letter into her pocket, planning to leave it when she left. She had carefully established her route to Beaumont, with the hopes of beginning a new life. *That's it!* She thought, as she gathered her things together; mostly mementos of what she had left of her father's. She packed only one suitcase and a large tote with her large dresses stuffed inside, and only a few changes of simple clothing.

She planned to make a clean break from East Texas and settle in a town large enough to become lost in, just in case Jonathan caught up to her whereabouts. She was wide-eyed and full of dreams, leaving obscurity behind and venturing into the unknown. Although she admired Ben, he was not the center of her world. She knew that leaving without a proper goodbye would hurt him, but she couldn't take the chance of looking him in the face. His eyes would make me melt, she feared.

The next morning, Ben awoke feeling somewhat depressed. He didn't know if it stemmed from the night before, or if it was something else. It was almost like he knew Aggie was gone. He made his coffee and waited for time to pass so he could see her.

True to his thoughts, he discovered the door open, and Aggie gone.

After searching through the cabin for any clue as to why she left, he checked the barn and found she had taken the horse and buggy. All that was left was Bradley's old nag.

Of course, he had money, but nothing else except a few clothes Aggie had helped him buy in town and some clothes that fit him that belonged to her Pa. He was puzzled that she would leave without a goodbye. He rechecked for a note, thinking it might have fallen on the floor, but he found nothing. Unbeknownst to both of them, the note Aggie had planned to leave was tucked away safely in her pocket. It wasn't until later that she discovered she had inadvertently failed to leave it.

Her original idea was to leave a note, hoping he would travel to Beaumont after her. At least he would know where to find her, that is, if wanted her badly enough.

I can't go back. I might never leave again, she thought.

In a spell of weakness, Aggie slowed the buggy, thinking she should go back, but again vacillated. She took the whip and lashed several times until she was driving her horse at full speed.

She traveled by day and slept in her buggy at night. It wasn't until she came to a sleepy little town called Woodville, Texas, that she stopped to spend some time.

It was midday when she arrived at this familiar-looking town. It was like home, she thought. Right away she noticed the luscious pine trees. It was a bustling little town, all intermingled with people going and coming in their automobiles. Although Woodville was a small town there were still some townspeople walking, while others were on horseback. Toward the end of the street there were people assembling booths for the big Fourth of July celebration. *Now I know why it reminds me of home. Yes, these folks are preparing for a festival, like we have in San Augustine when the pecans come into season. This is a perfect town for me,* she imagined. As she sat there in her buggy, her thoughts went back to her childhood. Picnics were another favorite pastime. Families would often gather for lunch on Saturday afternoon or after church on Sunday. Weather permitting; they would congregate in the churchyard or along a nearby riverbank. Those were good times when I didn't have to be alone. There were kids playing jump rope or hide-and-seek, and fields to romp and stroll through.

She had her mind set on Beaumont, but Woodville seemed to be asking her to stay. *Perhaps I'm not ready for a big town*, she thought. *Yes, Woodville is the perfect town* for *me right now.*

As she drove her buggy through town, she was on the lookout for a boarding house. She needed a place to eat and make arrangements for a night's stay. The activity of the town excited her, as she heard a piano playing from a nearby celebration.

It had been a long time since she had been in a town like Woodville, which was so much like San Augustine, the town she loved. The roads were well maintained, and all the stores seemed to be doing a good business. While searching for a boarding house, she walked by the bank. She thought about her large sum of money and the need to keep it safe.

The man sitting at his desk observed a young woman peering at him through the window and motioned for her to come in. She walked in appearing very unkempt, at least in the eyes of the banking clerk. She had no idea she was being judged by her appearance. He quickly sized her up as being poor and only there to waste his time.

Bunky Willams, the bank clerk, looked up at Aggie and thought she had no business in his bank. Nonetheless, he put on his most cordial and businesslike air.

"I'm Bunky Williams, ma'am. Can I help you?"

"Yes sir, I'm new in town and I want to put my money in the bank."

"You mean open an account, don't you?"

"Yes sir, an account."

Mr. Williams was doubtful this poor woman had the ten dollars required to open an account, and wanted to hurry and get her out of the bank so he could close for the celebration-taking place outside.

"Now tell me, your name Ms., ah…."

"Dawson, Ms. Aggie Dawson."

"Well Ms. Dawson, where do you live? I don't think I've seen you before."

"Oh, you haven't. I don't know where I'm going to live, not yet anyway."

Bunky was now very annoyed, hearing she didn't have a home.

"Miss, you can't just march in here without a place to live, no money and open an account. When you have money, you come back."

"Oh I'm sorry, but I do. I have money. Just a minute."

Aggie reached into her purse and pulled out hundreds of bills, laying them in the middle of his desk. Bunky was astonished as he watched all the bills piling up in front of him.

"Miss, please let me lock the door! We don't want anyone seeing this much money. Please excuse me."

Bunky quickly locked the door and pulled down the shade acting a bit nervous.

"I'm terribly sorry, Ms. Dawson," he said, as he scurried back to his desk.

Aggie knew very well the man had misjudged her, and she was amused upon seeing how quickly money gets one's attention.

"Now, Ms. Dawson, now that we're private, let's open that account for you, shall we?"

Before she left the bank, she had opened her account and had all the information she needed to possibly purchase property from a Ms. Lori Mixson who lived five miles outside of Woodville.

The next morning, after a good night's rest, Aggie drove her buggy out to the Mixson residence to speak with Ms. Lori.

When she entered the gate, she traversed a pebble pathway, which took her quite a distance. It seemed like forever before she came to a house situated in the midst of overgrown shrubbery and a narrow road leading to someone else's property. She stopped her buggy and sat there in front of a beautiful home that she was certain could not be the place Bunky Williams had told her about. Aggie thought, *There is no way I can afford a place like this. I must have turned in the wrong place.*

While Aggie considered what to do, the door opened and an older woman stood waiting for her visitor to say something. Seeing the confused young woman, she approached the buggy. "Miss, can I help you?"

"Well, it appears I'm lost. I was given directions to the Mixson place, but I must have taken a wrong turn," she said.

"This is the Mixson place. Is there something I can do for you?"

"Are you Ms. Lori Mixson?" Aggie asked.

"That's right. Are you here about my house and property?"

"Yes ma'am. Mr. Bunky Williams from the bank said you were selling your property, but I'm sure this place is more expensive than I can afford."

"My dear, why don't you come inside so we can talk?"

Aggie took her tote and went inside, feeling it was a waste of Ms. Mixson's time, but since she had been traveling, she was thirsty and needed water.

She was led to the parlor, where French doors opened onto a large sitting area with swings and large chairs, providing a perfect view of the back yard and the property around them.

"This is lovely, Ms. Mixson. You must enjoy this every day."

"Yes, I'm going to miss this view. Before my husband died I would have a cot rolled outside so he could lay and breathe fresh air. Mr. Mixson died last year of tuberculosis."

"Oh, I'm so sorry." The woman evidently was still mourning the loss of her husband, for her eyes welled up with tears. "I'm so sorry," Aggie said again. "I thank you for inviting me in, but I don't want to take your time, when your property is far more expensive than I can afford."

"I have one other offer from Parley Jackson, but it'll be a cold day in hell when I sell to a man like him," Ms. Lori spoke.

Aggie was surprised to see Ms. Mixson's attitude change so quickly. "He's got everybody in this town scared to buy my place 'cause his property adjoins mine. Well, I'd soon sell at a loss than sell to him. Do you know Mr. Parley?"

"No ma'am, I don't believe I do."

"Did you tell me your name?"

"Oh, I forgot my raising—excuse me for not introducing myself, but my name is Aggie Dawson and I was on my way to Beaumont. But when I rode through Woodville, it made me think of home. Thank you for your time, but I best be on my way."

Aggie had no idea the bad blood that Ms. Mixson and the entire town had toward Parley Jackson. This sweet widow was ready to sell at any cost, fearing that no one else would purchase her property, since it adjoined Parley Jackson's place.

She looked at Aggie and thought this young woman might be the very one who could stand up to a man like Parley. "Miss Dawson, are you married?"

"Oh, no ma'am, I'm single and I have a lot of living to do before I get married and have a bunch of babies."

"I don't know how much money you have Aggie, but this place is a little over a hundred acres. My sister is sick and lives in New York where I lived when I was a little girl. When Oliver was living, Violet would come each summer to see us. When my husband died I had no need to stay here. I suppose what I'm leading to is this—I need to sell. I've lived most of my life here and I don't have much time left. And with no children to leave my place to, I would be most grateful to hear your offer. I want this house to be in good hands."

Aggie's mind began to race. She didn't care that there might be a motive behind Ms. Mixson's madness; since the place was everything she could possibly want.

"I'm embarrassed to make such an offer, for I need some money to live on. And then I have to figure out a way to run this big place. I'd be taking on a big responsibility, being young and inexperienced." She stood and looked out the window, then turned to face Ms. Mixson. "It's so beautiful, but I don't think I have enough money."

"Aggie, I'm ready to sell, and if you are anywhere close to the figure I'm thinking, I'll gladly give up this place."

Aggie was thinking about the money Barney left her and how much she could afford to spend on a place. *I'm sure she will refuse my offer*, she thought. Finally, it was as though someone else was speaking for her.

"Ms. Mixson, I know this place is worth much more, but all I can offer is two thousand dollars."

The next conversation involved Ms. Mixson accepting her offer.

Suddenly realizing the enormity of what she had done on the spur of the moment, Aggie found a chair to sit in, overwhelmed that her offer had been accepted. *That was easy, but what now?* Aggie wondered.

In the back of her mind, Aggie had hoped Ms. Mixson would not accept her offer, since she understood her life would change, and much faster than she wanted it to. She sat for a moment thinking of how uncharacteristic it was of her to make such a rash decision.

Seeing Ms. Mixson's jubilation, Aggie felt she had no choice but to go through with the offer she made, even though this could end up being a poor decision for one being so young.

Before she knew it, she had agreed to meet the next day and sign the papers.

Bunky smiled knowing that he had finalized the sale of Ms. Mixson's property, but the icing on the cake was when Aggie read the fine print explaining that all furniture, canned goods, meat in the smokehouse, livestock and farm tools were all part of the deal.

She was ecstatic by the time she returned to her new home. She could not believe her good fortune as she walked through the rooms of what was a mansion compared to Bradley's little one-room cabin.

She carried a fan she was sure Ms. Mixson had used many times. Fanning herself she picked up a porcelain cup that was meant for the lips of a proper lady.

While Aggie was enjoying her new place in Woodville, just the opposite was happening in San Augustine.

Vick and Elizabeth had received notice that Jonathan Petty was the new benefactor of the Petty estate.

Chapter 14

VICK WAS WORKING IN THE FIELDS WHEN A LONE RIDER APPROACHED **the entryway to Pecan Plantation.** For a second he thought it might be Cain, but as the man drew closer his hopes vanished upon seeing someone else who looked strangely familiar.

I've seen that man before, he thought, as he studied the rider from afar. Although he racked his brain, his memory failed him. Who the hell is he? I know him from somewhere.

Seeing the stranger in a completely different setting, the name Hop Babcock, the man for whom he had worked on the lease program while serving his time in the New Orleans prison, did not come to mind.

Hop rode slowly, giving Vick a chance to collect his thoughts.

When Cain failed to show up in Memphis, Hop had only one option, and that was to seek out his job offer in San Augustine. Hop had given notice to his former employer that he had taken another job and it was time for him to move on.

As Hop got closer, Vick was still struggling to identify him.

Hop stopped his horse short of Vick and dismounted, looking into the face of a man he thought he would never have occasion to see again.

"Can I help you?" Vick asked, studying the man's face.

"No, but I'm here to help you," said Hop.

Once up close, it took only a few seconds for Vick to recognize Hop, the only man who treated him with respect while he was in prison. That was the only normalcy he experienced during the 20 years he spent behind bars.

"Mr. Babcock! Is that you?" Vick hurried over and shook his hand.

"Don't give me any of that 'mister' stuff, I'm here to help you run your plantation. Your son hired me some time ago, and I'm here to give you a hand."

"You say Cain arranged this?" Vick was a little confused, since Cain was missing.

"Your son was coming to Memphis with a man named Orson, a former Sheriff, and we were all planning to travel back together. He wanted to surprise you, but when they didn't show, I figured I should come on and see if I still had a job."

"I can't believe this. You're here." Vick took his hat off and brushed his brow in disbelief.

Hop looked around the place and then turned to Vick.

"This is some kinda place you got here. Looks like you did well for yourself while you were in prison. No, I'm just jawin' with you." The men chuckled at the thought.

"Well, all is not as it seems, Hop. It's going to take me a few minutes to wrap my mind around you being here. I lost contact with you years ago after I heard you sold your plantation and moved to Memphis."

"That telegram your son sent me explained everything about you being framed. I never knew that. You should have told me."

"Prisoners that talked didn't live long. I'm surprised I walked out of that hell hole alive."

"Well, you survived, and that's what counts."

"Yeah, I reckon it does."

They carried on polite conversation, but all Vick could think about was how things had changed, and that Hop traveled a long way for nothing.

"Hop, you haven't heard about Cain."

The way Vick looked at him, he knew it wasn't good.

"Well, we've had a turn of events since Cain contacted you. Why don't you come in and let me introduce you to my wife, Elizabeth?"

Hop had already begun to think the worst, when he looked up to see Elizabeth approaching them, smiling.

His first thought was how beautiful she was and how lucky Vick was to have such a woman. Hop looked very important dressed in his signature clothing of tweed pants and boots that laced up to his knees. He was a few years older than Vick but had hardly changed at all from when Vick last saw him.

Elizabeth knew immediately who the stranger was. "You must be Hop Babcock, I'm Elizabeth, Vick's wife," she said.

"Nice to meet you," Hop said politely.

Vick turned sharply when he heard Elizabeth mention Hop's name.

"Elizabeth, you knew about Hop and didn't tell me?"

"I did know about Hop, but when Cain was ambushed things got out of hand, and I completely forgot about Mr. Babcock.

"Ambushed, you say?" asked Hop.

"Yes, Cain and Orson were on their way to Memphis when it happened. Orson was injured but survived, while we think Cain may have been killed. We know he was injured but his body was never recovered," Elizabeth explained. Vick added, "We hope he comes riding up one day."

Vick disliked hearing Elizabeth speak of Cain as dead.

"Hop, come on in so we can talk," Vick suggested.

The kitchen was very comfortable, and before long the men were having drinks and talking about the old days when Vick was in prison. Elizabeth could tell the men had a genuine fondness for each other, but she hated hearing about the negativity of such a dark time in Vick's life.

Hop eventually changed the subject back to Cain.

"That's too bad about your boy. I thought when he contacted me that he was a good kid to arrange this surprise for his Pa."

"We're slowly piecing together what happened, and why. Orson said he thinks he saw one of the men who was from back home, but we don't see why that man would be so far away and involved in an ambush where it happened. It doesn't make sense."

"But that's a clue. Maybe what he saw is worth thinking about. That man could have followed you here, and the reason might be right under your nose. Just think about it."

"We hadn't thought of someone following us. What we do know is Johnson Petty's twin brother is behind Cain missing."

"Did I hear you right—Johnson Petty? Me and him used to meet in New Orleans when I had my plantation. Johnson was one of the richest men in Texas and liked to flaunt it. I heard he was murdered, but I never knew you all had connections."

"Yeah, we had a connection alright. Johnson Petty left his entire estate to Cain and cut his twin brother out. Our problem now is his brother Jonathan Petty, who owns the Circle J Ranch about 3 miles from here. We've already received word that Jonathan is protesting his brother's Will, and without Cain—well, I guess Elizabeth and me will be moving out. So you can see I have no job to offer you at this point."

"What are you and Elizabeth planning to do?"

"Move in that small house next door near the lake."

Hop nodded.

"We own it and the five acres. Jonathan's not going to like us being neighbors, but we're staying here until we find out what happened to our son," Vick said.

"Do you mind me asking how Cain became involved with Johnson Petty?"

"It's a long story but Cain married Johnson's daughter, Eileen. After the wedding Eileen and her daddy were driving back to Texas when the man that framed me, and who was responsible for me going to prison, murdered them. There's more to the story but I'll keep that until another time."

"Sorry about that. It had to be devastating to your boy after his wife was murdered."

"Yep, Cain's had a rough go. You can imagine how surprised he was when he learned he was the beneficiary to the entire Petty fortune," Vick shared.

"And his brother didn't get a penny?" Hop asked. "There must have been bad blood between Johnson and his brother for him to cut his brother out."

"Jonathan was willed the house and five acres next door but he ended up selling it to Cain after he learned he was cut out of his brother's estate. Cain offered him a deal he couldn't refuse. We sure didn't want Jonathan living next door to us anymore than it's going to be when Jonathan finds out we're his neighbor.

My boy got caught right in the middle. This whole damn thing has turned into a nightmare, and all because of Jonathan Petty's greed."

"Sounds like Cain was doomed from the beginning with this much wealth and a scorned brother that thought he should have gotten what your son inherited. Did you say Jonathan lives about three miles from here?"

"Yeah, he has the Circle J Ranch and 40 acres. What I want to do is make Jonathan's life a living hell," Vick vowed. "I've been doing some thinking. I know that bastard's behind the ambush and Cain's disappearance."

"Vick, whatcha' say I ride out to Circle J and talk to Jonathan about a job? If he hires me, I'll try to win his trust, and if he doesn't, I'll come back and we'll put our heads together about finding your boy."

"You'd do that? I hate for you to get mixed up in this. I have a feeling it's not going to turn out pretty. Know what I mean?"

"I don't want you worrying. He doesn't know me from Adam and if I can, I'm gonna win him over. All I have to do is get him to open up and start talking."

Hop and Vick talked at length about how Cain encouraged them into coming to Texas.

"Hop, you mentioned clues. The man Orson saw looked like Lonnie James from Jonesboro. I can't imagine him following us here. When you go to Circle J to talk to Jonathan keep your eyes open for two men. Lonnie wouldn't be here without his brother Dudley."

I'll keep a look out for 'em—so you sold out and came to Texas with your son?"

"We sold the lumber company, but the land we kept. It had been in Elizabeth's family since she was a little girl. We couldn't part with it."

Elizabeth explained to Hop about the manor and how she had mixed emotions about leaving Jonesboro, the town she was raised in.

"There's no place like home," she said.

"Do you think y'all will ever go back?" Hop asked.

"Not now. We're not leaving here till we know what happened to Cain. He is a good man, as good as they come, and he deserves better than what he got," Vick shared.

Elizabeth had never seen Vick's passion regarding Cain, until now. He's not leaving this place until he sees Jonathan pay, she was certain.

The next morning Hop woke up to a wonderful smell of breakfast being prepared by Elizabeth. There was something about this couple that made him want to help solve Cain's murder. He had a feeling he was in the right place and was there for a reason.

Before he left Memphis, he knew he was taking a chance coming to San Augustine unannounced. However, since he was here, he was glad he came to give Vick the support he desperately needed.

Before Hop left his room, he stood at the window and gazed over the beautiful cotton fields. His mind raced back to the time he met Vick, who was a young man in prison. He had heard of the brutality of the New Orleans Prison and was amazed how Vick survived seemingly unscathed. He had to have emotional scars, Hop imagined.

Hop continued to reflect on memories of Vick. This man's made out of pure steel, living in a hellhole of a prison. Ain't nobody I've ever seen walk through the gates of the New Orleans Prison and live to talk about it. Hop then thought about the new Vick. Something is downright special about him, and the man's still fighting, but this time it's for his son.

When Hop came into the kitchen, Vick stood and shook his hand. That strong, sincere handshake told Hop he was here to stay. No matter what the man has on his shoulders he still has that smile that makes you want to be his friend. There's no way I'm turning my back on Vick this time. If he's going to be fighting Jonathan Petty, I'm going to be right by his side, Hop averred.

"How about a cup of coffee?" Vick asked.

After a very large and tasty breakfast, Hop laid out his plan to help Vick and Elizabeth.

"I know working for Jonathan might sound crazy to you, but if I can I'll find a way to get him talking. I'll be there to keep my eyes and ears open. A new man in town needs a job," Hop chuckled.

"At least you'll have a job," Vick kidded. Elizabeth saw calmness come over Vick she had not seen since Cain's disappearance. He finally had someone who could help him find proof that Jonathan arranged the ambush and killed their son.

"Hop, you know Jonathan's plan is to take over this place."

"Maybe not, if I can find out enough to keep that from happening."

"One other thing—keep your eyes open for a paint horse with white markings on his left hind leg. That's another clue that Orson noticed."

"Orson, must be quite a man. When I got Cain's telegram, he told me he was traveling with Orson and he wanted to warn me about him."

"Oh, that's Cain messing with Orson. He was with Cain when they were ambushed. That's when Orson recognized one of the men who shot them. But, it's just hard to believe the fella followed us here.

Hop thought a minute about what he said.

"I wouldn't discount anything Orson saw."

"Why's that?" asked Vick.

"The man's a Sheriff, and has trained himself to be observant and gather clues. That's in his nature, and if he saw someone familiar, I would take notice."

Vick knew Orson was shrewd, but all Vick's attention was on the whereabouts of his son, and hadn't given serious thought to that clue.

"Well— Orson was Sheriff of Jonesboro for over 20 years, so he bound to have learned something. He's an ornery cuss, but he does surprise me with his knowledge of the law sometimes."

Hearing about the Sheriff, Hop thought they could possibly be missing something important that could help them find Cain.

"Like I said, don't discount anything your Sheriff friend has told you. He's got a whole lot more experience in this sort of thing than both of us put together.

Elizabeth, let's talk about those James brother's again."

"Vick, why don't you and Elizabeth think about the last time you saw these men. Perhaps you can come up with a reason they might both be here. Can you think of anything that has happened that could involve these men? Any grudge they would have against you or your son?"

Elizabeth was scratching her head trying to think. "Well, the manor was burned to the ground, but I don't think that was arson. And what reason would they have to do something like that?"

"Why not?" asked Hop.

Elizabeth was shocked at the thought. "Surely they wouldn't be so evil to burn down our home?" she said. "Orson's daughter Lucy, who was to be married to our son, died in the fire on their wedding day. We still mourn her loss."

Hop was stunned hearing that Orson's daughter was a casualty of the manor fire. "That's tragic! You all have had more than your share

of bad luck. I don't know what to say, except I'm sorry for your losses."
Hop could see the sadness in the eyes of Elizabeth and Vick.

"What's so difficult is Cain had finally come to terms with Eileen's death, Johnson's daughter. Marrying Lucy was the highlight of his life until the tragedy happened in the manor. You can't imagine how hard it's been on our families, and poor Orson. The man will never be the same."

After they explained their sorrow, Hop went to saddle his horse and ride to Jonathan's ranch.

"Before I go, think back to the last time you saw those James boys?"

Vick thought a minute and then remembered he had seen them after they returned from Panther Holler. He then remembered what Orson had said; about the brother's being there to possibly rob Buck whom they thought had the treasure. Could it be this entire debacle was because of the treasure that they had lied to Johnny about? Perhaps Lonnie and Dudley broke into the manor and killed Lucy when they were trying to find the treasure.

Now alone, Elizabeth and Vick discussed the fire and the possibility of it being arson.

"Vick, do you think the James'would deliberately set fire to the manor?"

"I wish I knew. If I did, maybe some of this would make some sense," Vick stated.

"If that's possible, do you think Lucy was murdered before the house was set on fire? That would be more merciful for her, Elizabeth said.

"Lizzy, this is the first time I've considered arson. And as for someone murdering Lucy…truthfully, I find that hard to believe."

He comforted Elizabeth, but there was no one to comfort him.

It was midday when Hop approached the Circle J Ranch, just in time to see two men heading to the bunkhouse. He remembered the James brothers Elizabeth had spoken about, and wondered if those were the two men.

Those could be the men that killed Cain, or at least be Jonathan's pawns, he thought.

Hop did his best to get into character before knocking on Jonathan's door.

He'd never been nervous asking for a job, but the idea that he would be spying more than working put him a bit on edge. Helping Vick was paramount, and it rested on him to be convincing enough to win Jonathan over. *I'll keep my eyes open and see what I can learn.*

Dudley and Lonnie saw Hop at the door and wondered who the stranger might be. "Maybe he's the marshal and has news about Cain. If that's the case, we might need to be on the lookout," Lonnie warned.

After Hop knocked, the door opened shortly and out stepped Jonathan, dressed all in black, his usual attire.

"You lost?"

"No sir, I'm new in town and looking for work. My name's Hop Babcock."

He stuck his hand out but Jonathan paused before he shook it.

"I ain't used to men just showing up looking for a job."

"I guess they ain't needing a job." Hop was quick to answer, which was impressive.

Right away, Jonathan gave a half smile and realized he liked this man. *I ain't never had anyone work for me with any sense,* he thought. He didn't realize how bored he had become with his hired help, who failed miserably at any task requiring intelligence. As he mentally examined Hop, he thought, *this might be somebody I can use.* However, in reality, he was starved for a challenging conversation. He had become tired of the "huh" and "uh huh" of men like Dudley and Lonnie. I need another man who understands me when I talk, Jonathan reasoned.

He also liked the fact that Hop was a stranger, and would not be influenced by what others knew of him. Thinking ahead, he presumed that Hop could help him build a case against Lonnie and Dudley if the marshal came calling. He might work out when I take over the plantation. All of this was devised in a minuscule of a second.

"I see you're armed?" Jonathan noticed.

"Yes sir, I always carry a weapon when I travel. You don't have anything against a man carrying a gun to protect himself, do you?"

"No, not at all. But just to warn you, they don't allow guns in San Augustine."

"You mentioned my gun, and it made me wonder what else you might have in mind?"

"We always have plenty of work around here, but I do have a problem. I have a couple of squatters on a place of mine that I might have to take care of if they don't leave peacefully. You any good with that gun?"

"I'm still standing. Any man that knows me—knows better. I'll put it that way."

"I like that, why don't you come in? Looks like you might need a drink."

"Don't mind if I do," replied Hop.

Lonnie and Dudley saw Jonathan invite the man in and they began hashing over the possibility of being arrested if they were caught. "I wonder who that feller is?" Dudley asked.

"Looks like the law to me. Better keep an eye on 'em jest in case Jonathan needs us."

When they entered the bunkhouse, Matilda was cleaning and Dudley, who had always had an eye for her, happened to notice her hand. The ring on her finger was familiar to him.

Enraged, he knew it was the same ring he took off Lucy's finger when they left her to die in the fire. He began questioning her.

"Hey Matilda, where did you get that ring?"

"Meestor Jonathan gave thees' ring to me. It's bee-yoo-tee-ful."

"Well now, do you know where Mr. Jonathan got that ring?"

Lonnie was looking at Dudley, trying to get his attention to stop him from harassing her with questions, but Dudley ignored him.

"Matilda, don't pay attention to Dudley, he just thinks it's a purdy ring."

"There you go tryin' to tell me what to do, and I don't like that!" Dudley shouted.

Lonnie had no idea his brother was about to lose it.

"Stay outta my business Lonnie! Matilda, that ain't yer ring, it's mine, and I want it back. Ya jest stole it from me." She could see the fire in Dudley's eyes, and was frightened and embarrassed by being accused of stealing.

She had shown the ring to everyone, and told them it had been given to her by Mr. Jonathan as a gift.

Dudley moved toward Matilda. She screamed and took off running toward the ranch house.

"Now, look what you've done. That man talkin' to Jonathan could be the law, and that ring could git us hung!"

"She's got my ring and I want it back," Dudley snapped. "Yore gettin' crazier by the minute…you know it? And if that damn ring backfires on us, yore goin' to end up gettin' us both in a heap of trouble. Watcha gonna do with that ring anyway? Ain't no woman around would have ya'."

"Maybe we better go to the house before Matilda starts trouble fer me," Dudley suggested.

It was too late to stop Matilda, for she had already gotten Jonathan's attention.

"Meestor Jonathan," Matilda cried, "Oh Meestor Jonathan, I am sorry. I did not know you had company."

The men stopped talking and gave Matilda their attention. Jonathan was annoyed at having been interrupted, but he could see she was upset. "Matilda, what's wrong? Why are you upset?"

"Meestor Dudley…he accused me of stealing thees' ring you give to me."

Jonathan was racking his brain, since he had not paid attention to her that day she asked him about the ring.

"I'm sorry Matilda, but you need to refresh my memory."

"When I found thees' ring you said, I could have it…don't you remember?"

"Do you mind if I see the ring?" Matilda walked over to Hop and Jonathan just when Lonnie and Dudley walked in.

Jonathan gave them a "go-to-hell" look for interrupting his meeting with Hop.

Seeing Dudley and Lonnie standing there reminded him of how low he had sunk entering into a partnership with them.

"Dudley, what do you mean accusing Matilda of stealing this ring, when I gave it to her weeks ago?" Jonathan scolded.

The brother's partnership began to crumble when Jonathan showed his true colors. He disappointed them when he took Matilda's side instead of theirs.

Hop, witnessing the confusion, decided to play along. "What a beautiful ring," he said. "I haven't seen a ring like this in a long time. It looks like a rare Australian opal." He looked at Jonathan. "You have very good taste and very expensive taste."

Jonathan had no knowledge of precious stones and was thinking of how he could get it back from Matilda, now that he knew it had value. He also admired the culture of this stranger who not only had substance, but could use a gun.

Lonnie sensed that Jonathan was hiring Hop, while Dudley was obsessed with the ring. There was no way that Jonathan would be that relaxed in the presence of a Marshal, Lonnie thought.

"Me and Lonnie came to tell Matilda we made a mistake. That ring of hers, ain't mine like I thought."

Jonathan enjoyed demoralizing Lonnie and Dudley because of the stunt they pulled. Seeing them shift from one foot to the other, he decided to announce Hop Babcock as his new foreman.

"I reckon we gonna be seeing a lot of each other," said Hop, evoking his responsibility.

The blood drained from Lonnie's face as he swallowed his pride. He was shocked at how fast he and Dudley had been demoted by the hiring of this stranger, and the incident with the ring.

Dudley did nothing but stare into space while Lonnie gave him a piercing look.

Hop studied the two. "So this is Lonnie and Dudley James, the men that Vick had told me about."

He imagined, since they were all tied together with Orson as an eyewitness, that Jonathan held the secret of the ambush. "All I have to do now is find out what happened."

"The task may not be easy, but if it's as easy as finding Lonnie and Dudley James, it'll be a breeze.

To further antagonize the James', Jonathan announced that Hop would be moving into his own private quarters attached to the bunkhouse, and would be allowed his privacy.

Days passed and the James boys were breathing down Hop's neck. There was something about the man they didn't like, and they followed him around like he was the Pied Piper. As much as he wanted to get the information about the James brothers to Vick, he knew he had to play it safe in order not to bring suspicion on himself. He felt trapped. I can't chance riding over there now.

One morning, Jonathan invited Hop to ride with him to town.

"I need to talk to you about what's going on, and I'd like you to hear me out."

"Sure, when would you like to go?" Hop asked.

"In a couple of hours. You ready for some good home cooking?"

"I reckon so. Hop chuckled.

When they rode off, Lonnie and Dudley got mad because they were left behind.

"I ain't likin' this one bit. I reckon we jest back to bein' his hired hands, doin' his dirty work."

"What we gonna do 'bout how he's treatin' us?"

"I don't know, I'm a thanking on it. Dudley, you shouldn't have gone accusing Matilda about that ring and got us on his bad side. Another thang, when we help run them Porter's off that plantation of his, he's gonna cut us loose faster than a man can skin a cat."

"What about the treasure back in Panther Holler? Ain't ya' planning on Jonathan goin' with us?" Dudley asked.

"You ready to hear my idea about that?" Lonnie asked.

"Ya' gonna tell me anyhow, so go ahead and spit it out!"

"Maybe if Jonathan don't believe us, his new partner will."

"Lonnie thank whatcha doin'. Ya' ain't planning on splittin' the treasure four ways are ya?"

"I'd rather have a fourth of something than half of nothin'. We ain't got nothin' as it is."

Dudley thought about it a few minutes, then agreed. "What I'm thanking 'bout is ole Vick Porter a'leadin' us to it. If we smart, we'd take 'em with us."

"So yer talking 'bout hog-tying 'em and taking him with us?"

"Ya' want to find the treasure don'tcha?"

"What if he don't talk?"

"He might if he wants his son back?"

"His son's dead. That ain't gonna work."

"Dudley it's a shame you were raised so damn dumb. Lawdy, He don't know that!

We'll make him think Cain's alive. Dudley, are you crazy, or just plain nuts? Think!"

"How ya' gonna make that happen?" Dudley asked.

"What would a man do to save his wife? We might jest have to hog-tie her too and take her with us. Then we'll kill 'em both."

"Even Jonathan and his new partner?" queried Dudley.

"Maybe." Lonnie took out his knife and began sharpening it on an Arkansas stone.

On the ride to San Augustine, Jonathan gave a slightly slanted version of his life, as Hop listened. Of course, he left out all the facts that could incriminate him from prior murders and other crimes. Hop smiled inwardly as he listened to Jonathan create the "poor me" story, embellished with lies to draw Hop into his web of deceit.

The more Jonathan talked, the more Hop noticed irregularities in his story. Hop was keenly aware that Jonathan was "blowing smoke," and had already exhibited plenty of idiosyncrasies, raising questions as to who he really was.

Jonathan's insecurities relating to his twin brother became obvious to Hop, as he spoke of his abuse from a father who never loved him, and also a mother who mentally abused him. Soon all of his complaints were infused with ramblings of lies that made no sense at all.

When Jonathan caught himself talking too much, getting too upset and loud, he would consciously try to control what he said, for fear he would be judged accordingly. By the time they arrived in town, Hop had heard enough.

When they rode past the café and preceded directly to the courthouse, this was a clue that Jonathan was not playing with a full deck, he kept referring to the Porters as "squatters." Hop could not tell fact from fiction when Jonathan spoke. It's one thing to discern the truth from a sane man, but trying to determine the truth from a ranting mentally disturbed man is just about impossible. I don't mind fighting someone I know, but I don't know who the hell this man is or what he's capable of. He could be capable of anything, even murder.

As planned, Jonathan obtained a copy of the papers to serve on Vick and Elizabeth, and having forgotten about the home-cooked meal at the café entirely, fixating on the service papers. Hop was starved by the time they got back to the ranch.

The next evening, Jonathan asked Hop to meet him at the house so they could talk. Another night of lies, he presumed. When he arrived, Jonathan had the drinks poured and proposed his plan.

"Hop, I can use your help to get those squatters off my place. Tomorrow I'm giving notice for 'em to move out. I want 'em as far away from here as possible. Understand?"

"What do you aim to do to make that happen?"

"Whatever it takes. That son of theirs that tried to weasel in and take what's rightfully mine learned who he was dealing with..."He stopped talking and looked away for a second.

He almost let it slip. *This is a good time to prod*, Hop told himself.

"Tell me Jonathan, what about that man who was the beneficiary?"

Jonathan looked at Hop like he resented the question.

Hop covered himself by throwing Jonathan off track.

"What if you move the family out and the missing man shows up to reclaim his property?" Hop asked the leading question and eagerly waited for the answer.

"That won't happen," Jonathan assured him.

"You sound awfully sure of yourself."

"That's all you need to know," Jonathan said emphatically. "I ain't giving up my property for nobody, dead or alive, understand? You mentioned how good you are with that gun. So how good are you?"

"I ain't used to having to prove myself, but if it's necessary to keep my job, I suppose I don't have a choice. Let's go outside and I'll show you."

Jonathan followed him out the front door while the James brothers came to see what was going on.

Standing there with his coat open, Hop took out a fifty-cent piece and gave it to Jonathan to throw into the air.

The coin didn't have time to fall before Hop had drawn his gun and hit it with a loud "ping." Jonathan chased it down and observed the indentation in the middle. To menace the James', he gave the coin to Dudley so he could be reminded of Hop's incredible aim.

"That's quite a show. I reckon you're what I've been looking for."

"You hiring me for my gun?"

"I don't know yet. When I find out, I'll let you know."

"Jonathan, tell me something. What if the man shows up to reclaim his property? Am I gonna be using this gun?"

The James boys were looking and listening. Lonnie thought, Let's see him git outta this one?

"Well now, since you asked, there's been a rumor that Cain Porter is dead, along with the man who was traveling with him."

"So you think that Porter feller is dead?"

"The truth is, I hold my brother responsible for everything."

"Who is your brother?" Hop asked.

Johnson Petty—have ya ever heard of him?

"Don't reckon I have."

"If he hadn't tried to beat me out of what is rightfully mine, none of this would have happened to 'em. I should have been named the beneficiary from the beginning!" he said fiercely.

Jonathan almost spilled the beans again but caught himself, "I mean, you know, all this trouble I've gone through."

Hop thought, Jonathan's crazy, but he isn't about to incriminate himself to me. Jonathan waited for Hop to speak up. Finally, he thought he should acknowledge Jonathan's statement. "Well now, if you're sure he's dead, then I'll do what I can to help," Hop said, in an effort to calm him down.

Hearing Jonathan all but say he knew Cain was dead played right into Hop's hands, and gave him hope that he would find what he was looking for. *This is going better than I thought.* But his problem was finding the right time to pay Vick a visit.

Back on the Pecan Plantation, Elizabeth and Vick had no idea what Hop's plans were, and trusted he had made some progress in his undercover work. They were worried, though, since they had not seen hide nor a hair of Hop since he rode away that day. They had no choice but to wait and trust that their friend had it all under control. After all, what else could they do, with Cain being assumed dead and the Will stating that the property would go to the next of kin? Jonathan still held all the cards.

While Vick and Elizabeth were in limbo, waiting for Jonathan to make his move, they were not standing by idling away their time. They were making plans of their own.

They were sure Jonathan would never entertain the possibility that they would move next door into the house that Cain had purchased for Orson. They assumed Jonathan would think it too small and uncomfortable for a sophisticated woman like Elizabeth. As a matter of fact, he had not even thought about the Porters living in the shadow of the plantation home. At the time Jonathan sold the small house and five acres to Cain, the water rights and the lake were more on Cain's property than the plantation land that was now in the custodial care of Jonathan. This could pose a big problem to Jonathan should he think about it.

It would be Vick's ultimate revenge living next door to Jonathan applying pressure.

Lonnie and Dudley stayed back at the Circle J, while Jonathan and Hop rode out to serve the property seizure papers on Vick and Elizabeth. All the papers were in order. Jonathan boasted to Hop, "If need be, I'll get the Sheriff to drive 'em off!"

Vick glanced at Hop riding up with Jonathan and assumed all was going as planned.

Vick had heard in town that Jonathan had seizure papers drawn up, so they began to move their furnishings before Jonathan could try to seize them, too.

Vick timed it just right moving his last bit of furnishings into the wagon parked in the barn. It was Vick's plan to drive the wagon out just at the right moment so Jonathan would not have the pleasure of ordering them to move.

When Jonathan and Hop were down the road in sight, one of the hands harnessed the mules to the wagon, and was standing by with all of Elizabeth and Vick's furniture as Hop and Jonathan rode up.

They watched as Jonathan grew closer, and when it was time, they walked over to Jonathan to hand him the key.

"What's this?" Jonathan asked.

"You came here for the key, didn't you? We were waiting for you," Vick clarified. You could have had the place a week ago, if you would have said you wanted it. We have no rights, since our son is not here to defend himself and his property."

"Well, where is your son?"

"It's none of your business where my son is. The house is all yours; isn't that what you wanted?"

Jonathan had a speech planned to show Hop how tough he was, but now that the Porters had jumped the gun and moved out, he had nothing to say.

"Well, I guess you're going back where you belong?" Jonathan chided.

"Yeah, as a matter of fact we are."

"Shoulda thought about that before you left Arkansas…could'a saved yourself all those miles of backtracking."

Vick loved Jonathan's sarcasm, and especially this remark.

Oh, we don't mind the drive; we'll only be a stone's throw away. Anytime you need to borrow something, you won't have far to walk." At that, Vick gave Jonathan a big smile and hopped up in the driver's seat of the wagon.

Hop thought Jonathan's reaction to Vick was priceless. After seeing the hate in Jonathan's eyes he no longer doubted Jonathan killed Cain. Jonathan fumed as he watched Vick head toward the house adjacent to the plantation.

"Damn it to hell!" Jonathan whispered under his breath. "I thought they would be leaving and going back to Arkansas."

"What we gonna do now?" asked Hop.

"I reckon I'll think of something. By the time I get through with 'em, they'll wish they would have gone back to Arkansas where they belong."

Hop wanted to burst out laughing, seeing how Vick played Jonathan. It made him like Vick just that much more. The man's got class, he thought.

That night, when the last of the dishes were put away, Vick walked up behind Elizabeth and held her. She turned and looked into his eyes, searching as if she knew something was going on with him. She saw regret that he had moved her into Orson's home.

"Elizabeth, everything you've lost has been because of me," Vick lamented. "I'm going to make it up to you. You wait and see."

"Is this what's bothering you? After all this time— don't you realize that I have you, and that's all I've ever wanted. From the time I met you I prayed we would be together, and that's all that mattered to me."

"I don't deserve you," Vick said.

"But I deserve you," Elizabeth reassured him with a mischievous grin.

Once again, Vick whisked Elizabeth off her feet and took her to bed.

Chapter 15

AFTER AGGIE LEFT HENDERSON, BEN STAYED AROUND FOR A COUPLE **of days and then headed for Beaumont.** He tried to convince himself that Aggie's leaving was for the best, but deep inside he felt hurt and alone. He had grown to depend on her, having no knowledge of his past. The thing that Ben feared most was he knew someone out there wanted him dead and wondered if he had family who missed them. Somehow he missed them, though he didn't know who they were.

Leaving Henderson was a giant step, since he had become so familiar with his surroundings. Actually, he was unsure where to go, but the buzz was all about the Spindletop oil boom, but most of all he remembered Aggie mentioning Beaumont as a town she would like to live in.

When he rode through the thoroughfare of Beaumont he kept a firm grip on his reigns as he maneuvered his horse amid buggies, cars and horsemen, until he found Ms. Josey's Boarding House. Beaumont was a thriving little town with all the money the oil boom had pumped into it.

His concern was that he might be a hunted man, and that required him to keep a low profile, just in case there were posters with his picture on them.

What if I'm a fugitive, and the laws after me? I could have robbed a bank or maybe even killed someone. *Going to the Sheriff for information could turn out to be a bad idea, and I'm not ready to be hung*, Ben thought. *All the loot I had on me came from somewhere. No ordinary cowboy would be carrying that kind of money on him*, Ben reasoned. He hoped and prayed he had come by it legally.

Perhaps the reason Aggie left so abruptly was she knew something of my past and refused to tell me. So many questions when I don't even know why she left.

Ms. Josey's boarding house was a busy little place, and as it happened, he was the last guest of the evening. He signed the registration book as Ben "Gentry." He had seen that name on a sign during his travels and thought it sounded noble and would be easy for him to remember. The aromas from Josey's kitchen were nostalgic, but still there was no memory of from where he might have known those smells. *Maybe its Aggie's cooking causing me to reflect.*

Ms. Josey took an immediate liking to Ben after she signed him in and noticed he was new to her boarding house. He followed her into the dining room for a meal before he retired for the evening.

"So what brings you to Beaumont?" she asked.

"Work…I need to find a job." Ben was enjoying the food, helping himself to a second helping while she fussed around her kitchen. The jolly little woman in her printed apron enjoyed making over him.

"Do you mind if I finish these potatoes off?" he asked.

"Help yerself, I'm glad you're enjoying my cooking. I noticed your name on the roster."

Cain finally had nerve enough to call himself Ben.

"Yes ma'am, Ben's been my name as long as I can remember." She had no idea how truthfully accurate that statement was and wondered why he said it that way.

"I've been riding almost non-stop for several days. Guess you can tell."

Ben, you made a good choice 'cause Beaumont is about to bust its' seams. I'd say, after a hearty meal, hot bath, and a good night's sleep on a soft bed, you'll be just like new. We used to be a quiet little town before the oil boom, and now we've tripled our population since

Spindletop. Yep, the town is growing in leaps and bounds. Everybody in the world is coming here. All on account of that 'black gold." Ms. Josey said.

"Yes ma'am, where I came from they were talking about the oil business in Beaumont."

"You ain't in the lumber business are ya'? 'Cause the oil business done ruined logging around here."

"No ma'am, I'm afraid I don't know anything about logging."

Well, at least we don't have them giant potholes from them logging wagons nomore'. But we shore got a crazy bunch of people nailing up buildings right and left, and foreigners moving in that we can't even understand." Ms. Josey shook her head.

Ben thought she was a storehouse of knowledge by the way she was talking his ears off.

"It looks like you have a thriving business due to all that growth you been talking about…so it can't be all bad," Ben noticed.

"You're right, but it's forcing me to go bigger myself. Used to, I was lucky to have two rooms a night, but now I stay full. It might be my cooking," she laughed. "I got a piece of apple pie fer ya' when you finish them dumplings."

"Thank you Ms. Josey. I heard that man call you 'Ms. Josey'."

"Oh, I'm sorry, I didn't even introduce myself. I've always been Ms. Josey. Looks like yer ready for that piece of pie." She took his plate and replaced it with the most delicious piece of dessert he had ever tasted.

"You've been awfully kind to me. I appreciate it," Cain said.

"You know they got all kinds of oil companies in town ya' could probably work fer. Yeah, when Spindletop blew, it put Beaumont on the map. But I reckon ya' know all about Spindletop."

"Ms. Josey, I think I'm going to be looking for ranch work. That's what I'm good at."

"Seems like I heard of somebody needing a ranch hand. I'll give it some thought and tell you in the morning."

The next day Ms. Josey was as bright and cheery as she was the night before.

"Ben, I got some news fer ya'. I been knowing these people fer over thirty years and they might be lookin' fer someone like you. It's a sad story about them folks." Her demeanor changed to melancholy, as she spoke of this family that had lost a son Ben's age.

"Ben, do you think you'd be interested? I could write a little note stating I know you, if you think that would help?"

"Yes ma'am, it would, especially since I'm new in town. I don't know how to thank you. I really appreciate you looking out for me."

She patted him on the shoulder and smiled.

"Ben, I can tell good people when I see 'em."

The next day he had his note and headed out of town. It was mid-afternoon when he arrived at the Cormack ranch.

A couple of dogs came running out to meet him as he rode up to a large ranch that looked like it could use his help. Before he could dismount, a woman and older gentleman greeted him. *The dogs warned them*, he thought.

"What can we do fer ya'?" asked the gentleman.

"You all must be Mr. and Mrs. Cormack."

"Yes, I'm Martha, and this is my husband Glen."

"Nice spread y'all have out here."

"All this land and cattle has been in our family fer' a long time. What can we do fer ya?"

Ben dismounted and approached the couple and handed them Ms. Josey's note.

"Nice to know you folks. I'm Ben Gentry. Ms. Josey told me that you all might need somebody to help out around here. I'm a good worker and can do most anything that needs done."

Glen was sizing up Ben and his horse. The young man reminded him of the son he and his wife had lost.

Glen noticed a sparkle in Martha's eye, which was a good sign. I know this young man must remind her of Billy.

"So you're good with a horse, 'eh?"

"As you probably noticed, this isn't the best horse, but I know how to handle horses well."

"Well then, if it's alright with Martha, I'd say you got yourself a job."

Martha smiled with approval.

"Now Ben, we're all family here. I'll clear a place for you out in the bunkhouse with the other men. Butch Clark is the foreman and Wendell Young…well, we don't know about Wendell, other than we like him. We all get along, so I think you'll be just fine working with these men."

Glen continued to study Martha as she smiled and chatted, walking Ben to the bunkhouse. *I ain't seen her this happy since before Billy died*, he thought.

~

It bothered Aggie that she left Ben so abruptly. If only she had been more careful and left that note as planned, it would have made all the difference in the world to Ben, and her peace of mind. *I guess it was meant to be that I forgot to leave the note.*

Aggie had been in her new home two months when she woke up sick one morning. This was the most horrible sickness she had ever had. It was the kind of sick that made her wonder if she could be expecting a child. Each night thereafter, she would lay awake for hours, praying there was an explanation for her sickness other than having a baby, though she had other signs that indicated the same. She continued to deny it and prayed it wasn't so.

She thought about her feelings for Ben, but while she was in Henderson she was not ready for marriage. At that time, her head was spinning with doubt because of the promise she made to her daddy about marriage. However, now, since she had her new home and was all settled, she could think of no one she'd rather be with, especially since Ben was the only one possible who could be the daddy of her unborn child. That is, if it turns out she is with child! Aggie knew she wanted to see Ben again, but his feelings could have changed since she left so abruptly.

How could she even find him? All she knew was a first name, no last name, no idea where he came from. She didn't know if he had regained his memory and moved on back to his home and family. The thought of a single woman explaining her pregnancy made her more depressed.

Within a few weeks, Aggie had to hire two ranch hands in order to keep up with the work that needed to be done on her ranch. It didn't take long for her to realize that running a ranch was more of a man's job than a woman's, due to the endless backbreaking chores that were impossible for her to do without help.

She was also beginning to experience sustained signs of depression—partly out of sheer loneliness, and partly from knowing how people will look down on her and her child for not being married. By now, she knew for sure she was going to have a baby. She was far enough along that she didn't need a doctor to confirm her diagnosis. *So much for being determined not to be tied down by children*, she thought.

The seasons began to change, and her worst enemy for the time being, turned out to be nature itself—typical Texas weather. There were all kinds of storms that would loom out of nowhere; some so severe she would hide under her covers like a child. Many times Aggie got caught out in a rain and lightning storm, and have to struggle quickly to move her milk cow to shelter in the barn.

Aggie was three months along, but not showing, when Pappy came running into the house reporting that 10 Angus were missing, and her fence had been cut in several places.

"Are you sure the Angus didn't push through the fence?"

"Ms. Aggie, we know a cut fence when we see it," Pappy insisted.

She was furious. At long last, Parley Jackson had reared his ugly head. She remembered that she was warned about him, and the possibility he would try to cause her trouble. *He's been toying with me all along. He thinks I don't know what's been going on? The scoundrel has allowed me to become comfortable before starting his antics. It's his game.*

Aggie put on a long coat to avoid any suspicions one would have with her condition and then waited for the men to bring her horse and buggy around. She knew she had to speak to Mr. Parley and let him know she was on to him.

Pappy hated her to meet with Parley alone.

"Ms. Aggie, me and Kenny will go with you if you want us to."

"I'll handle Parley, but if I'm not back in an hour—come looking."

"I don't thank ya' need ta go over there by yerself," Pappy insisted.

"Before the day's over, this Parley Jackson fella is going to know not to mess with Aggie Dawson." She gave her horse a swift whip. The men stood there and watched as she sped away.

Aggie knew how to handle a horse and buggy well. She rode rapidly down the open road, then over the cattle gap that led up to the Jackson ranch.

She couldn't wait to look Parley Jackson in the eyes. As she brought the rig to a stop, she saw a curtain move. *He knows he has company*, she thought, as she walked up to his door and knocked loudly. "Mr. Jackson, I need to talk with you!" Aggie waited a few minutes, and then heard the sound of boots walking toward the door.

She took a deep breath just as a very handsome man with a mustache stood before her. *This can't be Parley*, she thought, *He appears to be a man of class, who would be too upstanding to destroy my fence and steal my cattle.* Her heart skipped a beat when his clear blue eyes met hers.

The stranger smiled at her; but instead of a cunning smile, it was guileless. She was at a loss for words until she remembered the reason she was there.

"Uh, I'm Aggie Dawson, your neighbor."

"I know who you are. My father has told me about you. Are you here to see him?"

"Yes, ah, I am. Is he here?"

The man reeked of whiskey. *Ah ha*, she thought, *he's nothing but a sorry drunk. I knew I could find something wrong with him.*

"I'm Seth, his son. My father isn't here." He took a moment to look her over and then pondered, So this is Aggie! I've never seen such a beauty.

Seth had heard of Aggie from his father—who was furious that the ranch she purchased was sold before he could buy or steal it. He had been trying to drive old lady Mixson off her ranch for years.

Aggie acknowledged Seth with a simple nod.

"Please, Ms. Dawson, have a seat. My father is expected home soon."

She took a seat in a cushioned chair, but was not comfortable. She felt awfully uneasy in the strange home, as she waited for Parley's arrival.

"Would you like a drink while you wait?"

"No thank you, I can't wait long," she said. She turned her head and stared out the window.

"Why don't you relax? I'm not going to bite you. Have you ever had a drink before?" "Look Seth, this is not a social call. I'm here to find out about 10 missing Angus and my cut fence."

"Ms. Dawson, are you here accusing?" Aggie had not expected to meet those steel blue eyes staring at her. A shiver she could not explain came over her. *What is it with this man? I better gather my senses or I'll appear like a complete fool, she calculated, while turning her gaze to avoid his disarming eyes.*

"Let me say this: I've heard of your father's reputation."

"Then perhaps you need to hold your questioning for my father."

About that time, a man rode past the window and she caught a glimpse of an older version of Seth. *This has to be Parley*, she presumed.

"Looks like you're going to have your chance," Seth said.

The door opened quicker than she anticipated, and before she could speak, a tall arrogant looking man walked toward her. He walked with a slight limp, but she could tell he was confident and used to getting his way.

Seth, did not like the look on his father's face as he stood before Aggie.

"Father, this is Aggie Dawson, our next-door neighbor."

"I know who she is," he said rudely. Parley barely looked at her, as he took off his hat. Aggie noticed the indentation from his hatband on his forehead, and the beads of sweat rolling down the side of his face from the Texas heat.

"What can I do for you, Miss Dawson?" he asked, while again failing to look her in the eyes. Aggie was infuriated by his lack of respect.

"First, you can own up to stealing 10 of my Angus, and second, you can agree to repair my fence, return my cattle and then never step foot on my property again."

"Let's see, I think I counted four things. Seth didn't you hear four things?"

Aggie looked at Seth, who had a half-smile on his lips.

"Father, I think you ought to give her a straight answer. Did you steal her Angus? If you did, tell her, and don't play games."

"Seth, why don't you get the hell outta here? You're like your Mother. You could never stand the heat in the kitchen."

Seth stood and walked out. As he passed by Aggie, he looked at her sympathetically.

Parley was a cynical character and did not own up to anything.

"Miss Dawson, I don't take kindly to anyone coming in my house accusing me of stealing. So when you get tired of playing rancher, let me know, and I'll buy the place from you."

"I didn't come to sell, but I did come to warn you to stay off my land. I have a trespassing sign, big as Texas, and I expect you to obey it."

"Or you'll what?" He glared at her. "You have a good day Ms. Dawson."

"And sir, you remember that I warned you."

Parley watched Aggie as she marched out the door, and wondered why she was in a coat on such a warm day. He chuckled under his breath at the idea that she thought she could frighten him. *She has no idea who she's dealing with*, he thought.

Aggie was very much aware of the slight change in her weight, but felt sure she could conceal her condition a little longer. She also knew it would not be long before her largest coat may not fit. On what had become almost a nightly ritual following supper, her only company, Pappy and Kenny would sit with her on the front porch talking about their life in Louisiana. She loved hearing their stories about living in small Louisiana towns such as Erath and Abbeville. On one particular night, she decided to clear the air by opening up about her pregnancy. She told them her husband had left her. Unbeknownst to Aggie, they already knew she was expecting. Her first inclination was to say her husband was dead, but she quickly realized she couldn't use that lie because sometimes in the future Ben might find her and want to claim his child.

As time passed, she grew more desperate to save her baby from ridicule. Finding Ben was the only thing that made sense to her, for the moment.

Perhaps I can pay someone to go to the cabin and see if he's still there. She felt it might be a wild goose chase, but it was worth it to ease her mind.

Aggie was right in her assumption; for when the man she hired returned, he reported that the old cabin was vacant, and that he'd inquired in town and learned that someone by the name of Ben had lived there but left for Beaumont.

She began to accept how hopeless it would be to find a man who might have already regained his memory and gone home. For all she knew, Ben could be married with a house full of children.

Ben's presence had breathed new life into Martha, who had grieved herself sick since their son had died. Since Ben had begun working for the Cormacks, Glen had decided to do whatever it took to make sure that Martha stayed happy, even if it meant lying to protect her.

Ben eventually confided in them concerning his amnesia, and what little past he knew. This greatly disturbed Glen—knowing at any time Ben could regain his memory and leave. *That would be devastating for Martha*, he thought.

Should Ben regain his memory Glen was certain that there were no skeletons in his past. Ben was too nice a young man for anything like that.

After their son died, Martha shut Glen out, and would not leave her room. She felt her world had stopped, and Glen could not get through to her no matter what he did.

When Ben arrived Martha bounced back, and started cooking and cleaning like her old self. *Just like the old days*, Glen thought.

After a few months of Ben being the center of attention, Butch Clark, the foreman, left without any warning. This would leave Wendell in line for the promotion to foreman, and that simply would not do, since he was not much of a worker.

Glen asked Ben to ride out to the north pasture with him to check on a bull that continuously pushed down his fence.

Buddy was an ornery old bull that Glen had paid handsomely for and used for breeding purposes. He thought many times that he should have Buddy slaughtered, but couldn't come around to having it done.

After they repaired the fence, Glen decided it was a good time to talk with Ben.

"Let's ride on up to the top of that hill. I want to show you something." After they raced, as they often did, Glen stopped and began his conversation. Ben could tell it was getting serious.

"Ben, I know you didn't know Martha before, but she's like her old self again. Our son Billy was about your age when he died, and I know your being here reminded her of him. This is one reason I want to talk to you, about running the ranch."

"What about Butch? He might come back, and I wouldn't want to come between you and him."

"Naw, I know Butch, he ain't comin' back. He's that kind of man. When he leaves, he's gone."

"What about Wendell? He's been here longer than me."

"Son, do you want the job or not? I'm offering it to you, and besides, when I git through with you, yer gonna make a hellava foreman."

"Well Mr. Cormack, since you put it that way, I'd be happy to take the job."

Ben and Glen shook hands and raced their horses back to the ranch house, just like father and son.

"I told you I could beat you," Glen said with a chuckle.

What he didn't know was Ben held his horse back so Glen could win. Before they went into the house, Glen asked him one other question.

"Ben, I been meaning to ask, do you know how to use a gun?"

"I'm not sure if I do or not. I'd like to try sometime."

"Working on the ranch…you need a gun. We got all kinds of critters, and it's best that you know how to protect yourself."

"Let's go to the tack room. I have something for you."

Ben couldn't believe Glen would give him a beautiful hand-tooled leather holster, with a brand new .45 pistol.

"Son, I want you to have this." Ben noticed something in him he had not seen before—Glen was having the same problem with the death of his son as his wife.

Ben thought, *Why not let them treat me like a son?* He felt it was as good for him as it was for this family who had a lot of love to give.

That evening, after supper, Glen and Ben went out back to do a little target practicing. Ben strapped the holster on his hip as if he knew what he was doing, and he thought to himself how natural it felt.

"Okay now, let's see how you do. You ready?"

Ben was standing there with his legs slightly apart when Glen said "go." Ben drew the gun with legendary prowess, just like his father Vick, of whom he had no memory. He was picking the cans off with such speed and accuracy that Glen became frightened of who this young man might be. He had never seen a hand that fast and accurate with a gun. Ben surprised himself at his marksmanship and figured that shooting a gun must be pretty easy to learn.

Glen was speechless, and Ben wondered why Glen was suddenly quiet.

The speed of Ben's quick draw made Glen think he could be a professional gunfighter, which made him wonder if his acumen for figuring Ben's character might have been way off. *This could be the secret to his past, and why someone wants him dead*, Glen thought.

If Glen only knew Ben's past, he would know that before Ben's amnesia, he was a fumbling kid with a gun. Apparently, along with his loss of memory, he lost his inhibitions too. Now Cain possessed the same natural ability with a gun as his father.

Chapter 16

Tʜᴇ ʏᴇᴀʀ ᴡᴀs ᴄᴏᴍɪɴɢ ᴛᴏ ᴀɴ ᴇɴᴅ, ᴀɴᴅ ɪᴛ ᴡᴀs ɪᴍᴘᴏʀᴛᴀɴᴛ ғᴏʀ Vɪᴄᴋ **to call on a few more Texas towns before the frost set in.** Orson usually traveled with him, but since he had returned to Arkansas, Elizabeth would be his sidekick on this adventure. She insisted they take the Model T to make their rounds. This time they were more prepared, carrying with them posters containing Cain's picture.

When they pulled out, Jonathan saw them and wondered where they were going.

∽

After Orson returned home, he was having moments of second-guessing himself over leaving Lizzie and Vick. After all, they were the only "family" he had left in his world. He thought he would be happy when he got back to Jonesboro, but it wasn't working out that way. He figured he'd gain some contentment and solace by living in his tiny cabin because it was only a few feet away from the graves of Lucy and her mother. Truth was, he was still grieving, and felt he had left sooner than he should have after Lucy's death. Now he was back to take care of the graves, and he was still unhappy. Orson's wife had died giving birth to Lucy, and her grave had always been taken care of, just as he intended to do with Lucy's. *Now they're together, and there ain't no more I can do*, he thought.

172

Although Orson missed Vick and Elizabeth, he was back home in Jonesboro, the place he loved. But things had changed for him since Lucy's death. *Texas is a nice place to visit, but it ain't home to me,* Orson kept reminding himself. Then he would think of Lucy's death and think, *But this ain't home to me no more without my little Lucy.* In Orson's mind, she would always be his little girl.

After Orson retired as Sheriff, everything seemed to fall apart. Lucy died in the fire, and after that, he didn't even want to go to town. "That's jest a'killin' time," he would say. Soon the town thought of Orson as someone of the past. Charlie B his old time friend had stepped up to take his job, and few people now bothered to give a thought of the man who had given his life's blood for the safety of their town. Even though Orson was back home the word had already spread that Orson and Cain Porter had moved to Texas, and were both killed in an ambush.

Being away from Vick and Elizabeth caused a deep loneliness to set in, mainly because he had become somewhat of a recluse. He knew a lot of folks, but he had only one friend who understood him, and that was Vick Porter.

One afternoon, while Orson was sitting on the porch, two men rode up to his cabin and introduced themselves. They were working men, leading a packhorse that was weighted down with tools.

"Howdy mister. What can I do fer ya'?" Orson asked.

"We been sent here by Vick Porter, and I wonder if we can sit an' talk a spell."

"Vick sent y'all here jest to talk?"

"No, that ain't the only reason. He told us we could move into that house near the one that burned up."

"That's the carriage house he's talkin' 'bout by the manor that burned a while back.

"Vick said ya' knew all 'bout that carriage house as ya' call it."

Orson hated being reminded of the fire, and had not been out to see the place since Lucy died.

"We been riding all the way from San Augustine, Texas, and we're mighty tired. I wonder if ya' got some coffee we kin have. We ran out two days ago and ain't too used to being without it."

"Why don't y'all come on in and have a cup and eat a bite. I reckon y'all like pork, don't ya?

"Mister, beggars ain't choosers is what I always say. By the way, I'm Buster Sykes, and this is Pat Day."

"Glad to meet y'all. I'm Orson Cargill and I been knowing the Porters fer a long time."

After the men had a good meal they stood up ready to go.

"We know it ain't polite to eat and run, but we want to get settled in that place a'fore dark."

"It ain't that fer down the road, why don't I ride out a ways and show ya' the place."

"That'll be mighty nice of ya', Orson."

Orson wondered why Vick offered the carriage house to two workers. It didn't make sense, but it was none of his business to ask. That's how Orson was. A man's business is his own.

~

Cain and Elizabeth hated being away from their new home by the plantation for any length of time, for fear that Jonathan might destroy it. It gave them some consolation knowing Hop was now at the plantation to watch over things. They drove several hundred miles, while diligently distributing the posters about Cain. Every place they stopped it was the same bad news, which was difficult to hear. The trip seemed hopeless, but Elizabeth and Vick needed to exhaust every effort. They tried to remain positive, and refused to give up.

After a week on the road, and with no leads, they turned the automobile around and headed back to San Augustine. "Lizzie, I think we've done all we can do. From now on, it's out of our hands." She could see how difficult it was for him to admit that he could do no more.

Hop desperately wanted to tell Vick about his suspicions, but there were no opportunities to do so. Acutely aware of Jonathan's extreme paranoia, he was careful not to draw suspicion on himself.

Before Hop left Circle J and moved to the plantation, Dudley and Lonnie had approached him about the treasure at Panther Holler. Suddenly it clicked that this might have something to do with Vick, and the burning of the manor. They didn't say much, but just enough to get a feel of where his head was in case they included him in searching for the treasure. Hop didn't know what they were up to, but he acted interested without committing to learn more about their plan. They said just enough for him to know they believed Vick was to be involved in some way with them finding the treasure.

During their conversation, Lonnie noticed hesitation on Hop's part, and stopped talking before revealing more of their plan.

When Hop left, Dudley and Lonnie discussed their feelings. "I don't know 'bout him. He might not be one we'd want to help us. Time will tell," was all Lonnie said, but Dudley felt his brother was uneasy about how much they had revealed.

"Maybe we messed up talkin' to Hop 'bout the treasure. Now he might say somethin' ta git us in trouble with Jonathan."

"There ain't no way we can keep an eye on Hop and Jonathan with them Porters living close to the plantation," Lonnie pointed out.

"As long as they're alive, we're gonna be lookin' over our shoulder. We might need ta git rid of everyone one of 'em 'fore they git rid of us. Ain'tcha gittin' tired of dancing around, tryin' to keep them Porters from knowing we're here?" Dudley anguished.

"What if Hop and Jonathan decide to go after the treasure without us, now that we been stupid enough to tell 'em both, thinkin' they'd help get it?"

"Lonnie, you should have thought about that 'fore you went and opened yore big mouth," shaking his head as he chastised his brother.

"Don't worry, we'll work it out" Lonnie tried to convince himself.

Jonathan continued to regret and stew about selling the little house to Cain. "Now I have them Porters knowing every move I make, living right under my nose."

One morning, Matilda was making biscuits when she placed her ring on the sill of the kitchen window. When she got through, she went about her cleaning and forgot all about it.

Hours later, Hop passed through the kitchen and noticed the ring she had carelessly left. He didn't stop to think, as he took the ring and placed it in his pocket. He knew it was the same ring Dudley had accused Matilda of stealing. Most probably, the ring has something to do with Elizabeth and Vick, he imagined, since the James' were so eager to get it that day.

Somehow I have to get this ring to Vick and Elizabeth, Hop thought. *It may have some*thing to do with the manor burning. The more he thought about it he was sure the ring was an important part of the puzzle, and he aimed to find out at any cost.

By this time, Hop was certain Lonnie and Dudley had burned down the manor, based on what they told him about the treasure. *They're the men that killed Cain's wife, and the ring has to be the evidence in some way*, he postulated.

It was the wee hours of the morning before Hop left his room to slip out of the house. When sufficient time had passed and he was sure Jonathan was asleep, he walked quietly down the hall past Jonathan's room. He froze when the floor creaked just as he walked by the door. Jonathan, who rarely slept soundly, sat straight up in bed, wondering if it was a dream or if someone was outside his door. Hop stood there momentarily before he took another step, then walked to the stairs as quietly as possible. Suddenly, the floor creaked again. Standing near the stairs and no sound coming from Jonathan's room, he was sure he had made it without being heard. Even if he was, there was no turning back now. Beside, he could just be going to get some fresh air.

It was still dark outside, and the moon had a haze of dark clouds over it. The dew was heavy, and a thick fog lay over the lake, making him shudder. He felt a blanket of moisture envelope his face as he stood silently, looking around to see if there were any movements within the house. Every so often he would hear the sound of the horses that were bedded down in the barn. The fog was so thick he could not see Vick's house. Knowing well the landscape, he walked through the fog toward Vick's house, disappearing into the night. Although uneasy, he was not frightened. *Perhaps it's because I'm breaking into Elizabeth and Vick's home,* he smiled at the thought. He was almost to the house when it suddenly appeared out of the darkness. Looking behind him, not even the stately plantation home was visible, as he moved toward Vick's house. He was sure all was calm, as he walked into the shadows. He took his knife and pried open the window on the backside that led into Elizabeth's bedroom. After climbing through the window, he passed by a mirror and was startled by his own image. Looking around, he spied a pair of Elizabeth's gloves, which was a perfect place to leave the ring. She'll see the ring right away, he thought.

Climbing out of the window, Hop noticed the fog coming off the water that seemed even thicker than before. What an eerie morning, he thought, as he was nearing the barn. Suddenly he heard horses snickering, and wondered if they sensed him nearby. As he passed by a wagon loaded with bales of hay, a dark figure sprung from the top of the wagon, knocking him to the ground. In an instant, the man was on top of him, holding a very large knife. The man's face was hardly recognizable in the dark, but he could tell it was Jonathan. Hop had to wince to make sure he was seeing correctly, as the man looked deeply into his eyes with the gaze of a madman. They struggled, but there was no need, since Jonathan was wielding the knife, and Hop had been caught off guard. It was then that Hop's life passed before his eyes.

"Jonathan, please don't do this," he cried out.

"You're in with the Porters, and here to spy on me!" Jonathan shouted.

"I don't know what you're talking about. You're mistaken! Get the hell off me and let me explain."

"You're here to trick me! I know you're a con, just like your friend! Too bad you're not going to be around to tell him that he and his little bride are next!"

Hop felt the thrust of the sharp blade enter his stomach, and then another in his chest. He then lost consciousness. Jonathan stood, as Hop's blood drained off the knife onto his clothing. "The dirty bastard's dead," Jonathan whispered, while wiping the knife off on his coat.

He had forgotten how it felt to murder someone. He remembered the sense of power it gave him when he raped Aggie, and when he murdered her mother and Phillip Bradford. He felt fulfilled, as he relived stabbing his own father.

It took a while, but he managed to drag the body to the lake. His first thought was hiding the body in the barn until morning, but decided some of the hired help might see him. He thought of the lake; a perfect place. The body will sink and never be found, he murmured to himself.

After dumping Hop's body into the body of water, he thought his problems would be over, if he added a couple more bodies to his list. He looked over at Elizabeth and Vick's house and imagined watching them take their last breaths.

"In time..." he laughed, in a sick sadistic way, "in time."

Hours later, when daylight came, Jonathan saw Elizabeth and Vick drive up in their Model T. He wondered where Vick would have met Hop—*were they both in prison together, gambling buddies, or what? I should have made him talk before I killed him.*

Later that morning, Jonathan rode out to the Circle J to get away from the crime scene. Telling Lonnie and Dudley that he murdered Hop was out of the question, since he thought the least they know, the better. Jonathan still held a grudge against the brothers for not telling him about the opal ring that Matilda now owned. *A woman like her doesn't need a valuable ring like that*, Jonathan bemoaned.

When he arrived at the ranch, the boys were caught off guard. They had reverted back to their old habits of being dirty, unkempt, and wearing old clothing. Because of his fixation with cleanliness, he was repulsed. *Too bad Hop messed up, for he was the kind of man I needed to work for me. Unlike these stupid Arkansas hillbillies I can't trust*, he thought.

The James' could see changes in Jonathan they didn't understand, and wondered what had happened. They had no idea the man was sinking little by little into a deep hole of psychotic behavior.

Jonathan knew he had to be careful, and not allow Vick to know he had any connection with the James boys other than their boss—if so, it could foil his plan. Before he left, he scolded them like children again.

"From now on, when you come for your pay, come after the sun goes down, just before dark so no one will recognize you. Them Porters are watching every move I make."

This was the first time they had seen Jonathan without Hop, which surprised them. "Where's Hop, he's usually with ya'?" asked Lonnie.

"Don't question me about things that's none of your business!" Jonathan snapped back. "And clean yourself up so you don't stink!" The men looked at each other, again wondering what was going on with him.

"It ain't your business about Hop, you hear!"

The man's a squirrel, Lonnie thought.

Each time the brothers asked questions, it raised his level of paranoia. After a long pause, Jonathan said, "I don't know. Hop upped and left. Said he was going hunting and never came back. Guess he just decided to move on. Why you want to know?" Lonnie and Dudley had never seen Jonathan in this frame of mind.

"Jest a wonderin' boss. We ain't seen him neither."

After Jonathan left, Lonnie said, "He's hiding something from us."

"Maybe Hop left and went looking for the treasure," Dudley said.

"Dudley, think! Hop don't know where Panther Holler is. Hell, we don't even know where it is. We need to keep an eye on them Porters 'cause when they leave, we want to be right behind 'em."

~

Elizabeth and Vick were glad to be back home even though it was next door to Jonathan. While she was unpacking her suitcase, Elizabeth saw a ring on one of her gloves. She looked closer and then screamed, "Vick come quick!"

He could hear the panic in her voice. She was sitting on the edge of her bed pointing at the gloves.

"Lizzie, what's wrong?" he asked.

She couldn't speak. She just pointed at the gloves.

"It's only gloves," he said, until he saw the ring.

They both stood approached the chest, staring at the ring, afraid to pick it up.

"My God, that looks like Lucy's ring. How did it get here?" Elizabeth had no explanation, and thought Lucy must have visited them from the grave. What other explanation did they have, since the ring was on Lucy's finger when she died?

They were both trying to recover from the shock, when it finally registered that someone selectively placed the ring there. "Yet, who?" Elizabeth wondered. Vick never found the body, nor the ring, and they knew Lucy had it on the day she died in the fire. Vick assumed the ring had been destroyed with Lucy, yet there must be someone else in the equation who knew of the ring. Still the question was, who?

"Vick, Lucy wants us to know something. It's a clue," Elizabeth said.

"Lizzie, you're talking like you believe in ghosts."

"Well, you tell me how this ring got here. We both know that Cain placed the ring on Lucy's finger before she died, and I saw it on her finger the day of the fire."

"Someone must have come into the house when we were gone and left it here. It could have been Hop. He would be the logical one, leaving it here to let us know he is onto something. It has to be—for there's no one else... The more I think about it, it has to be Hop. I haven't seen him since before we left on our trip. Perhaps it's time we do a little digging to see what the hell's going on."

The next morning, Vick saw Jonathan leave.

Since Vick had not seen Hop with Jonathan his curiosity got the best of him. Making sure that Jonathan was out of sight he walked down by the lake where a man carrying two bales of hay was working.

"Naw, Mister Vick, I ain't seen the man fer a couple of days." Vick's mind began to race. What if something happened to Hop?

"If you see him, let me know. But remember, it's between me and you, and no one else."

"Yes sir, Mister Porter. I shore will," said the field hand.

In the meantime, Matilda, who had left her ring on the windowsill, had forgotten she had left it there overnight. At first she couldn't remember where she had taken it off until it dawned on her that she had left it at the plantation on the windowsill. Her heart was in her throat until she arrived for work. She went into the house and quickly ran to the window in the kitchen to fetch it but it wasn't there. After retracing her footsteps of the previous day, she became extremely upset, realizing that someone had taken her beautiful ring.

She began to panic, when she looked out the window and saw one of the workers talking with Vick.

She didn't want to be accusing, but someone had to know about the ring. Maybe they saw someone come in the house who wasn't supposed to be there. Vick was about to walk away, when Matilda approached them.

"Clarence, my bea-u-ti-ful ring is missing. Do you know anyone that has seen my ring?"

"No ma'am, Ms. Matilda. Ain't nobody ever go in Mr. Jonathan's house. Ain't nobody got no ring that I know of."

Vick saw the tears well up in her eyes as she turned to walk away.

"Just a minute," he said. "Wait! Let me ask you about your ring. What kind of ring did you lose?"

"It was a bea-u-ti-ful ring that Meester Jonathan gave me, and I think I know who has it."

Vick thought she was going to name Hop as the culprit.

"Meester Jonathan's men working for him came in and stole it. His brother say, 'cause they t'ink I stole the ring, but Meester Jonathan gave me the ring."

"You're not talking about Mr. Hop are you?"

Matilda looked shocked that this stranger was asking about Hop as if he knew him.

"Oh no, not Meester Hop. He is so nice. It is Dudley and Lonnie, who live at Meester Jonathan's ranch."

Vick could have been knocked over by a feather. Finally things began to make sense.

Hop, with all his probing, stumbled onto something, and that's how the ring got in our house. He wondered if Hop was in some kind of trouble, and what may have happened to him.

Vick began forming a plan. Something that Elizabeth said, about ghosts. If she could believe in ghosts, certainly others could as well. Vick smiled for the first time since Cain's disappearance, when he thought about Jonathan and the James brothers working together. When I get through with them they'll wish they'd never heard of the Porters.

∽

Weather in Arkansas had been storming for two weeks before it finally stopped. Orson had cabin fever and was getting antsy, being stuck in his cabin for so long. He began thinking of Vick, and missing their friendship. *Life's too short and I shoulda' never left Vick and Lizzie. Ain't nothin' fer me here.* This was all it took for him to pack up and take a little trip after the storm. Ever since Lucy died, it was hard for him to sit still. *I guess it's time fer' me to git' outta here, he convinced himself.*

A week later, just as the sun was going down, Orson was on the same road outside the entrance to Pecan Plantation, when he happened to run into Dudley, who was coming after Lonnie and his pay. He was following orders that Jonathan had given them about riding out separately before dark, and it was near dusk.

Evening was fading fast, with a cool breeze kicking up dust when Dudley who didn't have a care in the world, was approaching the cattle gap on his horse. Orson was nearing the same entrance to the plantation.

With the brim of his hat pulled down, Orson did not notice Dudley riding toward him until the two riders nearly collided at the plantation entrance. When they met, within six feet of each other, Orson looked up and said, "Howdy," to Dudley.

"Holy God Almighty," said Dudley, as he turned his horse and sped away.

Orson couldn't see the man well enough to recognize him since it was near nightfall, but he wondered why the man acted frightened.

"That damn man must be goin' to a hanging, or running from one," Orson chuckled.

"That was damn peculiar, the way that man took off. Something spooked him alright." Orson had no idea the man thought he was seeing a ghost or apparition, since he was sure Orson was dead.

By the time Orson got to the plantation, he experienced a flashback when that menacing face had appeared before him on another night, but he couldn't put his finger on when and where that was.

Bedding down his horse for the night, he took the small bag filled with his clothes and walked to his little house. He still had the keys to let himself in to get a good night's sleep. His plan was to surprise Vick and Elizabeth in the morning when he showed up at the big house.

While sitting around the table talking about the mysterious ring they heard a key turn in the lock on their door. Vick grabbed his .45 pistol and was ready to shoot, when Orson opened the door. Vick shoved the gun to Orson's head when he walked in.

"Hey, it's me don't shoot!" Orson shouted.

"What the hell! You almost got yourself shot!" It startled Orson, too.

"You're the one who's breaking and entering. I'm a little skittish 'cause I already been dry-gulched once. What you and Lizzie doin' down here in my place? Did the sonavobitch kick y'all out?"

"Sorry, but I didn't know it was you. Lucky I didn't shoot you."

"I guess I have that kind of face, 'cause I pert near scared one feller to death down by the cattle gap. All I said was 'howdy,' and he skedaddled like a scalded rabbit."

Vick knew it had to be one of the James boys, or perhaps Jonathan. Orson had shown up at the right time, just as he was about to put his ghost idea into action. Apparently, it'll work, now that Orson already gave it a test run, Vick thought. He couldn't help but grin.

Elizabeth gave Orson a big hug. "I'm glad you finally came to your senses and returned." Orson looked down at the floor because Elizabeth was making over him and kissed him on the cheek. He quickly changed the subject.

"You know that feller I ran into on the cattle gap shore looked familiar, but I can't remember where I seen him."

"Orson, you shouldn't be traveling alone at your age."

"Hot dang! Don't go talkin' 'bout that age thang, 'cause as long as I'm kickin', I'm gonna be doin' what I wanna do. I just came to ask y'all what's goin' on with those two men coming to Jonesboro?"

"What two men?" Elizabeth asked.

Vick interrupted Orson by giving him the old "evil-eye" before he went any further.

Orson was quick to pick up on it and did a good job of recovering.

"You know Vick, 'bout those men tryin' to take away Cain's property he inherited?"

Elizabeth thought the questioning was a little strange, but it was Orson, and one would expect a little peculiarity.

"You never said, but I reckon Jonathan already kicked y'all out."

"That's why we're here. Hope you don't mind. Your bedroom is just like you left it."

"It'll be good ta have a little company, so make yerself at home. Oh, by the way,

I'm glad you brought the cook with ya'."

Elizabeth sensed Orson was more like himself, since he had returned from Jonesboro.

"I hate to ask 'cause I thank I already know the answer, but have y'all heard from Cain?"

Vick shook his head "no." He wanted to tell Orson about the James boys but telling him at this time would be a mistake. *It's best I not tell him just yet*, Vick decided.

"Orson, I have an apple pie in the oven."

"I smelled it the minute I stepped in the house. Y'all ain't eat supper yet have ya'?"

"We been waitin' on you. It's suppertime. We had a feeling you'd be riding up," Lizzie laughed.

"Now I know yer jest pullin' my leg," Orson mused.

"It's good you're home." Elizabeth patted him on his back as he sat at the table.

Chapter 17

ORSON COULD HARDLY SLEEP HIS FIRST NIGHT BACK IN SAN AUGUSTINE. He lay there wondering whether his pain from the loss of Lucy would ever subside. It was good to be back with old friends, but it wasn't home, the place where he had raised Lucy and watched her grow up. He couldn't figure out why he didn't seem like himself at either place.

Orson was an early riser, so, before daylight he decided to make coffee and step outside to stretch and take in the fresh air. It was still dark outside, but he liked that time of the morning to clear his head. As he gazed over the small lake suddenly his thoughts were of Cain. The boy was like a son, he recollected.

Cain is dead, but I'll never forget him lookin' out fer me, Orson thought.

Orson thought about Vick's plan and wondered how long he was expected to play dead. *I ain't gonna git ta go a damn place if I'm dead*, Orson reflected. He was anxious for everything to get back to normal. Patience was not his virtue, and he was never one to sit around and wait. With coffee in hand, he strolled alongside the lake, just like he had done many mornings before, walking and drinking coffee. "Cain my boy, what happened to you after we got dry-gulched?" Orson mumbled under his breath. *It's a puzzle we may never piece together*, he thought. *The boy would have been my son-in-law if Lucy hadn't died. Now they're together, and he can take care of her.*

The lake always had a mist of fog over it, but this morning it had settled right on top of the water. It was inviting, almost beckoning him to come closer to the water's edge. *It's a might purdy place*, Orson thought.

Orson was still thinking of Cain. *The boy shouldn't have died the way he did*, he kept thinking. He was sure Jonathan had something to do with ambushing him and Cain, but he was perplexed as to why he didn't find a body.

As he sauntered along, he listened as a fish jumped, making a splash. *I should be fishing. They'd be jumpin' in my bucket.*

When Orson got near the edge of the lake, a bird flew from the bush, startling him enough to spill his coffee. "Damn bird," he said." Now I gotta go and git me another cup."

Orson was about to head back to the house when he heard a rustling in the brush. He turned sharply, thinking it might be a big snake, but instead he saw something larger moving. *There's something mighty big coming at me*, he thought, as he turned to run. But as he turned, he saw a human arm reach out to him.

"Good Lord! That's somebody down ther" he said. Orson walked slowly toward the water, unable to even imagine whom it could be. The hand grabbed for him again, and this time Orson grabbed it, pulling whoever it was out of the bushes. Part of the body was in the water, but his upper body was on dry ground. *Perhaps the man was trying to crawl out and couldn't quite make it,*" Orson thought.

"Hold on feller, while I help ya'." Orson struggled, but was not able to pull him up onto the bank.

"I can't getcha by myself. Now don'tcha' move, while I go fer help," he ordered.

The man was trying to speak, but couldn't make any sense. Orson was sure it was no one he knew. No matter if he did know him. The man was completely unrecognizable with his face and clothing covered with mud.

Hop was still alive after two days of lying near the water's edge. The cold water helped keep him alive and the mud and sludge had apparently plugged his wounds, stopping the blood flow.

Hop was completely irrational and thought Orson might be going to fetch Jonathan. Fearing for his life, he mustered enough strength to drag himself out of the lake and crawl in the direction of the barn. He thought Orson was one of Jonathan's workers.

Orson woke Vick and the two-hurried back to the lake to help the injured man. When they got there, the body was gone.

"He ain't here. I pulled him out of them weeds right down there. Half of 'em was still in the water and I thought he was a damn snake. I told 'em to stay until I went fer help and now he's gone." Had it been daylight they would have seen the drag marks and sludge of water.

"Orson, are you sure you pulled a man from the lake?"

"Now don't go thanking I'm losin' it. I pulled the man out of them weeds and laid 'em right here." Orson enunciated each word to make sure he made his point "Okay, don't shout…I believe you. But if he was here, now he's gone. What could have happened to him?"

"Hell, I don't know! I guess I scared 'em off, jest like that feller last night I told ya' 'bout when I passed him on the road. "

"Who you saw last night may have recognized you. After all, you're supposed to be dead…remember? Orson, that man you pulled out of the lake could have been Hop."

"Hop? You talkin' 'bout the man me and Cain wer' gonna meet in Memphis?"

About that time Vick heard a noise. "Listen!" Vick whispered as they stopped dead in their tracks. "That sound came from over near the barn."

Vick ran toward the sound and saw the man trying to get away.

He was cowering down with one hand up trying to protect himself.

Vick saw some familiarities in his body style. "Hop, is that you?"

"Vick?" Hop asked, as he lowered his hand to see him. "Settle down, let me help you. It's me, Vick."

"I thought I was a goner," Hop said.

"Who did this to you? Was it Jonathan?" asked Vick.

Hop could barely talk. "Yeah, was Jonathan...Jumped me... stabbed... threw me in..." He slumped in relief to be rescued by friends.

Elizabeth was waiting in the kitchen when the men helped Hop amble into the house.

"My God! Is that Hop?"

"Lizzie, I need you to turn back the bedding and get some hot water and towels, then get the medicine from the cabinet. We've gotta check his wounds."

No one said a word as they administered to Hop. Vick cut away his muddy clothes while Elizabeth was busy heating water. Hop was breathing and conscious during the entire ordeal of cleaning and patching his wounds, feeling embarrassed.

"Let me take a look," said Orson. Vick stepped aside and Orson examined Hop like he knew what he was doing. He noticed there was hardly any blood draining from the wounds.

"I jest don't know if he's gonna make it. We have to wait and see," Orson determined. Vick felt all along that Jonathan had something to do with Hop's disappearance. He was seething as he watched his long-time friend fight to stay alive.

"Lucky for Hop he survived these wounds," observed Orson.

"Orson, what do you think?" asked Vick.

"I ain't no doctor, and don't profess to be. All I can tell ya' is he must have bled a lot, since there ain't much blood coming out after you cleaned 'em up. The water and mud must have 'co-agga-lated' the blood, 'cause I ain't never seen nothin' like it," he regretfully answered.

"Orson, where did you learn about coagulating?" Elizabeth asked.

"I seen Dr. Lewis patch up many a gunshot wound, and Lucy knew a few thangs 'bout doctoring, too."

Hop opened his eyes and looked at Orson.

"Why y'all talking like I'm already dead? I'm still here ain't I?"

Orson flexed his hands. "It must be these healing hands," he said, and looked skyward as Hop grinned.

Vick would have laughed if Hop hadn't been in such bad shape. He was furious with Jonathan and wished he was dead.

Vick marveled at how coherent Hop was.

"Buddy, you have a lot more to do before you kick the bucket."

Hop gave him the thumbs up like he knew he was going to make it. Vick patted him on the shoulder as he prepared to leave the room. "Hop, we're gonna' let you rest a bit, but later this morning we expect you to be better… a lot better," he lied.

They all breathed a sigh of relief and were about to walk away when Hop spoke again but still very weak. "Elizabeth, before you go, can I have a drink of water? I've had enough of that ditch water to last a lifetime."

"You think you can drink?" asked Vick.

"You damn right I can drink. My mouth tastes like a nest of craw-dads been in it."

The next day was spent taking care of Hop and helping him walk around the house. By late evening, he was doing so much better that Vick thought it was time to unveil his plan.

He helped Hop to the table, where he explained how important it was for everyone to continue thinking Orson and Hop were dead. " It's a little crazy, but it might work. As far as Jonathan will know, you're dead, and that includes you Orson."

"You want me in on this dead man walking thang?" asked Orson.

"Yeah, I been holding back telling you about Lonnie and Dudley James being here. Orson flinched when he was told the entire story about the James brothers being in San Augustine. "Whatcha' tryin' to tell me?"

"Orson, now don't jump to conclusions, 'cause I haven't known long that Lonnie and Dudley James followed us to San Augustine."

"Why would they foller' us here?" Orson asked.

"I ain't figured it out yet, but more than ever I know it has some-thing to do with the manor burning down." Vick said.

Hop had plenty to tell them about what he knew. "I think Lonnie and Dudley may have had something to do with the connection of a treasure in Panther Holler, because they spoke of a treasure. Then, there was the ring that might help tie this all together." Elizabeth gasped when she and Vick began making the connection of the treasure and the ring. Hop noticed their reactions but continued, "Before Jonathan jumped me, those brothers asked if I would go with them to Panther Holler to find the treasure."

"Well now, that does shed light on why they burned down the manor," Vick concluded. "There was a time when we had a treasure at the manor but the Governor had a courier pick it up over a year ago. Orson, from what I've learned and what Hop told me, I think those boys had something to do with Lucy's death."

Orson's head was reeling upon learning that the boys had killed his daughter. His knees began to weaken, so he sat in a nearby chair.

"That's right Orson, I heard Dudley claim the ring was his," Hop explained. "Y'all have seen Jonathan's maid haven't you?"

"Yes, we've seen her from a distance."

"Matilda found the ring outside the tack house at the Circle J and Jonathan claimed he had given it to her to keep the James" from having it. The brother's were claiming it as their own. "

"What on earth did the James" have to do with the ring?"

"Matilda stole it," Dudley said.

I didn't know if the ring would mean anything to either one of you but when I saw it sitting in the windowsill I decided to take it and bring it to your house. It was pitch black after I broke in here and then afterwards, Jonathan attacked me.

"I wonder just how many people that man has murdered?" Vick said.

He turned to Orson; "Elizabeth was frightened at finding the ring on her glove. It was apparent someone had placed it there. The only thing that made sense was someone or some thing was sending her a message.

He showed Orson the ring who became infuriated, learning that the two good-for-nothing brothers who took the ring from Lucy's finger and killed her were in San Augustine staying at Jonathan's ranch. He was outraged thinking about Lucy and how they intentionally let her die a horrible death.

He hung his head, clinched his fists and hid his tears. "So to git this straight, you're tellin' me them boys came looking for the treasure, and when they didn't find it in the manor they killed my little girl and burnt the manor down?"

By this time Orson was standing again, beating his fist on the table. He began pacing the room like a caged cat, breathing so hard that Elizabeth felt he might have a heart attack.

"Orson, I'm afraid that's what happened."

"Let me at 'em! They don't deserve no mercy! I want 'em both dead, you hear? Dead!" Orson shouted, as he pounded on the table again, then started for the door.

Vick tried to calm him. "Orson, I know you want to bring them to justice, but your justice is outside the law."

"I ain't no Sheriff no more, ya' hear? So don't give me none of that law business." Orson started out the door and Vick had to manhandle him to keep him from leaving and blowing their cover.

He held his shoulders in a half hug. "Now Orson, you have to listen. This ain't the way. A lot's riding on what you're about to do. Think of Cain and how this could hurt him. There could be consequences if you go out to Jonathan's ranch and start an all-out war and those boys will get away with Lucy's murder!" Vick insisted.

Hop could see Vick struggling to get through to Orson, and poor Elizabeth was near tears watching Orson go through a meltdown. She had never seen anyone so angry.

"I got a right to go after 'em," he said.

Elizabeth had seen Orson cry only one other time. It tore her to pieces seeing tears streaming down his face.

"My little girl. They had no right! They had no right!" he cried out.

Elizabeth walked over and wrapped her arms around Orson as he wept. "Lizzie, they killed my little girl. She never did no harm to nobody and they murdered her in cold blood. What am I suppose to do, stay here and let 'em live, with me knowing what they did?"

Elizabeth saw how heartbroken he was. "Orson, I understand. Don't forget, they murdered Cain and almost killed you, but Vick's right. We have to be strong a little while longer. They'll get their due. You know how we felt about Lucy and the heartbreak of losing her."

Vick kept explaining the harm it would do if Orson took the law into his own hands.

"Orson, we're not going to let 'em get away with what they did. You can rest assured of that. And that goes for what they did to you and Cain. They're all going to get what's coming to them, but we have to do this right, like we did with Buck Dupree. My plan is to lure 'em back to Panther Holler, and when we get 'em there, we'll take care of 'em."

Orson calmed down and finally asked, "How do you plan to do that?"

"Them knowing about the treasure and how bad they want it."

"When we gonna do this?" asked Orson.

"I want to give Cain a little more time, just in case he's out there some place and trying to make it back home. We have to be here in case someone recognizes Cain from the pictures on the posters.

If he returns, I want him to know we never gave up on 'em."

"I know yer right, but I don't want to pussyfoot around before we do something and I'll be damned if them James brothers will get away with murdering my Lucy," Orson declared.

"There's plenty we can do. Just try and have a little patience."

Hop felt the need to reinforce what he knew about Jonathan.

"Vick, before you go messing with Jonathan, I want you to be careful, 'cause that man's insane. He ain't operating with a full deck. When he stabbed me, I hardly recognized his voice—he sounded crazy."

That night, when everyone had gone to bed, Vick fell into a deep sleep. At first he thought he was awake and working in the cotton fields, loading the wagon used to haul cotton to the gin. After the load was secured, a rope was hanging loose and Vick tripped over it, falling backwards. When he hit the ground his head began spinning. In the midst of the circles in this apparition appeared a beautiful hawk. The same hawk he remembered from Panther Holler. It has to be my Indian friend who has promised to always protect me, he assumed.

Vick felt he was conscious as he began to talk. In his heart he knew it was Hawk.

"Hawk, I don't understand."

"*Harken and listen closely to what I tell you. Many years ago this land belonged to our fathers. My people walked this land with the buffalo and the antelope and when we went up river we found the white man chopping our wood and killing our buffalo. Many of our people went hungry and died because of the white man. My ancestors died that winter eating roots and mushrooms that had been frozen. The next year we went up river again and this time a group of white people joined with us and killed our enemies that were trying to rob us of our food. It was your ancestors that helped our people...When you saved me and faced your fear fighting the panther, my people chose you to give back what the white man took from us.*"

"What am I to do?"

"Vick, you will know when the time is right."

Vick saw the apparition dissolving and Hawk turned to fly away. "No, wait! Please don't go! I need to ask you about Cain. Hawk! Hawk!" Vick shouted. He had no idea that he was talking in his sleep and had awakened Elizabeth.

"Vick, wake up. You're dreaming." Elizabeth knew he was troubled. She assured him he was home and safe.

"Vick laid there thinking of what Hawk had told him."

Elizabeth could see that Vick was upset about his dream.

"Perhaps it's because of all the years you were in prison that's causing you to have these reoccurrences." Once fully awake, Vick doubted what he had seen and heard. "There's no way I can commune with the dead," he thought. Hawk died when he was a boy many years ago. Vick thought about the promise Hawk had made to him when he saved Hawk's life. "I will always be your protector," he said to Vick.

When morning came, and the effects of the dream began to wear off, Vick explained to Orson and Hop that his first plan of action was to torment Jonathan. They had been observing him walking around the lake each morning possibly making sure Hop's body didn't surface.

The following morning, they were ready for Jonathan as he walked out to the edge of the lake. They observed him peering in and around areas of the lake he seemed most concerned about.

Hop stood directly across the lake under a large oak tree, in the same muddy wet clothing he had on when Orson pulled him out of the lake. Elizabeth had done a superb job at costuming Hop and making him look "dead."

With outstretched arms, Hop beckoned Jonathan to come to him. Once certain that Jonathan had sight of him, he slowly turned and walked away. They watched carefully as Jonathan took the bait.

Hop was amused with the outcome, but he knew it was serious business tricking a man who attempted to savagely murder him. He watched Jonathan strain to see if what he saw was real, or if it was a fabrication of his mind.

Finally, after Jonathan was shocked back into reality, he hurried away, stumbling on the rough terrain. Frightened that he had seen Hop, Jonathan was sure that Hop had come back from the dead to haunt him.

Vick was pleased with the success of the first phase of his plan. Now it was time to go after Lonnie and Dudley with some mind tricks. Vick knew that each Friday evening, one of the brothers would ride alone to pick up their pay from Jonathan.

The plan was for Orson to ride by around dusk, stop briefly, stare, and then say, "howdy."

They hoped that he would again yell, "Holy God Almighty," and ride off frightened that he had seen Orson's ghost.

Paydays came and went, giving Orson the opportunity to pull off his ruse on both brothers. And it went off perfectly every time.

Oftentimes, Jonathan would ride to the Circle J for an "overnight" just to get away from the usual surroundings happening at the plantation. He would never let on to Lonnie or Dudley that he was seeing things, nor would the brothers complain about what they saw to each other, for fear the other would think they were going crazy. They independently of each other sure weren't going to tell Jonathan about those sightings. Consequently, each man began living his own private nightmare, being instigated, of course, by Vick, Orson, and Hop.

When Jonathan returned to the plantation after several days of being away, he would find a pair of Hop's muddy boots on the back porch. Sometimes even a shirt or pair of pants was left in a puddle of water outside his door. Jonathan, who felt the pressure of his sick mind, took all these games very seriously.

The plantation became a frightening place to live, as the men made Jonathan's existence pure hell. They threw pebbles at the windows, and other times rattled the pipes that led up to the house. Sometimes they would have all the piped water running outside. Unexplained things happened, and Jonathan began thinking the place was haunted. Was the ghost that of his father, Aggie's mother, Phillip Bradbury, Hop?... Or, had they all joined together to haunt him?

The constant harassment was definitely beginning to take its toll on him, and the James brothers experienced first handedly its effects, as it became more and more difficult to deal with Jonathan.

Chapter 18

A BAND OF RIDERS AND THEIR LEADER WAITED ON A KNOLL ABOVE THE town of Trumann, Arkansas, while one of their women scurried into the hospital to beg for medicine. Lucy, who was helping out, immediately recognized the vile odor of the Clan that had been her captors. She feared them, for they had captured and tortured her after she escaped the manor fire. Seeing Mila again, one of the Clan women sent a chill through her as she remembered her harrowing experience, and the brutal treatment of these villainous people. No one should ever have to endure what I went through, while they had me captive, she disgustingly reflected.

Birdie was confused by Lucy's reaction, since all she did was whimper. She watched as Lucy hurriedly left the office to escape the woman's stares. Birdie thought there was something strange going on with Lucy, who ran down the corridor to get away. Jason intercepted her and was alarmed by the fear on her face. She wanted to speak but was unable to. *If only I could warn Jason that these people are the ones who held me captive and now will pursue me, since they know I am here.* Try as she might, her severely bruised vocal cords were not healed, and all she could do was make humming sounds. Her heart was racing, knowing the Clan would stop at nothing to recapture her. She remembered Munk, the head of the Clan, and how cruel he was to her. *He'll never give up until he kills me, and now he knows where I am!* She remembered how he announced that he was taking her as his woman, and she would stay with him until she died.

Jason determined that Lucy's flight had something to do with the woman who was begging for medicine. He hurried to the office to address the problem, while Birdie endured the woman and her foul odor. Birdie listened carefully as she tried to understand what the woman was saying. When Jason saw the hunched over species, he began quizzing her about who she was and why she was there. He had seen and heard of mountain people before, but this woman was more of a creature than human, and she had the smell of death.

"Who are you, and what do you want?" he asked.

"Somepin' for sick. Me people sick." Then she pointed in the direction of where Lucy had gone. "Woman, Munk's woman," she said as she continued to mumble incessantly.

"Birdie, you give this woman medicine and get her out of here, and fast!" Mila stared at him with dark hollow eyes. Birdie quickly bagged up the medicine and opened the door for her to leave. And good riddance to an odor that reminded her of a very large chicken house she once visited. The smell was horrendous.

They watched as she limped toward the door, looking back at them as she fled.

Birdie was not sure she understood the woman correctly.

"Jason, was she saying Lucy was Munk's woman?"

"The woman is crazy...couldn't you tell? She made no sense."

Birdie thought Jason was in a state of denial where Lucy was concerned. She had never seen her brother so enraptured with a woman, and that stood to jeopardize her and Jason's future plans together as a medical team. She tried to hold her tongue, but what just happened brought on a reaction. "Jason, you should have listened to me. I told you Lucy was well enough to leave, and now look who she's bringing into our hospital."

"Birdie, you don't honestly think Lucy had anything to do with these people coming here. I have a feeling they're responsible for her injuries."

"You know nothing about Lucy, and we should have released her weeks ago, but you've insisted on her staying here. Why?" Birdie quizzed. "Can you answer me that?"

He disliked arguing with her and wanted to shut her up before Lucy heard them. "I don't know what you're talking about," he whispered. "Keep your voice down! I'll be the one to decide when a patient is ready to be discharged. Now, I don't want to hear another word about Lucy… do you understand?"

Birdie was surprised at how defensive he had become regarding Lucy.

"Brother, why don't you tell me what's really going on. I can sense you have feelings for this woman. Please tell me it's my imagination."

Jason hesitated before answering her, but he knew she had a right to know.

"Birdie, I know you are not going to like this, but I intend to ask Lucy to marry me when she's well enough to have me."

"Marriage?" Birdie picked up her papers and walked out of the hospital toward her house in disgust.

In the distance, the Clan was watching her leave the hospital.

By the time Jason found Lucy, she had removed all the bandages from her hands and was writing a scratchy note explaining what happened to her after she survived the fire inside the manor. Her hands and fingers were still very raw and stiff, but he could see they were now healing nicely. Lucy explained everything to Jason, and how they caged her like and animal. It was painful reading how they tied a noose around her neck and feet. "The days were long without hardly any food, and then the worst would happen when Munk would take me into his tent for the night," she wrote. "He was like a savage. No one can imagine what I went through," she continued.

As she struggled to inform him, he could read between the lines. She confirmed with nods that her burn injuries came from the fire in the manor after Lonnie and Dudley James knocked her unconscious, leaving her to burn with the manor. She wrote that after the manor went up in flames, she revived herself, and ran through the flames until she found refuge in a closet underneath the stairwell. It was there where she moved a bookcase and discovered a small escape hatch in the floor. She imagined Elizabeth's father had installed it for an easy escape. She was able to drop herself into the chute, then scoot herself to safety.

By the time she freed herself, she was consumed with pain from the burns on various parts of her body. She lay exhausted near the woods in a semi-conscious state. Drawn to the manor by the site of fire and smoke billowing high in the sky, a Clan of wild and savage misfits, known as the Jackson Whites, picked her up and carried her to their camp.

After hogtying her with rope, the tightness cut into her neck, injuring her vocal cords. Lucy continued to write and explain that Munk was part of a passel of thieves who had escaped prison and found refuge among the Clan, a race of people who led an isolated existence removed from civilization. There he felt safe, and used them as a shield to escape the law. He masterminded their crimes and cleverly manipulated them, teaching and coercing them to do his dirty work. He stayed mainly in the background and only revealed himself when it was absolutely necessary. The Clan was made up mostly of illiterates who were inbred to the point of mutation; therefore, they had their own crude way of communicating. Lucy had been captured only a few days when Munk took her as his woman. Adopting the ways of the Jackson Whites, he simply had to declare her as his property, and it was so.

The late nights, when he took her to his tent, were the only freedom she got from the ropes. However, she preferred the ropes rather than face the atrocities committed on her body that she was sure ruined her chances of ever having children. She would have killed herself before having any of his children. Before escaping, she learned that Munk had murdered a number of people who tried to escape. Lucy no longer feared death, but looked upon it as an escape from the hell she was living. The executions were informally ceremonial, and a time of celebration.

Mila finally loosened Lucy's ropes after they considered her too frightened to run. One night, after the Clan had gotten drunk on their homemade brew, she freed herself and ran away as fast and far as she could until she passed out along the road where Birdie found her.

After Lucy told Jason the story of her capture, it only made him love her more. Her wounds were mostly healed except for the ones she carried in her heart. Afterwards, he took her by the arm and pulled her from her chair. This was the first time she had ventured to tell what had happened and the first time she felt safe, as he drew her close to him., "Could it be that Jason will want me, a defective woman?" she wondered. Caught in his spell, she looked into his eyes with a tenderness that melted his heart but her heart was with Cain whom she had loved.

It was only natural that he tilted her head back to kiss her. She couldn't believe that Jason had feelings for her, especially after hearing she was so tainted, scarred and mute, but this was not a dream. It was really happening. The embrace seemed like forever as he poured his heart out to her. "Lucy, you are the woman I have been waiting for. There can be no one for me but you. You've captured my heart." Lucy could sense his sincerity as he knelt on one knee. *"Is he about to do what I think he's doing?"* she presumed.

"Lucy, I know this must come as a shock, but will you do me the honor of marrying me?" She saw the love and kindness in his eyes as she stared at him in disbelief. Then she smiled and shook her head "yes." She wanted to say there was so much he did not know about her, and even ask if he was sure. But all she could do was embrace him and smile with approval.

Those scars don't matter," Jason whispered in her ear.

She tried to talk but just a squeak came out. He cupped her face in his hands, looked into her eyes. "Lucy, I know I love you, and that's all I care about. I want you to be my wife." It didn't matter to Jason that he had only known her for a very short time and wanted to cure her hurt as well as her injuries. It didn't even matter that her heart was with another man. He had enough for the both of them.

She smiled with tears running down her cheeks as Jason cupped her elbows in his hands helping her stand and then kissed her. The kiss felt right. She knew she was marrying someone who would love and protect her. *"What more could a girl want, but a good man like Jason,"* she happily accepted.

Birdie was not happy when she learned of Jason's intention of marrying Lucy. Her relationship with her brother was so strong yet neurotic, that she was jealous of any woman who might vie for his attention. She was smart, though, and knowing her brother as she did, she knew it would be in her best interest to give the couple a chance. It took a while before she realized she could never stand between their love; that is, if she intended to continue her profession as her brother's medical assistant. Although she was heartbroken, she knew she must embrace the couple and support them if and when they married. Besides, Lucy was so grateful to Birdie for saving her, she helped all she could at the hospital and was devoted to Birdie as well as to Jason.

Lucy had changed since her ordeal with the Clan. She was no longer the self-assured girl who could conquer the world and do tasks, which were once considered a welcomed challenge. She felt vulnerable and needed Jason's guidance and protection, especially now, since she knew her father and Cain were both dead and unable to protect her. *There's no need for me to wait for a happy reunion when the man I originally loved is dead. My world has been destroyed, but with Jason I have a chance to regain a portion of my dignity. I have no one else except Jason and Birdie*, she rationalized.

Jonesboro, the town she was raised in, was now a town she wanted to forget.

As the days passed, Birdie tried to change her attitude about Lucy and Jason marrying. *I need to give them a chance*, she kept telling herself.

She had time to see how happy Lucy made her brother. *He's happier than he's ever been,* and that's all she ever really wanted for him. It helped that he continued to depend on Birdie for so much at the hospital and showed her just as much attention as before. Her final decision was to make it work.

The day of the wedding, Lucy was beside herself, wondering if she was doing the right thing. The wedding was simple, but beautiful, with Lucy wearing the wedding dress of Jason's and Birdie's mother. Walking toward him in her long lace dress, she was prettier than any picture he had ever seen. She was absolutely stunning, even with the veil that covered her beautiful blue eyes. *All I want is to love, protect and make her happy,* he reasoned. He knew she did not fully respond to his love the way he wanted, but in time he felt she would come around.

The small, private ceremony took place in a beautiful rose garden, only a short distance from the hospital. Birdie had gone to extra trouble to make their wedding day one that they would remember and Jason and Lucy showed their appreciation. She had invited a few important townspeople who brought gifts, and then she adorned her lace-clothed dining room table with roses and a three-layer cake, everything a couple would want for a very special wedding day. Lucy kissed Birdie's cheek when she saw what she had done for them, knowing she had sensed Birdie's reluctance to give her blessings.

After they were married, unbeknownst to them, a band of riders were on a hillside looking down on the happy couple. After the wedding was over, Munk reined his horse and he and the Clan rode away deep into the forest.

～

In the meantime, a very much alive Ben was trying to find out who he was, but he was worried that such information might not all be good. *Going to the Sheriff could end up being a mistake should I discover I am a fugitive on the run.* Finding out his past could possibly cost him his life without him even knowing the circumstances of what happened to him, or who he was. All the loot he had on him came from somewhere, and no ordinary cowboy would be carrying that kind of wealth on him, unless he robbed a bank. And in that case, the law would be after him. It just so happened that Cain was planning to replenish his livestock.

Ben imagined all kinds of scenarios that frightened him. He sought to find anything familiar that might give him a jolt of reality to help him remember.

Although he did not feel like a criminal, he thought it wise to keep a low profile, and stay away from small towns where someone might possibly know who he is. Occasionally, he would think of Aggie and wonder why she left. I had genuine feelings for her, he recalled.

~

About three months passed, and Aggie was still not showing any signs of expecting a baby. She continued to work around her house just like her hired hands, wearing baggy clothes and large aprons to look like she was just gaining some weight, she concealed any hints of being in the family way. It was only in her mind that she was showing.

One day her milk cow broke through the fence and was standing in the middle of the road. This was a stubborn cow and Aggie knew she had her hands full trying to get the cow back into the barn.

She began waving her apron trying to shoo the cow in the direction of the barn, but the stubborn thing would not move. She finally managed to loop a rope around its neck and pulled hard, but the stubborn beast just stood there. After her efforts failed, she decided to push from the rear. She was pushing away when Seth Jackson rode up. Concerned at seeing a woman exert herself like that, he offered to help.

"Ms. Dawson, I think you need my help." Her pregnancy made her very uneasy, so Aggie was hoping he would go away and mind his own business.

"Mr. Jackson, you are preventing me from doing my work. What I do is of no concern of yours".

Seth noticed how spirited and determined she was, all the characteristics he admired in a woman.

He slid out of his saddle, placed the reins over a fence post, and then took the rope from Aggie. She watched as he pulled on the rope with the cow following without giving any resistance whatsoever. *That stupid cow*, she thought.

"Ms. Dawson, where do you want me to take her?"

"Just take her to the barn," she said in disgust.

Seth walked the cow to the barn and returned to find Aggie leaning against the fence, weak from the ordeal. She tried to keep from displaying her sickness, but pulling on the cow left her lightheaded. Concerned about her condition, he helped her make it to the porch, said goodbye, and then went on his way.

Two days later, Seth called on her again to see how she was. This time, she invited him in, hoping to pick his brain regarding his father, Parley, who had been trying to buy the ranch she snapped up before he could. She thought he seemed genuinely concerned, and this impressed her.

Seth had a way about him that broke the ice with Aggie. Seeing that he was not at all like his father; Aggie became a gracious hostess spoiling him with tea and her baking she had made that morning. Before Seth left, they were so relaxed in each other's company that she surprised herself by sharing information—nothing about her pregnancy, but troubles she had when she left San Augustine. There was something very trusting about Seth, unlike his father, whom she detested for the way he had treated her. In turn, he shared that he and Parley had never had a real father-son relationship. She could see that since she was witness to how Parley talked down to him when they first met. Aggie and Seth were drawn to each other. She came to know that he would be one she could count on if ever she needed him. Marriage though, was the farthest thing from her mind.

Trying to hide his romantic feelings for Aggie, Seth talked about everything other than his feelings when he visited with her. Their friendship was moving very fast and finally he asked her to join him one evening for a play that had come to Woodville.

Before Aggie knew it, she was saying yes, hoping she would be able to squeeze in one of the dresses she had purchased from Ms. Jones in Henderson. That evening, she was on pins and needles as she lifted the beautiful dress over her head to button it. She breathed a sigh of relief, for it was a tight squeeze. *My shawl will cover up the areas that are tight*, she hoped.

When Seth came calling, he was mesmerized at how stunning she looked, the most beautiful woman he had ever seen.

"You look beautiful," he said. She immediately thought of Ben and how shy he was when he first saw her in her dress. *Seth is a man with experience and knows how to treat a proper lady*, she compared.

The night was beautiful as he led her to his buggy. "Aggie, I hope you don't mind the buggy. It's such a clear night and I thought you might enjoy taking a ride." There on the floor of the buggy was a beautiful basket that he gave to her. She quickly opened the top and saw it was filled with different kinds of edible delicacies that intrigued her. "Seth, you shouldn't have. You're spoiling me."

"You're worth it," he said. Later she learned that he had the owner of the local boarding house make them for him.

Aggie had never had anyone make over her like Seth, and this was all so romantic. As they rode back to her house she did not want the evening to end, and neither did Seth, but he knew he had to play his cards right if he wanted her to like him.

After Aggie went to bed, she felt like a woman in love. He was a man who could change her life, and he just happened to be her arch-enemy's son.

There was something electrifying about Seth, and try as she might, Aggie could not put her finger on why this man fascinated her so.

He was certainly handsome enough, but there was something else; the way he looked into her eyes and the magical tone of his voice. It was articulate and raspy, characteristics she had not seen before in anyone she knew.

The next time Seth came calling, he was a little more aggressive, even though it was only a kiss. At this point she realized for sure that there was something between them that could not be impeded.

After several more visits, he told her he was falling in love with her, but out of respect, he promised not to pressure her. This greatly impressed her to know they could enjoy their new romance without his advances. At that time she had not planned to marry him, because obviously there was the unborn child she was carrying that threw a monkey wrench into any plans she might have in taking their relationship to another level.

Before the day was over, Seth asked her to marry him.

She thought, *Can I pull this off without him ever knowing this is another man's child?* The question plagued her mind. She could not believe Seth, whom she adored, was asking for her hand in marriage so soon. She did not want him to think her acceptance of his proposal was for any other reason than she loved him, and for that reason she did not want to tell him about the baby.

Aggie loved him, but she also needed a father for her baby. If only he wasn't Parley Jackson's son... she worried. Her concern was how she would fit into the Jackson family, with the war she had going on with his father.

When Seth told her he had not told his father about their involvement, this gave her reason to question whether she was doing the right thing. She knew Parley would not want a bastard child in the family.

She was caught in a terrible dilemma. She was afraid being truthful about the baby would ruin things between them, and she would lose Seth. Finally, after considerable anguish, she convinced herself that she should do what was best for the baby, and that was to pretend the baby was born prematurely.

Aggie hated to begin their marriage with a lie, but the only thing she could think about was the baby and her good name.

It was on a warm summer day when Aggie and Seth exchanged their vows. They were married before a small group of church ladies, and of course, Parley Jackson. As much as Parley hated his son marrying Aggie, he decided that this might be for the best, since he was certain black gold lay beneath the soil in her back pasture. He'd be closer to the oil, and now all he had to do was figure out a way to get the property signed over in his name.

Seth couldn't help but notice Aggie's protruding stomach right away after they consummated their marriage, and naturally wondered if Aggie had been with another man and was pregnant before he married her. He didn't want to question her for fear she might be gaining weight instead of being pregnant, which would be insulting.

But within a few more weeks, it became evident that she was going to have a baby, when the morning sickness that she continued to have became noticeable. He knew his suspicions were correct. Eventually, he asked her if she was pregnant, and she began to cry.

She admitted to him what happened and he was deeply concerned. He logically assumed Aggie only married him because she needed a father for her unborn child.

They spent over a week talking about dissolving their marriage, but when it came down to doing it, Seth loved her too much to let her go. His love was enough for both of them, even if she did marry him just to have a father for her baby.

She saw Seth's hurt, and regretted she had not been truthful with him, but his tenderness and love made her happier than she had ever been, and this only made her love him more. She was also determined to make sure he realized she married him because she loved him so much. Now, her focus was on the community and what they might think if they found out she had to get married.

On one occasion, not too long after the wedding, Parley saw Aggie struggling with a sack of flour as she tried to lift it onto her buggy. He was shocked to see that she had gained so much weight, and all in her abdominal area. So this was the reason for the hasty wedding, he murmured to himself, disgustedly.

He walked over to her buggy and offered help.

She was embarrassed when his eyes focused directly on her stomach.

"Looks like you could have used my help getting that sack of flour in your buggy. I ain't seen you since your wedding. Now, how long has it been?" Parley asked tauntingly.

"Thank you Parley, I didn't need you then, and I don't need you now."

"Looks like you might be needing a doctor to deliver that baby, though, maybe even before nine months is up. There ain't been enough time for you to blame this one on my son."

Aggie was caught completely off guard with the outspoken Parley, as he pointed to her stomach.

"Excuse me Parley, but I don't have time for your accusations. I have to be on my way home."

She left him with his mouth agape as she whipped her horse all the way to her ranch. By the time she arrived, tears were streaming down her face. *Soon the entire town will know this baby is not Seth's and think I bedded him to trap him into marriage; thanks to Parley Jackson, who will spin the rumor to hurt me.*

Seeing Aggie so upset, Seth wanted to kill his Pa after he heard what happened and how distraught his wife was. He was fit to be tied, and rode his horse over to make sure Parley knew he wasn't going to stand for the mistreatment of his wife.

When he walked in, his Pa was waiting for him.

"Congratulations son, looks like you're going to be a daddy. How about a drink? Do you know who the bastard baby's father is?"

"That's why I'm here to talk to you. I'm the father."

"Don't be ridiculous. I can count. And if I remember correctly, you and Ms. "Patty Perfect" ain't been married that long. You want to tell me how that's happened? Now I know why she didn't object to waiting awhile to get married. I wondered what the hurry was, and now I know."

"Okay, you've said your piece, so now you listen to me. Whether you believe this or not, I'm happier than I've ever been, and I want you to be respectful and give Aggie a break. Since you think you know it all, I'm asking you to keep quiet and let us be. You think you can do that?

"It might come with a price."

"And what would that be?"

"You and Aggie take over the ranch here, and sign over her place and deed to me. If she'll do that, I'll let you two love birds live happily ever after. Take it or leave it."

"Why you sorry sonavobitch. I should have known you would try to pull something like that."

"Well, I think it's a fair price for exchange of your kid not being labeled a bastard, don't you think?"

Seth went for Parley's throat and had him pinned to the wall before he regained his senses, knowing he would be making matters worse. "I could kill you, but I realize something." He released his father's throat and stabbed a finger into his chest, menacingly. "I'm a better man than you'll ever be. You are not my father," he declared with emphasis.

Parley pulled himself together and then watched Seth walk out. He had never seen his son so angry. Although Parley wanted to smear Aggie, he thought she might eventually pay him for his silence, so he kept what he knew to himself.

Aggie suffered through the next few months, knowing Parley was out to ruin her, but there was nothing she could do about it. After many tearful nights, she decided to let things fall where they may. Seth kept telling her all that mattered was her and the baby. So after a time, she refocused her energy on her husband and the life they would have together.

As the months passed, and Aggie got closer to term, her love continued to grow for Seth. He made her heart pound furiously as she looked at him, thankful she had found her true love.

When the baby boy came, Seth was right by her side and helped her through the delivery. He took the baby from the midwife and held him in his arms, bathing him just like any father who was anticipating the birth of his first child. Fortunately, their baby boy was about 6.5 pounds, making it easier to pass him off as a premature.

~

Martha and Glen Cormack were wonderful people and accepted Ben like a son, but there were concerns on Glen's part as to who Ben really was. *A young man who can use a gun like that is bound to be a professional,* he summized He was worried that Ben could bring danger into their home, making it doubly hard on Martha, if she found out he was running from the law.

Glen had been putting feelers out each time he went to Beaumont, but no one had come up with any answers, not a clue as to what Ben Gentry's story was.

My next trip, I'm going to try harder to find out if anyone knows of a man meeting Ben's description, since he didn't know what his real name was, he planned.

It had been nearly a year since Glen had been on his last buying trip, and there was need for more cattle.

"I have to go. Martha. The stock needs replenishing and I'll talk to Ben about staying up at the house while I'm gone. By the way, I'm taking the Model T to Houston when I go."

She agreed with him, and thought this would give her the opportunity to have Ben move into the house permanently.

Glen walked out to the tack house to discuss his trip with Ben, which he explained about the need for another 50 head of cattle.

"Ben, do you mind moving into the house and keep an eye on Martha while I'm gone? I've already talked to her and we want you to have the bedroom with its own private entrance. You'll be doing us a favor living up at the house 'cause we ain't gettin' no younger."

"Why, certainly, Glen. I'll be happy to keep an eye on Martha. Are you talking about me moving in permanently?"

"Yeah son, for as long as you feel comfortable."

Ben didn't know what to say about such generosity, and if he could repay their kindness by accommodating them, he was pleased to do so.

"Thanks Glen, you and Martha sure have made me feel like part of the family."

On the first day of Glen's trip he stayed at Ms. Josey's boarding house in Beaumont. This was the first chance they had to talk since Ben had come to work for them, and he wanted to thank her for thinking of them. They talked about Ben's amnesia, which was a surprise to her, since she had not known he had been injured.

"Glen, why don't you go to the Sheriff's Office. They may know something about Ben."

"Josey, I know he ain't no criminal."

"I do too. I'm sure the Sheriff hears about missing people. I knew he was good the first time I laid eyes on 'em, but he's somebody's boy, and maybe somebody's husband who might be a'lookin fer 'em," Josey offered.

When Glen left Josey's, he decided to do as she suggested, since he knew she would go behind him and do the same. He felt guilty deceiving Ben by poking into his business, but he had to know who he was, Glen rationalized.

The Sheriff brought out a bunch of papers and laid them before Glen.

"I got these posters, but I don't remember nobody by that name," the Sheriff said.

"Do you mind if I thumb through and see for myself?"

"You go right ahead and take yer time." Glen began reading poster after poster. Finally, he came across a picture and description that sounded like Ben. The name was Cain Porter. The more he read, the more he thought this young man might be him. He thought the image of the young man on the poster looked like Cain who matched the description being the same age, height, hair color with bullet wounds. He was possibly murdered or injured, and his family was Vick and Elizabeth Porter from San Augustine, Texas, who were eagerly waiting to hear from him. The Sheriff had several copies of each poster, and he was obliged to let Glen take one of the Cain Porter posters. There were a couple other missing person posters, but the one with with the image of Ben was the one that interested him.

After Glen left Beaumont, his entire trip was consumed with Cain and the dilemma he now faced.

Perhaps this man, Cain Porter, is not Ben, and me stirring up things will cause Martha to go off the deep end. By the time Glen returned home, he had convinced himself to never tell Ben he had suspicions of who he was. *It's not worth me losing Martha,* he finally decided.

Chapter 19

SAN AUGUSTINE WAS A BEAUTIFUL LITTLE TOWN, BUT ELIZABETH'S **heart yearned to be back in Arkansas.** Her uneasiness was growing, and she was slowly giving up hope that Cain would ever be found alive.

Since Jonathan pushed them out of the plantation home, the small frame house that Cain bought for Orson was getting smaller and smaller. Vick and two other men under the same roof was becoming too much for her.

It was necessary though, in order for Orson and Hop to carry out the hoax of frightening Jonathan. While these two dear friends had to stay hidden, they were under-foot for Elizabeth every day, all day.

Elizabeth had never been one to nag, but the plan to set up Jonathan and the James brothers was taking too long. She had become impatient after nearly two years of Cain missing. "Vick, how much longer will this take?" she asked. "It doesn't appear your plan is working." Vick hated to admit it but he felt the same.

At first they were excited at watching Hop pose as a dead person but after frightening Jonathan and the chance of Hop being shot; they figured that in time, Jonathan, along with the James brothers, would figure things out, but they showed no sign of doing so.

"Vick, we have to make a move or do something different. Might be a good time to lead them boys to Panther Holler," Orson suggested.

Elizabeth and Vick discussed other alternatives but only one thing made sense to them and that was leaving San Augustine.

"I'm ready to move back to Arkansas," Elizabeth said.

"Lizzie, you're not ready to give up on Cain, are you?"

"No, but it's going to take time to overturn the court's decision to get Jonathan off this property when and if our son does come back. At that time, we'll return and help Cain win back Pecan Plantation."

She could tell Vick, too, was still in denial about Cain being dead.

At this point, they still had no clue that there was another heir to Pecan Plantation—now by the name of Aggie Dawson Jackson. Although Orson knew of Aggie, he had promised Cain he would not tell Elizabeth and Vick, but keeping the secret turned out to be too much for Orson.

The next morning, when Elizabeth was serving coffee, Orson proposed another plan, since he was getting antsy.

"Whatcha' got in mind?" Vick asked.

"There's somethin' I ain't told y'all bout a girl that Jonathan raped."

"Were did you hear that?" Vick questioned in shock.

"Cain told me but swore me to secrecy. I know, I shoulda told y'all but I was afraid of what Jonathan would do if he found out where that Aggie girl lived."

"Maybe we need to find Aggie and have her come back and testify against Jonathan and send the bastard to jail," Vick suggested.

"It ain't no need to confront him without the letter and it could be dangerous to have Jonathan know we have proof who Aggie is," Orson stated.

Even though much time had passed, they still didn't know for sure that Aggie was Jonathan's half-sister, and without Cain and Johnson's letter, this would continue to be a well-kept family secret.

"Vick, I know ya' know how big Texas is, and fer yer information, that Aggie woman is a waste of time, when we don't know where she could be," Orson explained.

"Maybe you're right, but if we left, I'd be leaving Lizzie by herself, with a madman next door."

"Yep, we'd probably be goin' on a wild goose chase tryin' ta find that girl, anyway."

Hop was listening to Orson and Vick, and he agreed they had to do something else or be found out.

That evening, Orson remembered the two men in Jonesboro that showed up at his cabin to borrow coffee. Why *would Vick offer them the carriage house as a place to stay?* Orson thought. Once again, he asked Vick why the men were staying in the carriage house back in Jonesboro.

"I ain't ready to talk about it yet—maybe soon," said Vick.

"Ain't nobody can say ya' can't keep a secret, that's fer shore!" Orson responded.

Vick thought it best to change the subject.

"What about you and that little retired school teacher, Irene?"

"Now ain't that a damn crazy thang yer askin'? Did ya' ever hear of a dead man calling on a woman? I'm supposed to be dead, remember? I jest wonder if she grieved any fer me?"

Vick laughed. "Orson, did I ever tell you that you're good for me?"

"In what way?"

"Well, it's that craziness in you."

"You mean that same kinda crazy that's saved yer ass more times than I can count on my fangers?"

"I guess you're right about that!"

"Yer damn right I'm right, so don't ya' fergit it. It wouldn't hurt ya' ta show some respect—now, why ya' got those men livin' in that carriage house of yers back in Jonesboro?"

Vick smiled and patted Orson on the back. "I'm ready to call it a night, how 'bout you?"

"Damn you, Vick Porter. When you git ready ta tell me why them men are livin' in the carriage house, I ain't gonna listen. Ferget I ever asked!"

⌣

Lucy had become a big help to Birdie and Jason, running errands and freeing them to work in the hospital. This gave Lucy a chance to regain her independence and feel she was becoming her own woman. She realized she was changing little by little, and she credited Jason for that.

It was a cold, brisk day when Lucy left the hospital to run errands. After parking in front of the local mercantile, she grabbed her shawl and walked into the store to purchase supplies—when a strong odor hit her. It was the Clan. They were there.

She wanted to run, but instead, hid behind one of the shelves that divided the aisles. She edged her way around the end of the aisle, only to come face to face with Mila, who stood staring at her. Frightened and surprised, Lucy tried to scream, but nothing came out. Lucy ran out of the store to get into her car but the Clan were on horseback waiting outside to grab her and return her to Munk. *Evidently, they have been following me.* The driver's side was blocked, so she jumped in through the passenger side and was struggling to get into the driver's seat just as one man managed to grab onto her clothing. After frantically fumbling with the key, she was able to start the car. It jerked into gear and she sped off with two of the men hanging onto the side of the car. One was holding a sleeve that he had torn away from Lucy's blouse. When she picked up enough speed, she jerked the steering wheel back and forth, causing the men to fall off. She looked back to make sure they were not following her. Once out of town she was relieved, but still terrified from the experience when she arrived at the hospital. She ran into the hospital calling for Birdie: "Bir-die...Clan..."This was a tremendous breakthrough, since she had not been able to speak in a year since Birdie had found her. For the first time, Lucy began to form words.

"Lucy, you can talk," Birdie said. "Jason, come quick?" He was with a patient, but he recognized the excitement in Birdie's voice. As soon as Lucy saw him, she ran into his arms.

"Lucy spoke to me," Birdie said.

"I know, I heard her call my name." Lucy nodded her head "yes," as tears rolled down her cheeks.

Lucy clearly said the word, "yes," then slowly mouthed out what had happened. She was difficult to understand, but they were able to piece together that Munk was after her.

"Lucy, tomorrow I'm going to do something about these people." She grabbed his arm and shook her head "no."

"No…can't reason…with them…dangerous for you," Lucy struggled to whisper her words.

"Jason, I know you want to address this problem, but these people are dangerous, and you cannot do this alone," Birdie also pleaded.

"I know, but I must try to protect my wife. I'll meet with the Sheriff tomorrow and see if I can get a posse to hunt them down. This has got to stop!"

It was a huge step Lucy made that day speaking for the first time. Finally Jason thought their life together would be normal since he had never heard her lovely voice. Through the months of being married he had been patient and loving with Lucy. Jason had to give her time to heal from the ordeal she suffered by the hand of Munk and the Clan. He knew going into the marriage that it would take time for her to return his love, but slowly and surely after winning her trust Lucy was able to be a wife to Jason in everyway except for the deep love that she had for another man. She doubted she would ever get over Cain and what they shared together.

Even though Lucy's mind was still on her recent ordeal, Jason's thoughts had turned to the miracle of his wife speaking for the first time since they'd met. "Lucy, I am so happy that you can speak."

The next day, he learned from the Sheriff that several young women in the area were either kidnapped or missing. And there also had been bodies found of young women who were badly beaten and raped.

"I'll git a posse together and we'll hunt 'em down!" the Sheriff said.

That night, after all had gone to bed, Jason heard a noise outside. First it sounded like someone running. Jason followed the sound of the footsteps, which led to the rose gardens and got only a glimpse of someone, obviously up to no good, circling the hospital. Jason ran back to the bedroom. "Lucy, wake up, someone's trying to break into the hospital."

Several patients were already out of bed and concerned that someone was hurt. Jason ushered them back into their rooms.

"Please go back to bed," Jason spoke. "Be sure and shut the door behind you, and don't come out." When everyone was settled in, Jason insisted that Lucy hide herself. "Lucy, follow me, quickly." They hurried down the corridor with lanterns, then walked into the dispensary where the medicine was stored. Lucy passed in front of a glass door and mistook her own reflection for an intruder. She screamed. "Oh, Jason, I'm sorry. I didn't mean to scream. After she was settled down, she was sure it was the Clan. They kept hearing what sounded like pebbles being thrown against the windows. They stayed hidden there in the dispensary for what seemed like hours, until it was suddenly quiet again.

Lucy whispered. "Do you think they've gone?"

"I think so. Here, let me help you back to bed." They were afraid to light any lanterns for fear it might attract the Clan, who might still be outside.

"What about Birdie? Do you think she's safe?"

"Lucy, I need to go check on her. Will you be okay if I leave you long enough to go see about her?"

"Just promise me you'll be careful. Bring her back with you."

As soon as Jason went out the door, a rope was slipped around his throat. The rope tightened around his neck. It was Munk sitting on his horse, staring down on him.

"Teach you to steal my woman!"

Jason looked into Munk's filthy face and could hardly see his eyes. He tried to free himself, but it was no use. The rope continued to tighten as the horse galloped away, pulling Jason to the ground. All the while, Birdie was screaming at the top of her lungs for the man to free her brother. Jason was fighting to free himself, grasping at the rope while rolling over and over as Munk spurred his horse to run faster, with Jason's body being pulled behind him. Munk dragged Jason over stumps and through ditches, as he rolled and tumbled. He knew he had very serious injuries as he tried to hold onto the rope with his hands, but he was losing the battle as the noose was squeezing the life out of him. Slowly he could feel himself losing consciousness. Munk continued dragging him until he was satisfied that Jason was dead.

Seeing Munk ride off with her husband at the end of his rope, Lucy was forced into thinking fast. She retrieved guns from the cabinet and was shooting at the Clan, while Birdie ran to safety at the hospital. Lucy fell into character as she remembered what her daddy had taught her about loading and firing a weapon. When Birdie reached the door, Lucy nailed one of the Clan right between the eyes. Another Clan member saw Lucy with a gun, and thought he had time to overtake her. He was foolish to think so with Lucy's training. She raised the rifle, took careful aim, and shot him in the head. The man slumped in his saddle as the horse ran away.

Birdie could not believe what a good shot Lucy was, and how comfortable she was with a rifle in her hands. Then she remembered that Lucy's father was the Sheriff in Jonesboro, and that's probably where she learned to shoot so well.

"Birdie, we have to go after Jason!"

"One of the Clan got him! They had a rope around his neck. I think they killed him!" Birdie cried out.

Lucy's eyes filled with tears as she tried not to be upset. "Birdie, I hope you're wrong, but we don't have time to think about that now, 'cause I'm going after him."

"Not without me," Birdie insisted.

"Are you sure? It's dangerous. Don't you think you should stay with the patients?"

"No, you need me now more than they do. She was sorry she had misjudged Lucy, for she proved to be a woman of incredible strength. And for the first time, she recognized Lucy as someone just as passionate about dedication as she was.

"Birdie, I want you to stay right behind me when we run for the car." Before they left, she told her again, "Remember, stay behind me." Birdie was frightened, but she knew she had to be there for Lucy whom she had grown to admire. They ran to the car with Birdie carrying the rifle and Lucy aiming a six-shooter that she had taken from the gun cabinet Birdie trailed closely behind her while Lucy shot at serveral of the Clan.

She was amazed at how exceptional Lucy responded in a crisis.

When they got to the car, Lucy asked Birdie what the man looked like who took Jason.

"Lucy, he didn't look like the others. He looked more like us, but filthy."

"Oh No! That's probably Munk," Lucy said. "I need you to drive. Can you?" Asked Lucy.

Birdie slid over into the driver's seat and started the car. "What are you going to do?"

"We're going to hunt 'em down, and I'm going to kill 'em," Lucy said. She took the rifle, cocked it, and positioned herself ready to shoot.

They drove until they saw riders ahead. "That's them, Birdie! Try to get as close as you can, and don't be upset when I start firing."

"Lucy, please be careful, and don't take any chances." Lucy was hanging out of the window, aiming her gun at the riders who were whipping their horses, trying to get away. She took aim and shot one of them as the car gained on them. The headlights were glaring on the riders, but she did not see Jason.

"Lucy," Birdie cried out, "that's the man who was dragging Jason."

Lucy was halfway out of the window when she saw Munk turn and shoot at them. Birdie swerved the car and Lucy fell hard against the seat. "I'm sorry Lucy, I didn't want him to shoot you."

"Don't worry about the gunfire, just try to keep the car steady," Lucy insisted. "I'm going to shoot him."

Birdie was alarmed, watching Lucy risk her life, not paying attention to her own safety. Suddenly Lucy cried out, "Birdie, watch out!" It was too late. The car skidded off the road and down the embankment.

It had been raining heavily upstream, and the normally quiet river below had now turned to whitewater. Bouncing and rolling down the embankment made it seem like an eternity till they reached the bottom. On its final flip, the car plunged into the icecold turbulence of the raging rapids.

Lucy watched in horror as the wreck of their car began filling up with water. "Birdie, are you alright?" Lucy cried out. Birdie did not answer, but lay motionless with her head on the steering wheel. Lucy reached over and shook her, trying to wake her, but she appeared to be unconscious.

"Oh my God, please help me." Cold water kept finding its way inside the car, and they needed to get out before the car totally sank and before Munk had a chance to get to them.

She looked up toward the embankment where the Clan was standing, watching should they drown. Miraculously, the headlights were beaming upward, temporarily blinding Munk but lighting the way as he reined his horse down the embankment toward Lucy. *I've got to wake Birdie and get her out before he reaches us*, she thought.

She fought against the current in an effort to get around to the driver's side of the car. "Birdie, please wake up!" she screamed. In an instant, the current began pulling her into the rapids, but not before she grabbed Birdie and pulled her with her. Whether dead, or just unconscious, she was not going to allow the violent waters swallow up Birdie.

Munk made it down the embankment, but to his disappointment, the two women were lost to the rapids.

Even more danger lay ahead, as they were swept downstream towards a very dangerous ledge that would drop them onto boulders and rocks. The moon shone through the foggy mist as Birdie and Lucy slipped away into the night, bobbing like two corks, Lucy trying to keep both their heads above the water. Munk could see them on top of the water but he could not reach them. He was familiar with the falls ahead, and he didn't want to miss the moment they plunged over and perished below.

The water was freezing, as the two women gave in to the power of the rapids. Birdie had gulped water and awoke coughing, trying to clear her throat. She grabbed Lucy and held on tight. She was confused and didn't know what was going on or how they got in the river.

"Birdie, hang on, we've got to find a way to shore!" They were rushing through the turbulent rapids very fast when Birdie remembered they were headed for the ledge.

Again Birdie shouted, "We got to get to shore, there's a waterfall up ahead!" They were getting closer to the ledge as Birdie recognized the loud roar of water hitting against the rocks. The sound was deafening. She remembered having played in the stream as a child, but through years of erosion, it had become treacherous; with boulders and rocks that formed eddy lines, creating problems for canoes and fisherman who were sucked under the water. Lucy struggled to keep out of the eddy lines as they tugged at her and Birdie. Their long dresses made it doubly difficult to fight the current. She couldn't believe this was happening, but by their sheer will and determination, and with their lives at stake, they mustered the strength to swim closer to the shoreline. Each time they were about to approach land, they would ricochet off the side, and the rapids would again take them downstream.

Munk followed after them, keeping watch on their struggles.

He had hopes of apprehending them alive so he could kill them, but he would also revel in seeing them sucked over the ledge and plunging to their deaths among the rocks and boulders below the waterfall.

Lucy saw a protruding limb from a tree that was growing out into the water. *I have to reach it!* By this time, Birdie was ably fighting the waters on her own, and staying right behind Lucy. "Just a little more Birdie!" Both made it to the limb and grabbed on with what little strength they had left.

Birdie turned out to be just as much a fighter as Lucy, and neither was going to die without giving it all they had. Lucy amazed herself with the strength she had to save Birdie. The women embraced each other and then floated under branches that stemmed from the tree, watching and waiting to see if Munk had seen them escape. They huddled together without saying a word. Fortunately, the rushing waters drowned out the noise from the chattering of their teeth.

"Thank God we made it! Lucy, I was so frightened. But now we're going to freeze to death, if we don't get out of this water and wet clothes."

"I'm afraid we've got more than that to worry about right now, Birdie."

At that moment, they heard movement in the brush, and knew it was Munk looking for them. He was pushing himself through the branches and tall grass, edging himself along in the dark. Step by step they could hear him getting closer, until he was practically on top of them. Before Munk took another step, Lucy sprung up from her hiding spot and pushed him into the raging rapids.

Birdie was holding onto Lucy to make sure she didn't go with him. They stood and watched as Munk fought the current, a futile effort under the circumstances. He made loud sounds of distress as he bobbed above the whitewater that was taking him towards the ledge. Finally, it was a relief to see him swallowed by the rapids—caught in eddy lines, which sucked him over the ledge. His deep, throaty yell echoed through the trees as he plummeted toward the rocks below. They were sure he would not survive. They watched as the Clan rode toward the ledge in an effort to save their leader, but, seeing his goliath of a body hitting the rocks, they rode away without retrieving his body.

Lucy and Birdie rested long enough to regain the strength needed to climb up the embankment to the road. Both were shivering and holding on to each other as they crossed the road and disappeared into the woods.

"Birdie, do you know how far away we are from the hospital?"

"About two miles, but we can't go back…they might be waiting for us," she pointed out.

"Lucy, I think there's a cabin nearby."

They walked through the wooded area until they came to the cabin that belonged to a friend of Jason's from childhood.

Lucy hoped the inhabitants were friendly, for she was not sure if Jeb still lived there. Shaking from the cold, Birdie knocked until they heard footsteps coming to the door. Jeb Harris was aghast at their soaked clothing and both shaking from the cold.

"Birdie…is that you? Here, y'all, come on in. I'll put some more wood on the fire and get a pot of hot coffee going. Y'all must be freezing to death. What on earth happened?

"Thank you Jeb, we just had a terrible experience." He rushed them in and placed seats by the fire.

"Jeb, this is my sister-in-law, Lucy. I don't know if you've heard of a Clan living near here called the Jackson Whites, but they just killed Jason." Birdie's voice cracked as she told him about how he died. Lucy, too, was in tears, thinking of Jason and her being responsible for him dying. "If it hadn't been for me, Jason would still be alive," she stated to Birdie and Jeb, then broke into tears.

"Lucy, I will not allow you to blame yourself. What happened was not your fault. If anyone's to blame, it's those Clan people."

"I'm so very sorry about Jason! I been hearing some stories 'bout those folks, but didn't know if them rumors were true," Jeb said. "Your brother was a good man, Birdie. I know you want to git back to yer' place, but y'all don't need to go back till morning. First thang I gotta do is git y'all some dry clothes. All I got is some of my brother's clothes he left behind. You remember Terry, don'tcha Birdie?"

"I think I do; it's been a long time."

Jeb was in the logging business, just an average man with a broad smile. Lucy thought he looked German. Birdie and Jeb hadn't seen each other since they finished school.

"Jeb, it's kind of you to help us out."

He listened as she explained about the Clan and what happened to Jason. Lucy was wide-eyed and still dazed, as she relived the specific details of what happened to Jason.

"I'm sure sorry about your husband. I read all about y'all's wedding." Lucy was still in tears, thinking about poor Jason dying in such a horrible manner.

"Birdie, I got a place fer ya' here tonight, and we'll go looking for Jason in the morning. Ain't nothing we can do in the dark." Birdie shook her head in agreement.

When morning came, Jeb saddled an extra horse and accompanied Lucy and Birdie back to the hospital. When they arrived, two town folk were standing there with a body they had found. They knew whom it might be as they took time to examine the corpse. He was hardly recognizable, but there was no doubt the body was Jason.

"Thank you boys for bringing Jason home to me. Now we can bury him properly," Birdie cried. Both of the women were visibly upset and in tears as Lucy with a cloth bent over and lovingly removed the blood from Jason's face. This is when Birdie witnessed the love Lucy had for Jason as she kissed his lips.

"We're real sorry fer yer loss. We had no idea that this would be yer husband, Ms. Lucy.

If y'all need anybody goin' huntin' 'em down, me and Lonny will join the party. We heard of some mean goings on here and it's about time we did something ta end this once and fer all. Jeb, you let us know when we be goin' after 'em."

227

The funeral was very difficult for both Lucy and Birdie. Afterwards, when the women had a chance to talk, Lucy confided in Birdie that she wanted no claim to Jason's estate, and that she was going back to Jonesboro to live. "Birdie, I don't belong here. This is yours and Jason's family estate, and I'm not claiming any part of it."

"I don't want to hear another word about this. You were my brother's wife, and it was his wish that you be his heir. Lucy, you can't leave. I need you now, more than ever before. Mrs. Lucy Crumb, you're like my sister, and besides, you know more about birthing babies than me. And what you don't know about the other things…I'll be teaching you. Please… you have to stay." Lucy paused and then said, "Well, since you put it that way, I guess I'll give it a try. I just don't know how we will do without Jason."

Lucy hugged Birdie as they agreed to look for each other.

The next few weeks were busy with paperwork, and taking care of the car that had been mangled and submerged in the stream. Lucy and Birdie both needed a car since they would be making house calls, delivering babies and taking care of the sick. So each purchased a new Model T.

A few days later, Jeb stopped by the hospital and told them that the Sheriff and his posse had rounded up what was left of the Clan. They had two volunteer scouts who searched from Trumann to Jonesboro. The camp was found in a secluded area not too far from the manor where Vick and Elizabeth once lived.

Lucy had no idea the Clan was so close to the manor. She had lost consciousness after her escape from the fire, and when she came to, she was in a cage with a noose around her neck.

"Jeb, what about their camp?" she asked.

"Ms. Lucy, we already took care of the Clan, and rescued two young women who were kidnapped over a year ago. The girls hadn't even had their eighteenth birthdays, and they have already lived a lifetime. Seems to me like the Clan wanted 'em young. We ended up killing pert near all of 'em in the shootout."

"I imagine they were confused without their leader," said Lucy.

"Ms. Lucy, I seen members of a Clan before, but these were the worst I've seen. They all had that same kinda hollow look."

"Did anyone see a man who looked like us?"

"No…they all looked like they were from the same cloth."

"Then it's safe to say their leader, called Munk, died when the rapids got him," Lucy assumed.

"Ms. Lucy, we heard about that man bein' caught in the rapids and goin' over the ledge, but no body was ever recovered. We were lookin' downstream but never found 'em. I guess he got caught up in some of the brush near the bank. We'll be keepin' an eye out, and if we find 'em, we'll let ya' know. He's bound to show up sooner or later."

"Do you know of anyone ever surviving the fall?" She asked.

"No, don't reckon I ever heard of nobody ever makin' it over that ledge. Them boulders and rocks would have got 'em, if them rapids didn't."

"Don't worry, I'm sure he's dead, and now perhaps we can get back to living," Birdie reassured her.

For the first time in a long time, Lucy and Birdie felt normal, except for their heavy hearts.

After sharing their ordeal, Lucy began regaining her confidence. She even got homesick for Jonesboro, but it was not a good time to leave Birdie.

She would often close her eyes and visualize her daddy smiling at her in their little cabin back home. He was one of a kind, she reminisced, and it was hard for her to think about living the rest of her life without him. Then there was Cain. She had loved him with all her heart, but it was Jason who saved her. He was the kindest man, and he would occupy a special place in her heart.

Lucy and Jason had been married only a short time when Jason told her she would never be able to have children. At the time, she thought it was terribly unfair. *All I ever wanted was to be happily married, and have a family, she reflected. Now, since Jason is dead, my life will take on a different meaning. Perhaps my earthly calling is to work with Birdie and take care of the sick.*

During her full recovery, Lucy resigned herself to nursing, and gave little thought to the future.

Several weeks passed as normalcy set in, but Lucy continued to think of home. There was really no plan for her to drive to Jonesboro, but that morning, nothing could have stopped her from getting into the Model T and driving there. Too much time had now passed, and she longed to visit the town she loved. As she drove along, she enjoyed cool, fresh air as it wisped across her face. She was glad to be alive, and loved each mile she drove, as a rush of excitement came over her. She missed Jonesboro and the gossip of the town, with its stories being told and retold. It went without saying, that she enjoyed her tiny town because it was kinder than any other town in which she had lived.

As her car puttered down the narrow dirt road bypassing the manor, Lucy was unaware that someone had seen her.

When she arrived at their old cabin, she had a change of heart. *I'm not ready for this,* she thought. Instead of stopping, she drove past the house until she saw workers in a pasture working on their fence. She pulled over and asked if they would nail boards over the windows of the cabin until she decided what she would do with the place. After they agreed, Lucy paid them for their help, and drove back to Trumann.

When Lucy returned, Birdie asked, "what happened?"

"I thought I was ready, but, when I got to the place, and it looked like someone still lived there, I couldn't make myself stop. It would have been too painful."

"Lucy, don't try and rush yourself. You have time to recover, and then you can go again."

"I tried to find my daddy's grave but all I found was my own. I desperately wanted to place flowers on daddy's grave but they must have buried him in Texas."

Chapter 20

Parley Jackson had known for years that oil lay beneath the surface of Aggie's land, but he never shared that information with anyone for fear that pandemonium would break out, and he would lose any chance at acquiring it. So he just bided his time until the right opportunity came along for him to step in and grab it.

He was careful to guard the secret, even from his son, Seth. Parley was tenacious in harassing the prior owners, knowing the riches that lay beyond the surface of the ground—that is, until young Aggie Dawson edged one up and beat him to the punch. When he learned that Ms. Mixson sold the property to Aggie and what she paid for it, this infuriated him who was willing to do anything to become owner of the Mixson property.

Seth did not like his father, but he continued to love him in spite of their estrangement. More than a year had gone by since he distanced himself from his father, and his marriage to Aggie did not stop Parley's mistreatment of her.

One afternoon, while Seth was working in the yard, a sunny breeze with a scent of oil wafted up his nose. Even the fragrance of wild bluebonnets, entwined with the scent, could not overpower that distinct smell. He began following the scent, and found not just a little oil, but a lot of bubbly oil, oozing out of the ground.

Finally, Parley's secret was out, and Seth guessed his Pa might have known all along that oil resided there. He now knew the real reason for the dispute with the Mixsons', and also, Aggie. He fancied how this new discovery of oil would change the dynamics of Beaumont, with Spindletop not being that far away. *This could be big*, he thought.

Seth threw his hat up in the air and hollered "Hot dang, we struck oil!" He ran to the house to tell Aggie but had momentarily forgotten that she had taken their son, who was now walking, to town to attend a work session with other women of the church. She had planned to be gone all afternoon. Seth was terribly excited, and felt the need to share the news of his good fortune with his father. Maybe this will change his negativity about me, he thought. He may even accept my marriage to Aggie, and for once, work with us instead of against us. But then he began second guessing himself and looking at it from another perspective. Maybe I shouldn't tell anyone, not even my Pa, and take a chance of the word getting out.

His ultimate decision was to confide in his father and hope he would do right by Aggie and him. It really didn't take much convincing, for Seth already had his horse saddled and ready to ride. When he arrived at his Pa's ranch, he jumped out of the saddle and ran to the door.

Seth knocked until the door opened. There was a pleasant expression on Seth's face—one that Parley had not seen in a long time. He decided to take a momentary break from their estrangement and responded in kind. He imagined that Seth might be there to patch things up. Whatever it was, Parley was eager to find out what was on his son's mind.

"Come on in, I got coffee made," Parley coached enthusiastically.

This was different, Seth thought, having his father act like he was glad to see him.

"I need to talk to you, if you have time," Seth exclaimed.

"Sure, let's talk. Had you rather have coffee or a drink?" Parley asked.

He thought of the nice reception and chose to celebrate. This effort on my part could be a new beginning for me, Aggie and Pa, he supposed.

"I ain't had a drink in a long time. How about a whiskey, that is if you'll join me."

"Sure, glad to see you son, it's been a long time."

Seth had never felt so optimistic, and thought it was about time they made peace with one another and win his father's affection.

Actually, Parley was manipulating Seth just like he'd always done. Since his son was vulnerable, he overlooked Parley's lies and deceptions, as he allowed himself to fall into the same old trap.

Before the afternoon was over, Seth managed to divulge information that he shouldn't have. Not only did he deliver information about the oil, but also about Aggie's past and her fear of Jonathan Petty, who lived in San Augustine and wanted her dead.

"Pa, this man raped Aggie and murdered her mother. He's nothing but a cold blood killer."

The more Seth talked, the more he elaborated on information that was shared to him in confidence by Aggie who loved and trusted him.

Of all people, she would never have approved of Parley knowing her background and where she had come from.

He listened and seemed concerned, but he was more interested about the oil on their land, and how he could prosper if he could manage to steal it out from under them.

Being a good son, Seth had completely misunderstood his father's interest, and indulged him in most of Aggie's family secrets.

"You can't imagine how Aggie's been hurt, never knowing who her real father was until the man she thought was her Pa told the truth to her on his deathbed."

With this newfound knowledge about Aggie's past, Parley began developing a plan to get Jonathan Petty do his dirty work. But he had to be careful, since he did not know whether the story Aggie told Seth was true. *The girl could be making up the part that she was a rich man's daughter. All I want is that Jonathan feller to kill Aggie, which would end my troubles once and for all*, Parley conspired.

That night, when the house was quiet, Parley planned his trip to San Augustine to talk with Jonathan.

At first light of the next day, he left his home in Woodville and rode his horse in the direction of San Augustine. He planned to take several days to clear the cobwebs and travel through the backwoods in areas he had never explored.

Parley was ten miles from the plantation when he stopped for the night. He had been on the road for three days. *Tomorrow, after a good night's sleep, I'll plan to meet Jonathan Petty.*

Parley had no idea what to expect when he rode into Pecan Plantation. He had never seen such wealth, with the vast fields of cotton among a magnificent setting. *So this was Aggie's daddy's place,* Parley thought, admiringly. *Hamp Petty must have been rolling in the dough. He doubted that Aggie was part of this wealth. I don't believe the story that she made up about a man like Jonathan being capable of raping her and murdering her mother.* Still, he was a bit uneasy about his reception and what he might find.

Matilda, who saw the stranger ride up, ran out to greet him in order to protect Jonathan, because of his paranoia.

Vick also became interested seeing a stranger ride, which was unusual since no one had called on Jonathan that he could recall.

"If the man has news about Cain, I have to find out," Vick said under his breath.

Matilda announced to Parley who was still mounted on his horse. "Meester Jonathan is not seeing anyone today,"

"I see...if you don't mind, tell Mr. Petty that I've come a long way to see him about a woman named Aggie. It's important that he sees me, since I hold some valuable information that might be of interest to him."

"You wait here, and I will see if Meester Jonathan will see you."

Jonathan had been listening from inside and heard the name Aggie.

His heart sank when he heard the rider mention the woman who could send him to prison or better yet have him hung. *The man could be the Sheriff,* he thought. He knew sooner or later he would have Aggie to deal with, but considering his troubles, he was furious of the timing. He was concerned that the lawman might be there to arrest him. Feeling the urgency he felt he had no choice but to pull myself together and act like an innocent man who had been wrongly accused.

He walked to the door with his gun on his hip, just in case. Parley spoke first when Jonathan showed himself.

"Howdy Mister Petty...you are Jonathan Petty aren't you?"

Jonathan was careful not to show emotion.

"Yes, I'm Jonathan. What can I do for you?"

"I need to ask you about my son's wife, Aggie Dawson."

Jonathan finally knew why he was never able to locate her; she was using her mother's maiden name and not that of her father, Barney Simmons. Jonathan still had no clue that Aggie was his half-sister.

"This woman you're talking about ain't nothing to me, so I suggest you leave and let me get back to my work." Jonathan was sure he had not seen the man before. "You ain't from these parts, are you?"

"No, I rode here from Woodville, Texas. By the way, my name is Parley Jackson," he said as he extended his hand but Jonathan ignored Parley's gentlemanly gesture. Parley dropped his hand and continued, "This Aggie woman married my son Seth, and I ain't too happy about it."

"Why you here to see me?"

"She said she knows you and used to live here. I'm nosing in her business, 'cause there's something about her that bothers me. I think she's hiding something, and I aim to find out. I'm hoping you can help me."

Parley kept talking while Jonathan began to sweat. He tried to hear what Parley was saying but all he could think about was Aggie and his troubles should she talk. "She drove a wedge between me and my son, and I ain't seen him in over a year, since she had that bastard child of hers. She forgot to tell my son she was pregnant when he married her. That's why I'm here. I need to know if you're the baby's daddy."

"I don't know any Aggie Dawson, and I'm certainly not her baby's daddy, so if you don't mind, I'm busy taking care of my business. So you need to turn that horse around and stop wasting my time. I spec' you've come a long way for nothing. Ain't nothing I can do for you here."

Jonathan felt his heart sink, knowing that Aggie was alive, and talking, when she should be keeping her mouth shut.

"You be careful now," Jonathan said with a sinister look that sent shivers through Parley's body.

There was something about Jonathan's eyes that frightened him. He knew one thing for certain: he did not want to tangle with the man. After their meeting, he wondered if he had made a mistake by contacting him.

Parley didn't quibble, as he turned his horse and headed back toward San Augustine.

Vick and Orson were watching the entire time, and as the man rode off, he wondered what Jonathan and the man had in common. Vick couldn't shake the feeling that the man might have news about Cain. This was the first time he'd seen an outsider contact Jonathan, and he felt compelled to examine why the visitor was there. Vick was looking for a break since it had been over two years of seeking the whereabouts of his son.

Since time had passed Vick was not going to allow any stone to be unturned if it was a chance that information could surface about Cain. So, seeing the stranger speaking with Jonathan aroused his attention.

Elizabeth had seen the man too, but did not want to alarm Vick with her apprehensiveness. After Parley left, Elizabeth told Vick she had an errand to run in town. She deliberately drove out the opposite road, so Jonathan would not see her leave heading toward San Augustine.

Soon afterwards, Vick saw Jonathan saddling his horse, and leaving the plantation as if to follow the stranger. He was concerned for Elizabeth safety, and so was Orson; seeing the two men who could intercept her, even though she was in a faster mode of transportation.

"You better go see after Lizzie, 'cause you can't tell 'bout those two men or what they're up to," Orson said.

Vick didn't waste any time saddling his horse to follow them.

Elizabeth was speeding along as she passed the stranger on the road. As soon as she drove out of sight, she stopped her car; pretending to have car trouble. She said a silent prayer, *Help me God*, as she waited for Parley to catch up with her standing beside her car.

Slowing down as he went by, he stopped, believing she needed help.

"Ma'am, looks like you can use a little help."

Elizabeth tried to act coy and annoyed for being stranded.

"Thank you, sir, but this happens all the time. It just needs to cool off. Then it will start up again. Now, you go ahead and don't let me hold you up."

Parley noticed how beautiful she was, and wasn't about to leave her in distress.

"I don't know much about cars, but I can take a look for you."

"You're too kind. It will start in a few minutes. I'm used to it."

"I can at least wait and make sure you're not stranded. It's a long walk to town."

In spite of her bold effort, she was nervous, not knowing with whom she might be dealing, but it did not deter her from asking questions.

"I think I saw you back at the plantation."

Parley assumed Elizabeth was Jonathan's wife, and since his meeting did not go as intended, he commenced telling Elizabeth about his son's wife whose name is Aggie.

Elizabeth would have learned more had she not seen Jonathan riding towards them.

"Sir, please excuse me, but I'm late for my appointment." Elizabeth hurriedly jumped into her car and drove off, just in the nick of time.

Parley thought she was certainly right about her car, and didn't question her hasty departure. Parley rode away a few minutes before Jonathan could reach him, but not before Jonathan saw the stranger and Elizabeth talking. Again his paranoia kicked into high gear. *I should have invited the man in and killed him when I had a chance.* The Porters are behind him coming here, and now I know I have to get rid of all of 'em. He was boiling with rage, and at the same time, plotting how the James boys would help him do it.

Jonathan turned his horse around and ran into Vick, who had been purposely lagging behind.

When the two men met, Jonathan held up his hand for Vick to stop.

"Porter, I need you to tell me what the hell is going on?"

Vick was as smooth as silk. "You tell me, since I don't know what you're talking about."

"You and that wife of yours are both keeping this road hot today!"

Vick was concerned that he had mentioned Elizabeth. "Are you following my wife?"

"Guess you didn't have anything to do with that stranger coming up to the house today. And now I just saw Elizabeth talking to the man."

Vick was alarmed, wondering what could have happened to Elizabeth, since she had been talking to the stranger. *Things are getting crazier by the minute*, he thought. He studied Jonathan, and saw a change he didn't understand. Jonathan had always been so well dressed, but now he was unkempt.

"Well now Jonathan… if I did know something, I don't think I'd be talking to you about it." Vick was in a hurry to cut loose and try to find Elizabeth.

"I shoulda' had you and that wife of yours run off of Petty land a long time ago. I know 'bout that reputation of yours. You ain't nothing but a small-town hustler. You hustled my brother! If it had been me, I would've wiped that cocky smile off your face and taught you a thing or two about playing poker."

Jonathan spurred his horse and took off to Circle J.

After arriving at the ranch, Jonathan made himself at home, since Dudley and Lonnie were nowhere to be found. The Circle J was the place he felt safe, and he thought he would have a drink to drown the pain. One whiskey didn't seem to do it, so he had several, as he studied his plight.

The James boys had been in town killing time. When they returned to the tack house, they noticed Jonathan's horse. They knew he wouldn't approve of the way they looked, so they took time to make themselves presentable. They arrived at the main house and knocked on the door, waking Jonathan, who had fallen asleep in his chair. He walked to the door hardly recognizable, with his long crumpled hair and sloppy clothing. The boys had never seen him in such disarray.

"Whatcha staring at? Come on in here…we need to talk," Jonathan ordered, as he staggered back to his chair.

"What's up, boss?" Their eyes were darting back and forth, seeing the man who was obsessed with cleanliness take on such a shabby appearance.

"I got a job for you. A big job."

Jonathan took another swig of whiskey.

Slurring his words, he spoke, "Them Porters…they know way too much about my business, and I want 'em gone."

"What kinda gone…like dead gone?"

"Don't do the stupid act. What do you think?"

"Boss, we can't git rid of Vick before he leads us to the treasure. That was always our plan, remember? We gotta git 'em back to Panther Holler where the treasure's hid, and then we can take care of 'em and make it clean fer all of us." Dudley looked at Lonnie when he said the word, "clean". "I suppose he said that for Jonathans benefit," Dudley thought.

"Y'all do that...the sooner the better," Jonathan slurred. He then walked over to the bottle of whiskey and poured himself another drink.

"There's one other thing I'd like to do before I kill the bastard."

"What's that boss?"

"Kick his ass at a game of poker, something my brother couldn't do."

"Vick Porter's got a reputation of beating every man he sits down with. Ha! I could show him a thing or two about the game. Oh, before I forget, I got somebody else for you to take care of...Aggie Dawson. I know where she lives."

"Is that the girl you know?" asked Lonnie.

"Go ahead and say it. I raped her and killed her mother." Jonathan took a big gulp and continued his downhill spiral.

He turned and stared out the window, like he was drifting back to another time. "Yeah, my old man was something else alright. One time, I walked in on him kissing Aggie's bitch of a mother. That's when I knew something was going on. They both got what they deserved...my old man, too."

Lonnie and Dudley rolled their eyes, having to stand there at attention and listen to a man, who had gone raving mad.

"You boys find that Aggie gal, and I'll make it worth your while. Ain't neither one of you had a woman, have you?"

Dudley and Lonnie looked at one another. Finally, Jonathan answered the question for them.

"I know you boys ain't never had a woman. Well, don't you worry 'cause it's all overrated. Ain't ne'r one of 'em worth it, accept maybe that little woman that belongs to Vick Porter. Now she's mighty fine and the kind of woman I'd like to have around for a while."

Jonathan took another swig of whiskey and said. "Well, it ain't any need to tell y'all what I'm thinking." Jonathan had begun to chatter obscenities that even embarrassed Lonnie and Dudley.

The brothers kept waiting for the rant to be over, but it continued on and on, while they just stood and listened. Jonathan was in rare form, talking crazy, when all that interested them was keeping Vick alive, so he could lead them to the treasure.

He made them promise to take care of Aggie before he agreed to dry gulch Vick.

When Jonathan finally collapsed on the couch, they took off his boots and carried him to bed.

"Lonnie, do you reckon Jonathan was serious about us killing that woman he raped?"

"He's serious alright but I think he ought to do his own damn killing."

"We don't need Jonathan," Dudley suggested.

"We might not need him, but he could cause us a world of trouble, and he'd do it if he thought we lied to 'em."

"What about that Porter woman? It sounds like he wants to kill her too," said Dudley.

"She'd be a little spitfire. Can't ya' jest see 'em together?"

Dudley and Lonnie helped themselves to Jonathan's whiskey, and then planned how they intended to kill Aggie.

"We take care of the woman fer 'em, and then Vick Porter's taking us to Panther Holler."

"Dudley, if we play our cards right, we might end up with a lot more than we thank. Have ya' ever thought of that? We git Jonathan and Porter back to Panther Holler, find the treasure, then we'll kill 'em all. That shore would make me feel good ta put a bullet twixt their eyes."

Lonnie, smiled at the thought.

"I reckon it'll be payback if we can git Jonathan drunk enough to sign every thang over to us. He's crazy enough ta do it, too."

"I wouldn't mind having the ranch, but over at the plantation some mighty strange thangs are happening." This was the first time either of the two had alluded to the eerie sightings of the dead.

Lonnie's ears perked up, relieved to hear he might not be the only one seeing ghosts. "Whatcha talking about?"

"I been wonderin' if ya' been seein' anythang strange over at that plantation? Well, it ain't exactly at the plantation, but jest outside where ya' turn in."

Lonnie started playing dumb while he was feeling out Dudley. He wasn't quite ready to admit that he'd been seeing Orson's ghost.

"Uh, ah, uh, why you ask? You been seein' thangs?"

"You thank people ever see the dead?" asked Dudley.

"What makes you ask that?" Lonnie played along so Dudley would open up more to him.

"Because, if Orson ain't dead, he's still alive. That's what I'm talkin' about."

Yer' crazy, 'cause we did everythang but plant daisies on his grave. Ya' gotta be seein' thangs," Lonnie lectured, even though the same things had been happening to him.

"I been seein' Orson when I go to the plantation fer our pay," Dudley expressed.

That's jest plain nuts. We seen him and Porter both dead on the ground. Do ya' thank if that Porter boy was still alive, that crazy Jonathan would be back livin' on that plantation?"

Lonnie had never believed in ghosts before, but now, Dudley seeing Orson made him wonder. He still wasn't ready to come clean about him seeing Orson, too.

"There's something else; it's about Jonathan. Ever since he moved to the plantation, he's acting like a crazy man. That place may be spooked."

"Ya' mean with ghosts?" Lonnie asked.

"Yeah, with ghosts, or maybe them evil spirits our old man used to tell us about.

Something else, did you hear Matilda say somebody over at the plantation stole that ring she took from ya'?" Lonnie recalled.

"My ring? The one I took off of Lucy's finger?" Dudley queried.

"That's right! Somebody don't want either one of ya' ta have it."

"Maybe Orson came ta steal back Lucy's ring," Dudley imagined. "Or maybe Lucy came to git it herself."

"Jest listen, yer' talkin' as crazy as Jonathan. There ain't no damn ghosts.

Hearing Dudley's confession frightened him.

"Now Dudley, settle down…ya' might need another drink."

"No, I jest need ta git outta here. That's what I need. All these people are goin' crazy and maybe me, too."

"Ya' have been actin' a little off lately," Lonnie teased.

"I knew I should never told ya' 'bout me seein' Orson. I'm thankin' I'd rather live by daddy's old still than I had ta be in Texas livin' in a place wher' I have to mark down ever time I take a bath. Lonnie, whatcha say we do our business here and git back to Arkansas?"

"Once we take care of that Aggie girl fer Jonathan, I'll be ready to leave this God forsaken place myself," Lonnie admitted. For once, they agreed it was time to go back home and get serious about finding the treasure.

The next morning, Jonathan walked out to the tack house to see what the boys were up to.

"You boys taking care of this place?"

"We tryin' boss, but working here and out in the fields is real hard. Sorry fer ya' seeing it this way." Clothes and clutter were scattered everywhere. Lonnie looked at Dudley and rolled his eyes, for they were not expecting to have a visit from Jonathan.

"Ya' know I don't stand for filth! Cleanliness is Godliness and it looks like hell in here!"

"We tryin' boss," said Lonnie, who rolled his eyes again. Lucky his back was turned so Jonathan could not see him.

Dudley diverted Jonathan's attention by changing the subject to Aggie.

"What about that woman ya' asked us to take care of?"

"What woman?" Jonathan asked.

"That Aggie woman you said you wanted us to take care of."

"That's nonsense! I ain't asked no such thing."

"You don't remember sayin' to take care of her? You even told us to take care of them Porters."

"Don't y'all know how Vick stayed alive in prison? He played poker, that's what kept him alive."

Lonnie thought, "Here we go again." Jonathan was completely off subject.

"Are ya' plannin' on havin; a little poker game with Vick?" asked Dudley.

"In time, I plan to do just that." Jonathan spoke with a militant speech pattern when he spoke, which was different than the boys had heard before.

"Member we gotta git the treasure 'fore we go killin' 'em."

That night, when Jonathan had retired for the evening, he dreamed of playing poker with Vick. Jonathan won every hand, and at the end of the card game, he stood, drew his gun, and shot Vick through the heart. He remembered feeling a sense of satisfaction killing the man that he had grown to despise.

~

Seth felt like a new man after patching things up with his Pa. He was certain that sharing secrets about Aggie's personal life, (not to mention the oil on her land), had restored their relationship.

The meeting had gone well he thought, until he found out his Pa had left town without a word. Parley's sudden departure, after Seth confided in him, was very unsettling.

After several trips to check the ranch and his father's whereabouts, he began imagining the worse. He had betrayed his wife's confidence to his father, and now he imagined his Pa was using it against him and her, a particularly worrisome thought. How could I have been so stupid to believe I could win my father over by telling him the truth about Aggie's past. No telling what he's going to do with the information I gave him.

Seth became consumed with guilt, knowing Aggie would be furious to know that he broke her confidence.

After a week passed and still there was no Parley, Seth had a hunch and thought it was time to question the men who worked for his Pa.

"Mr. Parley said he was going to San Augustine and would be gone over a week one of the ranch hands reported.

"Are you sure?" Seth felt a shiver run through him, thinking of what Parley was capable of. *I can't believe he would put my wife in danger by talking to the man that raped her, and murdered her mother.*

Each day thereafter, Seth would ride over to see if Parley was home. After the second week passed, he saw his Pa's horse hitched to the post out in front of the house. "He's home!" Seth felt the blood rush to his face. "He's not going to lie his way out of this one," he said, secretly.

By the time he reached the door, his boiling point had reached the maximum. All the years of mental anguish his Pa had caused him surfaced, and he could not ever remember being so enraged. *I've had it with this man! I'm tired of the careless disregard he's given me through the years, and it's time I confront him.* Seth walked into the house calling out.

"Pa! I need to talk to you! Now!" he yelled. Parley came out of the kitchen with wet hands and a half-smile on his face. Seth had seen that smile before, when he knew he was hiding something.

"Son, you didn't give me a chance to dry my hands, what on earth is wrong?"

"Dry 'em on your shirt. I want to know why you went to San Augustine?"

"Who told you I went to San Augustine?"

"Your foreman, and unlike you, he wasn't lying."

"Well, what you so worked up for?"

"Why did you do it Pa? Now my wife is in danger on account of you."

"Son, I wanted to know who you're really married to. I'm concerned about you."

"What you've done is put a target on Aggie's back."

"Awwww, that's not so. All I asked Jonathan Petty was what he knew about Aggie, and you know what he said? He said he didn't even know who the hell I was talking about. So you got this all wrong. Your wife is the one lying to ya'."

"Aggie ain't lying, you're the one lying...like you always do. I know what you're up to. I fear you've placed my wife in harm's way, and I'm not going to stand for it!"

"Well, you need to wise up son, 'cause the woman you're married to ain't nothing but a whore. That son of hers is a bastard, and you need to face it."

Seth was angry, as tears welled up in his eyes. He couldn't discern if his tears were from his father disappointing him, or if it was because of Aggie being in danger. He was sure it was some of both.

"Look at you, now you're crying just like your Ma, who was weak and pitiful. You're both shameful."

Seth turned, and as he did, he saw his Pa's new rifle leaning against the wall. All he wanted to do was shut Parley up, not thinking of the consequences of his actions. He ran over to the gun and picked it up. Parley turned away to go for his gun, and when he did, Seth shot him in the back.

Seth turned with the look of surprise on his face.

"Sonnnn, I can't believe you shot me!"

He threw the gun down as soon as his Pa hit the floor. He stood over him with his hand over his mouth as Parley twitched, with blood running from the wound onto the floor. Before Seth bent down he knew Parley was dead and that he would most likely be charged with murder.

"What have I done? Oh, my God, I've shot my Pa." As Seth stood and turned, he saw two ranch hands standing behind him. They had witnessed him kill his father.

"We heard yer Pa and you yelling, and we thought we needed to come break up a fight, but Seth, you shot yer Pa in the back. We seen ya'."

"Seth, yore daddy probably had it comin', but ya' shot him in the back!" the other ranch hand said.

Seth just stared at them with tears streaming down his face. He tried to speak, but he couldn't, so he ran out of the house and jumped on his horse, riding as fast as he could to Aggie's.

The men didn't know what to make out of what had just happened, as they stood in the doorway watching Seth ride away.

They had no choice but to ride into town with Parley's body. As they rode to the Sheriff's office, the deputy came out to see whose body they had.

"Well, I be damn, if it ain't Parley Jackson. Y'all say ya' seen what happened?" asked the deputy. About that time, the Sheriff walked out.

"Yep, we seen the boy shoot his Pa. They was arguing real loud, and me and Lonnie thought we needed to go in the house and pull 'em apart. Seth ran off before we could get 'em settled down enough to talk any sense into 'em."

"Where do you think Seth went?" asked the Sheriff.

"I have ta tell ya' that Seth was mighty upset." We think he headed to the old Mixson place where him and that wife of his lives."

"Hey Duncan, I reckon ya' need to git a posse together and let's ride out toward that Dawson woman's house, since that's where Seth was headed."

Seth rode his horse into the barn and ran to the house, taking Aggie in his arms. "Sweetheart, I don't know what to say, but I have to leave."

Aggie thought she was hearing things. "You have to leave? Why?" she asked.

"I shot my Pa. He's dead!"

"Seth, you what? I can't believe what you're telling me!"

"I can't stay, but, Aggie, you need to prepare yourself 'cause Jonathan knows you're here. Parley went to see him."

"Just a minute, slow down. How does Jonathan know I'm here?"

"Pa told him! He went to see Jonathan in San Augustine, and it's just a matter of time that he'll be coming here. And I can't be here to protect you. The Sheriff is probably on his way now to arrest me."

Seth was out of breath and trying to talk at the same time.

"You told Parley what I told you in confidence? Is that what you're trying to say... that you broke my confidence, and now me and my son are in danger?"

"I'm sorry Aggie, I thought Pa had changed. When I discovered oil on our land, I went to tell Pa, thinking he might be happy for us."

"You told your Pa that we have oil, when you haven't even told me?"

"I should have known Pa would never change. Aggie, please try to understand. I didn't mean to hurt you. I thought he would feel the same as I do about you whenever he heard the truth. Aggie, I'm so sorry."

She turned away from him. Had I been mistaken about Seth? she anguished. Despite her efforts to turn her back on her husband, she couldn't. She knew he did not intentionally set out to hurt her.

This was the man she loved, and wondered how he could have been so stupid. Now I don't know what I'm going to do, she thought. There was no doubt of the feeling between them that drew them together like a magnet, and even though he had disappointed her, she loved him beyond measure.

"Seth, you don't worry about me and Jared. Worry about yourself...now go." She went to him and kissed him, possibly one last time, then watched him ride off.

The next day she heard that Seth was arrested south of Henderson, and placed in jail to face murder charges. The town was shaken that a son would shoot his father in the back, even though he might have reason. Everyone disliked Parley, but for a son to take the law in his own hands and shoot his father in the back, was intolerable. He would either be hanged, or spend the rest of his life in prison.

Aggie loved Seth, and to think she would spend her life without him was more than she could bear.

As it turned out, the public could not get enough of the story about the handsome young man who turned his gun on his father. Aggie and Seth's forbidden love became a sensation to many bored housewives, and their love soon grew into a scandalous relationship, full of intriguing bits and pieces, which were embellished and fueled by fast moving gossip.

After the case gained so much notoriety, Aggie felt unsafe because of Jonathan. Of more concern was her son's welfare.

The trial was expeditious, and Seth was on his way to serve 20 years in the Huntsville State Prison for murdering his father. The only thing that saved him from hanging was his lawyer's reading of scripture from the Bible, before sentencing.

Eph. 6-4 "And ye father, Provoke not your children to wrath: but bring them up in the nurture and admonition of the Lord."

The jurors knew the kind of man Parley was, and felt if he had not provoked Seth, he would have never shot his father.

Aggie was heartbroken, but felt relieved when the jurors gave Seth only a 20-year sentence.

After she watched her husband taken away in shackles, she vowed to support him, and promised to run the ranch until Seth won his freedom.

Chapter 21

AFTER GLEN HAD BECOME OBSESSED WITH LEARNING THE TRUTH ABOUT **Ben's identity, he wished he had left well enough alone.** He became guilt ridden, knowing Ben had a family and another life before coming to work for him and Martha. His selfishness and love for Martha prevented him from telling Ben and her the truth of who he felt he knew Ben to be.

Glen had been through some bad times with Martha, and he was fearful that the news would devastate her. She had accepted Ben as a replacement for the son they lost several years before, and that was all that mattered to her.

Glen had seen the change in Martha, and credited Ben for her recovery. A shock could send her reeling back to the depressed state she was in before Ben came along, and I don't want that to happen. Glen justified in his mind that he could not chance Martha relapsing into her depression.

When he returned home from Beaumont, he opened his suitcase in the privacy of his own room and took out the poster that he was sure identified Ben as Cain Porter. He carefully placed it in a drawer with the other mementos he had once hoped to pass on to his son Billy.

As the weeks passed, Glen became more preoccupied and agitated with guilt, thinking about how he was deceiving both Ben and Martha by keeping Ben's secret.

After work one rainy evening, all the men came in for supper, except Glen. They waited for him until Martha grew concerned about supper getting cold.

"You boys go ahead and eat your supper. Glen can eat when he gets in."

Ben could see the worry in her face, knowing that Glen was never late.

"Martha, I ain't seen him since morning. It's kinda grim out there, since it stopped raining," Wendell said.

"Well, he probably got sidetracked someplace, but it ain't like Glen being late," Martha worried.

Seeing her concern, Ben grabbed his rain gear, a couple of biscuits, and headed to the barn. When the men got through with supper, they joined him with lanterns and a stretcher, ready to go looking for Glen. "Boys, this doesn't look good. I got a bad feeling about Glen," Ben admitted.

It was almost dusk when more dense fog moved in, typical Texas weather that time of the year.

"How about we split up and shoot twice if we find Glen?" Ben instructed.

Heading to different parts of the ranch than where they had worked that day. Ben had one other section of the pasture in mind that the men had not covered, so he decided to check it himself.

"I didn't want to say anything in front of Martha, but something's bound to have happened to him." The men agreed, and then split up, going their separate ways.

The trail became very unpredictable as dark set in, and still there were no traces of Glen or his horse.

The men probed everywhere: the fields, corral, and areas all around the ranch, but all seemed in vain. They continued to call out Glen's name as they went about searching in various places he could have traveled. Finally, when Ben arrived at the one area they had yet to search, he saw part of the fence down. Stopping his horse short of a grove of trees, he heard a horse neigh. *That has to be Glen's horse*, he thought. Sitting quietly, listening, he heard a soft muffled sound. "Somebody help me." Ben knew it was Glen, although the voice was no more than a whisper.

When he heard the voice again, he drew his gun and shot two times in the air. He first came upon Glen's horse, lying on its side, dying from huge open wounds over parts of his body. He fired a couple more rounds to put down the injured horse. No sooner had he holstered his gun, he heard a loud rushing noise coming towards him at lightning speed. There was no time for him to think; only react. Ben dropped the lantern, and with one swift motion, drew his gun and shot Buddy (the old bull Glen had refused to slaughter) right between the eyes. He knew it had to be Buddy who trampled the fence, gored the horse, and apparently, Glen, too.

The lantern fell into the briar bushes, but the dampness from the rain kept it from igniting. Glen was on the opposite side, farther away from the brush, wrapped in barbed wire. Ben rushed toward the voice of his injured friend.

"Glen, where are you?" he shouted! Then he heard the very weak voice again.

"Over here, I'm all tangled in this damn mess of barbwire."

About that time, Wendell and the other boys rode up with the stretcher to transport Glen home.

"Boys, bring the stretcher closer so we don't have to carry him so far. Glen, you hang in there 'cause you got some broken bones, and it's bound to hurt." The first thing they had to do was get him out of the wire that entangled his body.

"Just get me home boys, that's all I ask."

Glen cried out when they moved him, but it was necessary in order to free him from the wire. There was blood and scratches all over his body from his writhing movements, where he had tried to free himself from the barbs. He didn't realize it, but the wire was what saved him from the bull. If Buddy had been able to get through the wire, he would have killed him for sure.

Once free, they lifted his broken body onto the stretcher. "Thank God y'all got to me when you did. I couldn't have lasted much longer. Thank you boys, for finding me."

Glen could see Ben's concern for him.

Later he described how Buddy frightened his horse and caused him to be thrown into the barbed wire.

"I shore thought he was going to finish me off," Glen repeated himself, as euphoria set in. "I sure hate you had to put my horse down, but I knew he was a goner from that damn bulls attack."

"Glen, you don't worry about your horse, we'll get you another one as soon as you're able to ride."

Being dragged on the back of the stretcher was rough going with the injuries he had sustained. But finally, Glen became quiet.

"I think he passed out," said one of the men.

Wendell shouted, "I'm on my way to fetch Doctor Wells. I'll meet y'all back at the house. The doctor was an old friend of Glen's, and by the time they arrived, he was there waiting for his patient.

Martha was wringing her hands while her husband was being examined. They were all worried, but Ben was there for her when she received the news about Glen's condition.

Dr. Wells addressed Martha, "I want you to be brave, Martha. Glen would want that."

"Why? Is Glen going to be alright?"

"I wish it was good news, but that old bull did some real damage when he gored him. Glen's in bad shape and I suspect he ain't gonna walk again. There ain't nothing we can do to make him better, just wait and see how he comes out of this," said Doc Wells. Martha felt her world crashing around her as she heard the news.

"If you got kin, best let 'em know, and Martha, you best get Glen's house in order in case we lose him."

Her fear was losing Glen, just like her son. *"Thank God I have Ben to help me through this,"* she contemplated. She turned to Ben and saw the gentle look in his eyes and knew she could count on him helping her through this crisis.

The weeks that followed were difficult for the man who had been so active and now had reconciled to never walk again. They thought it best to hide the truth that he was dying, but sometimes a man just knows these things. So Glen went about preparing for his death without anyone knowing.

The physical pain he suffered didn't compare to the heartfelt pain he anguished for Martha. He worried about what would happen to her with him not around to care for her. He also felt the burden of guilt, spun from deceiving Ben of his identity. Seeing the goodness in this young man did not ease his conscience. Even knowing Ben was a bright aspiring lawyer was not enough for him to break Martha's heart, should he tell Ben the truth.

The days ahead were tough going around the ranch. Work went on under the circumstances, but in the meantime, Glen's body continued to wither away.

It was mid-afternoon one day when one of the neighbors came to fetch Ben. *Glen must be worse*, he thought.

"Thank God I found you. Martha needs you now! The doctor's with Glen, but it ain't lookin' good." Ben jumped on his horse and headed back to the ranch. Martha met him as soon as he rode up.

"Come quick, Glen needs to see you. I'm afraid he ain't gonna be here much longer."

The doctor and Martha were praying that Glen would last until Ben arrived, and were relieved when he rode up. He saw Martha as he ran into the house.

"Ben, he's still holding on waiting fer ya'."

"Martha, are you sure? Ben asked. "I don't want to take time away from you."

"Don't you worry. I've been with Glen all morning, and he asked to speak to you alone. He's got something important to tell you, but he won't tell anybody but you. I think he's holding on to say goodbye."

With hat in hand, Ben walked in close to Glen's bed. He was surprised to see him somewhat coherent.

"Hey Glen, how are you doing?"

"I've seen better days, son."

"You hang in there, you hear? We need you to get well and help us run this ranch."

"It ain't likely to happen, and that's why I needed to see you. Before I go, I need to come clean with ya'. Ben, you go over to that third drawer and pull out that poster under my clothes." Glen pointed in the direction of the chest of drawers.

Ben walked over and opened the drawer, wondering what Glen knew that he didn't. He found the poster, but had no idea what it meant.

"I didn't mean to hurt you by keeping this poster a secret," Glen said. "I was thinking of Martha, and how you reminded her of Billy. I know it was wrong of me." Glen was speaking so softly that Ben could hardly understand him. "I knew I should have told you, but I couldn't bring myself to break Martha's heart. I know it ain't no excuse, and all I can do is hope you can forgive me."

Ben held up the poster and saw the picture that resembled him.

"Is this about me?" he asked.

"Yeah…I've had it checked out, and son, this is your past. Ben, I had no right ta keep this from you. You had every right to know who you are, and it was wrong of me to keep it from you and Martha."

Ben could see Glen slipping away as he laid the poster down.

"You don't worry about me and what's on that poster, you hear? Glen, let me set your mind at ease; if it hadn't been for you and Martha, no telling what would have come of me." Ben couldn't hold back the tears as he choked up. "Glen, you're like a father."

Ben was broken up, seeing the man he came to love, beg for his forgiveness.

"I don't deserve your forgiveness, but now I can die in peace, knowing you know." Glen tried to laugh, but got strangled. "Ben, be careful when you tell Martha 'cause she still doesn't know about this. This was all my doing."

Ben tried to comfort him, but with each word he spoke he could tell Glen was slipping away. Ben picked up the poster and put it away for another time.

As soon as he explained about Martha, he closed his eyes and never regained consciousness.

He lasted until that evening, when he took his last breath. Ben and Martha were by his side. "Now you're with Billy," Ben said, as he placed his hand on Glen's forehead.

For now, all he could think about was the man who treated him like his son. How could he begrudge him for trying to protect his wife. Martha and Glen had become his family.

That night, after he and Martha planned the funeral, she excused herself and went to bed. Ben took the opportunity to examine the poster. He read enough to get a good sense of who he was, but now it didn't seem to matter, since he still couldn't remember his name or his family.

He had always been sure that when, or if he got news of who he was and where he belonged, that the memories would come flooding in. That didn't happen. The man described on the poster seemed like someone else, except for the physical description and the picture. He still felt like Ben Gentry with a short life story. He wondered if that would ever change as time went on. For now, though, it was life as usual helping Martha get over the death of her life-long husband.

Glen had been dead over a month when the news of a shocking murder took center stage in Beaumont. Everyone and his neighbor was gossiping about a man in Woodville who killed his father over a woman. The papers had painted Aggie as a conniving wench who manipulated her husband into killing his own father to take over his estate. They mercifully left out the question of her son or his parentage. Every woman waited to hear the news that had become embellished and blown out of proportion by the news.

Martha was caught up in the hype just like everyone else—talking about it incessantly around Ben. She read about the torrid love affair between the man's son and a woman who married the son for his money, who drew 20 years in jail. Not letting the facts get in the way of a good story, the newspaper had put their own spin on things in order to sell more papers.

For fear of tarnishing Glen's memory, Ben had been withholding from Martha the information concerning his true identity.

They had just finished supper one evening, when Martha began asking Ben if he had heard about the murder in Woodville, only 60 miles North of Beaumont.

"I heard some of the men talking about it, but I don't pay attention to gossip like that."

"This ain't gossip. Why don't you read fer yourself?"

Ben read the headlines and then decided to read more of the details.

"Yeah, that's pretty bad when a son takes a gun to his own father. I haven't had time to read this until now," Ben said.

As he continued to read, he caught the name Aggie Dawson. He couldn't believe it was the same Aggie that had saved him two years earlier. He knew there had to be a mistake, for the Aggie he knew would not be involved in a murder case. He remembered how she ran away without saying goodbye to him and how rejected he felt. The more he read, the more he learned about her husband, and what drove him to kill his Pa.

Perhaps she was married, and that's why she left without telling me goodbye, he reconciled himself.

Ben thought back to the time when he and Aggie were intimate, and how beautiful she was. *I never thought I would hear from her like this*, he kept thinking.

Martha saw Ben's expression change as he continued to read.

"Ben, is there something wrong? You look like you've seen a ghost," Martha said.

He couldn't speak at first, lost in the thought of Aggie and her plight.

"Martha, it's this woman everyone is talking about... I think I might know her."

"Noooo," she said. "How on earth could you possibly know Aggie Dawson a girl like this?"

"Remember me telling you the story about the young woman who found me when I was near death? This has to be the same woman, unless there's more than one Aggie Dawson in this area."

"But that's been a long time. Perhaps ya' got her mixed up."

"Martha, I know you may not understand this, but I have to go and see if this is the Aggie I know. I think she may need my help." He was thinking about the poster that indicated he had a law background, wondering if his apparent legal mind might come forth. Occasionally, Ben had flashes of memory, but what he remembered were bits and pieces of his past that made no sense, no connecting points. Still he had no clear memory of anyone connected to him, other than Aggie.

Martha did not fully understand why Ben felt the need to rescue Aggie Dawson, but she wasn't going to stand in his way, nor question him.

"I know you well enough to know I ain't gonna change your mind, so you go ahead and don't worry 'bout me. Wendell has been doing better since Glen's been gone. I think he sees now that he has to pull his own weight."

The next morning, Martha saw Ben off on his trip north to Woodville. When he got to the cattle gap, he stopped and waved goodbye to her again.

After Ben left, Martha was cleaning Ben's room when she opened a drawer to place some of his clothes inside. It was there she saw a rolled up poster that evidently belonged to him. She unrolled it with complete disregard for Ben's privacy. Curiosity took control of her senses. She read it and wondered why he had not told her he knew his identity. "Cain Porter," she said quietly to herself. After carefully studying the poster, for an instant she imagined he had used Aggie Dawson as an excuse to leave without saying goodbye. She immediately felt ashamed for even thinking he would leave without telling her goodbye. *He'll be back, but he won't be Ben, he'll be Cain Porter.*

It was late evening when Cain rode into Woodville. He first stopped and asked for directions to Aggie's home. Of course, everyone knew where she lived, which was no surprise to him, since her name had been splashed all over the papers. Impressed with how large and beautiful her ranch was, he had no idea Aggie could afford such a place. *Not bad at all*, he thought.

He dismounted and approached the front door and knocked. When he got no response, he went around back to see if anyone was there. As he turned to go back to the front of the house, he walked right into the barrel of a shotgun.

"Mister, don't even think about moving!" A startled Ben froze in his tracks.

Aggie could not believe her eyes, nor could Cain believe his. It was Aggie, and she was more beautiful than she was before she left Henderson. Startled to see him, she dropped the gun and wrapped her arms around him. "Oh Ben…"

He held her. "Aggie, I came as soon as I heard."

She thought he was talking about the baby, and that he had somehow found out through the papers that she had a young toddler that could be his.

"When you left I didn't think I would ever see you again," Ben said.

She backed away and looked into his eyes. "Have you regained your memory?"

"No, I'm still the same, but at least I know my real name and that I am a lawyer. I found out from a poster that my real name is Cain Porter, and that my family lives in San Augustine. I'm not married, but I'm the son of Elizabeth and Vick Porter.

"San Augustine?" Ben, that's where I'm from. Remember me telling you about San Augustine when we were in Henderson?"

"I'm not sure, it's been so long ago."

"You must have come when you heard about the baby."

Cain didn't think anything of what she was saying. "So, she and Seth had a baby together. What was so unusual about that?"

Although trusting the man she thought to be Ben; she wondered how he would react learning he is a father.

"Cain... I like the name, it has a nice ring to it. It suits you.

"As far as I'm concerned, I'm still Ben Gentry."

"Where did the Gentry name come from?" she asked.

"I saw it on a sign," Cain laughed. "You know... I needed a last name," he chuckled.

He looked at her and thought how strange it was to find her through the paper.

"Aggie, I read what happened to your husband and that's why I'm here."

"Thank you, but I need to talk to you about something else that's more important. I only ask for your understanding and not be upset with me."

He studied her as he saw a look that he had not seen on her before. She suddenly appeared a bit gloomy as she approached what appeared to be a bedroom or study. Cain could not imagine what she was trying to tell him. "How could I be upset with you, when you saved my life?" he said.

He followed her down the hall until she opened the door to a child's room. There in the corner of the room was a toddler hanging onto the railing of his bed looking at him. At first it did not register, but there was something very familiar about his smile. It was like looking into a mirror. Cain suddenly remembered baby pictures of himself from his past. Finally, he was beginning to remember a few things, but not nearly enough.

He walked over to the child and saw the most piercing blue eyes, just like his. There was no doubt he was looking into the face of his son, or someone who looked very much like a son he imagined he would have. He turned and looked at Aggie, who had tears running down her face. She began shaking her head, "yes." "Cain, I want you to meet Jared— your son. I didn't know how to find you and explain. I did make an effort. I sent someone back to the cabin where we lived to find out if they knew your whereabouts. When they failed to find you, I was sure you had regained your memory and left. I didn't know what else to do. I even thought you might have a family of your own. Please forgive me and try to understand," she sobbed.

Cain took a step back, for he was in complete surprise. "Aggie, I don't know what to say." He picked up his son and held him close, and in that second, he knew he could never let him go. He tried to understand what Aggie must have gone through. "Does your husband know about Jared?" Cain Asked. Aggie shook her head yes.

After Jared went to sleep, they talked seriously about what was in store for their son if she should keep him.

"Cain before we discuss Jared there is something we need to talk about," she urged.

"Aggie, why don't we talk about your husband and what happened?"

"Cain please, I first need to explain about a man called Jonathan Petty, my half brother. When I was a young girl he raped me and murdered my mother. He didn't know at the time that I was his half sister. Since I'm a threat he wants me dead and will kill anyone who gets in his way. I'm a threat to be dealt with." Hearing the word Jonathan struck a nerve with Cain.

"Cain, it's important for you to know that I'm very much in love with my husband. When you and I were together I wasn't ready for marriage. Seth is a good man and didn't deserve a father like Parley Jackson. And now he's in the Huntsville Prison and doesn't belong there.

"I'm sorry about your husband but Aggie, I need to know why you left Henderson without saying goodbye? You just up and left!"

"I know, but I was mixed up at the time. I was 5 miles down the road when I felt the note I planned to leave for you in my pocket. I started to turn around and go back, but I knew if I did I would never have the courage to leave again, and I was determined to get away. I'm sure I have the note around here someplace, I'll look so you can see that I'm telling the truth." As she explained, he began to understand. Then she told him about Seth and why he shot his father. She rambled on jumping from one subject to the other. "Cain, you have to believe me Jonathan will kill our son and me. He's the devil, and he will kill all the heirs who stand in the way of his birthright he was denied of. I'm also worried about Johnson, and his daughter Eileen. Aggie had no recollection that Johnson and Eileen were already dead. When Cain heard the name Eileen, cold chills ran over him. There was something familiar about the name and he wondered why. "Aggie, I think I know Eileen. Can you tell me something about her family?"

The more she spoke of her plight, the more empathy he had for her, and a connection with the Petty name. "Cain, I'm the one who can send Jonathan to prison. When you were in San Augustine, did you ever hear of Johnson and Jonathan Petty? It seems so long ago, but we all lived on a cotton farm called Pecan Plantation in San Augustine. You've heard of San Augustine, haven't you? Anyway, I learned that my mother was the mistress of Hamp Petty, Johnson and Jonathan's father. That's how I was conceived. Jonathan must have found out about my mother and their father just before he raped me and murdered my mother. I was so naïve when I lived there. Of course, everything was kept secret, and I'm sure, my brothers still don't know I'm their half-sister. Barney, who married my mother, did a good job keeping it confidential until he was on his deathbed. That's how I found out who I am, and who my real father was."

"So Barney married your mother and raised you as his very own?" Cain asked.

"Yes, he married my mama and Hamp paid him $5,000 to keep the family secret. I never knew the difference until Barney was dying. That was just before I found you on the side of the road. I never told you, but he left the entire $5000 to me upon his death. He never spent a cent of it…just saved it all for me. That money is what I used to buy this place."

"But Aggie, this place is worth 10 times more than five thousand dollars."

"I know, but Ms. Mixson was ready to sell, since Seth was harassing her. She had been putting up with him for years, and when her husband died, she wanted to get out. She knew no one would buy her property with a troublemaker like Parley Jackson living next door. Ms. Mixson would have never sold the property to Parley, and when I came along, she seized the opportunity. Quite frankly, I thought I could handle Parley Jackson. He gave me time to settle in and that's when he began creating problems for me, cutting my fence and stealing some of my Herefords."

"You've been through it, haven't you Aggie?"

"You don't know the half of it. The town knew Parley wanted my property, and now that he's dead, they're blaming me. I'm sure you've read all the stories in the papers."

"Aggie, they'll get over it. You just have to remain strong within yourself."

"In the meantime, they are destroying me and my child. Cain I know my husband, and he would never purposely kill anyone. He snapped from all the years of abuse. I know he didn't mean to shoot his father in the back and was probably protecting me. The way I feel,

Parley Jackson won, even though he's dead. I don't know if I'm thick skinned enough to stay here?"

"Aggie, you don't give up on this place. I have a feeling everything is going to work out for you, if you just hang in there."

"But Cain, there's more…I need you to take Jared as far away from here as possible. It's for our son's safety. My husband needs me. I love him too much, and I want to be as close to him as possible. I can't put our son through this."

"Aggie I don't think you realize that Seth is in prison for the next twenty years, and how a man changes during that period of time."

"The way you talk you must have known someone in prison." Aggie said.

Later that night Cain wondered why he suddenly had a deep connection with prison life. "How would I know—unless I've been there?

~

Jonathan returned to Circle J one last time to discuss Aggie Dawson with the James brothers. After hearing the news of her being alive, it began eating away at him about what she was capable of, if she went to the Sheriff.

He became paranoid after seeing Elizabeth talk to Parley, it unleashed a beast inside him that even frightened Lonnie and Dudley.

"I want you boys to hunt Aggie down and kill her…you hear?" He spoke in a newly adopted combative tone.

"Does that mean if we kill 'er, that we be going ta Panther Holler fer the treasure?"

"You damn right, and I'm here to tell you that Vick Porter will be leading us every step of the way. We'll take care of him and that wife of his when they least expect it. Y'all understand what I'm telling ya'?"

The men looked at each and smiled. Lonnie however, had another plan and that was to kill Jonathan as soon as he fulfilled his usefulness.

The next morning, the James' set out at first light on their way to murder Aggie. They had been riding for two days when they entered the town of Woodville, Texas. Concerned about killing a woman they had never met, they began second-guessing why they were chosen to carry out Jonathan's dirty work, risking their lives and freedom.

Before they walked into the local boarding house, Dudley decided to talk seriously about his part in killing her.

"Jonathan ought to be doing his own dirty work. Something tells me killin' that woman is gonna be a big bad mistake."

Lonnie knew his brother would start in with his bellyaching, re-neging as usual. "You don't have to worry about killin' 'er. I don't thank I wanna hear ya' crying cause ya' got a little blood on yer hands. Ya' always leave it ta me... every dang time. Yer nothing but dead weight I'm carryin' around."

"Well, I ain't the one that volunteered ta kill 'er. Yer the one that opened yer big mouth volunteerin' ta do Jonathan's dirty work. Can't ya' tell he's nuttier than a fruit cake? What if he doubts ya' killed 'er after she's dead. Then what?" Lonnie ignored him.

~

Cain had the strangest feeling that he knew Eileen. I have to find out, he thought, and the court records would be the best place. He supposed that was the lawyer in him. He knew his best protection taking Jared from Aggie, was to have adoption papers drawn up. When asked what she thought of an adoption, she fully agreed that it was best for their boy to make everything legal. She understood completely and insisted that he go into town alone to draw up the papers, since she did not want the townfolk knowing her business.

Cain also thought this would be a good time to inquire about Eileen Petty, and possibly find out how he might know her.

As he rode into town, unbeknownst to the James boys, Cain was riding toward them on the same road. They knew Aggie's place was close by but they were not sure of the exact location. Seeing the man approaching them, they thought it would be a good idea to ask.

By this time, bits and pieces of Cain's memory began to resurface. He knew there was something connected to the Petty name that puzzled him. *Could it be that he knew the Pettys? What if returning to San Augustine placed Jared in danger?* These were questions that needed to be answered before bringing his son into harms way. He could not shake the feeling that someone wanted him dead.

Riding into town, Cain would never have guessed the two men approaching him might give him answers regarding his identity. As the James boys got closer, their minds were consumed with the task of killing Aggie, and not to the approaching rider.

When they finally met Cain face to face, every drop of blood drained from their faces consumed with the thought that they were seeing a ghost. They were sure seeing Cain was a warning of what could happen if they carried out their plan to kill Aggie. The boys turned their horses around and galloped away. Simultaneously, their hasty about face triggered a flashback to the night of the ambush and it registered to Cain that these men were responsible for his injuries. That's Lonnie and Dudley James, he said out loud. As soon as he said their names, most of his forgotten memories came flooding back to him. He remembered Lucy's death, and of course, all the pain associated with losing her. Then he thought of Orson, who died when they were both ambushed.

After the James' were out of sight, Dudley shouted, "Lonnie, you know who that was?" "Yeah, I know… it's a warning. Let's git the hell outta here." The men were running like two scared rabbits frightened that they had seen a ghost.

Seeing the men and recognizing them, Cain now remembered everything. *My mother and father must think I'm dead*, he thought.

Finally, he remembered his wedding to Eileen Petty and how Buck Dupree murdered her and their unborn child. The memories were heartbreaking as he recalled having to move to San Augustine in order to manage the Petty estate in which he was named the beneficiary.

He was reeling as the memories flashed through his mind like a speeding train, so much to absorb, the tragic events of Lucy's death. He remember it all; the love of his parents and Orson and then finally, Jonathan who orchestrated the ambush that killed Orson and left him for dead. His heart was heavy thinking of Lucy and the manor that went up in flames—such a senseless death. Cain was devastated for Lucy was his true love. *How can I go on without her?* This was a question that lingered with him as each thought became a reality.

Cain felt empty, losing both Lucy, and Orson. Still, it was bittersweet recollecting his past and preparing for the future. "Oh, my God! What have I missed since then?" he said out loud.

Seeing Lonnie and Dudley in Woodville puzzled him, unless they were one up on him and followed him there. *Why would they turn and run away if they were looking for me? It has to do with Aggie*, he thought. Suddenly, he remembered the letter that accused Jonathan of raping Aggie and murdering her mother. *Now it makes sense. Jonathan must have sent Lonnie and Dudley to kill Aggie, since he knew she could testify against him and have him hanged or sent to prison, but how and why did the James brothers get involved and end up in San Augustine? There's a connection and I intend to find out*, Cain thought. Paramount on his mind was the imminent danger Aggie and Jared were in, which was all the more reason for him to take his son and find refuge someplace where Jared could not be found. He thought of Martha, and knew she would be the one to take care of Jared until the problem with Jonathan and the brothers were solved. Cain now knew that Jonathan and the boys were responsible for the murder of Orson, and him being left for dead.

After the two men were out of sight, he continued his journey into town, while planning his next move.

When Cain returned to Aggie's place, he told her about running into the two men that ambushed Orson and him. "Those two men murdered my friend and left me for dead. This is when you found me and nursed me back to health. Aggie, I think Jonathan sent them here to possibly do you harm."

She was quiet, but then became frightened for her son.

"This is all the more reason you have to take Jared and leave. Get him as far away as possible, and promise me you won't be going back to San Augustine with Jared as long as those two men and Jonathan are alive. Can you do that?"

"Aggie, I promise you that I will not ever expose our son to danger. You can count on that."

"Thank you, I knew if I ever found you that I could count on you to protect our son."

"Aggie, there's a little more that you should know."

As his story unfolded, she could not believe everything he was telling her.

"Cain, I can't believe this. You were married to Eileen, my niece?"

"Aggie, I had no idea you were the heir to Pecan Plantation, and when they told me my marriage to Eileen made me the beneficiary, I could hardly believe it. That's the reason Jonathan wanted me dead… so he could step in and reclaim what he thinks is his."

"Cain, you listen to me. I don't want any part of Pecan Plantation. It's yours and Jared's. There are too many bad memories, and I just as soon stay away. I have all I can handle right here… so, don't go worrying about me. I have two men working for me that can deal with anyone who steps foot on this ranch.

One other thing you need to know is Seth discovered oil on my land, and I'm not about to sell and leave. Then there's Parley's place… believe me, I have plenty going on without adding more. Just take care of yourself, and love our son. He needs his daddy."

Aggie signed the papers for she wanted to do the right thing by protecting Jared.

The next morning, she could hardly accept her baby leaving with Cain.

She held on to her emotions, trying to be strong in front of Cain and Jared, but afterwards she crumbled emotionally. She will always remember her little boy straddled in the saddle in front of his daddy. They belong together, she justified. For a moment, she wished she had never left Ben when they were together in Henderson. *My life has turned into a complete mess since then*, she bemoaned.

The trip was not as bad as Cain thought it would be, but telling Martha that he would be leaving again was something he was not looking forward to. *This is going to be hard, since Martha doesn't know that I've regained my memory.*

Martha was curious when she saw Cain ride up with a child. Puzzled, she took the boy, as Cain slid out of the saddle.

"Well now, what have we got here, Ben?" She began to question Cain with her eyes. Cain blinked reminding him he had a lot to impart to Martha.

"Martha, I guess you've figured out why I had to go see Aggie. This is my son, Jared." "Your son?" she asked.

Martha could have been knocked over with a feather. "I had no idea you had a son." "Neither did I," Cain replied. "He's a happy little boy 'cause now he's with his daddy, where he belongs," Cain assured Jared.

"So your son's name is Jared?" Martha asked. "Yes, this is little Jared Porter." She smiled at the boy sweetly.

"Now Jared's with his Aunt Martha, and I'm going to make sure he has one of my fresh baked cookies. Have ya' fed him?" Cain had no reason to worry about leaving Jared with Martha, for he saw her instant love for the boy.

She picked him up and held him close. "How 'bout it, little fella, let's go get you something to eat. I bet yer hungry as a bear." He watched as she carried him into the house, and thought once again how sad it's going to be when he has to leave Jared with her.

That evening, after Jared was put to bed, Martha opened up to Cain about the poster she found while cleaning his room. *She deserves to know the truth*, he decided.

"Martha, you remember when I talked to Glen the day he died? He wanted me to know that he knew who I was. I reckon he thought I was a gunfighter, the way I handled a gun, and that's why he began his inquiry. Glen had run across the poster that told him about Cain Porter missing. All the pieces fit, and he knew it had to be me since there was a picture."

"So Glen knew who you were and didn't tell you...Cain?" she asked, to see how it felt calling him by his given name. It would take some time getting used to it...

"Martha, Glen knew, but I'm not telling you this because I feel bad. Glen was a good man and he was afraid that you would have a setback if I left. He knew how unhappy you were when you lost Billy, and he didn't want you to relapse into the state you were in before. I don't blame him."

"Still, he should have told you what he knew and he shoulda told me, too."

Martha smiled and patted Cain on the back. "I don't know if I'll ever get used to calling you Cain. Ben seems to suit you better."

She thought a minute and then said, "I want to apologize to you for Glen. He should never have kept that poster from you. I hope you can forgive him."

"Martha, I don't blame Glen, and I told him that before he died. You and Glen mean everything to me, and I don't know what would have become of me if y'all hadn't taken me in. You're like family, and this is why I want to leave Jared with you. I know you will love him and take care of him until I return."

"Why of course, but can you tell me where yer going?"

"Let's just say I have some unfinished business."

"I hope you're not going to put yourself in danger. This boy needs his daddy."

"It's because of Jared I have to do this. I hope you can trust me."

"Well, you don't worry. Little Jared and me will be here when you come back. As for the ranch, Wendell has been helping more and I think he'll do jest fine."

"I'll talk to him before I leave, and there's something else. After I get settled, you and me are going to have a long talk. But it will have to wait until I get back before we can. Do you think you can wait?"

"Ben... I mean Cain, you know I'm going to be wondering the whole time you're gone about that secret of yers. I been thinking... when you leave I want you to go in Glen's old Model T. As a matter of fact, I want you to have it."

"Thank you Martha, but I think I need my horse where I'm going."

"I guessed you'd be leaving when you came back. I'm really gonna miss you, but at least I'm going to have Jared here to keep me company. So you go, and come back when you're done."

The workings of the brain will never be fully understood, and amnesia is just one of those mysteries. Attempts to understand by the use of logic are destined to end in failure. So it goes with Cain's use of a pistol. Before he lost his memory, he was lucky to hit the side of a barn. But somehow, amnesia wiped out his ineptness to the point where he was considered to have the prowess of a professional gunslinger. And now, even though all other memories have returned, his confidence and skills with a pistol remained with him. He was now as good as his Pa—maybe even better.

Chapter 22

It was quiet as a grave the day Elizabeth returned home after running into Jonathan Petty. He frightened her so, that she was ready to leave San Augustine prematurely if she had to, getting as far away as possible.

After Vick and Elizabeth retired to bed, she had difficulty falling asleep. During the night, her fears were manifested in her subconscious, causing her to awaken, screaming Jonathan's name.

Vick was startled awake when Elizabeth called out. "Something's wrong!" he said. He had no idea she was living her own nightmare.

"Elizabeth, you're dreaming. Is it Jonathan whot has you so upset?"

"I dreamt he was chasing me."

Vick tried to reassure her of her safety and to comfort her.

"Lizzie…you're safe… don't be frightened. No one's going to hurt you as long as I'm around. Jonathan would know better to even show a hint of an intent to harm you."

He could see she was deeply upset.

"Vick, we have to leave and go back to Jonesboro, and the sooner the better," Elizabeth cried.

"How long have you been thinking this way?" Vick asked.

"I know you want to stay and wait for Cain, but I'm afraid it's time we accept he's not coming back. And the man responsible lives right next door."

Vick sensed Lizzie had had enough of San Augustine, and her mind was set on leaving.

He understood her point was justified, but he had no idea she felt as strongly as she did.

"Lizzie, you're right. Yesterday, seeing Jonathan's agitation, made me realize it's not worth risking more lives. I know you've been unhappy ever since you've come to Texas."

"If Cain was alive, everything would be different. But when he went missing, this town changed for us, and living next door to this killer makes it even worse," she explained.

He had never seen Elizabeth so worried and in this state of mind. It was apparent living near Jonathan was having its toll on her. He knew she would continue being troubled until they left.

"You know I want to make you happy, and if leaving is the answer, then so be it," Vick said.

"You know I'm not one to complain, but without Cain, I don't feel this is home. And I know Orson would rather be back in Arkansas if we are there," she said between sobs.

Vick felt sorry for her and knew he had to do something—and quick.

"Was it that stranger I saw you talking with today?"

"No, it was Jonathan…he frightened me. I've never seen such evil in a man's eyes. He's up to no good, and when he finally loses it, I don't want to be anywhere around. I can't stand the way he stares at me."

"What do you mean?"

"He makes me feel unclean, like he's undressing me."

"You should have told me about this! Tell you what, tomorrow we'll talk to Orson about leaving."

"What about Hop?"

"I've been aiming to talk to you about that. You know he has no place to go and I wouldn't feel right telling him we're moving on without him. You know he's risked a lot for us going up against Jonathan. It just wouldn't be right in my estimation."

"But Vick… where will he stay? Our place is not large enough for us, let alone another man living with us."

"You let me worry about that. Maybe he can stay with Orson. He'd be good for him."

"Don't you think that would be imposing? You best let Orson do his own inviting."

"Right now, I want you to stop worrying. I promise tomorrow I will get this all worked out."

"Ohhh you! You think you have it all figured out."

Lizzie, I know you want to leave soon, but can you give me about a week to get repairs done on the house before we go?" he asked as she kissed his cheek. "Okay, now curl up here with me and let's get some sleep."

While the Porters were getting ready to make their move, Jonathan was on the verge of a meltdown. He had such contempt for the Porters that he began obsessing about Elizabeth. He wanted everything Vick had, including his wife.

Vick had noticed Jonathan "packing" his silver plated .45, and wondered what it would take for him to use it. This made him concerned for Elizabeth's safety. The next morning, Vick did as he promised, and suggested to Orson and Hop that they should all go to Arkansas because of Jonathan's volatile behavior. "Hop, we sure hope you will give Arkansas a try." They all agreed it was time to distance themselves from a man exhibiting psychotic behavior. Hop responded, "I'm happy you asked, and I'll help out all I can."

Jonathan secluded himself inside his home, continuing his rampages behind closed doors by destroying expensive works of art, paintings, lamps, and memorabilia that were known treasures of his childhood home. He went into a hallway and blasted glass containers full of silver, overturning curio cabinets filled with precious collectibles. It was there that he discovered a large painting of his mother.

He stopped momentarily, looked at it, and began to cry. "Mother," he said softly. He touched her face, then ran his hand across the picture as if to show his affection. His exaggerated mood swings were out of control, when suddenly, he picked up a fireplace poker and began smashing the painting to bits. After realizing he had destroyed her picture, he fell on his knees and wept, totally unpredictable. "Mother…why did you leave me?" he cried out. Whimpering like a child, he rolled up in a fetal position and drifted off to sleep. When he awoke, he saw his house in shambles, and wondered who could have trashed it. As he looked at the mess, he remembered bits and pieces of the night before. "It's because of the Porter's! They've caused me this distress!" he sickly rationalized.

Jonathan went about cleaning up the broken glass, when Matilda walked into the house, ready for a day's work. She was stunned at seeing the wreckage, and wondered what was wrong with the man she knew who was obsessed with cleanliness.

"Meester Jonathan… what happen?" she asked.

"None of your business! You're late! You need to show up on time!"

"I'm sorry. My mother is sick, and I had to care for her."

Jonathan looked at Matilda as if she was lying. He noticed she was not wearing her beautiful opal ring. "Where is that ring of yours… that opal?" Jonathan had planned to take it from her.

"Oh my beau' ti' ful ring is lost. Someone stole it when I was cleaning."

Again he thought she was lying. "You had no business with a ring like that in the first place. A girl like you doesn't need an opal ring. You're nothing but a housekeeper."

"But Meester Jonathan, you were the one who gave me the ring. Don't you remember?" Matilda sensed she could be in danger. She had seen changes in him, but had no idea he was going loco.

"Meester Jonathan, I tink' I need to go take care of my mother. I will come back tomorrow and work for you."

Jonathan had no intention of letting her leave, after he saw the fear that transcended from her face and throughout her body. This excited him, and the animal inside him, that only his victims had seen, came alive. She was a young innocent, weak girl, which made him feel powerful over his prey. Walking toward her, Jonathan began to hallucinate, and suddenly, in his mind, Matilda became Elizabeth. She began shaking uncontrollably as he walked toward her.

"Elizabeth, you are frightened. Are you afraid of me?" he asked.

She did not respond, as she surveyed all the exits that stood between her and Jonathan. "There's no place to run," she thought.

"I must leave Mr. Jonathan. I 'tink you are not well. Maybe I go and come back tomorrow." She began edging her way to the door. Jonathan reached in back of her and bolted it so she could not escape.

"Elizabeth, forget about leaving. You're staying."

"Meester Jonathan, I am Matilda. Why do you call me Elizabeth?"

There was terror in her eyes as he took her face and squeezed it in his hand.

"Elizabeth, don't try and play games." Jonathan could feel the desire within as he grabbed Matilda. She struggled violently as he dragged her down to the wine cellar. He unlocked the door as she continued to squirm, trying to free herself.

Alarmed by his violent aggression, she began screaming at the top of her lungs, before he placed his hand over her mouth. "Scream all you want...no one will hear you. Not even Vick."

She could see he was suffering from delusions, and tried to convince him that she was Matilda, and that she should leave.

He pulled her around in front of him and began kissing her. She was repulsed at kissing a man old enough to be her father. In a moment's time, he had her down on the floor, trying to rape her.

"Please Meester Jonathan, I am Matilda. Don't you know who I am?"

He looked at her like he did not understand. Suddenly, he sprang to his feet when he recognized Matilda.

"You don't move, you hear?" he ordered. Afraid of his advances, she tried to keep him talking.

"Why are you doing this? Please let me go."

He went about pulling out drawers and scattering its contents on the floor. Then he found a rope and began holding it out in front of him, as if testing its strength, as he walked slowly towards her. In an attempt to save her, she ducked and ran around in back of a shelf containing several wine barrels. She pushed the barrels one at a time, sending them rolling in his direction. But her efforts were in vain. Jonathan kept walking around them and pushing them aside. Finally, she realized it was hopeless, for there was no place to run.

When he reached her, he was so angry that he grabbed her hands and struggled to bind her them with rope. Once done, he dragged her to a chair, making her sit while he bound her feet.

Matilda begged for her life. "Please let me go! I promise I won't tell anyone. You're a good man Meester Jonathan."

He took her face in his hands again. "You're not going anywhere, so stop your crying. Women…you're all alike."

"What are you going to do to me?" she asked.

Toying with her again, he thought about the beautiful ring.

"You tell me where the ring is and I may let you go."

"I told you already that someone came in and stole my ring. I don't know who it could be unless it was Meester Dudley. He tinks I stole the ring from him—remember?" Jonathan began pacing, as he wondered if she was telling the truth.

"Can I go now? Please, my mother is sick and she needs me."

Jonathan ignored her and walked out, leaving her alone in the cellar. He knew she wasn't going anywhere with her hands and feet bound. He needed time to think whether or not the James brothers were holding out on him. They ain't nothing but Arkansas trash, and the reason they came to San Augustine was to blackmail me.

It's all coming together, he thought. His mind was going a mile a minute, thinking of how two stupid gourd-heads were trying to outsmart him. He thought about their faces and how they would look when he finished them off. *They've been playing me all along, but now it's payback*, he schemed.

Jonathan began laughing, thinking about the brothers. He was so delighted with the thought of killing them that he went to the humidor and pulled out one of his finest cigars. He walked over to a shelf and got a new bottle of whiskey to have while he smoked.

Matilda knew she had to loosen her bindings in order to save herself. She kept twisting her small wrists, loosening them little by little. She had freed her hands completely when she heard footsteps coming down the cellar stairs. The bindings lay loosely across her wrists. "It's him," she feared. Jonathan arrived in the cellar with a large knife he used to gut sheep.

Matilda saw the knife and screamed. He ran the sharp blade underneath her chin, lightly scraping her skin.

"Please Meester Jonathan, don't do theese."

He toyed with her like a cat toys with a ball of twine.

"Matilda, how old are you?"

"Seventeen, eighteen next month," she whispered, "Now let me go!"

"See this knife? Can you imagine what mind-numbing pain you will feel in the most sensitive part of your body?" There was terror in Matilda's eyes as she twisted around in her chair. She prayed, *Holy Mother, please give me strength to fight to the end.*

The young girl wasn't going down without a fight, and as the adrenalin began to flow, she slipped her hands back out of the bindings. Before Jonathan knew it, she sprung forth with her feet still bound and scratched him with her long fingernails. They embedded deep into his flesh, and blood began running down the side of his face.

"Why you little bitch!" he shouted. Jonathan was furious, and slapped her so hard her small-frame body went flying across the cellar floor. Seeing her laying there helplessly, the wild beast in him came alive again. The last time that beast was unleashed was when he raped Aggie and murdered her mother with a pitchfork. It had reared its ugly head again, and it was time to feed his cravings.

Pain shot through Jonathan's face as he saw the blood on his hands. "Why don't you scream again? Go ahead…but it won't do you any good." He began telling her to scream over and over until he nearly choked the life out of her. Matilda, too afraid to cry, began coughing uncontrollably from lack of air.

There was hatred in his eyes as he began taunting her with the knife again. Now too weak to move, she was sure that one little tug might force him to kill her.

"Please, I will do as you want. Just let me live". This was the last thing Matilda said, as the knife was thrust through her heart.

As she took her last breath, the terrified expression on her face changed into a peaceful one.

"All you women are alike. None of you deserve to live," he said. He then laid her out on the floor of the wine cellar, and desecrated her young body.

Late that night, Jonathan took Matilda's cold stiff body out to the barn he shared with the Porters. Fear of being seen he hid her body and planned to dispose of it later the next day.

Plans often go asunder, for each time he planned to retrieve her body, the Porters were working outside their house. He couldn't afford to draw attention to himself; therefore, Matilda's body was left to decay.

When Matilda didn't come home, her father, Senor Galvez, came around asking questions about his daughter.

No one could tell him where she had gone, and Jonathan made up a lame excuse that she had run away to get married. Of course, Senor Galvez did not believe a word Jonathan said.

The Senor then asked the Porters if they had seen Matilda, which they had not. Vick took this opportunity to ask the Mexican if he would keep his horse while he was gone to Arkansas. He also asked him to keep a lookout for Cain, should he return to Pecan Plantation.

Finally it was time to go and all the necessary preparations had been made. Vick had to go to the barn and saddle his horse, since he planned to ride it to Senor Galvez's house.

During the early morning hours, just before sunrise, Hop and Vick walked out to the barn to fetch Vick's horse and saddle. Even before reaching the barn, a very familiar odor hit Vick in the face. Hop thought it was an animal that had died in the barn, but Vick knew it was no animal. That same odor had been etched in his mind forever, when as a young boy, he and his brother Sam found that family of four murdered at Panther Holler.

Once inside the barn, the stench was stifling.

"Vick...what in the hell is that? I need to git out of here," Hop said.

Walking away Hop said, "Sorry, Vick, but my stomach won't take this smell."

"Do what you have to do, but that smell is no animal," Vick assured him. They both walked from the barn.

"You telling me someone has died in the barn?"

"Died or murdered." Vick had a feeling this was the handiwork of Jonathan, but he knew he couldn't stay around to prove it, since Elizabeth was packed and ready to go. He could not disappoint her, when she was set on leaving.

The men walked back to the house and informed Elizabeth and Orson that a dead body was in the barn.

"Oh nooo...who could it be?" asked Elizabeth.

Vick had an idea, but he didn't want to say.

Orson, who never disappointed anyone about his theories, knew immediately who it was.

"That damn renegade outlaw next door done killed that Senor Galvez's girl, I betcha."

"What makes you say that?" Elizabeth asked

"Lizzie, Orson's right, because Senor Galvez was over here asking about her last week.

"Vick, do you really think it's Matilda?" asked Elizabeth.

"Likely so, and if that's the case, we can't leave until we take her body home to Senor Galvez."

"I hate it's Matilda. She was a sweet little thing." I don't know what Jonathan was thinking, leaving her body in the barn," Hop said.

"That's jest it, the damn fool ain't thanking. He's done lost it if ya ask me. Now, we gotta figure out what to do with the body in the shape it's in."

"I got to get her home so her family can bury her, and if y'all can't help, I'll do it myself" Vick said somberly.

"You thank we jest gonna stand by and let ya do it yerself? Jest don't go gitten yerself in an uproar."

Orson was well aware that Vick had learned early on about the sacredness of burial from the Indians.

Knowing what to do, he asked Lizzie for a blanket in which to wrap the girl's body. That's the least they could do for a young girl who had never hurt anyone.

"I hope you don't mind parting with one of your quilts."

Vick was surprised when Lizzie had chosen one of her favorites that her Aunt had made for her.

"Are you sure you want to part with this nice quilt?" he asked.

"These are just things, so please use it for Matilda." Vick took the quilt; the three men wrapped handkerchiefs around their faces, all looking like they were going to rob the barn instead of recovering this girl's body.

"This is gonna' be hard, taking her back to her family. I ain't lookin' forward ta seeing that family so upset," Orson lamented.

Vick knew he was thinking about Lucy, and wished he hadn't had to involve Orson with the task of seeing Matilda's body.

The three men entered the barn with Hop carrying a lantern; ready to light when they got to the barn. With no time to waste, they hurried, knowing Jonathan would be walking the lake early in the morning.

Vick bent down and immediately recognized the decaying body as Matilda and shook his head. "Ya shore that's the Galvez girl?" Orson asked.

"Yeah, I'm afraid so," Vick replied.

He and Orson quickly covered her body, placing it over the saddled horse that Senor Galvez agreed to look after while Vick was gone. When they led the horses out, they tied Vick's horse with Matilda's body behind the Model T, while Orson and Hop planned to ride their horses all the way to Jonesboro.

The additional room will give Elizabeth and Vick more room for their personal property inside the car, Hop thought.

Slowly they drove out of Pecan Plantation with Orson and Hop trotting their horses behind the car. It was like a funeral procession as they carried Matilda's body to its final resting place

Vick would like to be a fly on the wall when Jonathan finds that Matilda's body is missing. *Just another way to spook him*, Vick imagined.

After delivering the body to Senor Galvez and his family, they thanked Vick for bringing their Matilda to them. They wept, unable to comprehend that someone could do such a vile thing. They vowed to go to the Sheriff and tell him where her body was found.

In leaving, Vick once again reminded Senor Galvez of his request to be on the lookout for Cain, should he return, and to tell him they had gone back to Arkansas.

It was a tight squeeze in the Model T as it puttered through Texas towns and back over the state line to Arkansas, filled with as much of their personal property as possible. They stopped in Texarkana for the night, waiting for Hop and Orson to show, but they knew that they would be too far ahead of them. Afterwards, they talked about how they were going to get Jonathan and the James boys back to Panther Holler.

The next morning they journeyed on to Jonesboro without Orson and Hop.

Orson was glad to be going back home, but he wasn't happy about the James' returning to cause them trouble.

"One thang we know, is them James boys are headed ta wher' they think there's a treasure."

"Orson, you're right about that, and if they're the ones who killed Cain, they're not going to stop until they come after everyone involved. And when they do, me, you and Vick will take care of 'em."

"Vick promised me I could take care of them boys for what they did to Lucy, and I ain't fergitten."

"You're going to get your chance if Dudley and Lonnie take the bait," said Hop.

"Vick thinks them boys are gonna come looking for us, and when they do they won't know what hit 'em."

Vick and Elizabeth had plenty to talk about while they were driving, and most of it was about Jonathan and the James'.

"The only good thing Buck Dupree ever taught me was how to read people, and I can still hear Buck saying, 'Mate, it's a cat and mouse game, and that's what makes it fun.' Then he'd lean back in his chair, speaking with that deep Australian accent, 'A man who thinks he's winning, hungers for more, and that's when we feed him until we make him starve.' Understand what I'm saying?"

Elizabeth knew Vick was getting ready for a showdown and this concerned her.

The next morning Vick decided to wait and give Orson and Hop a chance to catch up. There was one mercantile place that he knew Orson and Hop would probably stop at and sure enough he was right.

Before they headed out again, Orson noticed Vick looked preoccupied by something. He thought it might be because he allowed those two men to move into the carriage house without Elizabeth's knowledge. Finally, Orson stood it as long as he could, and asked Vick about the men. "What about them two men you let move into the carriage house about a year ago?" Elizabeth turned toward Vick. "Is this a joke, Orson? Are you trying to start something?" Vick said. "Oops, guess I let the cat out of the bag."

Orson saw Vick's face turn white as he gave him that certain look, one that he knew wouldn't have a happy ending.

"Well, is somebody going to tell me what's going on?" Elizabeth asked.

"Lizzie, you know Orson; he's always trying to start something."

"Yeah Lizzie…I wuz jest a kiddin' ya'. Trying to git a rise outta ya'."

Orson, nervous for nearly spilling the beans, began whistling his annoying whistle as he and Hop rode on in front of the Model T.

Vick and Elizabeth took their time waiting along the way for Orson and Hop to catch up. They intended to ride through Jonesboro at the same time.

After arriving at Orson's cabin, they saw it all boarded up, like someone was trying to protect it. It was dark, so Orson failed to see the "for sale" sign in front of the small cabin.

"Well, I'll be damned! Looks like somebody done broke into my house and is doin' a little homesteadin'. I don't even have a claw hammer to take 'em boards off my winders."

"Orson, don't worry about it tonight. Tomorrow we can take care of everything but tonight let's plan on bedding down in the carriage house."

Elizabeth looked sharply at Vick, noticing that little grin on his face she never quite understood.

"Are y'all sure?" Orson asked. "If I remember right, there ain't much room in that place of yers."

"Now, don't worry," Vick said. "Orson, if we run out of room, you can camp outside. Maybe that'll serve you right for always starting trouble."

"Jest a reminder...when we git to the carriage house, ya' might be camping out with me," Orson jokingly threatened.

"Do you mind telling me what's going on...anybody?" a puzzled Elizabeth asked.

"Beats me, it's that peculiar husband of yers," Orson continued to rant.

When they entered the long drive and archway that led up to the manor, Elizabeth cautioned Vick that he had taken the wrong way because the carriage house had its own private entrance.

"Vick, you missed our road. This is the way to the manor."

"Well whataya know—I guess I'm just a creature of habit. Spare me while I drive until I can find a place to turn around."

When they turned into the final drive, she could not believe what she saw. It was such a shock to Elizabeth that it took some time to register.

"Holy cow, somebody done rebuilt the manor," Orson said.

"So this is the manor," Hop admired.

Elizabeth was so overwhelmed she started to cry. *How was this accomplished without me knowing?* she wondered.

She looked at Vick. "I can't believe you did this. How did you do this and keep it a secret?"

"Orson, did you and Hop know about this?" she asked accusatorily.

"No ma'am, I knew them men were stayin' in the carriage house, but I shore didn't know nothing about rebuilding the manor."

"Vick, you did this all for me?"

"You ready to see the inside?" he asked. Vick hopped out of the car and ran around to Elizabeth's side of the car to help her out.

As soon as she got out of the car she hugged and kissed him for his thoughtfullness. He took off his hat and threw it on the seat of the car, then grabbed her again.

Elizabeth was taken-in by the stately beauty of the manor, since he had restored everything, even the outside.

"Look, you even thought of my feathery yellow bushes that were burned, and look at the ferns. They're as full and green as before.

Elizabeth noticed the brisk summer breeze as it swayed the mimosa trees, dropping seedlings around the walkway as they walked up the steps to the porch. She noticed everything. Everything was perfect, she thought.

When Vick swung open the doors, all of his apprehensions vanished when he saw her face. She was glowing with happiness.

Elizabeth turned to Vick, "I can't believe this. It's more beautiful than before, and all because of you."

Orson looked at the two lovebirds, as Vick led her from room to room. *How in the hell did he pull this off?* he thought.

"You've taken my breath away. I can't believe you did this. I could have never done this for myself," Elizabeth remarked.

He walked with her as she admired all the fine architecture and beautiful antiques. "Vick, when did you plan this?"

"Lizzie, I knew I had to rebuild the manor for you. Now you know why I had to keep you in Texas so long. I was afraid you were going to want to come home before I had the place finished. You will notice there is still room for you to buy plenty more furniture to your liking, and to add your special touch."

She was overcome with emotion, and kissed him again in front of Orson and Hop.

"What if we give y'all two lovebirds yer space, and me and Hop kin stay out in the carriage house."

"Don't be silly. We've got plenty of room." For the first time in a long time, Elizabeth felt safe. She was home.

Chapter 23

After Munk murdered Jason, the little hospital in Trumann gained recognition because of its two lady doctors. Even though Birdie and Lucy did not have licenses to practice, they gave such good care that people overlooked the fact they were not accredited.

Within months, the news of the hospital traveled outside Trumann to surrounding towns, all the way to Memphis, and even into smaller towns, including Lucy's home town of Jonesboro. Soon people were coming from near and far for their medical care, and the hospital beds stayed full. Birdie was pleased with its success, but also saddened, because Jason wasn't there to share in the success, since it had been their lifelong dream to convert the family estate into a hospital.

After several months, Birdie became increasingly concerned about operating the hospital without a certified physician. She was aware of the risk of not being accredited.

She worried that she might jeopardize the entire hospital and all the good work they were doing by not having a doctor on staff.

She decided to take the steps necessary to find a doctor willing to fill the position. Birdie contacted one of Jason's doctor friends, and as luck would have it, he happened to know of a young doctor from Memphis who was looking for such a position. The doctor in question jumped at the opportunity and began making preparations for his trip to Trumann. Once on staff, she and Lucy would act as his assistants, and also run the office.

A week before the new doctor's arrival, a man hurried into the hospital requesting help for his wife who was having trouble delivering her baby. She had been in labor for over 8 hours, and thought to be near death.

The man was frantic, trying to hurry Birdie to follow him to his cabin.

"My wife needs help fast, 'cause she ain't able to travel. She's sufferin' a lot, and I don't know how much more she can take."

Birdie nodded to Lucy to go and deliver the woman's baby while she stayed to take care of her patients.

The man cranked up his old car and led the way, while Lucy traveled close behind in her Model T.

It seemed like forever, traveling on the narrow road, deep into the woods where the stranger's cabin was located. When they finally arrived, Lucy immediately heard a cry for help coming from inside the cabin. She wasted no time in examining the young woman, who was exhausted from twisting and turning, trying to deliver her baby without a midwife.

She opened her medical bag after immediately recognizing what to do in order to save the mother and the unborn child.

"The baby needs to be turned," she said to the husband.

"What's your wife's name?"

"Mary, and I'm Mitchell."

"Nice to meet you Mitchell."

"Is she gonna make it?" the concerned husband asked.

"If you can help me…here, take the smelling salts and have Mary breathe it to keep her conscious. I need her awake so she can push. Do you understand?"

"Yeah…I reckon I do," said the husband.

He took the smelling salts and administered it, while Lucy proceeded to turn the baby.

"Now Mary…this is going to hurt a bit, but I have to do this for the baby to come out."

She could see the pain in the young woman's face as she turned the encumbered baby. Harold's eyes got big as saucers when Mary's last push was successful in delivering a baby boy. Exhausted from her experience, she gave Lucy a faint smile, and thanked her for saving her baby's life. Mary didn't realize that it was more her life that Lucy was saving. Afterwards, the baby was cleaned and given to the mother in a soft blanket. Mary examined him from head to toe, showing the love a mother had for her newborn.

Lucy was happy for the couple, but she couldn't control her anguish and disappointment, remembering Munk, and what he had done to her. *Because of him, I'll never have a child of my own*, she reflected.

After gathering her instruments, she gave Mary some last minute instructions on how to take care of her newborn, and urged her to come into the hospital if there were any complications.

"Thank you, Ms. Lucy. You saved my baby and me. I don't know what I'd done if ya' hadn't come ta help me."

Lucy patted the woman on the shoulder and followed her husband as he accompanied her to her car. "How much do we owe you for our little boy? he asked.

Lucy replied, "Well, Mr. ...uh, Mitchell, you can pay what you can spare. I know times are tough."

He fished in his pocket and handed over a few wadded bills and some coins. Lucy handed most of the money back to him.

Mitchell looked at her and said, "I know we owe you more than that, a whole lot more."

Lucy replied, "Seeing your baby healthy is all the pay I need. Congratulations on your new little boy."

"You sure you gonna be alright finding yer' way outta here? It shore got dark in a hurry."

It had been daylight when they arrived, but now it was pitch black, with only a few stars shining from above. Lucy assured him that she could find her way back to the hospital.

"I'll be fine. Just take care of Mary and the baby," she replied.

On the way back, she felt great satisfaction knowing she saved Mary and delivered a healthy baby boy.

The lonely winding trail back to the hospital was more difficult than she anticipated. Now she understood why the man questioned her about finding her way back to town. *He was right about that*, she thought. Driving continued to be more difficult, as the road narrowed, and soon she became disoriented. It was frightening, driving at a snail's pace in order to keep from trailing off the road and veering into a ditch.

Lucy had just slowed down when she noticed a man on horseback following her. Driving slowly increased the chances of the horseman overtaking her, she thought.

Her immediate concern was Munk, should he be alive. *Was it possible he survived the waterfall?* she worried.

As the rider continued to gain on her, she prayed there was another reason the horseman was pursuing her. She tried to drive faster, but the conditions were such that to do so would not be safe. Her eyes were constantly jumping from the mirror to the trail, then back to the mirror. Whomever it was approaching her, was riding at a very fast pace. Suddenly, there was a loud thud and she knew someone had jumped onto her car. There was nothing she could do but floorboard it, as the man was climbing toward the window. When he stuck his head inside, she screamed. For her worst fear had become a startling reality. It was definitely Munk. The stench emanating from him, and shared by all members of the Clan, filled the inside of her automobile.

She instinctively went into survival mode. "You'll never hurt me again you sonovabitch!" So without hesitation, she pressed hard on the gas pedal and went off the road into a wooded area. Munk screamed "nooooooo!" The little Model T hit the tree with such impact that their two bodies were shoved together in the wreckage. It was a horrible scene, as it gave the appearance of nothing but a pile of chaotic metal rubble.

That night, Birdie became concerned when Lucy failed to return after dark. The hours ticked by and she wondered what she should do next? She blamed herself for sending her off with a virtual stranger, but the thought never entered her mind that she could be hurt in a wreck.

Birdie did not sleep at all that night, and the next morning she drove to Jed's cabin to ask if he would conduct a search. After she explained the details, a team of men set out with hound dogs to find any clue that could lead them to Lucy.

After a day of disappointment, the search was called off until the next morning.

On the second day of the search, they found their first clue: car tracks that left the road and went into the woods. Following the tracks, they spotted the mangled wreck with two bodies thrown together. They felt sure both people were dead, since there was so much blood, and the car was torn to bits.

Without checking for a pulse, they loaded them up and rushed toward the hospital. As they approached the hospital, they saw movement from one of the bodies. "It's Lucy," one of the men said.

As Birdie approached the vehicle, she recognized Lucy's blouse. She hurriedly examined her, and found a faint heartbeat, giving her hope that Lucy would survive. "Lucy's alive!" she hollered.

Birdie spent hours meticulously examining her broken body. Meanwhile, she sent Jed to Memphis to fetch the new doctor, who wasn't due to come to work until the following week. Lucy's crisis dictated that they needed him, now.

When Dr. Mark Cohen arrived, he reexamined Lucy and concurred with Birdie's assessment that she had severe head trauma with broken bones. After Lucy's arms were set, and her leg placed in a splint, she was wheeled into a hospital room.

Dr. Cohen was uncertain Lucy would survive, but thought it best not to tell Birdie the entire truth. "Why destroy her hopes?" he thought. After a few days, when Lucy wasn't improving as he'd hoped, he decided to tell her the truth. "Birdie, I've seen injuries like this before, and I have to warn you that she may never wake up."

She suspected as much after her own examination, but she was not going to give up on Lucy, who had become like a sister to her. Birdie was aware recovery could take as long as a year, if she recovered at all.

"Birdie, I know you want a quick fix, but there is some slight swelling in her brain that could take some time to subside, so don't expect a miracle for we're going to have to do what's required to eliminate the swelling. He explained to her about case studies where patients with head trauma stayed in a coma until they died. We'll keep an eye on her and make sure she rests comfortably while she heals. I think if you were to ask Lucy now, she would trade places with the chap who died."

"No doctor...you don't know what all this girl has been through. She's a fighter, and she's not about to die on me now."

"Well then, Birdie, you keep talking to her...she might just hear you and try to wake up."

~

After Jonathan murdered Matilda and destroyed some of his furnishings, he spent the entire day cleaning up his mess, wishing Matilda was there to clean it up for him. He had several flashbacks of his bazaar behavior from the night before, but he could no longer decipher dreams from reality. As he looked over the destruction of his boyhood home, he imagined the Porters had something to do with it. *They must have come in while I was sleeping*, he thought.

At nightfall, Jonathan's mind often retreated to a secret place where he felt safe. He always accompanied these illusionary excursions with a bottle of whiskey. When the first signs of daylight appeared, he was relieved, and much less afraid.

It had been over a week since he had sent Lonnie and Dudley to kill Aggie, and he was growing more anxious for them to return. He wanted to hear the details of what happened. His main concern, though, was whether or not they eliminated her.

Thinking of Aggie's final moments, he was swept away in thought of her taking her last breath. He imagined her begging for her life.

As he grew more impatient for the brothers' return, he continued to dwell on her death. He fretted that he had made the wrong decision in sending two idiots to do the job of a man. *I should have taken care of her long ago when I had the chance,* Jonathan regretted.

It was late afternoon of the same day when the brothers finally rode up at Circle J. They immediately saw Jonathan's horse tied in front of the ranch house and presumed Jonathan was waiting to drill them of every detail of how they snuffed the life out of Aggie.

Concerned that Jonathan might sense they were lying, the boys knew they would have to be careful in hiding their deception.

"Dudley, if he asks ya', stick ta the story and don't git all balled up," stated Lonnie.

"Don't worry 'bout me... jest worry 'bout yerself," Dudley replied.

They were right about Jonathan. For as soon as the men knocked on the door, he met them with a slew of questions. "Well...what happened? Is she dead?"

"Yeah boss, it's all done, and now ya' kin rest easy." Dudley was twirling his hat on one hand, trying to relieve his nerves.

"Do you mind being more specific, and tell me what happened?" Jonathan asked.

"Well boss...we first asked around 'bout where that Aggie woman lived, and then rode out ta her place. Me and Dudley went to her winder and looked in ta see if we could see 'er. She was damn good looking, too." Lonnie looked at Dudley and shook his head "yes," as if to agree with his opinion. "Yeah, she was a sweet lookin' thang," Dudley bragged.

"You're getting off subject, so get on with it," Jonathan sassed.

"We gitten to it boss...like I said, she didn't know what hit 'er. She came to the door when we knocked...you know, like we were asking fer' a job or sometin'. She opened the door, so we went in talkin' to her 'bout fixin' a chicken house that needed some chicken wire stretched around it."

About that time, Dudley chimed in. "You know…stretching the wire under the roost, so the chickens won't fall off when their asleepin'."

"I don't want to know about no damn chicken house. Just tell me what in the hell happened. Did you kill her?"

"Yes sir, we did what ya' asked." Dudley rolled his eyes, sure that he wasn't seen. Jonathan then asked the big question, which neither of them were prepared to answer.

"Well…what did you do with the body?"

Lonnie looked at Dudley as if he was stumped. His mouth was moving but no words came out. Seeing his brother in a tight spot, Dudley spoke up. "Well boss, I wanted ta make shore she was dead, so I grabbed the knife from Lonnie and finished her off right then and there. She kicked till we picked 'er up and threw 'er in the well." Lonnie looked at Dudley and winced, unsure that Jonathan would believe them about the "well" story.

Dudley could read his brother and knew he was worried.

"You boys threw her in the well? Ha!" was Jonathan's reply.

"Well now, ya' have ta understand… it was a big well and we made shore she sunk all the way ta the bottom. No sir, we didn't wanna leave no signs that any killin' took place. That's the reason we made shore she sunk ta the bottom," Lonnie hesitantly expressed.

"Of the well," Jonathan finished their statement.

"Yes sir, real deep." Dudley added.

If Jonathan had been operating with a full deck, he would have known they were lying, after seeing their eyes shift back and forth. He wanted desperately to believe that Aggie finally got what was coming to her.

"You boys are thinking for a change, and I'm glad y'all covered your tracks, but asking where Aggie lived could end up biting you boys in the butt. That's good cause it wouldn't set well if the law came looking for ya'."

"Don'tcha worry, 'cause ain't no law comin' around lookin," Lonnie reassured Jonathan. "We jest here ta collect our pay fer doin' yer' job.

"You'll get your pay. Don't worry about that." Jonathan seemed a bit disgusted with the question.

Believing the boys killed Aggie, Jonathan paid them generously, which concerned them, since they lied about murdering Aggie. After they left, Lonnie explained, "So what if he pays us? We've done plenty of dirty work for 'em." Feeling somewhat guilty, and afraid of what might happen if Jonathan found out they lied, they wanted to get as far away from Jonathan as possible. But they had to be careful, for he could still create big problems for them if he let it out that they're the ones who burned down the manor, and killed Orson Cargill's daughter, Lucy.

The Petty brothers shoved their pay in their pockets and rode into town to hang out at the saloon and discuss their plan to go after the treasure.

The next day, Jonathan rode from Circle J back to the plantation, and was met by Matilda's father, who was asking questions about his daughter. He pointed over to where the Porters lived, and then prodded Jonathan for answers. Of course, Senor Galvez knew the Porters were on their way to Arkansas, since they had delivered Matilda to him.

At first the Senor had planned to contact the Sheriff about Matilda's murder. He imagined involving Jonathan with the Sheriff might cause trouble for them that they did not need. It took every bit of self-control he had to keep from jumping Jonathan. He kept saying under his breath that Jonathan will pay for murdering his daughter.

"Meester Jonathan," he said. "I went to Meester Vick's house to ask about Matilda, but they must have left. Here's the sign I found on the porch. Vick wanted to make sure Jonathan found out that he and Elizabeth had gone back to Arkansas.

Jonathan took the sign and read that Vick and Elizabeth were, in fact, gone. *No wonder I haven't seen them around here in a few days. Good riddance*, he thought.

Surprised to learn the Porters had left, he told Mr. Galvez that he heard Matilda had left with one of the men to get married.

"Senor, which man was that?"

"How in the hell do I know? She left…that's all I know. She was a lousy housekeeper anyway."

Senor Galvez cringed, hearing Jonathan speak of his dead daughter that way. Jonathan's face had given him away, and Matilda's father instantly knew he was in the presence of the man who possibly raped and murdered his daughter. Her clothing was ripped off and the Senor thought the worst.

Preoccupied with the sign from Vick's porch, Jonathan wanted to get rid of the Mexican in order to plan what he wanted to do next, now that the Porters had left town. The old man kept standing there with his hat in his hand. He couldn't move. "I told you before that I heard she ran away. Now move on…I have work to do."

"Si, Meester Jonathan. I will talk to the workers and ask if they know where my Matilda has gone."

"You do that! But right now there's work to be done, and those field hands have plenty to do other than worry about what's going on with Matilda."

Senor Galvez wanted to kill Jonathan, but instead, he turned and mounted his horse and rode away. He knew he had just looked into the eyes of an evil man.

Jonathan's immediate reaction to the Porters leaving town was one of frustration. First, he had planned on kicking Vick's ass playing poker, and then take care of him and Elizabeth before they had a chance to leave. *Now, I'll have to go after them*, he thought.

Jonathan had to be careful that the Porters' leaving town wasn't a set-up just to catch him spying on them. *I'll have Lonnie and Dudley do my snooping, in case it's a trap.*

Later that day, Jonathan went into the barn to remove Matilda's body, but she was gone. He began to panic wondering why there was no body. Again, he felt a deep insecurity that a power he did not understand was working against him. Shaken because of her missing body, he made a trip into town and spotted the James boys eating in his favorite café. He wondered what business they had in town when they were supposed to be back at the ranch working. It didn't take long to figure it out, since he had paid them handsomely for killing Aggie. That money was burning a hole in their pocket, he thought.

When the boys saw Jonathan walk into the café, they stood instantly, as if they were finished and on their way out.

"Wait, what's your rush?" Jonathan said." The boys couldn't believe the lilt in his voice, something they had never heard. "You don't have to run off just because I'm here. Please keep your seats. I need to talk to ya'. It's about my neighbors…and I need your help."

"Ya' talkin' 'bout them Porters?"

"Who else, since they're the only ones living next to me?"

"It ain't likely we would be seeing 'em since we been laying low at the Circle J," Lonnie said.

"Well it ain't likely we'll see 'em again unless we go to Arkansas, 'cause they sneaked out in the night. Left a sign on the porch saying they gone back to Arkansas," Jonathan said, sarcastically. Except, I don't know if they're pulling a fast one.

"Ya' mean they ain't there no more?" Dudley asked.

"That's what 'leaving during the night' usually means," Jonathan said.

Dudley disregarded the insult, thinking only of the treasure.

"Lonnie, ya' know what that means…they gone after the treasure. Dang it! They done got the jump on us, and 'fore we got a chance ta make Porter tell us where the treasure is." Dudley was visibly upset.

"Dudley, keep your damn voice down. We don't want the whole town a hearing ya'."

Dudley looked around the room that was empty.

"I guess you're talking 'bout all them empty chairs in here a'listenin' to me."

"Yer a hollerin', and people can hear," Lonnie chastised.

Hearing this exchange, Jonathan once again thought about his mistake of getting mixed up with the James'. "For my sake, can you both keep your mouths shut, and let me talk?" Jonathan scolded.

"We listenin' boss. Go ahead and tell us what yer' plannin' on doin' since they gone."

Dudley's mind was working overtime, thinking they were wasting time with Jonathan who sat speechless.

"I know what I'm gonna do…I'm gonna' go after 'em and beat the pulp' out of 'em until he takes me to the treasure," Lonnie said.

For the first time, Jonathan noticed something about Lonnie and Dudley he had never seen before. "The stupid misfits are passionate, so there must be some truth to this phantom treasure they're always talking about." Jonathan knew he had to calm him down to keep from them going off half-cocked.

"Take it easy…don't go getting impatient, 'cause we're still going after 'em, Jonathan said. "And boys let's don't get the cart before the horse looking for 'em until we know for sure they're gone."

Jonathan thought a minute and then patted Lonnie on the back so he could continue to manipulate them. "What I want y'all to do is check out their house and see if it looks like there's a sign of life."

"So yer not shore they're gone? What if it's a trap? We ain't ready ta let 'em know we're around," Lonnie worried. The men were both reluctant, since they had already seen Cain, who's supposed to be dead. And then there were ghostly sightings around the plantation they didn't quite understand.

"We let them Porters know we're here, and it could ruin ever-thang fer us," Dudley responded. "Yeah, that could blow our plan 'bout the treasure," Lonnie agreed. Jonathan perceived the brother's obsession, which reinforced to him that there was, in fact, a treasure. After all, the boys killed a girl and burned down the Porter's home, which was enough to substantiate its veracity.

The next day, the brothers staked out the Porter's home to see if there was any sign of life coming from that direction.

"Dudley, see…they've already boarded up the place."

"I told y'all they've gone after the treasure. Now do ya believe me?"

"That dab blame Jonathan and his craziness has done run 'em off. Shoulda know'd they'd git a head start on us."

"We need ta git the hell outta here and go after Vick ourselves, and fergit about that nut cake holdin' us back."

"Dudley…ya fergit' one thang', he could cause us trouble… 'cause he knows too much. We need 'em until we git' the treasure. Then we settle the score with Jonathan."

Jonathan figured as much when Lonnie reported that the Porters were gone. "Yup…they gone all right. Me and Dudley seen the wind-ers boarded up, and the door had a big board nailed across it."

"So they're bound to be headed back to Arkansas," Jonathan stated.

"Boss, we can't waste no time 'cause the Porters done gone after the treasure. That's the reason he left." Dudley was like a dog with a bone—he wasn't going to let loose.

Jonathan knew he had to take care of Vick, and there was no other way but to follow the brothers to Jonesboro. If there's a treasure to be found, well that's just icing on the cake. He imagined if they led him to a treasure, it would be a good time to take care of Vick and the James boys together. *After all, they're as lethal to me as Aggie, since they know too much about me masterminding the killing of Cain and their friend, the Sheriff.*

"Well boys, I did give my word about going with you for that treasure y'all been talking about."

The brothers looked at one another and smiled. Jonathan had no idea what lay behind that devious smile of theirs.

Now it's time to let these boys in on my plan, Jonathan supposed.

"In fact, I have a plan if you care to listen."

"A plan about what?" asked Dudley, who was concerned that Jonathan would screw up things for them, since he had been acting crazy.

"Y'all want a sure way of dry-gulching him, don't ya?" Jonathan asked.

"I guess we do, but we have ta be real careful and not have 'em see us."

"Don't worry about that 'cause I want you boys to go with me to Jonesboro. When I get there, I'll send a message to Vick that I want to make a deal with him."

"What kind of deal we talkin' 'bout?" asked Dudley.

"I'll tell him I want to buy back that house I sold him."

"What if he won't deal?" Lonnie asked.

"Oh, he'll deal, 'cause I aim to make it worth his while."

"The other part of the plan involves you ambushing me along with Porter. After we have our little talk I'll follow him outside and that's when you and Dudley make your move. Remember you have to stick with the plan to make it work.

"Dudley wasn't following along to good and asked for it to be clarified. "Ya sayin' ya' don't want Porter ta know yer' in cahoots with us?"

"Once again Dudley…you've figured it out. When y'all cold-cock Porter I'll make him think I'm as surprised as he is. Then you do what you have to do to make him talk about that treasure and where it's buried. When we get to this Panther Holler place, that's when I'll beat his ass in a game of poker. After that, I'll let him know that I'm who masterminded the plan to kill his son and that Sheriff Cargill you boys are afraid of."

"Is that it?" Dudley asked.

"Not quite," responded Jonathan. Suddenly he got louder... "That's when I'll send Porter to hell to join his son."

Lonnie and Dudley were shocked to see Jonathan's piercing eyes change right before them. Seeing his rage there was no doubt they were in the company of a madman.

Chapter 24

IT WAS THE EARLY MORNING HOURS WHEN THE NOISE FROM HEAVY RAIN **awakened little Jared.** Hearing the cry of a child was still new to Cain, and for a second he thought he was dreaming. Martha was in the kitchen preparing breakfast when she heard the boy. But in total contrast, his cry was like music to her ears, knowing there was another child on the place. Jared's little cry brought back memories she savored of her son, Billy, who had died before his time.

Early breakfast for the ranch hands were always part of Martha's routine, and for years she had followed the same tedious task of preparing food for Wendell and the rest of the gang.

After breakfast it was work as usual: rounding up Herefords, mending fences, and adapting to whatever happened in the life of a cowboy running a ranch. Martha had already taken out a second pan of hot biscuits, and was getting ready to start the bacon and eggs, when Cain came into the kitchen to discuss leaving Jared with her.

He had just found his son, and now he had to leave him behind because of a promise he made to Aggie. It was a difficult choice, since it might be some time before he would see him again. His concern was also for Martha, whom he wanted to spare, since he knew her history of being shattered when she lost Billy. She had become like a mother to him and now a grandmother to Jared, and if at all possible, he wanted to alleviate her pain when it came time to return and take Jared back home with him. The promise he made to Aggie about protecting Jared from Jonathan left him with no choice, and he wanted to make sure Martha understood what she was getting herself into taking care of a toddler.

After they talked, Cain tiptoed into his room very quietly to keep from waking Jared. But much to his surprise his young son was standing up in his bed, hanging onto the railing. At seeing his daddy, he broke into a huge smile. Cain's heart burst with joy at seeing the strong Porter resemblance that he could never deny. He walked over to Jared just in time for him to cry out for his mama. Of course, the boy did not understand why she was not there. Cain's heart broke, knowing he would have to say goodbye to this child with whom he had developed such an attachment in such a short time.

Watching through a crack in the door Martha's heart went out to Cain as he admired his son. She wondered what he might be going through. As she kept out of sight, she was considerate of that special moment between father and son. She was careful not to disturb the rapport they were developing. It was certainly a tender moment. Finally, she could stand it no longer, and walked into the room. "Cain, you want me to take the boy?" He turned and walked out of the room to keep her from seeing how upset he was.

The boy and Cain had been together less than a week, but the connection between the two was undeniable. *I don't know if I'm going to be brave enough to leave my boy*, Cain thought. He knew he would miss him, but it was out of the question to take his son with him. Aggie's greatest fear was Jonathan finding her son and killing him, with the true intent of causing her lifelong unbearable pain.

She knew how sadistic Jonathan was, and she did not want Cain taking Jared anywhere close to the danger he would face with a man who was determined to see her dead.

Cain had the business of tending to Jonathan before he could even think about bringing Jared to San Augustine. Dealing with Jonathan came first. In the meantime, the existence of Jared had to remain a secret, even to those he loved and trusted. He wanted to make sure Jonathan and the James brothers whom he had recognized when he left Aggie's were out of the picture before he told anyone about Jared being his son. By this time it had become abundantly clear that the James' were working with Jonathan. *It's best I not even tell Vick or Elizabeth*, he reasoned.

Knowing how they'll feel about having a grandson, he imagined they would want to see the child, and perhaps insist on bringing him to San Augustine where Jared might be in danger.

When Martha returned to the kitchen, Cain was sitting at the table, waiting for her to help him figure things out. "Cain, do you mind me asking when you're leaving?" she quizzed.

He shook his head and shrugged his shoulders, indicating that he did not know. "It's funny how attached I've become to Jared—when a week ago I had no idea he even existed." Cain thought of Vick, and how he must have felt when he learned he had a grown son he had missed out on raising. *Now I understand*, he thought.

Martha could see what Cain was going through. "Son, do you mind if I give you some advice?"

"Of course not," he replied.

"If I were you, I'd leave as soon as possible so Jared won't have time to get more attached. I can see he's gonna be a daddy's boy, and the longer you wait, the harder it's going to be to leave. Understand? He's gonna' be fine so don'tcha worry. I even have him calling me grandma she said proudly— I hope you don't mind, but I already feel he's my grandson."

He considered what she said. "Martha, my head tells me one thing, but my heart tells me another. I know the longer I stay the harder it's going to be for me to leave. I just wish I could take the boy with me— and I can't."

"Now don't you fret, I promise I'll spoil him jest like he was my own. Everyday we'll talk about you until you get back home." Of course, Martha considered the ranch as Cain's home.

Cain hugged Martha and then walked outside to check the weather pattern and see if it had changed. He knew it was time.

"Martha, I'm not going to wait. My bedroll is ready to go, but I reckon I need to have you nudge me out the door." Martha smiled seeing Cain act just like a daddy.

"I hope you don't mind but I need to ask you one more time if you'll be okay taking care of little Jared?"

"That's silly for you to even think. You know how I feel about you and that little boy. I'm glad you've gonna go now, and I don't want you to have a minute's worry 'bout Jared and me. We'll be just fine... Cain, I wish you would reconsider about taking the Model T. It would save you a lot of time."

"I appreciate it Martha, but my horse can take me places that Model T can't go."

Saying goodbye to Martha was the most difficult thing he had ever done, since he knew she had come to depend on him. She's been like a mother to me, and I don't want to hurt her, he agonized.

"Well, if you've made up your mind...while you get ready I'll pack you a few day's rations to tide you over until you git to wher' you're goin'."

"Thank you, Martha. I can see why Glen was so good to you. You had him spoiled." She turned and went to work stuffing biscuits with bacon. When his gear was ready, and the saddlebags were packed, Martha gave him a number of wrapped biscuits, a canteen and cookies for his journey.

"Now you got plenty to eat. You're gonna love the cookies I packed. There's enough to last you all the way to San Augustine. I suppose that's wher' ya goin'?"

Cain gave her a big hug. "I imagine you're going to spoil Jared so much he's not going to leave with me when I come back."

Martha smiled, seeing Cain take on the role of a real father, but her heart hurt, hearing him talk about leaving with little Jared.

"Jest you don't worry about me and your little one. We'll be just fine, and he'll be waiting for you with open arms."

Cain's mind reverted back to Aggie, and the pain she must have suffered, seeing her son ride off with him. *And now I'm about to suffer the same hurt, and I've only just begun to know my son. Aggie's pain must have been ten times worse,* Cain empathized.

It was before daybreak when Cain loaded his gear on the back of his horse and rode away. Martha envisioned the reunion between him and his family, since they had not seen him in over two years. She guessed, after that long, his family may have given up; assuming he was dead.

Riding the trail between Beaumont and Woodville, Cain decided to stop by Aggie's to reassure her that their son was safe under the care of Martha. It's the least I can do, he thought. It took almost two full days to ride from Beaumont to Woodville, but when he did, he was disturbed to see Aggie's house boarded up. Two of the caretakers walked out of the tiny house in back and told Cain that Aggie had moved to Huntsville to be near her husband in prison. Cain had no idea that she was in such a hurry to leave, but seeing how the town was against her, it all made sense.

After leaving the ranch, the sun was brighter and the day grew hotter, but his horse was strong and fast-of-pace.

Leaving Woodville, Cain spent two more nights on the trail before arriving in San Augustine. Reigning his horse into a trot, he rode through town. He observed that everything looked just as it did before. *It's as though I've never been gone,* he reflected. As he followed the road to the plantation, uneasiness came about him. He assumed it was because he had been away for two long years, and Vick and Elizabeth might have assumed he was dead. When he arrived at the cutoff that fed into the final road through the pecan trees, he felt greater anticipation, knowing they might be stunned at seeing him. He now wished he had prepared them for his homecoming, as he knew they would be shocked. A telegram seemed so impersonal for such an important message, but now he was wishing he had sent one after all.

When the stately plantation came into view, he took a deep breath, while preparing himself for what he might find. As he got closer, the cotton fields looked as though they had been neglected. Several of the field hands came out to greet the stranger not recognizing it was Cain.

One old-timer pondered, as if he was trying to remember. Finally, a big smile came across his face.

"Well I'll be danged...if it don't look like Mr. Cain. Am I seein' thangs? Is that you?" the man asked. "Mr. Cain...we heard you was dead. I'm shore glad you're alive!" Cain was somewhat amused at seeing a preview of what was to come when others would find that he was very much alive. He remembered the reaction of the James brothers when they saw him on the road from Aggie's. They either thought he was a ghost, or that they failed to make sure him and Orson were dead.

Cain bent down from the horse and shook hands with the man who recognized him. He had been gone too long, and did not remember his name. "Yeah, it's me. It's been a long time, and you can see I'm still kicking."

"Where ya' been Mr. Cain? Yer' mama and Pa heard ya' was dead, and I could tell it shore tore 'em up. They ain't been gone long. It was just the other morning they set out riding in that Model T Ms. Elizabeth drives. I got to tell ya'...it ain't the same since Mr. Jonathan come in and took over the place. Some mighty bad thangs been goin' on, and Mr. Jonathan ain't acting right with nobody." Cain dismounted to talk face-to-face to be sure to get the facts right.

"Sure wish thangs would git back ta the way they used ta be when yore Pa ran the place. Mr. Jonathan done run everybody off, and ain't no way we can keep the place up without no help." Cain finally recalled the old man's name.

"Sammy, since you've seen me and know I'm alive, can I count on you to keep this between me and you that I was here?"

"Mr. Cain, I ain't tellin' nobody nothin'…jest between me and you."

"Where is Jonathan now?" Cain asked.

"Him and them two men he rides wit', can't rightly remember their names, but they left ta go somewher' in Arkansas, right after Ms. Elizabeth and Mr. Vick left. All Mr. Jonathan tol' me is ta keep doin' my job. And I reckon that's what we tryin' to do. I wish I had more to tell ya', but that's all I know. Oh, one other thang, Senor Galvez gave me a message fer ya'. Yore Pa ain't never accepted yore death, and he told 'em that if ya' ever come home ta tell ya' they waited as long as they could, and fer ya' to ride that horse of yer' Pa's back to Arkansas. You ain't heard but the Senor Galvez's girl Matilda got herself killed. Somebody done snuffed the life outta her. "

"Some one killed Matilda? I never did meet her when I was here."

"Miss Matilda wer' a housekeeper ta Mr. Jonathan"

"Thanks for telling me Sammy. Have you got Pa's horse here?"

"No sir…Mr. Vick left it wit' Senor Galvez. I spec' on account of Mr. Jonathan. Yer Pa's horse needed good pasture ta run in. He shore didn't want to leave his horse, but there weren't nothing else he could do."

"Does Senor Galvez live in the same place?"

"Shore does…ya' member don'tcha? Ya' passed it when ya' cut off from the main road that goes into town."

"Yes, I think I rode past it on the way. Sammy, those two men that left with Jonathan…do you remember their names?"

"I heared one of 'em called Lonnie. Yeah…it shore was, but I don't 'member the other name."

Cain thought, *I reckon I was right about Lonnie and Dudley when I saw them on the road from Aggie. So, Lonnie and Dudley made it to San Augustine, a perfect pair to run with Jonathan.*

"You said Jonathan took over the place here?"

"Yep, that's when yer Pa and Ma moved in that little house that belonged ta' Mr. Orson 'fore he died." This statement caused Cain to grimace. Sammy paused a second and continued, "Shore made Mr. Jonathan mad a livin' next door to ya Pa.", Everybody knew that weren't gonna work. No sir, ain't the same working fer Mr. Jonathan.. Yep, we shore hated ta see ya' Pa and Ma go, but the way thangs stood 'tween yer Pa and Mr. Jonathan, somebody bound ta' git hurt."

Cain's horse began getting restless, so he tightened the rein and patted his neck. "Well, I best be on my way. I have a lot of miles to cover before I get to Arkansas. Sammy, I need to make sure, if Jonathan returns, that you remember... not a word about me being back."

"Yes sir, Mr. Cain, we ain't sayin' nothin'. Don't you worry none."

Cain presumed Jonathan and the James brothers were going after Vick, or God forbid, his mother. All he could think about was Orson not being around to help Vick, in case things flared up and got out of hand. The more he thought about the James', the more he knew there was another reason they had come to San Augustine to make trouble. It had not yet occurred to him, until now, that they might have been involved in Lucy's murder. Cain recalled that his Pa and Orson suspected the James' of knowing about the treasure since their brother Johnny had possibly told them about the treasure that Buck was sure Vick hid in Panther Holler. What the brother's didn't know was Orson and his Pa made up the phony story about a treasure in order for Johnny to lure Buck back to Panther Holler for a show down. It was all for making things right, for the brutal killings Buck was guilty of and the harm he had done to the Porter family. Connecting the dots Cain figured the James' and Jonathan were all in cahoots to find a treasure that did not exist.

When Cain made it to the main road, he took time to ride by Senor Galvez's house and trade horses. Heartbroken about Matilda's murder, Cain hoped the Sheriff would arrest the one man that was capable of such a crime. He was sure Jonathan murdered the girl.

Now, more than ever, he was overwhelmed with fear for his own family's safety. Cain pushed Jasper into a hard run. It was like Vick's horse knew he was going home.

〜

Approaching sundown, after more than two weeks on the trail, Jonathan and the James' rode into Jonesboro. Much to Jonathan's surprise, the town was thriving and showing signs of growth, unlike San Augustine. The brother's also noticed the change. There were no longer potholes in the street as they remembered, and the town had grown to be very modern, as they called it.

The riders were weary and in need of food and a bath when they rode side by side through town. "Where's a good place to stay?" Jonathan asked.

"Lonnie, what about that boarding house called the Dinner Bell?" Dudley suggested.

"I ain't staying in no damn boarding house when I can stay at the saloon," Jonathan spoke up. In reality, Jonathan needed whiskey to calm the "darkness" he felt within.

"Ain't gonna find no saloon lest ya' ride outside town a ways."

"We can ride out there wit' ya," Lonnie replied. Jonathan was ready for some space, and needed to get as far away from his idiot misfits as possible, but he needed them to show him the way.

"Well, lead the way, if you know where you're going." Jonathan said with disgust.

Dudley was sick and tired of cowering down to Jonathan, but until they kidnapped Vick, they knew they had to play along for a while.

When they reached the saloon, Jonathan planned to enter alone and have the James' come in later.

Observing the stranger enter the saloon, the locals wondered who the man was. Most of the drifters that came into town generally had a story, and they wondered what Jonathan's might be. They could see he had been on the road for a while, since his coat and hat were covered with trail dust.

Standing at the bar, a young woman kept giving Jonathan the eye. He had disdain for women like her and could care less that the woman was trying to get his attention unless, of course, he was in the right mood. He perceived her interest out of the corner of his eye, but he was tired, and all he wanted was a drink and to be left alone. A few minutes later, the came into the bar and sat down at a table, hardly being noticed. They watched the flirtatious woman in action, as she inched her way closer to Jonathan.

"I hope she knows what she's gitten herself into," Lonnie whispered.

They wondered how the evening would play out. Jonathan could smell her harsh cheap perfume, mixed with an equally strong odor of whiskey, further turning him off.

Every eye in the place was on him, as he stood at the bar soaking in his own paranoia. He detested anyone gawking at him, so he turned his back to his audience and hailed the bartender's attention, pointing to his favorite bottle of whiskey. He had never come to understand that whiskey was his enemy, especially when mixing it with his instability.

"Can I git anythang else fer ya'," the bartender asked.

"Just a room for tonight," Jonathan ordered. After a few drinks in him, he turned around with his back to the bar and noticed the old man at the piano pounding out old songs he had heard a million times before. Trying to avoid making contact with the "lady of the night," Jonathan wanted her to find some other cowboy to annoy, perhaps the James'. The thought of her and the brothers made him laugh inwardly. Jonathan kept drinking and losing himself in the bottle, as the warm brew trickled down his throat. The effects of the whiskey rushed to his brain, slowly transforming him into the mental case that no one would recognize. The woman was playing her part well as a master in the art of seduction, smiling and twisting as she continued to move from one cowboy to the other, exchanging smiles, patting them on the back as though she was popular among them. Jonathan was well aware that she had singled him out for the night. All the while, Lonnie and Dudley were intrigued, watching her game playing as she moved in the direction of Jonathan. Clandestinely, Lonnie and Dudley were living their own fantasies of women they knew only in their dreams.

The saloon was exceptionally noisy with the laughter of all the rowdy cowboys, as she made her way to the bar. In her mind, she had already chosen Jonathan as her bed partner, figuring he had enough money to pay for her time, and she had been through most of the regulars. He could see the wanton look in her eyes, as she moved in his direction. After the whiskey had time to take its effect on Jonathan, his and the woman's eyes locked. He was startled to see a resemblance of another young woman he had known. The more he squinted, the surer he was that the woman was Matilda. She's supposed to be dead, he thought. His mind had become transfixed into thinking Matilda had come back from the dead to haunt him. Everything about her looked like the young Matilda he had murdered. Even when she laughed, it was Matilda. *My mind is playing tricks on me, because Matilda is dead*, he thought, causing a frightened look on his face. The young woman wondered why he acted afraid of her all of a sudden. Those watching were taking it all in, and the James brothers shared knowing looks indicating, He's off his rocker again.

Jonathan took his bottle of whiskey and the room key, and then walked hurriedly upstairs, as though he had seen a ghost. When he got to the top of the stairway, he peered back over his shoulder in the direction of the woman, who mistakenly thought Jonathan was luring her up to his room. The "painted lady" planned to allow him time to get settled before she made her way to his door. There was something very mysterious and attractive about Jonathan that she liked, and wanted to explore. Not too many men of his caliber, she thought. The woman, who had been every cowboy's delight, wasn't about to allow Jonathan's sophistication stop her from pursuing him who could possibly take her away from the profession she longed to forsake.

Once in his room, Jonathan sat near the window, staring into the night, becoming more frightened and drunker by the minute. Before he left San Augustine, his physical condition had begun deteriorating, but now his eyes had become nothing but a hollow stare, and they had acquired an unhealthy brightness.

Visions of Matilda filled his mind. He took another drink, then paced around the room, trying to get her image out of his head. Matilda's dead body filled his every thought, and he was sick with fear that he might meet with the same fate. *Matilda has come for me.* He was sure of that. Trembling, he heard a soft tap on the door. *It's Matilda, she's here.*

Crouching behind a chair to hide, he listened as the tapping became louder and more rapid. *I have to make her stop... once and for all!* he thought.

He moved recklessly toward the loud knocking, stumbling under the influence of whiskey. When he opened the door, the woman he thought was Matilda walked in like a hypnotic cat, reaching for him and slowly placing her arms around his neck. She looked at him with a smile that he construed as taunting.

"Matilda, why have you come back?" he asked. The woman thought he was being playful, calling her by another name. "I'm here because I want you," she said, giving him her seductive smile, while unbuttoning his shirt at the same time. She was too drunk to see the fear he had in his eyes. He was a stranger who might take her away from the small town where she had become so well known, is all she knew.

"I want you," she whispered again in his ear. She looked up and noticed the curtains were open, then pranced over to the window to close them. Jonathan stared at her, horrified of what her next move might be. Continuing in his state of delusion, he grabbed her, throwing her on the bed. *Oh, he likes to play rough,* she thought. Jonathan jumped on her so hard it knocked the breath out of her. Stunned, she could do nothing to defend herself when he began choking her. "You have to stay dead," he said. He choked harder as she clawed at him with bulging eyes that quickly turned to horror. She was helpless, as death was only moments away. "You should have stayed dead!" he taunted. "Now, I have to kill you again!"

Jonathan continued his hold on her throat until the life was squeezed out of her.

Afterwards, he lay for hours planning how to get rid of her body. He knew there was a possibility of being seen if he took her body from the saloon. So that was out of the question. After a time of stewing, he peeked out the door to make sure the coast was clear. In the middle of the night, Jonathan wrestled with the body, as he carried her down the stairs and into the closed, dark saloon. Only the James' knew what happened, since they heard the shuffling from next door. Cracking open their door just enough to see Jonathan wrestling with the body, they watched as he carried the dead woman down the stairs. He staged her in a chair to give the impression she drank herself to death. His desire was that whomever discovered her would think she died of natural causes, and no one would guess she was murdered.

Lonnie pulled Dudley back from staring. "The man's crazier than we thought. He's the devil. We gotta take care of him 'fore he kills the both of us." Dudley had begun to shake. "Git a hold of yerself Dudley! As long as Mr. Crazy needs us, we don't need to worry 'bout that. Remember, we're the ones that do his dirty work. The time ain't right."

"Jest listen at ya'. Do ya' know how many times ya' say the time ain't right? Waitin' is gonna git us killed."

"Dudley, he ain't gonna do anythang until he gits the treasure."

"Eh, and if we ain't careful, he could blow it fer us," Dudley argued back.

Jonathan believed no one would think his victim had been murdered.

And he was precisely right. For after examination, the undertaker concluded that the marks around her neck were probably from an overly passionate cowboy. "Besides, she ain't worth no man being hanged over," he was heard to say. That was the general consensus since no one cared anyway.

Mornings seemed easier for Jonathan to cope, and after cleaning himself up and dressing in a fresh shirt, everything about Matilda seemed vague. He then met the brothers and hurried into town for breakfast, ignoring the hubbub in the saloon over some floozy who had died.

When they arrived at the boarding house, Jonathan excused himself and walked over to the Sheriff's office to quietly check the postings for any wanted posters, just in case the town had found out Lonnie and Dudley were the ones who burned down the Porter home, killing the Sheriff's daughter. It had been over two years since the s committed the murders and burned the manor. Jonathan thought it was good that the town may have finally given up. After he found there were no posters with their names or pictures, he returned to the boarding house to find Lonnie and Dudley deep in conversation. They're up to something, he concluded. The three were alone, since the morning crowd had already eaten and dispersed. This would make it easy to discuss the plan to trick Vick into coming to town.

Jonathan was upset when he noticed right away that Lonnie and Dudley had slipped back into their dirty habits of greasy hair and dirty clothes. He hated to be seen with them, and seated himself in such a way that no one knew for sure if they were connected. The boys saw Jonathan's look change, and had a notion what he was thinking. Jonathan hadn't figured out that since the James' were back on their own turf, that the rules might have changed a bit. Being back home, the brothers had developed a sense of security, and their attitude was something Jonathan hadn't planned on.

He suddenly realized that he might have underestimated them, as they appeared to have minds of their own. *This is hardly what I expected... which is all the more reason for me to kill them.* After calming himself down, he knew he had to first make sure they followed through with his plan to kill Vick and kidnap Elizabeth, which was a thought he could not shake. Jonathan had become so jealous of Vick, coveting his wife. It had become his secret obsession daily, and into the nights.

"Okay boys, this is what we have to do if we want the treasure."

"What about Vick, ain't we gonna kill him?" Dudley asked.

Jonathan had learned to ignore Dudley when he asked senseless questions.

"Here's what we have to do. I'll have a message delivered to Vick that I'm in town to make him an offer he can't refuse."

"What kind of offer?" Lonnie asked.

"Don't y'all remember me telling you that I'm gonna offer to buy the house and five acres from him.?"

"You mean that place next ta the plantation?" Lonnie asked.

"That's right, the place by the lake," Jonathan replied tauntingly thinking the two men were the idiots of the century.

"On his way to town I want you to go after Elizabeth and kidnap her. Can I count on you to do that?"

"We ain't talked 'bout no woman involved."

"Well, now you know," Jonathan stated. "Besides, she'll be good leverage if Vick fails to tell us about the treasure."

"Hmm, I ain't thought about that," Dudley admitted.

"Of course you haven't," Jonathan said, sarcastically.

"After I meet with Vick, that's when I want him ambushed."

"And who's gonna do the ambushing?" Dudley asked.

"You boys, of course. Remember the plan?" Jonathan could not believe the two partners he had.

"Maybe ya jest want that Porter woman thanking yer innocent and we the ones that killed her son?"

"Not bad Dudley—of course not, you dummy!" Jonathan was furious. "I've already told you that when we get to Panther Holler, or whatever that damn place is, that I'm coming clean with Vick and his little wife. I'm gonna beat his ass playing poker and then I'm telling them that I'm the one who masterminded the plan to murder Cain and his friend Orson. Now, the other part of the plan is killing Elizabeth right before Vick's eyes. That's when he'll tell us where he buried the treasure. After we get Vick, we'll show him Elizabeth, and that's when I want you to rough her up a bit.

The plan is when Vick comes into town to meet me that's when you and Dudley kidnap Elizabeth. Didn't ya say she's living in a house by the manor that was burned? I'm sure you all know where to find her. After we have the treasure I don't care what you do with either one of them. Do you understand?"

Lonnie and Dudley thought how easy it's going to be to kill Elizabeth and Vick. They began rattling off how much they despised Elizabeth since she was rich and they were poor.

"She always thought she was better than everbody else. It'll be 'bout time fer her ta git what's comin' to 'er, along with that jailbird husband of hers who killed her daddy. I still thank he killed all 'em fellers he was accused of killin'. How many was it Dudley?"

"All I heared was it was a bunch of 'em. I thank it was 'bout 8 or 9. He shoulda got more than 20 years if ya ask me."

"You boys have to remember that Vick is smart as a fox, and if he gets wind of what we're up to...we're dead in the water and he'll have the treasure. Do you understand what I'm sayin'?"

"Yeah, we git it." Lonnie reassured Jonathan, who smiled, knowing he would finally have his revenge.

Chapter 25

ORSON WAS OVERJOYED BEING BACK HOME IN JONESBORO, AND AFTER **removing the boards that had barricaded his windows, it appeared the contents of his home was still intact.** However, he remained puzzled that someone would board up his place, and then try to sell it out from under him. *Who would be bold enough to take another man's property, and try to sell it as his own? Times have shore changed*, he thought. While Vick, Elizabeth, and their two friends, Orson and Hop were busy settling down to make new starts of their lives, unbeknownst to them; Lucy was in a coma clinging to life a few miles away.

It was mid-morning, and chores were just beginning when a courier rode up to the manor. "It's me, ma'am," the courier shouted, while waiting near the front door.

Elizabeth was in the kitchen baking pies, while Vick was feeding the horses in the barn. Neither of them heard Rufus, but Vick spotted his old friend when he walked back to the house.

"Why, I'll be damned!...if it ain't Rufus Ward," Vick said.

Rufus went over to Vick and patted him on the shoulder.

"Good to see yer still a'kickin'."

"You ain't looking for Orson are you?"

"Hell no...I'm looking fer you. A man paid me a pretty dime ta ride out this way and bring this letter to ya'. I could tell he wasn't from these parts, 'cause he paid fer my time." Vick laughed, knowing how tight folks in Jonesboro were with their money.

"Why don't you come in for a spell? If you're nice, Lizzie might fix you up with a big piece of pie."

"Lead the way my friend…lead the way. Oh, 'fore I fergit…here's the letter."

Vick looked at the handwriting on the envelope, and imagined it might be a legal document, since the penmanship was very elaborate.

"Charlie, wait a minute before we see Lizzie. Would you read this for me? My eyes ain't that good, if you know what I mean." Vick was embarrassed that he never learned to read more than a just few words.

"I probably can't do no better, but I'll try. There ain't nothing in here that's gonna git me in trouble is there?"

"You tell me. I hope not! I'm just worried that it's something that might upset Lizzie. You know we lost our boy two years ago, and she doesn't need any surprises. I have to be careful not to upset her, so don't let on when you see her."

"Well then, let's see the letter." Vick handed Rufus the opened envelope.

He read over the letter to himself first.

"I reckon you know the man, Jonathan Petty?"

Vick wondered what Jonathan was up to now.

"He says he's here to make you a deal you can't refuse. So, it can't be that bad if he's wantin' ta deal with ya'."

"What kind of deal?"

"That's what I'm trying to figure out. Oh, it's about a house he sold ta Cain before he died. He's willing ta pay whatever ya' want."

Vick assumed Jonathan was up to more than what the letter said. *He wouldn't come this far just to talk about buying back the house.*

"This Jonathan feller says he wants ta meet you tomorrow at that boarding house across from that fancy mercantile store they jest built. Yep, he wants ta meet ya' at 2:00 o'clock. And if you don't come, he's riding out yer way."

Vick knew he had no choice but to go alone if he wanted to protect Elizabeth, and maintain the secret that Orson and Hop were alive. After he met with Jonathan, he would warn Orson and Hop to lay low until Jonathan was gone.

"Rufus, I want you to tell him I'll be there." Vick knew Elizabeth would be extremely upset if she knew Jonathan was nearby.

"Vick, mind me asking what this man is to ya'?"

"Let's just say me and Jonathan have some unfinished business."

"I don't thank I like the sound of that," Rufus said.

"Rufus, there's something important I want to ask you…"

"Sure, what's that?"

"It's about Orson. I want you to keep quiet about Orson being back. Jonathan Petty is up to no good and I don't want him to know Orson is anywhere around. Can you keep this between me and you?"

"As we speak," replied Rufus. The men shook hands and Vick knew he could trust him.

The next morning, Vick dressed, and then gave Lizzie an excuse as to why he had to ride into town. "You go on, I have plenty to do right here," Elizabeth said.

Vick knew she was still excited about making improvements to the manor and would hardly miss him.

"Are you sure you don't mind?" Vick asked.

"Of course not. Why don't you get Orson and Hop to go with you?"

Vick would have liked nothing better than have them ride into town with him, but he was not ready to let Jonathan know Orson and Hop were alive.

In a tight for words, Vick made up a lame excuse to throw Lizzie off. "You know, I've had my fill of Orson and Hop. Sometimes a man needs to be alone," he said playfully with a chuckle; thinking a little humor might do the trick. It apparently did.

On the way to town, Vick had to ride right past Orson's cabin. He had to take a chance at not being seen. But the Sheriff wasn't called

Ol' Eagle Eyes for nothing. There he was in full view, sitting on the porch with a morning cup of coffee when Vick passed by.

"Git yoreself over here and have some coffee," Orson invited. Vick imagined it was going to take some quick thinking to discourage Orson, who would surely want to tag along with him.

"Come on in, and I'll git ya' a cup of Arkansas's best."

"How you doing Orson?"

"Seen better days, but I'm still here, and a'breathin'."

Once again, Vick had to think of something quickly. He remembered how much Orson fancied Lizzie's pies. "Orson, I'm here because Lizzie just made your two favorite pies, peach and apple. She wants you to come over and have a little bite to eat with her."

Orson studied Vick's face for a moment.

"Yer a lyin'! What ya' lyin' ta me fer? I can tell when ya' got somepin' ya' don't want me ta know about...so come clean, and then I'll think about the pie."

"You ol' coot, you're hard to fool, aren't you?"

"You thank being Sheriff all those years didn't teach me somepin' 'bout reading a cowpoke when he's a lyin'? Now, you tell me what the hell's a'goin' on."

"Maybe when I get back, but not now."

"I ain't a pryin', but I want ya' ta know that yer' a hidin' somepin."

"Orson, for your information, there comes a time when words are better left unsaid...and this is one of those times."

"And who in the heck made that up?" Orson debated.

"If I'm not mistaken, I think it was you," Vick fired back.

"Well, I ain't always right. Hadn't ya' figured that out yet?"

Vick couldn't help but chuckle.

"Orson, why don't you go have pie and let me be, okay?"

"Don't let me hold you up. You mosey on, but be careful." "Don't go worryin' 'bout me," Vick insisted. He hated to disappoint Orson, but he wasn't about to tell him he was going to meet with Jonathan.

At least Orson would be going in the opposite direction of town, lessening the possibility of Jonathan seeing him.

Riding the road to Jonesboro, Vick began having regrets about leaving Orson with unanswered questions. He knew how impulsive Orson could be, and he wasn't about to allow him to mess up his plan.

Orson was a little too agressive at times and had a tendency to jump in with both feet when it's unnecessary. Vick figured if Orson knew Jonathan was around, he would surely go after him. Underestimating him he had no idea that Orson would go about trying to find out what was going on with Vick and his secret behavior.

As soon as Orson rode up to the manor, he could smell the fresh pies baking. "They calling fer me," he explained to his lusting stomach.

Lizzie greeted him, and figured Vick had something to do with Orson coming over. *Somehow, he always knows when I'm cooking supper, or baking.* Elizabeth thought, we're always glad to share with dear Orson.

He didn't get seated before he began his grilling.

"Lizzie, Vick was shore out early this mornin'."

"Oh, so you saw him?" Elizabeth said, sheepishly.

"Yeah, I was having my morning coffee when he came and said he was going somewher', and bein' real cagey. This is the first time he refused to tell me wher' he was a going."

Elizabeth remembered what Vick had said about having enough of Orson. "He didn't want to hurt Orson's feelings," she thought. She tried to cushion what would surely have been a blow to his ego if he knew the real reason Vick failed to mention where he was going.

"Orson, I think Vick wanted to go it alone today. Sometimes a man wants to be left to his own thoughts without having the people he cares most about knowing what he's thinking."

"So that's what it's all about...he's tired of his friends?"

"Now, don't go putting words in my mouth. You know better than that."

"Then why didn't he ask me ta go with 'em? He knows I don't have a thang ta do but rock in that damn rocking chair."

"Oh, alright. If you have to know. Vick wanted to be alone. So now, I've said it. He needed a little time to himself."

"Well, why didn't ya say that the first time. Ya' know I don't like people a sugar coatin' thangs. He jest didn't want me goin' with 'em."

"Orson, you ready for another piece of pie?"

"Yes ma'am, I thank I'll try the peach this time."

Vick rode through one stream after the other, and the day couldn't have been more beautiful. As he rode, occasionally he would look up at the blue sky and its majestic cloud formations, something he was unable to do while locked in a cell for 20 long years. As a result, the sky now represented freedom. While caught in awe of the vastness of the sky, he noticed a hawk soaring above. It was a magnificent creature, and he was reminded of the hawk he had seen at Panther Holler. He would never forget the serenity and beauty of the heavily wooded area that surrounded the small cabin he once lived in. His mind often reminisced of the last day he had at Panther Holler, before the Sheriff and his posse came looking for him. It was there he learned Buck had double-crossed him, and turned him in, falsely accusing him of killing that family and even his own brother.

Vick believed ridding himself of this nightmare would end his torment, but ironically, it had just manifested itself again, this time, in the form of Jonathan Petty, who was much like Buck Dupree. Besides sharing delight in killing, they both were cunning and unpredictable. As Vick rode through the last stream before riding into Jonesboro, he thought about Sam, his younger brother, who had died before his time. He would never understand why a father who was three times his size would beat a sweet innocent boy. *If it hadn't been for the beatings, I would never have left home with Sam and run away. My brother would still be alive.* As he reminisced, Vick observed the hawk continuing to circle above. Suddenly, out of the corner of his eye, he saw another hawk that appeared to be waiting to attack the first hawk for invading his space. The two large birds expanded their wings as they fought in mid-air. *What could possibly be the reason for the attack?*

Vick asked himself. He had never seen creatures exhibit such violence, and it became apparent that the hawks intended to fight until death. *One of the birds will die*, Vick thought. Their wings were flapping as they battled, which was a spectacle in itself, as the large birds made loud painful screeching noises. It was an unusual occurrence, and he was compelled to take time to watch the two birds fight for survival. Eventually, the weaker hawk gave up and fell from the sky, spiraling toward the ground. Vick felt the passion of the first hawk, as he fought to stay alive. At that moment, he sensed there was personal significance in what he had just witnessed: a fight for survival, symbolic of his own life, and the many times he had to overcome the forces that tried to destroy him. *This is my life, since I still have Jonathan to deal with.*

Earlier in the day, when Orson left the manor, Hop rode back with him to help with chores. There was a lot of lumber from the barricaded windows that still needed to be removed, and Hop offered to help, since Orson was older and showing his age. This left Elizabeth alone with no one to call, should she need protection.

As she busied herself in the kitchen, two riders were approaching the manor. As soon as Lonnie and Dudley got in sight, they thought they were seeing things.

They reined their horses to a stop, as they saw the manor that had been rebuilt.

"Well I be a cotton picker. They done gone and rebuilt the place!" Lonnie exclaimed.

"Why, I be, ain't that somepin'. Them Porters got money ta burn, ain't they?" responded Dudley.

"Money ta burn." Lonnie chuckled after recalling they had burned down the manor before.

"I been a wonderin', reckon Jonathan's got somepin' up his sleeve? I bet he's got a plan we don't know 'bout," Dudley remarked.

"But we got a better one, so don't ya' worry none," Lonnie reinforced.

"We need to git on with finding that treasure instead of wasting time findin' Elizabeth and killin' 'er," Dudley retorted.

"We did a good job makin' him thank we killed that Aggie woman," Lonnie bragged. "Well, when we find 'er are ya gonna be the one ta kill 'er? Ya' know I ain't no good at that," bellyached Dudley. Lonnie hated hearing his brother whine like a coward.

"This is one woman I don't mind killin', so you can watch. Her ol' daddy ruined Pa's bootlegging business, and that's why we never had nothin'. He wanted all that whiskey business fer hisself. I oughta burn that place down again. And I would if smoke didn't bring people out this way."

"We can't burn it down twice, 'cause that ain't nice," Dudley laughed.

"I didn't thank ya' had enough sense ta' make a rhyme like that," chuckled Lonnie.

"I best bet ther's a lot of thangs ya' don't know 'bout me," Dudley remarked.

"I know yer' crazy, and that's all I need ta know."

"But, you don't thank I'm crazy like that Jonathan nut, do ya?"

"Maybe a little, but ain't nobody that crazy. Jonathan needs ta be in one of them insane asylums, all locked up," Lonnie mumbled as they got closer to the manor.

"Dudley, when we git ther', let's head out back of the house where the barn is and make shur' that Vick ain't no place around. After we check you'll walk up to the house and tell Elizabeth that you need ta talk ta Vick. If he's there he'll show hisself. Anyway he ain't supposed to be ther'?"

"That's what we want. If he ain't ther' then we'll kill her."

"Oh, alright, as long as you do it," Dudley replied. Lonnie winced again when he heard his spineless brother show signs of cowardice.

"Lonnie, I gotta better plan. Let's do a little outsmarting ourselves. How bout we kidnap Elizabeth and keep her hid out jest in case we need ta have the upper hand."

"You mean with Jonathan?"

"Yeah, and Vick too."

"Why Dudley, yer smarter than I gave ya credit fer. Let's kidnap her and take 'er to our cabin. Ain't nobody around them parts. We'll tie 'er up good and if we don't like how thangs are playing out we'll threaten to kill 'er. Vick's bound to talk then. Jest before he talks we'll blow Mr. Crazy away. When he sees we mean business, he'll talk we know he will." Dudley smiled knowing his brother finally approved of a plan that can bring them closer to finding the treasure.

Elizabeth had no idea anyone was on the property until she stood near the window measuring a curtain she had just finished sewing. Out of the corner of her eye, she thought she saw movement. She wasn't sure, because it was still early, and the sun had created such a glare. *It might be Vick coming back to the house*, she thought. Elizabeth kept an eye on the barn, waiting to see if it might be Vick. When she failed to see anyone, she assumed the flickering sunlight was playing tricks on her. She picked up the curtain, admiring her work, when she saw a form near the barn. This time she was sure she saw movement, but it wasn't Vick. Instead, it was a man walking toward the house. She sensed the man was up to no good the way he was walking—very slow and deliberate. Elizabeth, overcome with fear, and wondering what to do, remembered the escape hatch in the secret closet under the stairwell. *Who could this man be?* She wondered. Lonnie and Dudley had not yet entered her mind. Briefly, she thought of screaming for Hop, but reminded herself that he had left with Orson.

Afraid of what might happen, she picked up her shawl, and then ran to the secret closet to escape. Vick had repaired the opening of the escape hatch after the fire, and made minor changes that were more concealing. *No one would know the secret passage was there*, she thought. *Thank God Vick repaired the chute.* She knew it would be difficult for anyone to come after her, not knowing about the secret hiding place.

Elizabeth sat frozen inside the closet, as she heard not one man but two walk throughout the house, looking in every crook and cranny. She then heard footsteps coming toward the closet, as if they knew it was there. *How did they know, unless they've been here before?* She thought back to the day Lucy died, when the manor burned. Vick had been right, and the men who walked in on Lucy were the ones who murdered her. The suspicions regarding the James brothers were correct and she knew the men were Lonnie and Dudley James. *They must have followed us to Jonesboro, which means Jonathan could be someplace close by.* Still, she did not understand how they knew about the closet, unless they were the ones who found Lucy hiding there. *Too bad Lucy didn't know about the escape hatch, she could have scooted herself to safety.* When she heard the closet door open, her heart sank, and her suspicions were confirmed. The two men, indeed, knew exactly where the closet was. She heard them as they were exploring the interior of her refuge. This caused her to scoot deeper, and more quickly, into the passage. When the men heard something, they had no idea it was Elizabeth scooting herself to safety.

"Lonnie, ya hear somepin'?" Lonnie winced, trying to figure out where the sounds were coming from. "Nah! Ain'tnothin' but some big rats in them walls."

"Well, she ain't here, and we best git goin'. We ain't got time fer no wild goose chase, if we planning on kidnapping Porter."

Elizabeth heard every word, and now she was in a panic to escape, and rush to Orson's cabin.

Lonnie was still scratching his head when he walked out the door toward the barn. "Dudley, ya don't thank that woman's a hidin' out in some secret place that we don't know about, do ya?"

"If she was here, we woulda found her."

By this time, Elizabeth had made her way through the chute and into the woods. Even though she felt safe, having escaped from the James', she was beside herself with fright, knowing they were going after Vick. *I have to get to Orson... and fast!* she shuddered.

Chapter 26

IT HAD BEEN MORE THAN A MONTH SINCE LUCY'S ACCIDENT, AND SHE **had not shown any signs of improvement.** Birdie wondered if she would ever regain consciousness, her injuries being so serious. Dr. Cohen examined Lucy each day, and noticed some signs of activity, but he was not sure she would ever be more than what she was at the time. Occasionally, she would open her eyes staring without seeing anything or anyone, but this would give them hope.

Birdie continued to look in on Lucy, and did as the doctor said, by sitting and holding her hand, talking to her about insignificant things that she knew would amuse her if she were well and coherent. The tragedies they suffered together created a bond that could easily rival that found in the strongest of families. There was no way Birdie was going to give up on Lucy, especially since she knew Lucy to be the stronger of the two.

"She's going to come out of this—you wait and see," she would often tell the doctor.

It was a cool crisp morning in November when Doctor Cohen looked in on Lucy, and he noticed a big change. *I think she's coming around,* he thought. The doctor heard footsteps coming down the hallway, and went to the door to see who it was. It was Birdie, walking towards him. "Come in Birdie. I don't want you getting your hopes up, but Lucy appears to be regaining consciousness." Birdie was ecstatic at hearing the news. She took Lucy's hand, and then bent down so she could whisper the news into her ear. "You're going to be alright, and when you open those big beautiful eyes of yours, we'll be right here waiting." In that moment, Lucy squeezed Birdie's hand.

"Mark, did you see that?" asked Birdie, now on a first-name basis with Dr. Cohen. "She squeezed my hand. She's going to be all right."

Mark smiled, "Well, what do you know! I think she's going to make it. Wonderful news."

That night, Birdie stayed with Lucy, just in case she opened her eyes again. Lucy was still in her splints, and Birdie was not sure she would remember the accident that killed Munk, and almost killed her.

But more weeks went by, and she remained in a coma with no more hopeful signs. Birdie had spent most days and nights close to Lucy's bedside, hoping she would squeeze her hand again, and give Birdie the chance to immediately encourage her to wake up, believing timing would help. Eventually, Dr. Cohen told Birdie that Lucy had relapsed, and reminded her of the possibility that she may never come out of the coma. "Then why would she squeeze my hand, if that were true?"

"Sometimes it's only a reflex," Dr. Cohen explained. This was the first time Birdie began losing hope of Lucy's recovery.

A few days thereafter brought torrential rains, and only added to Birdie's sadness concerning Lucy. She walked into her room, and was pulling the curtains closed, when she heard a weak voice say, "Birdie, you know I like to see the rain." She turned quickly, and rushed to the side of her bed. "Lucy, you're awake!"

"Of course I am; I like the rain."

"Well, if it takes a thunderstorm to wake you, then let it pour. I can't believe you've come back to us." Birdie was so happy, and wanted to immediately find Mark and tell him the good news.

"Lucy, don't go back to sleep, you hear?" Birdie all but ran through the door just in time to see Mark coming from another patient's room.

"Mark, come quick, I need you…now!"

Fearing the worst, he ran into Lucy's room. He too was elated to find Lucy awake and talking. Mark thought, *She's more beautiful than*

I imagined. Lucy's blue eyes were much larger than he remembered, and her lips had a natural pink to them now that her face registered conscious expressions and her eyes glistened. He couldn't believe, after being in a coma for that long, she would glow as healthfully as she did. Instead of the normally stoic and confident doctor, he turned into a bashful tongue-tied kid, something he had never experienced. He went to her bedside, almost embarrassed to touch her. When he bent down with his stethoscope to check her heart, she looked him in the eyes and spoke softly.

"I think I was in an accident...with Munk. Lucy's expression turned to fear as she relived Munk overtaking her car.

"You don't have to worry about him anymore. He's dead," he hurriedly put her fears to rest.

"Dead? Are you sure?"

Birdie spoke up. "Yes Lucy, he's dead as a doornail. We buried him, so don't worry about anyone trying to hurt you again."

Lucy realized she had been hurt and when she saw the splints she questioned.

"Birdie, am I going to be alright?"

"You're mending well, and now that you've regained consciousness, you'll heal faster than ever." Birdie looked at Mark for his support.

Finally, after a long pause, he said, "Yes, Lucy, you can rest assured that you will be okay. Just a little more healing, and you will be good as new."

Birdie sensed something going on with Mark, but she tried to ignore it. The last thing she needed was a doctor who couldn't maintain his professionalism because he was smitten with a patient's beauty. *Lucy has just been conscious a few minutes and already, this doctor was starting to act like Jason had toward Lucy.*

"Lucy, I want you to meet Doctor Mark Cohen. He's here because we needed a doctor to run the hospital, and, of course, to take care of you."

"Thank you for taking such good care of me. I hope I haven't been too much of a burden," Lucy whispered.

Mark tried to reassure her that she would be all right, but continued to be smitten with the most beautiful woman he had ever met.

"Ah…your body has, ah…continued to heal during the last two months while you've been in a coma."

Birdie thought, *Snap out of it!*

"You'll…ah…be out of the splints before you know it."

Good grief! Birdie thought. *What's wrong with you? Surely Lucy knows what's going on.*

Lucy looked into Mark's eyes and then questioned him about being in a coma for two full months.

"But you're fine now, and we will need to step up strengthening your leg and arm muscles, then we'll get you into a wheelchair and will be able to move you," Birdie encouragingly offered.

Lucy took Birdie's hand, whispering, "Thank you so much, Birdie."

Then, to the doctor, "Doctor Cohen, thank you again for taking such good care of me."

"Please, Lucy… call me Mark."

"I'll try," Lucy said in a weak, raspy voice.

All the while, Birdie was wondering, *How is this going to play out?*

Dr. Cohen reiterated, "I promise you that within two months, we'll have you well again, your bones fully healed."

Lucy smiled at him, thought how charming he was, and how much he reminded her of her late husband, Jason, who had been murdered.

"Birdie, let's see that Lucy is in a wheelchair by the end of the week. Do you think we can make that happen?"

"If our patient cooperates," Birdie replied, smiling at Lucy.

～

Elizabeth was too terrified to return to the manor, even though she watched the James brothers leave. *They must be the ones who killed Lucy, and if they find me, I could be next. I've got to get to Orson, and warn him that they're after Vick.*

Cain was only minutes away from seeing the manor when he thought of Lucy, and what would have been their wedding day. As he turned the bend he felt a wave of sadness come over him, recalling the tragedy that took sweet Lucy's life. Suddenly, there it was, the stately manor that had been rebuilt. He stopped his horse, and stared in near disbelief. *Vick must have had it rebuilt for mother,* he assumed. He sat motionless in his saddle, taking a few minutes to regain his composure. His mind and heart was reliving that tragic day of some two long years ago. *Somehow, it seems like only yesterday.* He forced himself back to the present, and nudged his horse forward.

Elizabeth was watching from the woods, too frightened to return to the manor, when she caught a glimpse of a man riding toward her. *Now I can ask for help,* she thought.

As she watched the distant rider coming towards her, she saw familiarity in his build and the way he rode the horse. *Who could that be?* she wondered. As she stared at the rider, she thought how much he looked like Vick. That's someone I've seen before, she recalled. As he rode closer, she clasped her hands, and her heart swelled with joy. "It can't be!" she blurted out. A feeling of relief swept through her as she ran toward Cain, riding in her direction. "Cain, Cain…oh, my goodness, you're alive!" Elizabeth shouted with tears running down her face. She was stunned and shaken. "Please, I can't be dreaming. Please don't let this be a dream," she sobbed.

As he approached, she knew for certain it was her son!

Cain pulled the reins and stopped sharply. Seeing his mother run from the woods, he knew something was wrong. Tears of joy filled his eyes seeing his mother for the first time since he left with Orson over two years earlier. He jumped from his horse and ran to her, grabbing her in his arms and swinging her around him. "Mother, oh mother, I'm back!"

"Cain, I can't believe it's you! My prayers have been answered. You're alive!" Elizabeth was sobbing, as she tried to speak. "We all hoped and prayed you would one day ride in like this. Where on earth have you been? We were so worried, fearing the worst since it has been so long."

She held his face in her hands, examining him as she wept uncontrollably. She was overwhelmed. "I can't believe it's you. Everyone thought you were dead, but we never gave up on you," she kept repeating herself.

Cain choked up, and wept at seeing his mother cry. "Ma, you wouldn't believe half of what's happened to me."

Elizabeth wanted to know, but she was afraid it would take away from the present. "Cain, you can tell me later—but right now, I want to savor this time with you. It must be God looking over me—and you, son."

With that statement, Cain knew something had happened.

"When I rode up, you were coming from the woods. Do you mind telling me what's going on?"

"Cain, I'm worried about your father. We need—Elizabeth hesitated before finishing her statement, for she knew that Cain needed to sit down to hear that Orson is alive and well. She quickly recovered and hugged him once again.

You're back, and that's all that matters. Come, let's go to the house." Cain led his horse to the hitching rail.

"I see you and Pa rebuilt the manor," Cain said, as he wondered what his mother was not telling him. He sensed something seriously was going on with her.

"This was all your father's doing. He sure knows how to keep a secret. He didn't tell anyone."

"Mother, why don't you tell me what's going on. I went by the plantation, and Sammy told me that you and Pa had moved back to Arkansas. Pa's alright, isn't he?"

"Yes, son. I don't want you worrying."

I guess Jonathan reclaimed the place after he killed Orson and left me for dead."

Elizabeth wanted to gradually lead up to what happened to Orson but she knew that Cain would want to leave right away to see Orson without understanding what all happened. She thought it was important for him to know some of the facts.

"Cain, Jonathan had to wait until everyone was sure you weren't coming back, and then the scoundrel moved quickly. We moved into Orson's place and stayed there until recently, hoping, by some miracle, that you were alive and would return home."

"Cain, come on in, and I'll try to catch you up."

The manor was so much like it was before, Cain thought. Elizabeth led him down the hallway to the library. "Son, can I get you anything? You must be hungry."

"Mother, why don't you start with why you were frightened when I came up. Did it have something to do with you being in the woods?"

Elizabeth looked away, but she knew she had to tell Cain about Orson and her ordeal.

"It's a good thing you came when you did. Do you remember the James brothers?"

"I reckon I do," Cain said, with sarcasm. They're the ones who killed Orson, and thought they killed me. It hit me in Woodville, Texas that they might have had something to do with the plot to murder Orson and me. When they ran away after seeing me, it was a dead give away that they were involved."

Cain didn't want to go into details regarding Aggie and the baby until he made sure that Jonathan was taken care of.

"Cain, I don't want this being too much of a shock, but Orson didn't die. He made his way back home thinking you had rode off without him."

"Orson's alive?"

"Yes, and he's living back at his cabin."

"I can't believe he's alive. He's all right isn't he?"

"Yes, Orson is fine, but I need you to know about your Pa. Cain, I'm sure he's in trouble. He rode into town to meet up with Jonathan. I didn't know for sure until Orson said your Pa rode by his house on the way to town acting very secretive. I think Jonathan and the James brothers are here to harm your Pa and me. Right before you rode up, Lonnie and Dudley broke into the manor looking for us. That's why I was in the woods when you first saw me. Do you remember the secret escape chute in the closet under the stairwell? That's how I escaped. I scooted all the way through the chute into the woods. I heard them talking about us. I was afraid to come back to the house for fear they might return. That's when I saw you riding up."

"Mother, you're okay now, aren't you?"

"Everything's going to be fine, now that you're home. One thing, though, since you're back, I don't want you getting mixed up with Jonathan and those James'. It's not me I'm afraid for, it's your Pa, and I don't want you getting involved. Now that you're back, I don't want anything happening to you."

"Is Orson home now?"

"Yes, he and Hop are working around Orson's place. You remember Hop, the man you hired from Memphis?"

"Oh yes, he's the man I was going to surprise Pa with."

"Well, you missed the surprise. You remember, he owned all those cotton farms in New Orleans. At least we have Hop with us now. So much has happened, I don't know where to begin. Jonathan and the James' think you and Orson are dead, and your Pa wants to keep it that way."

"Pa must have a reason."

"Orson can tell you all about it when he sees you."

"Mother, what I have to do now, is get you someplace safe, so me and Orson can go after Pa. What about my office in town? Have you seen it since you've been back?"

"I'm sorry, son, but I haven't even been to town."

"It's probably not a good idea, anyway. How would you feel about staying at Orson's until it's safe for you to come back home?"

"But what about you? I worry about your safety."

"You don't need to worry about me. I think by now, I can take care of myself."

Elizabeth saw the gun on Cain's hip, and wondered if he had learned to use it.

Orson and Hop were sitting on the porch when they saw a man and woman approaching the cabin. "Hop, ya' tell me if that woman riding up ther' don't look like Lizzie?"

"I think you're right. It is her."

"Who do ya' reckon is with her? I know it ain't Vick, 'cause he's on his way ta town, but it shore looks like him."

"Beats me, I ain't never seen that feller before," Hop said.

Orson got up from his chair, his mouth agape, trying to make out who the stranger was with Lizzie. This was highly unusual, seeing Lizzie on a horse. Orson kept staring. "Well, I be damn! That feller looks like…by George, I thank it is. That's Cain! Lord have mercy, if it ain't Cain! The boy's alive!" Orson couldn't move very fast, but he was running as fast as he could to get to Cain.

Hop stood on the porch and waited, to give Orson a chance to have a private moment with the young man who had just come alive before their very eyes. Orson had not shown much emotion since Lucy died, but seeing Cain was more than he could take. His eyes turned beet red as tears streamed down his face, seeing Cain after two years.

Orson dried his eyes on his shirt, and was a bit embarrassed about letting others see him cry. "Why I be danged…ain't you a sight fer my sore eyes." He kept rubbing his eyes. "Git down off that damn horse and let me at ya'." Orson grabbed Cain and gave him a big hug. "I can't believe yer here."

Cain, red-eyed as well, answered in kind, "Well, I can't believe you're here."

"Son, we 'bout gave up on ya', but one feller that never did was yer Pa, and of course, your Ma here."

"Orson, I thought you were dead, and when Mother told me you were alive, I had to come and see for myself." Cain alighted from his horse and grabbed Orson. The two hugged and patted each other's backs as Elizabeth and Hop wiped away their tears.

"Well, yer Pa kept sayin' Cain's out there somewhere,' and I guess ya' was. We covered many a mile a lookin' fer' ya'…I see ya' brought yer' Pa's horse home."

"Yeah, when Senor Galvez said 'your Pa wants you to ride his horse to Arkansas', I figured Pa might have a feeling I was alive. And then when Mother told me you were alive, I could hardly believe it. I was sure you didn't make it back."

"Yeah, I made it back, but it shore was a sad day when I thought ya was dead. Yer Pa ain't seen ya' yet, has he?"

"Not yet, he left for town before I arrived."

"He's shore gonna be surprised when he sees ya'."

Elizabeth allowed Cain and Orson a little time to have their reunion but was worried about Vick's safety.

"Orson, I hate to interrupt, but I had two visitors shortly before Cain rode up."

"I can tell it ain't good. Who was it?" Orson replied.

"It was the James brothers. They broke into the house, but not before I had time to escape. I hid in the chute that's in the closet under the stairwell. I could hear them talking about Vick and me. Since those brothers have been working for Jonathan, I think he's likely in town, too, and Orson, I think that's why Vick chose not to involve you. Vick didn't want Jonathan to find out you were alive. Jonathan and the James' are all up to no good."

Orson looked at Cain, and then Hop. "Well, I ain't gonna let him face the James boys and Jonathan alone. I'm going after 'em."

"It's about time we dealt with them," Hop said.

"You can count me in, too," Cain replied.

Orson looked at Elizabeth and knew she didn't want her son involved, after she had just gotten him back. "Cain, somebody needs to stay here with yer Ma, and keep her safe."

"Mother, would you be okay without me? Orson, maybe Mother can stay here at your place. No one would suspect she's here." Elizabeth could see the passion in Cain's eyes, and realized he had to do this for his Pa.

"Orson, do you mind if I stay here at your place? Cain's right. No one will be looking for me here."

"Lizzie, I thank ya know by now that my home is yours, too. Cain, ya' remember Hop, the man ya' hired ta come and work fer' ya' Pa?"

"So this is Hop...I'm sorry for the delay, but I see you found your way without us," Cain said in jest.

Cain shook Hop's hand. "Nice to meet you, Hop."

"Same to ya'. I've heard all about ya'," Hop said.

"When me and Orson headed for Memphis, we sure didn't expect to be ambushed."

"Well, you're home now, and that's what counts."

Cain couldn't take his eyes off Orson after thinking he was dead.

"Orson had a head start, and beat ya' home," Hop explained.

"After I was shot, it took me two years to regain my memory. I had no idea who I was until about a month ago."

"What do you mean, you didn't know who you were?"

"I had amnesia, a loss of memory. Thankfully, a nice older couple, Martha and Glen, took me in, gave me a job, and treated me like family. I ended up living on their ranch near Beaumont, until after Glen died, and that's when I found a poster that identified me as Cain Porter. That ambush description on the poster caused my memory to return. I began remembering right then, and now, I'm home. Glen and Martha turned out to be like parents to me while I was there." Cain thought it best not to mention Aggie, or that he had a young son, that made them grandparents. *After the dust settles, I'll fill in that part.*

Elizabeth was astonished to hear her son had suffered with amnesia. "Cain, I'm so sorry…are you all right now?"

"For the most part. There might be bits and pieces that I don't remember, but that'll come later. Right now, we need to get to Pa."

"Well, it looks like ya' done fell into another hornets nest with what Jonathan's put ya' through," Orson interjected.

Elizabeth gave up trying to convince Cain to not go. "I've talked 'til my throat's dry. I told Cain not to get involved, but there's no doubt that he's his father's son. Can you please talk some sense in his head?"

"Son, I know ya' want to help, but yer' Ma's right." echoed Orson.

Cain patted Orson on the back. "I guess you think I'm the same kid that got ambushed two years ago, but I'm not. I need to do this for myself, and for Vick." He looked at his mother earnestly and said, "You understand, don't you?"

Orson approached Elizabeth. "Well Lizzie, I tried. Now, I guess it's between you and Cain."

Chapter 27

Vᴵᴄᴋ ᴀʀʀɪᴠᴇᴅ ɪɴ Jᴏɴᴇsʙᴏʀᴏ sʜᴏʀᴛʟʏ ʙᴇꜰᴏʀᴇ 2:00ᴘ.ᴍ., ʀᴇᴀᴅʏ ᴛᴏ meet with Jonathan. As he rode through town, he hardly recognized Jonesboro with so much growth that had taken place during the years he was in prison, plus the two years he and Elizabeth spent in San Augustine. Signs of the "Old West" no longer existed, as the old era had passed and were replaced by the trappings of a new century.

Businesses had sprung up everywhere, with a new mercantile store, churches, schools, railroads, and telegraph wires strung up all over the place. Jonesboro was now a modern town, mostly with new residents, both young and old. There were kids playing in the street, playing new games that he was not familiar with. And then, instead of just wagons and horses, there were mostly new and old cars parked all over town, with many lined up in front of the bank and the stores. He could not believe this was his town of Jonesboro.

Vick, now in his mid-forties, felt he had already lived a lifetime. His redeeming grace was Elizabeth, and there was no way he would allow Jonathan or the James brothers spoil what happiness they shared, if he could help it.

Everything in my life is as it should be now, except for losing Cain, he reflected. Nothing in his troubled life was as bad as that; however, he had Elizabeth, and life would go on. Then there was Jonathan, who was just as evil as Buck Dupree. As he approached the boarding house, Vick wondered, *How many more Bucks am I going to have to kill to finally have a normal life? Perhaps there is no normal for me,* he wondered.

When Vick arrived at his destination, he recognized a much older man who had worked for him when he owned Porter Lumber Company.

"Why, I be damned, if it ain't Vick Porter," Clyde said. "I ain't seen you in a coon's age." They chatted for a few minutes, and then Clyde walked into the dining room of the boarding house to have a bite to eat.

Vick hardly recognized the man's face, since he had aged so much, but Vick had changed very little, even after so many years in prison.

Jonathan, who was waiting impatiently, kept looking at his pocket watch, wondering if Vick was going to show, or if he would have to track him down. Just as the second hand passed 2:00p.m. Vick and Clyde walked through the doors, and into the dining room. There, Vick saw the face of his archenemy. Jonathan was noticeably infuriated to see Vick with someone he did not know. He had specifically sent word for Vick to come alone, or least he thought he did. After Clyde took a seat at another table, Jonathan realized he had made a mistake. Vick was amused at the look on Jonathan's face. *He looks like a man who just learned someone shot his dog*, Vick laughed inwardly.

As he approached Jonathan, there was a cordial demeanor about him. At that moment, he imagined the meeting could turn dangerous, since Jonathan had some unknown motive for coming to Jonesboro. *There is something much bigger than the phony plan to purchase the house Cain bought for Orson*, Vick cleverly determined.

By the time Vick approached him, Jonathan had adapted into the character of a man who was there to meet an old friend. He stood and offered his hand for Vick to shake. Vick hated playing along with Jonathan's phony attempt at being a gentleman, but he wanted to see just how low Jonathan would stoop in order to accomplish his purpose.

"I see you got my letter," Jonathan quipped.

"There's no other reason for our meeting, so why don't you tell me what's really going on."

"What do you mean…going on?" Jonathan questioned.

"I've learned a thing or two about you in the last two years, and I know you wouldn't come all this way for just that small piece of land when that matter could be handled by the U.S. mail."

"Oh, but that's where you're wrong. You see, I don't want to live anywhere close to a Porter, but that's only one reason," Jonathan remarked.

"And the other reason?" Vick asked.

"I remember challenging you to a game of poker some time ago, and I think I owe it to my brother to whip your ass."

Clyde was observing the meeting between Vick and Jonathan, and sensed the meeting didn't appear to be friendly. He kept pondering what was going on. *Something jest ain't right*, Clyde thought. *When they smile, their eyes don't look friendly at all.*

He imagined Vick was in trouble as he continued to watch.

"You've got my attention, so what's your deal?" Vick asked Jonathan.

"I'll pay you five times what your son paid me, to purchase back the house and land after we have our little game."

Vick was amused, and took delight in seeing Jonathan sweat.

"We kinda like that property, and I think owning half the lake makes it worth a lot more."

"I should have known you'd ask a bundle, since you're a known cheater. Most men would consider my offer a bargain."

Jonathan imagined he got under Vick's skin, but Jonathan had no idea that a man who had spent 20 years of his life in prison knew all the tricks. Being locked up, and using your mind to stay alive had helped develop a mental toughness that no ordinary man would understand.

Jonathan was so angered by Vick's tough exterior that he allowed Vick to get under his skin.

"You did say you were going to make me a deal that I can't refuse, so let's hear it. I'm tired, and I don't have time for this."

Vick's remark further angered Jonathan, and he knew he had to jab harder to get Vick's attention. "I remember hearing the story of how you challenged your wife's daddy to a game of poker...and then stripped him of his wealth. Your wife must have been desperate to marry the man who cheated her father, and then caused him to kill himself."

Vick continued to show restraint even after hearing Elizabeth's name. He was not introspective enough to predict that the mention of his wife would enrage him to the point where he would become vulnerable to a plan that could cost him his life but he continued to remain stoic.

"I imagine we both have blood on our hands. Apparently, you know mine but I'm still waiting for you to confess to all the killings you've done," Vick chided him.

Jonathan was livid, but he managed to calm himself down after a few seconds. You could feel the tension at this table.

"Let's try not to be accusing, since we don't like each other. I prefer to keep the name calling to ourselves and work out this little proposition I'm going to offer you."

"Jonathan, why don't you cut out the games and get to the point."

"Well, I did send word that I was going to make you a deal you can't refuse," Jonathan reminded Vick.

"Then make it and let us get on with it."

"Here's the deal we meet and play at the saloon outside of town."

"What time," Vick asked.

"Let's meet at 6 o'clock this evening," Jonathan instructed.

Vick turned his back to Jonathan, and headed to the door, "See you at 6."

After Vick left, Clyde continued to eat, then followed Jonathan until he met up with the James boys. After hiding out and listening he got an ear full. *There's something shady going on with them James brothers*, Clyde believed.

He knew the background of Lonnie and Dudley, who were born and raised in Jonesboro, and suspected a man of Jonathan's caliber would not be dealing with them unless they were all up to no good.

Clyde wanted to hear what they were saying, and edged as close as he could without being seen. During the conversation, he heard mention of Elizabeth Porter.

"What about Elizabeth? Jonathan asked. "Where is she?"

"We had ta take care of her. We didn't have no choice!"

Lonnie looked at Dudley and gave him the eye to keep his mouth shut.

Their explanation appeared to be good enough for Jonathan for he was consumed with outsmarting Vick.

"Vick ain't ta know about Elizabeth, ya hear?"

"We ain't gonna say a word boss."

Lonnie bit his tongue trying to give Dudley the eye to keep quiet.

Clyde became alarmed hearing the men talk about Elizabeth.

Jonathan quickly assessed his scheme to kidnap Vick. His fear was that Lonnie and Dudley would ruin his plan.

"You remember what we talked about, and how important it is that you don't mess this up?"

"Yes indeedy, boss. We here ti make sure we don't foul up anythang."

"Now, y'all listen carefully. As soon as Porter hits the trail, y'all be close behind. When you see me step out of the woods and wait for Vick to approach me, be sure and give us a little time so Vick won't suspect we're partners. You have to be convincing, and make him believe you're kidnapping the two of us together. Understand? After kidnapping us, you make him believe that you and Dudley are acting alone. Do you understand?"

"We understand boss, ya' don't have a thang ta worry 'bout."

Just the mention of Lonnie saying Jonathan didn't have to worry made Jonathan worry.

Meanwhile, Clyde knew he had to help Vick get out of this mess, so he followed the brothers to spoil their plan.

~

November was a beautiful month in Arkansas, and Vick was enjoying the deep brilliant colors of a new season. Fall was always his favorite time of the year, and riding along to kill time before his card game with Jonathan, he thought of Elizabeth, and the dance the town had thrown for him after he was released from prison. *Those were good times*, he reminisced. He could still picture how beautiful Elizabeth was when he escorted her to the dance. Looking back, it seemed that everything was alive, and the world was beautiful and carefree. Recapturing those moments, and the excitement of his love for Elizabeth, he thought it was the best time of his life, which was the complete opposite of how he felt now. Vick wondered how his life had changed so drastically with the loss of Cain and with so much uncertainty lingering.

Lost in thought, Vick was unaware that the James boys were following him, waiting for the right time for Jonathan to encounter Vick on the trail to the saloon.

He had ridden nearly two miles when he was surprised to find Jonathan waiting on the side of the road. Vick approached him, wondering why he had stopped. He didn't want to ride with Jonathan, but it now looked like Jonathan wanted to ride along with him, probably to try to get into Vick's head and mess up his game. When the two men approached each other Jonathan acted as if there was no problem at all.

"I know we're not friends, but I hope you don't mind me riding along with you. I was told the saloon was three miles out of town, but seeing you, I figured you wouldn't mind if I tagged along, since I'm not familiar with the saloon's location."

Vick thought that was reasonable, but he still did not trust him and remained cautious. "We got another mile before we get there. You're a little early, aren't you?" asked Vick.

"I suppose…but since I didn't rightly know where I was going, I thought it best to be early than late."

"This game of ours must be real important to you, eh?" Vick asked.

"I guess we'll just have to wait and see."

Vick did not notice the cynical look on Jonathan's face.

They rode for another mile, when Vick saw two hawks circling above. *What's with all the hawks?* he wondered.

As they approached a stream, Lonnie and Dudley walked their horses quietly out of the brush, then mounted and rode up behind Jonathan and Vick. Hearing the sound of hooves coming up quickly behind him, Vick swirled around and tried to draw his gun, but not before Dudley grazed his shoulder with a bullet.

"Drop yer guns! I said, drop yer' guns…now!" Lonnie shouted. Turning toward Dudley, Lonnie yelled, "Hot dang it you stupid idiot, you almost killed Vick."

Vick didn't argue, concerned that the two brothers would most likely kill him if he didn't do as they said. Jonathan played along, dropping his gun, seeing his plan unfold before his eyes.

"You boys take it easy," Jonathan said. Dudley jumped off his horse and picked up the guns.

Clyde saw everything, but he wasn't about to act, not while the men had their guns trained on Vick. And, obviously, they were not afraid to use them. He had to play it safe until the time was right for him to catch them off guard, and rescue Vick. Clyde was living a pipe-dream, thinking he could get the jump on three men.

Vick had been in tight spots before, and since the James' had the upper hand, he had to wait to put up any kind of challenge.

Vick turned to face the brothers. "Seems like I've seen you boys before."

"And where was that?" asked Lonnie.

"I think you know," Vick answered, staring the men down. The brothers just looked at each other.

"What do you boys want with me?" Vick asked.

Jonathan pleaded his case. "Why y'all holding me when it's him you want?"

"Yer a witness, that's why," Lonnie replied. "Now keep yer mouth shut, if ya' know what's good fer' ya'."

For the first time, Jonathan was impressed with how well Lonnie and Dudley were playing their part. He didn't realize that what he saw was the men's true character, and it wasn't an act.

Vick was amused, at their stupid act when he knew they were all in cahoots together.

"Maybe this'll ring a bell fer'ya', You and ol' Eagle Eyes kilt our little brother, Johnny, and we're here ta collect, Lonnie retorted.

"So ya best start talkin' and tell us where you hid that treasure Johnny told us about?" Dudley demanded.

Vick had no answer, since the story about a treasure was a made one in order to have a showdown with Buck Dupree. He and Elizabeth had given the treasure to a courier years ago in order for the governor to redistribute the wealth to their rightful owners. However, now the rumor of a hidden treasure had doubled back and bit Vick in the butt. At this point he had no other alternative but to continue the charade of a treasure in order to stay alive.

"So where's the treasure, if ya' want ti see that purdy little wife of yours agin?" Lonnie threatened..

Looking on, Jonathan was pleased with the Jameses performance but Vick was concerned hearing the threat made against Elizabeth. He had no idea what to do. He needed time.

I've got to get them as far away from Jonesboro as possible to stall them, Vick thought.

"It was a long time ago and I'm not sure exactly where I buried it."

"It better come to ya' real fast if ya' know what's good fer that wife of yers."

Vick discerned that this was now a new game, a very serious game, and if he wanted to save his wife, he needed more time. *Panther Holler was a couple of days travel and this might give me enough time to free myself,* he thought. *With a miracle this might give Orson and Hop a chance to figure out what happened,"* Within a few seconds Vick calculated this. Of course, none of his plans included Cain since Vick had no idea that Cain was alive.

Jonathan continued to play the role of a kidnapped victim.

"You boys don't need me. Why don't you let me go?" Jonathan pleaded.

"I told ya' that yer a witness, and we don't like witnesses," Lonnie reiterated.

These idiots are so wrapped up in a treasure that there's no way they would believe me if I told them the truth about the treasure being a made up story, Vick thought. He began to wonder if he would ever have an opportunity to escape.

After Lonnie and Dudley had Vick's attention with their threats, Dudley rode up beside Vick and punched him in the back with the butt of his rifle.

"You got that treasure back at that Panther Holler place, so git a move on."

Eavesdropping on the outlaws, Clyde had positioned himself much closer than he first realized. When he heard they were taking Vick to Panther Holler, he thought, *Where in the hell is Panther Holler?* At that moment, Clyde's horse snickered, and the men knew they had company.

Dudley whispered, "Lonnie, I see somebody in that brush over there."

Clyde's horse snickered again. This time, Lonnie turned his horse sharply, and saw Clyde trying to get away. Without hesitation, he shot the old man in the back, knocking him from his saddle. Clyde lay on the ground playing dead, knowing he would most likely take another bullet. He had no choice, since his horse had run away. Lonnie dismounted and kicked Clyde in the stomach, testing to see if he was alive.

Dudley hollered, "Is he dead?" Another shot rang out.

"Now he is!" Lonnie replied.

Vick recognized the dead man as his friend Clyde. *He was a harmless, decent man, who died trying to help me*, Vick regretted.

Jonathan looked at Vick, and shook his head as though he was saddened that Clyde had been shot.

"Who else ya' got followin' us?" Lonnie asked Vick. When he failed to answer, Lonnie, again took his rifle and hit Vick in his back with the butt of the weapon.

"Don't kill 'em, we need 'em to find the treasure!" Dudley shouted.

Vick took quite a wallop, and reaffirmed to him the only thing keeping him alive was his captor's deluded belief that they were on a quest for a treasure worth a fortune.

Chapter 28

AFTER CAIN DISCUSSED WITH ORSON AND HOP ABOUT GOING AFTER **Vick, they agreed to leave the next morning at first light.** This would give Vick enough time to make it home, if he indeed was coming home. Vick would never stay away without telling Elizabeth; therefore, she knew there was something wrong. When the James brothers broke into the manor, Elizabeth narrowly escaped death. And now that Vick was missing, she was convinced that Jonathan and the brothers were in town to do harm to both her and Vick.

Elizabeth was thrilled at having Cain home, but his amazing homecoming was now dampened by Vick's disappearance. After they rode over to Orson's, and filled him in regarding the news about the James', they discussed what they should do next to find Vick, then rode back to the manor. Elizabeth wanted Cain to feel a sense of homecoming, and the best way was for him to return to the manor where he had spent most of his life. With heavy hearts they speculated about what might have happened to Vick. They all were sure that Jonathan Petty was responsible for Vick's absence.

It was very frightening for Elizabeth to even consider the possibility that the man she loved might be in some type of danger. *I can't lose Vick...not now!* she kept saying to herself. Cain was also uneasy, knowing the worst might have happened to his Pa before he got to see him and let him know he was alive. He and Orson knew firsthand what Jonathan and the James' were capable of. Cain and Elizabeth reasoned that the rumors of the treasure buried at Panther Holler and their hate for Vick was the brothers' motivation.

The next morning, Elizabeth was up early to see Cain and Hop off. She had made up several days' rations for them and had it all packed well to fit in their saddlebags.

"Miss Elizabeth, you always take care of us," Hop said.

"That's the least I can do, since I don't know when you all will be back. Cain, promise me you'll take good care of yourself. I can't afford to lose you a second time."

"You don't worry about Cain as long as Orson and me are around," Hop reassured her.

"Well, don't any of you take chances—just find Vick," Elizabeth managed to say and began crying, fearing the worst for Vick and all of them.

"Ma, please don't cry. We don't know for sure if Jonathan and the James brothers have Pa. He could have run into some other kind of trouble. Who really knows? That's why it's important that you be around, just in case he comes riding up." They knew how much Elizabeth loved Vick, and neither doubted that she might saddle up to conduct her own search.

"Don't worry about me. As soon as it's daylight, I'm going to Orsons'," Elizabeth said.

"Promise me you'll do that," Cain implored.

Elizabeth ignored the question, not wanting them to worry. "Y'all better git going—you know how Orson is. He's probably waiting for you now."

"Okay, but you take care of yourself, and use my gun if you have to."

Elizabeth managed a smile, and turned to go back into the manor.

"Hop, do you reckon she'll be alright?" Cain asked as they headed toward town.

"You're Ma's a smart woman, and I think she knows how to take care of herself."

"I know she's smart, but she's also feisty, and sometimes that gets her in trouble," Cain said.

"You got that right! She's a feisty one. That's fer sure."

They spurred their horses and took off for Orson's.

Sure enough, he was on the porch waiting and raring to go, just as Elizabeth said. He had a chew of tobacco, and was drinking his last cup of coffee when Cain and Hop rode up.

Orson stood up to chastise them. "Hot dang, ain't nobody ever gonna show up on time?"

"Orson, it's so dark I couldn't see my watch," Cain joked.

"Cain Porter, you don't even own a pocket watch, and I doubt Hop does either. I wear one, and that's why I'm always on time." Orson spit his tobacco and then took his last sip of coffee. "I've had ol' Nellie saddled and ready to go fer two hours, and it's a little chilly sittin' here a'waitin'."

"Ma told me to tell you she would be staying here at your place until we get back."

"Yeah, I tried ta pick up a few thangs... my drawers and such. I don't want her thankin' I'm not on the tidy side. Know what I mean?"

Cain looked at Hop, who was smiling ear to ear. *Orson was being Orson*, he thought.

"Hop, you've met Mr. Cargill haven't you?" Cain said in jest. "Well, if you haven't, I want you to know he's in rare form this morning. It's almost too early for all of this," Cain reprimanded.

Orson mounted up, and pulled the reign, jerking his horse around and ready to go.

"Well quit yer' mouthin,' and lets go find Vick!" he yelled leading the way at a fast pace. Teasing one another like they did helped Orson and Cain work off some tension, as they embarked on a venture they knew was no laughing matter.

The men rode the same route that Vick rode going to Jonesboro. It had turned daylight just about the time they crossed the last stream between them and town. It was there they saw a man lying in the road.

"Orson, that's not Pa is it?"

"We won't know til we git there. I shore hope it ain't."

They dismounted when they got to the body, and turned the man over.

"Well…it ain't yer Pa. But the feller shore looks familiar."

"Orson, that's ol' Clyde who used to work for Pa. I recognize him."

Cain bent down and placed his hand on Clyde's face. "He's still warm. I think he's still alive."

"Let me take a look at him," Orson said.

He bent down and held Clyde's head up. "Yer right! The man's still alive, and he's been shot." While Orson was holding him, Clyde opened his eyes, and tried to explain what happened. He kept saying Elizabeth was in trouble. But that didn't make sense since they had just left her. Orson looked up at Cain after Clyde mentioned her.

"Cain, Clyde's talkin' 'bout yer Ma being in trouble, but he ain't makin' no sense."

The old man tried to raise his head. "Them James boys got Vick."

"Clyde, tell us where they took him."

Clyde struggled to talk, and could only manage a whisper, "Panther Holler."

Cain bent over Clyde and looked him in the eye. "Clyde, was there another man with them?"

Clyde whispered, "Yes, a man…takin' yer Pa ta Panther Holler." Clyde held on just long enough to confirm Cain's and Orson's suspicions.

After they delivered Clyde's body to the undertaker, they rode the rest of the day before entering the thicket to Panther Holler. Since it was dark, they decided to stop and set up camp until morning.

The next day, they waited until daylight before entering the thicket. "Y'all take a look. These are fresh tracks, so they ain't that fer ahead of us," Orson pointed out.

"It must be them," Cain was convinced.

"They ain't more than 10 hours ahead of us, but I'm jest a'guessin'," Orson announced. "I spec' Vick's leadin' 'em on a wild goose chase ta give us time. See them tracks going away from the Holler?"

"I know Pa, and he's going to do whatever it takes until there's no other options."

"Yer Pa knew what he was doin' when he had me and Hop spookin' 'em."

"Spook 'em?" Cain asked with a puzzled look.

"Yeah...your Pa didn't want Jonathan Petty to know we were alive until the right time. I spec' this was his plan all along. We also spooked them James brothers."

Cain couldn't refrain from laughing. "Orson, I can just see you pretending to be a ghost."

"I reckon me and Hop did just that... and now we got you, too, if'n we need you to do the spookin."

"I guess whatever works. If we can't shoot 'em, we'll scare 'em to death," Hop said.

Orson took the time to explain to Cain how they had tested Jonathan's sanity by tricking him into thinking he was seeing the dead.

Cain then explained about seeing Lonnie and Dudley James on the road to Aggie's, and how frightened they were at seeing him. He now knew why they were scared.

"I spec' they thought they were seeing the dead." Orson smiled at the thought.

"I don't know what they were thinking. But I sure saw fear in their eyes. Y'all should have seen how fast they turned their horses around and hightailed it out of there."

"I don't know if it'll work now, but it might be the only way we can get the upper hand on them boys," Hop stated.

After they entered the thicket, they rode until they saw the scout camp, where they camped for the night. Everyone was quiet, consumed in their own thoughts.

"Let's turn in early tonight, and try to make it to the lake before nightfall tomorrow," Orson offered.

Cain thought about his Pa, and contemplated he might know they were coming for him.

Cain lay there and pondered over all the things that had happened to Vick. "When is this ever going to be over so we can all go back to living?" Orson could see the wheels turning in Cain's mind.

"Son, I learn't a long time ago that it don't do no good to question why thangs happen, when there ain't a damn thang we can do about it. Yer Pa can con his way out of trouble like nobody else can," Orson said optimistically.

Just before Vick, Jonathan and the James boys came to the mountain, a short distance from Panther Holler, Vick had managed to lead the men in circles, while claiming to have a lapse of memory. He was doing whatever he could to stall, as Orson had guessed, to give them more time to figure out that he had been kidnapped and where he was being taken.

When they came to that last mountain, Vick knew there was little time left to do what he needed to do in order to save him.

He remembered the same scenario as before; when he had to bluff Buck Dupree into thinking there was a treasure. Now, he had to do the same with Jonathan and the brothers. By this time, unbeknownst to Jonathan, Vick was certain they were all working together.

"Are we 'bout there?" asked Dudley.

"Patience. I didn't tell you it would be easy finding my way back," Vick lied. "I think we need to stop here for the night. My memory is a little fuzzy, since I was nursing a bullet the last time I was here. If I'm right, we'll be there tomorrow."

"Ya' better be right if ya' know what's good fer ya'," Dudley said.

"Seems like we been off the trail more than we've been on," Lonnie protested. We gonna give you till tomorrow, and if we ain't there, we gonna be jogging that memory of yers," Lonnie warned with a dirty look.

Every now and then Jonathan would nod to the boys when he thought Vick wasn't looking. That look meant, "get the show on the road." Lonnie knew that look ever so well. Jonathan felt things were not coming together quite like he planned, and because of that, he was having trouble keeping his temper under control and trying to act like he was a captive, too.

That night, they tied Vick's hands and feet to prevent him from escaping, while Lonnie stood guard.

It was a restless night, with hardly any sleep for anyone, but it didn't stop the brothers from an early departure.

Lonnie questioned Vick again, "Did you jog yer memory last night or are we going ta have ta jog it fer ya'?"

Vick knew they meant business, and it was now or never if he didn't want to be shot or beaten to death. He figured they wouldn't kill him at first, but he might wish himself dead before the beating was over.

"We gonna free yer hands, but we got a eye on ya', so don't go pulling anythang crazy," Lonnie instructed.

"You don't have to worry about that. It may surprise you, but I'd rather be with the likes of you than out here by myself."

Dudley and Lonnie looked at each other, confused by what Vick was saying.

"Some strange things happened the last time I was here."

Dudley, being the wimp, began to question Vick, thinking of their ghostly sightings. "Watcha talkin' about?"

"I don't like to talk about it," Vick said with a phony quiver in his voice.

Even Jonathan began taking note, and wondered what Vick meant, wondering if Hop's ghost would show up.

"Vick, why don't you tell us what you're talking about?" Jonathan asked.

"I vowed I would never come back to this place after what happened the last time we were here. That's why we left the treasure."

The men's curiosity began to stir, and Vick saw his plan working. "There's a legend about this place."

"What kind of legend," Jonathan asked.

"Haven't you heard of the 'Legend of Panther Holler'?"

They looked at each other as if they didn't believe what Vick was telling them.

"I know you boys don't believe a word I'm saying, but before we leave here… you will."

"Why don't ya' shut yore pie hole. Ain't no legend 'bout this place. If it was, me and Dudley would have heard about it."

The men became aware that several hawks were alighting in the trees around them. Soon the birds began squawking very loudly. The unusual noise and activity drew their full attention to the hawks, and their faces began to register fear.

"These are some noisy critters out here. I ain't never seen this many hawks in one place," said a confused Dudley.

Vick was making up stories as he went, and the hawks became part of it. "I know you don't believe me, but the hawks are part of the legend."

"You don't spec' us to believe that! You tellin' us some tall tales, and ain't nobody believin' a word ya' say," Dudley tried to convince himself.

Suddenly, the largest hawk among them flew down and circled the men.

"Dudley, you should have never questioned the spirits," Vick chastised.

The men were stunned at seeing the hawk and wondered if there might be a bit of truth to Vick's story after all. They became quiet as they rode, Vick smiling within as he presumed they were all trying not to believe his story. Lonnie rode in front, while Dudley, bringing up the rear, pushed along Jonathan and Vick.

Jonathan stood it as long as he could, and then asked another question. "Vick, how about telling us more about this legend of yours."

"Jonathan, it's not my legend. Some of the old-timers in town told me about it, and I expect that's why Lonnie and Dudley never heard of it."

"We ain't never heard of no legend, and me and Dudley ain't believin' nare a word Porter's sayin'," Lonnie told Jonathan.

Dudley, however, was soaking it all in. Vick stopped his horse and turned to look at Dudley.

"Why don't you tell us about it then," Jonathan insisted.

"The legend is about the treasure. People go mad trying to find it. It starts with people seeing things, and then little by little they go crazy."

"What kind of thangs?" Dudley questioned, hanging on every word.

"They begin seeing the dead, and shortly thereafter, they go mad. This is what happened to Carl Rhodes. He started seeing the dead people he murdered. Remember Carl Rhodes who was really Buck Dupree? He murdered your brother, while he was trying to find the treasure?"

"So yer sayin' that Carl Rhodes really did kill Johnny?"

"That's right, Carl murdered your brother. What we told y'all that day was true."

"Well, I remember you tellin' us that a panther drug Buck off and ate him fer his supper. And we know that's a made up story."

Jonathan thought hearing the ridiculous panther story indicated to him that Vick was conning them.

"To answer you, Jonathan…Buck Dupree will never die until he finds the treasure. He's still out here someplace just waiting. There have been unexplained deaths of people that have come here for the purpose of finding the treasure, but instead, suffered an untimely death. I've never told anyone, but when I was a boy, Buck came at me with a knife and cut my face. That's why I wear this beard. Lucky for me I could run faster than him. He accused me of stealing his treasure and hiding it here in Panther Holler. That's the only reason I'm alive. He knew if he killed me, he would never find the treasure." Vick hoped the hint about staying alive would be enough to bide him time.

Jonathan didn't know what to believe, but he was becoming more convinced that Lonnie and Dudley were idiots who had heard the legend of a phantom treasure, and were now leading him on a wild goose chase. *This complicates matters for me*, Jonathan thought. Believing the James brothers had duped him into participating in a senseless treasure hunt, intense anger began to stir deep inside his black soul. Because of the current circumstances, he tried his best to suppress the anger, only to feel it growing into rage, as an inner darkness began taking over his entire being.

Chapter 29

A LIGHT MIST OF RAIN BEGAN FALLING THROUGH THE TALL EVERGREENS, **as the trio made their way through thick greenery and brush on their way to find Vick.** It was a straggled ride, and for a time Cain thought they were lost, even assuming they had meandered off the trail, taking them in the opposite direction of the lake on the way to Panther Holler. He did not remember the distance between the first night's camp and the second, so by day's end, it turned out to be a painstaking ride.

After they came to the rapids, they made camp along the bank of the lake for their second night on the trail. Everyone was tired and hungry after fighting their way through the nearly impervious forest land.

"We should arrive at Panther Holler by mid-day tomorrow," Cain stated.

"Let's jest hope we find yer Pa in time. We don't need to be wastin' no bunch of time on the trail."

"Orson, quit your whining and have one of Ma's biscuits," Cain playfully quipped.

"Ya reckon ol' Clyde knew what he was a sayin when he told us 'bout Vick?"

"How else would Clyde know of Panther Holler if he didn't hear it from the men who took Pa?"

"I was jest a'askin'," Orson replied.

"If y'all are asking my opinion, which yer not, I would say we ride into Panther Holler during the night, so not to be seen," Hop suggested.

"That would be my thankin' too," Orson agreed.

To solidify their plan, Orson discussed how they would again trick Jonathan and the James' into thinking they were seeing the dead.

By dusk, Vick and his sentinels rode around the last mountain entering Panther Holler. In a distance, they saw the small cabin, which appeared to have been locked away in time. Even the little storm shelter was still intact, just as Vick pictured from his youth. The only difference was the heavy vines, which had grown up the sides of the cabin and over the storm shelter. Once again, he thought of his brother Sam, and the little grave that laid alongside the burial place of the family that was so brutally murdered by Buck Dupree. Vick was happy that devil was dead, but now he would have to dispatch three more killers if he hoped to see Elizabeth again. *It looks like I'll be doing this alone,* he conceded, glancing around at the bushes and trees, hoping to see friendly faces watching for a chance to rescue him.

Vick knew it was wishful thinking that somehow Orson and Hop would find out that he had been drygulched by Jonathan and the James'.

Seeing the cabin and storm shelter, Jonathan and the boys were not impressed.

"So this is Panther Holler?" Jonathan said.

"Ain't much to it," Dudley stated.

"Surely you didn't expect to see another Jonesboro tucked away on a trail that appeared to lead to nowhere," Jonathan scolded, still believing Vick was none the wiser to his working with the James'.

Dudley noticed several hawks again, they were now surrounding the cabin, as if settled in to roost in the trees overnight. "When we find that treasure, we need ta git the hell outta' here. Them hawks don't look too friendly," Dudley said. "They give me the willies."

Jonathan believed it was time to let Vick know that he had been the mastermind behind Cain's death. His mouth turned into a bitter smile, as his dark side began to take over.

By the time Jonathan and the boys unloaded for the night, it was too late to look for the treasure. As Vick walked through the cabin, he noticed everything was just as it was years earlier. By this time, Vick had convinced his captors that he wasn't going anywhere because of his fears regarding "the legend."

"We have some coal oil lamps here some place," Vick announced. He walked into the kitchen and brought out a couple of lanterns, which Lonnie lit. Afterwards, the boys went about helping themselves to beef jerky they had packed.

"Anybody want some jerky?" Lonnie asked.

Vick was starving, having eaten very little since his kidnapping. "Yeah, I'll have a piece," Vick said. Jonathan turned up his nose at the thought of eating anything the James' had on them. Besides, he was thinking more along the lines of a jug of whiskey, rather than any food that could sustain him.

"You boys don't have any whiskey on you, do you?"

Vick remembered the white jug he had from years ago, the potent stuff he had used for medicinal purposes. After Buck turned on Vick, he left Panther Holler abruptly, so the jug was likely still there. "Mind if I take a look? There used to be a jug I kept handy."

"You jest stay put. I'll do the looking, jes tell me wher ta look," Dudley demanded.

"In the kitchen," Vick responded, then he noticed the darkness that had now shrouded Jonathan's eyes and wondered what the un- predictable scumbag was up to. Vick watched him as he seemed to be having a silent argument with himself and acting like a caged animal.

Dudley walked back into the room with the white jug and two cups. "Here, y'all take the cups, and me and Lonnie will share the jug."

Jonathan poured two cups of aged whiskey, one for himself and the other for Vick and handed it over to him. Watching his captor drink the entire cup of strong whiskey in one gulp, Vick witnessed

Jonathan's demeanor change from stormy to calm but alert within a few seconds as the liquor began to take effect. *Good!* Vick thought.

It was dark when Orson and his companions entered Panther Holler. They had not expected to make it to the Holler before nightfall, but they made it with a little time to spare. They were on schedule, Cain believed.

They saw horses, including Vick's and waited until it was pitch dark before Orson moved cautiously to a spot just short of the cabin. Cain and Hop staked themselves in different positions, just in case they had a chance to spook Jonathan and the Porters.

The cool night air had made it very uncomfortable inside the cabin. "Ain't you boys cold?" Jonathan asked.

Lonnie knew it was a hint for one of them to go fetch wood. Luckily, they had noticed some wood close to the storm shelter. Dudley knew he would be the one to fetch the wood, but he didn't like the idea of going out into the night alone because of the "legend." Besides, he had grown used to his brother being with him for security.

"Git yer ass out there and git some wood," ordered Lonnie.

"What about them hawks? Ya' know, I ain't likin' going out there by myself."

"Dudley, ya' need to start doin' yer' share! Jest go and bring enough in so ya' don't have ta go back in a bit."

With the whiskey taking its full effect, Jonathan was feeling powerful and stimulated. Never before had he experienced a drink that burned his throat and brain at the same time. To the average man, one sip would have been enough. Vick saw Jonathan wince when he gulped the home brew down. *That's enough to choke a horse*, Vick thought. He watched as Jonathan's expression and mannerisms continued to change.

Jonathan stood up and walked over to Lonnie, taking his gun. "I think it's time I take over. Why don't both you boys go after the wood? Vick and me have a little business to settle."

Vick thought, "He's going to kill me, and there's not a thing I can do about it." But instead of shooting Vick when he had the chance, Jonathan took out a deck of cards, ready to play. Instead, Jonathan challenged, "Now, we gonna' play a little poker, and I'm gonna' whip ya like ya did my brother.

Vick had not expected Jonathan to show his colors quite so soon. *He brought me here to play poker? What the hell?* Vick thought, *the man really is mad. This is the actions of someone that is a raging lunatic.*

Lonnie and Dudley stood startled that Jonathan had jumped-the-gun, but never said a word.

"Don't just stand there like two idiots…go on and git the wood!" Jonathan demanded.

Lonnie had been so caught up in the role of being in charge, that he resented it when Jonathan took over. *I damn sure don't appreciate Jonathan talking down to me*, Lonnie thought. He grabbed a lantern and then headed to the shelter with Dudley. As they made their way toward the storm shelter, they heard hawks flapping their wings, and it was a bit disturbing.

"Let's git the wood and git back ta the cabin before one of them damn hawks gits us," said Lonnie, with the lantern shaking in his hand.

"Why did ya' let Jonathan take yer gun? Ya' was wrong ta let him do that," Dudley reprimanded.

"Don't worry, I'll git it back, and we'll take care of both of 'em once we have the treasure."

Cain and Orson were close enough to recognize Dudley and Lonnie as they walked toward the storm shelter. From total darkness, Orson walked his horse towards the glowing lantern. The brothers didn't hear the horse until it was right on them. Orson walked his horse right up to Lonnie and Dudley, then stopped momentarily. After they got a good look at Orson, it scared them so badly, Lonnie dropped the lantern, and both ran towards the cabin. They didn't look back until they got to the front door. At first, all they saw was the small fire, which was started by the lantern. Then the horseman appeared again to them.

"Lonnie, it's true what Vick said! They comin' after us 'cause we here fer the treasure."

"Dudley, keep yer' mouth shut about this. Jest back me up when I tell Jonathan what happened to the lantern."

"What about that fire...you reckon it might spread?"

"I ain't carin' 'bout no fire. Did ya' recognize who that was?"

"That looked like the ghost of ol' Eagle Eyes, if ya' ask me. I couldn't even shoot 'em with a empty holster."

On the other hand, Dudley was so frightened he held onto the wood instead of dropping it and drawing his gun.

"Lonnie, that legend must be true. That was ol' Eagle Eyes we seen, and we know he's dead. Maybe we already started going crazy."

"We ain't goin' crazy! The only crazy around here is that lunatic Jonathan who's more interested in playing poker than finding the treasure."

"Well, I thank we need ta fergit about that treasure and leave this God forsaken place. I ain't ready to die," Dudley insisted.

"Git a hold of yerself, we ain't leavin' without the treasure. That's why we here. Remember all them plans we made? We stayin', and we didn't come all this way fer nothin'. Tomorrow we'll git Vick digging, and once we have the treasure, we'll kill him, and the treasure will be all ours." They walked up the steps to the cabin door, "Remember, not nary a word, ya' hear?"

When the brothers walked back into the cabin, no one noticed that Lonnie didn't have the lantern. Jonathan's only interest was whiskey, cards and burning wood to keep him warm. "Hurry and git us a fire in this place," Jonathan ordered.

Vick noticed a change in the boys after they came back from getting the wood. "Something funny is going on," Vick thought. Lonnie repeatedly walked to the window and peered out, as though he was looking for something, or someone.

Jonathan, this time sipping another cup of whiskey, was too drunk to notice the difference. "I thought I would give you boys enough time to get the wood before I told Vick the real reason we brought him here," Jonathan stated.

Lonnie, somewhat preoccupied, thought, *What other reason is he talking about? We're here fer the treasure.*

Jonathan had put aside his thoughts of finding the treasure, now that he finally had the upper hand on Vick. His immediate concern was beating the man at poker, who had caused him misery for the last two years. Now he would watch Vick squirm, as he admitted he was the mastermind behind Cain, Orson and Hop being murdered. "This will give me great pleasure," Jonathan thought, *I think I've kept Vick waiting long enough.*

"Jonathan, why don't you stop your game-playing and tell me what's going on. If you think you've fooled me about you all working together—you haven't," Vick informed him.

"It doesn't matter what you think, as long as the results turn out the same."

Lonnie was angered by Jonathan's grandstanding. "The sooner we git rid of Jonathan, the better off we'll be."

The change in Jonathan's demeanor is enough to make one think someone else had stepped into his skin. " Vick thought.

"Just so you know… I'm the one that had your son and that Sheriff friend of yours killed. Yeah, we got a kick outta seeing 'em beg for their lives. Then I showed that sonavobitch Hop who worked for you a thing or two. He's probably turned into a frog paddy by now," Jonathan bragged, as he let out a sinister laugh.

Vick wanted to tear Jonathan to shreds, but the time wasn't right. He just let him rattle on.

"Yeah, tonight I'm going to beat your ass playing poker, then tomorrow I'm going to kill ya' and watch ya die."

Lonnie looked at Dudley and shook his head no. He knew come morning, Jonathan probably wouldn't remember what he said. Lonnie was a little smarter than his brother.

Vick had to think of something fast if he planned to change the course of events. He observed Jonathan closely. *I can handle him as long as he's sane, but when a man is living on the edge of reality, I'm not sure what Jonathan might do next. He could end up killing us all.*

It was apparent that Jonathan was now someone to be feared.

At one point Jonathan raked everything off the kitchen table onto the floor and patted the place where Vick was to sit for the card game. *I wonder if he's even sober enough to play.* Vick thought.

Jonathan took the jug of whiskey from Lonnie and then went about trying to impress Vick, stretching back in his chair with his cigar, fumbling to shuffle the cards.

Being a professional poker player, Vick noticed that Jonathan had marked some of the cards. "He's an amateur trying to be a con."

Every now and then Vick would take a hand, but mostly he intended to let Jonathan win just enough to keep him challenged, and he knew just how to do that. *No telling what he might do if he loses a hand that's important to him.* Vick could have wiped him out a number of times, but the idea was to set Jonathan up for more games. This would give Vick more time to figure out what he needed to do in order to free himself and save Elizabeth.

When Jonathan reached the point of total drunkenness, where he could no longer concentrate on the game, he called it a night. Vick made sure Jonathan was ahead in winnings, with hope he would want to continue the game in the morning.

After everyone had turned in for the night, Vick had another mysterious dream.

Again, he was thrust to the top of a mountain, just as before when his first vision manifested itself. Although still asleep, he questioned the purpose of these visions. Immediately, a white shimmering hawk flew toward him. It was Chaytan, his childhood protector. The hawk stopped before him, and the metamorphous took place again, as Hawk revealed himself. "Hawk?" Vick asked.

Chaytan stood in a mist of light while communicating with Vick. "My son, tomorrow you must tell the men that you are taking them to the treasure." Vick was overcome with a deep feeling of respect.

Vick thought Hawk was trying to give him more time to protect himself.

As Chaytan turned back into the magnificent hawk, Vick watched it fly away, but not before leaving Vick with one thought. "My son—look to the sky—look to the sky."

The next morning, Vick awoke with Jonathan standing over him with a gun.

"It's time," Jonathan instructed, as he aimed his gun between Vick's eyes.

Dudley and Lonnie saw that Jonathan was about to shoot Vick before they had a chance to find the treasure.

"No Jonathan! Put that gun down!" Lonnie shouted. Jonathan turned to see Dudley with his gun pointed at him.

"Don't worry boys, Jonathan ain't gonna shoot, because I've got the winning hand," Vick said.

"What are you talking about the winning hand?" Jonathan quizzed. "Looks like I'm the one with the winning hand, cause I have the gun. And what do you have, if I might ask?"

"A certain letter that you'd like to have back, for safe keeping if you know what I mean!"

"Of course the letter was Vick's bluff and it seemed to be working seeing the blood drain from Jonathan's face."

Jonathan was completely thrown as he held the pistol to Vick's head.

"What about this letter you talking about?"

Remember when you raped a young woman and her mother? I don't know if you were ever told but that girl was your half sister.'

It slowly hit Jonathan that Vick must know the truth, something that he never knew.

"You take it back, you're bluffing."

"Think about it! Aggie was your own sister and you raped her."

"You're lying," Jonathan screamed. Jonathan raised his gun toward Vick's head."

"The sucker is gonna kill me," Vick thought.

Lonnie pointed his gun at Jonathan for fear that he would kill Vick and they would never find the treasure.

"What you gonna do Lonnie, shoot me?" Jonathan asked.

"Not if ya' put yer gun down!"

Dudley walked over and took Jonathan's gun from him.

"You give me back my gun, you Arkansas hillbilly!" Jonathan screamed. He finally provoked Dudley to anger. Without a second thought, Dudley slowly aimed and shot Jonathan right between the eyes. They were all startled seing Jonathan hit the floor like a boulder.

"I'm the one with the winning hand," Dudley said, as he smirked.

Both Vick and Lonnie were stunned at seeing a coward like Dudley blow Jonathan's brains out. Blood was all over the floor, and part of his skull was lying beside the body that was now very much dead.

Vick thought, *Works for me! Maybe they'll end up killing each other.*

"Dudley, why'd ya' do that?" asked Lonnie.

"I don't know. I guess the devil made me do it!"

"Well, ya' jest blew his brain's out!" Lonnie laughed.

"Yeah, and I'm 'bout ready ta blow Vick's out too—if he don't hurry and take us ta the loot."

Observing the Jameses erratic behavior, Vick was uncertain, if by the end of the day, he would be dead, too.

"You boys brought me here for the treasure, so today I'm taking you to it."

Vick thought of Hawk's mysterious instruction, which he trusted. Instinctively, he knew he should pretend the treasure was not near the cabin.

"I know y'all think it's buried around the cabin, but it's a distance away."

"This ain't gonna be no wild goose chase, is it?" Lonnie asked.

"You want the treasure or not?" Vick scolded.

Cain and Orson heard the gunshot and hoped the bullet was not for Vick, since he should be safe as long as the James' are determined to find the treasure. They knew Vick could keep them guessing for a long while, since those boys didn't have one brain between them. They continued to spy on the cabin in hopes of seeing him.

A short time later, the James' and Vick walked out of the cabin, but not Jonathan.

"Cain, they must be heading out, but I wonder where Jonathan is?" Hop asked.

They continued to watch as the men saddled their horses. Orson and Cain did not understand why they were leaving the holler, unless Vick had instigated it.

The trio knew they had to follow, and saw there was an extra horse, indicating that Jonathan was still in the cabin.

"Orson, we can't let them get too far ahead of us."

"Yer right, but what about Jonathan? He's still in the cabin."

"Maybe that bullet we heard was fer Jonathan," Hop said.

"Well, let's hope so," Orson replied.

When Vick and the James' were out of sight, the men rode slowly and quietly up to the cabin and dismounted. Orson whispered, "Y'all stay here...I'm goin' in."

Of course, they didn't. They crept behind Orson as they made their way to the door. Once there, Orson hauled off and kicked the door off its hinges, ready to shoot. Instead, they found the dead crumpled body of Jonathan on the floor. They holstered their guns and examined the body.

"Well, I be damned if them James' didn't kill Jonathan!" Orson announced with no sadness in his voice.

"I wish I could say there's some love lost, but ther' ain't," Hop said sarcastically as he walked around the body, gently nudging it with his boot.

Cain wondered what happened to have caused them to turn on Jonathan. "It ain't no time to grieve if we plan to catch up with Vick," Cain said with a smirk.

"There ain't no way I'm grieving for that 'somabitch," Hop refuted.

Orson tried to pick up Jonathan's body.

"What ya' trying ta do?"

"I need one of ya' ta help me git Jonathan ta my horse."

"Orson, what are you going to do with Jonathan's body?"

"It might come in handy, so shut yer lip and give me a hand."

Cain and Hop helped Orson tie the body onto Orson's horse. Cain smiled.

"I can't wait to see how this is going to play out," Cain said.

"Jest pay attention and learn," Orson rode away with Jonathan's body, leaving a trail of blood as they went.

Hop rode up beside Cain and said, "I ain't never come across any man like Orson Cargill. Has he always been that way?"

"Always," Cain replied.

Vick led the James' deeper into the woods, without any knowledge of their destination. He was leading them solely based on Hawk's admonition. Every now and then Vick would glance over at the brothers, who each had a wad of tobacco inside their lip. Their mannerisms were the same, with both mouths moving, chewing tobacco, and then spitting about the same time.

"How fer is this place?" Lonnie asked.

Vick kept looking to the sky, as he was told to do in his dream. "I'll know when I get there, so drop the questions," Vick instructed.

Every now and then Vick would see a hawk in the sky leading the way.

"How big is that treasure you buried?" asked Dudley.

"Big enough that you'll have to make a couple of hauls," Vick answered.

The brothers smiled from ear to ear already counting their money.

Meanwhile, Orson, Cain and Hop devised a plan to let Vick know they were following them. Orson reined his horse off the trail, and rode hurriedly on ahead. It was tough going, but finally he was able to advance far enough ahead that he had time to display Jonathan's body. He quickly took out his knife and thrust it into Jonathan's chest, after tying him to a big tree. He barely finished with Jonathan when he heard the three approaching him. He quickly hid in the brush a short distance from the scene.

When Vick and the boys approached the tree where the body was attached, they stopped abruptly. The James" dismounted with guns drawn.

"Holy smoke—that's Jonathan! It's a sign we all gonna die!" Dudley beseeched. He was near panic. "It's that man that kilt' Johnny—the legend." "He's sliced Johnny's throat. Lonnie, I told ya' we shoulda left this place!— Vick warned us!"

"Dudley, shut yer' whining mouth! We ain't come this fer, fer nothing! Ther's a answer to this an it ain't cause of no spooks."

Lonnie walked over to the body, looking all around as he spit his tobacco. "Somebody's jest tryin' ta git us all rattled so's they can have the treasure, that's all," he said.

Dudley pleaded, "No! It's jest like Vick said, that knife in Jonathan proves that man Buck is killing anyone who's here fer the treasure"

"Something else is going on, and I ain't gonna let a body with a knife in it spook me! Now, shut up, and let's ride!"

Lonnie walked over to Vick and looked into his eyes. "You talk, 'cause I know you got something ta do with this." Vick recognized Orson's knife in Jonathan's chest.

"How can you accuse me, when I've been your prisoner all this time. I told y'all about Buck Dupree!" Vick said staring at the corpse and acting very concerned. "I believe that Dudley has summoned the spirits, and now he's a marked man."

Dudley looked terrified. "Lonnie, ya' heard what Vick said, we gotta git outta here, and fast."

Chapter 30

Lucy had shown remarkable improvement since the wreck **that almost claimed her life.** She was feeling so good that Birdie was having a difficult time keeping her from overdoing things.

"You need to take it easy," she scolded.

"I can't just sit around and do nothing."

"Honey, you may feel okay, but those bones need to heal properly. You still have a limp, and if you were completely healed, you wouldn't limp at all." Birdie tried to convince Lucy to go at a slower pace, but Lucy was much too headstrong to "take it easy". Birdie was well aware of this girl's grit. "Only Lucy could survive the things she's been through," she thought in amazement.

Mark Cohen, as her doctor, had also been noticing Lucy and her remarkable improvement. Unlike Birdie, he encouraged Lucy to do whatever she could in order to strengthen her leg muscles so she could walk without a limp.

He also noticed how fussy and protective Birdie was about Lucy.

"Birdie, I know you're very protective of her, but I think our patient can decide for herself what she can do."

"Well, I guess I'm outnumbered, so if the doctor says it's okay for you to resume your duties, then who am I to hold you back?"

Lucy gave Birdie a big hug.

"I'm grateful you care," she replied.

It was evident that Mark was smitten with Lucy. Birdie knew sooner or later she would have to address him concerning those feelings, since he was unwilling to tell her how he felt.

One evening, after the day's chores were done, Birdie caught Mark alone while cleaning up after a rush of patients.

"Dr. Cohen, can I please talk to you about something personal?" He gave her one of those half-smiles, as if to say, "now what?"

"You say something personal?" Mark asked.

"Well, yes...I don't know if anyone else has noticed, but I see you are paying way more attention to Lucy than the other patients."

"Do I have to remind you that I'm her doctor?

"Mark, I did expect more of an honest answer. I can see how much you care for her. It's in your eyes every time you're around her."

Mark knew she was right, but did not know how to go about discussing such things with her. *Sooner or later I'm going to have to come clean with Birdie, so I may as well do it now.*

"You know, perhaps you're right, and I should discuss my feelings.

Lucy is a very beautiful woman, and any man would be fascinated around such a beauty. And yes, I am developing feelings for her, but I don't know if she feels the same."

Birdie listened to him, however, she did not know if Lucy's feelings were mutual.

"Mark, if I can offer a suggestion. Why don't you tell her how you feel? At least you will know, and there's no harm in asking."

He thought a minute.

"Maybe I will. Our little talk may have given me courage to do just that."

"Birdie thought, *this will be the end to it when Lucy tells him she's not interested.*

Mark had studied Lucy's habits for over a month, and every night after supper she would take a stroll through the rose gardens. This was going to be a special evening, for he had been practicing over and over how he would approach her and explain how he felt. He was willing to take a chance, for he felt she was worth it. All evening he imagined she would say yes to his proposal, but he wasn't sure, since neither of them had spent time together away from the hospital. That evening, after supper, when all was quiet, Mark waited patiently in the rose garden for Lucy to show herself. He did not want to discourage her, but he wanted her to know how special she was to him.

Lucy arrived wearing a beautiful dress that Jason had purchased for her when he was alive. It was her favorite, and she was feeling coquettish, knowing there was a handsome doctor working with her and Birdie. When Mark walked toward Lucy they both seemed a bit embarrassed at seeing each other. It was as though they were thrust together on the exact night when their desire for affection was at its' highest peak.

Finally, Mark decided to take the bull by the horns and tell Lucy how he felt about her.

"Oh Mark, I didn't expect to see you here tonight."

His demeanor surprised her, as he fumbled for words to speak.

"It's a beautiful night, isn't it?" he said.

The conversation continued down this path of awkwardness for some time; exchanging trivial nonsense while attempting to feel each other out.

Lucy thought Mark wanted only friendship until now.

He gazed at her beauty and longed to tell her how he felt.

I have to make my move soon, or the entire night will be wasted. It's now or never, he imagined.

"Lucy, I'm at a loss for words, but I need to talk to you about something very important."

She gathered that he was serious.

"Is something wrong?" she asked.

"We've known each other for only a short time but I've watched you regain your health after the accident. I hope I don't mess this up, but you've become very important to me. Having you as my patient seems to have awakened a desire that I have never experienced for any other woman. I've loved every moment we've been together. What I'm trying to ask is if you feel the same?"

Lucy's reaction was filled with mixed emotion. *I don't know if I have a lifetime of love to give him*, she thought. She looked at him in awkward silence, as Mark had taken her completely by surprise.

Finally, she spoke. But the words were not exactly what Mark was hoping to hear.

"Mark, I'm flattered that you feel this way towards me, but honestly, I don't know how I feel. It wasn't that long ago that I lost my husband, and to give you an answer without examining my feelings would be unfair to both of us."

Mark was embarrassed that he had shown his vulnerability to Lucy, but he was still glad he had expressed his feelings to her.

For the next few weeks, Mark and Lucy hardly spoke. Both were confused: Lucy, about her feelings for Mark, and Mark, about whether or not he should pursue Lucy's affection.

Birdie noticed the silence between them, and thought it was for the best, since they worked together.

Each night before falling asleep, Lucy would lie there thinking of Cain, whom she had hoped to grow old with. *Cain was the only man I have truly loved, and I was taken away from him.* She then thought of Jason and how he had been taken from her. Lucy anguished thinking her life may not be meant for marriage or another.

If only I had not been lost after the fire and we had married. We would never have *experienced the awful pain of losing each other*, Lucy regretted.

The next morning, Lucy had a different attitude about Mark. She was trying her best to be logical. *He knows I cannot have children, and he loves me enough to accept a childless marriage*, she conceded.

What more could I expect, since I have no one but Birdie? Perhaps I can learn to love Mark. She was afraid if she refused his proposal that he might turn to someone else. *After all, he's a good man, and I don't question his love for me.*

Before the day was over, Lucy decided she would accept Mark's proposal when he asked her again.

That evening, Birdie and Lucy took an evening stroll in the garden, where they talked.

"You know, don't you?" Lucy asked.

"Know what? I don't know what you're talking about."

"It's about Mark. I know he thinks he loves me, but honestly, I don't feel the same. Birdie, I'm afraid of being left without anyone. He knows my medical history, and I'll always be childless, and yet he's willing to marry me anyway."

"Now Lucy, you know I don't know a thing about love. My only love is medicine, so I can't help you in the matters of the heart. You'll know what's best when the time comes. One word of advice, when it's right, you'll know it."

"That's pretty good advice. Maybe you know more about love than you think." Lucy and Birdie laughed, and then walked arm in arm back into Lucy's living quarters.

At this time Birdie resigned herself not to meddle in Mark and Lucy's business. *What will happen will happen but not with any help one way or the other from me.*

More than a week passed, and Lucy was waiting for Mark to approach the subject with her again. He had taken a breather; deciding to give Lucy plenty of unpressured time with which to make up her mind.

The very next evening, after what seemed to be an extra long workday, Lucy went for a stroll in the gardens, hoping that Mark would join her. No sooner had she thought of him, he suddenly came around the corner of the rose garden, startling her.

"Mark, you frightened me!" she said.

"Oh, I'm sorry…I didn't mean to scare you. I was hoping I would find you here." There was a short reservation, while Mark mustered up enough confidence to ask her.

"Lucy, I don't know if you've thought about our conversation. I stayed away, for I wanted you to make your own decision without feeling pressure from me."

Before Lucy knew it, Mark was on one knee with a beautiful ring, asking her to marry him. She was touched to see that Mark had purchased a ring without knowing for sure if she would accept his engagement.

"Mark, I've been thinking…and yes, I would love to be your wife. Mark stood and slipped the ring onto Lucy's finger, and then gave her a sweet kiss."

Although Lucy felt no passion she presumed after marriage she would be able to return Mark's love.

In the days that followed, there was an announcement about the engagement and upcoming marriage of Lucy Cargill and Dr. Mark Cohen, who lived in Trumann a short distance away from Jonesboro. Because of Dr. Cohen's importance, newspapers in the surrounding area printed the article.

Reading the Jonesboro newspaper Elizabeth came across the article announcing Lucy Cargill's engagement to Dr. Cohen. She was astonished that the woman had the very same name as Orson's daughter, Lucy Cargill. *It has to be someone else, because Lucy died in the fire when the manor burned.* As she read on she convinced herself that it was merely a coincidence, for Lucy was such a common name. She imagined it was foolish of her to think it was the Lucy she had known, and thought it would be irresponsible of her to mention the article to Orson or Cain. It wouldn't be fair to get Orson's hopes up, and then have him fall back into his depression that he suffered after Lucy died. And telling Cain would cause him to be crushed after the disappointment of finding out it was someone else. It simply wasn't worth the confusion, she thought.

Her thoughts quickly switched to Vick and Cain; praying that they return home safely.

Chapter 31

DUDLEY'S UNPREDICTABLE BEHAVIOR WAS EXTREMELY FRUSTRATING for Lonnie, who was constantly busy trying to keep him under control. He saw his brother the same as others did; weak and unpredictable.

"Dudley, ya' gotta git hold ta yerself. Ain't no such thang as ghosts. Orson is out there alive somewhere, and if I see him I'm gonna kill 'em—again!"

Under normal circumstances Vick would have been amused, seeing the brothers react to a dead man tied to a tree, but these two scalawags could lose their temper and shoot him, treasure or no treasure. Although Vick had not seen anyone, he was sure Jonathan's body being there was the handiwork of Orson.

Hop encouraged Orson to take it slow and easy, so as to lessen the chance of spooking the James'. Hop reminded him, "At least one of 'um is trigger happy, and that means Vick is in a worse situation than we figured,"

Lonnie and Dudley's horses were restless, pawing at the ground and prancing in one place, while their riders tried to figure out how a dead body traveled from the cabin to be found tied to a tree. The knife that pierced Jonathan's heart had significant meaning to Dudley, who Vick had frightened with the tale of a knife happy Buck Dupree. The story about a dead man running through the woods murdering anyone, who was in search of the treasure, was pretty gruesome and terrifying. Lonnie and Dudley believed the treasure was real, but they weren't sure who out there was coming after them. Dudley was hesitant to move on, out of fear of the unknown. Vick listened to the two argue until he'd had enough.

"Are we gonna waste time trying to figure out how Jonathan got tied around this tree, or are we going to find the treasure before dark? I sure don't want to be forced to spend another night in these woods if we don't have to," Vick added.

Lonnie kept yelling at Dudley to calm down.

"See here Dudley, we don't need ya' messin' this up fer us. Vick's finally showing us where he buried the treasure, and I need ya' ta fergit about all them stories 'bout a dead man with a knife. Ain't no such thang'."

Vick was worried about Dudley since he saw how easy it was for him to kill Jonathan. "I've got to get away in order to save Elizabeth," he thought, and the sooner the better."

"Dudley, we need to keep moving if you don't want to be digging in the dark," Vick warned.

"Me… digging? It's gonna be you digging, Mr. know-it-all Porter."

Vick had to be careful to not tip off the brothers while he was looking for signs of Orson and Hop. Vick was sure the knife in Jonathan belonged to Orson. "They're gonna be making their move anytime now," Vick anticipated.

"When we gonna git there? And I don't want no more of yer lies, if ya' know what's good fer ya'," Lonnie asked, as he was becoming more agitated.

"Well then, let's go, and quit wasting time," Vick responded.

~

Subsequently, Cain and Hop saw Orson ahead, standing near Jonathan's dead body, which was tied around the tree with a knife in him. "That's bound to have scared the day lights out of the James'," Cain said. It was a pretty gruesome sight, even for them, especially with the knife stuck through Jonathan's heart.

Orson walked over and pulled the knife out of Jonathan's body after Cain and Hop rode up.

"It's about time y'all showed. Vick ain't too fer ahead; leadin' them boys on a wild goose chase… I spec' in circles."

"Orson, what you trying to do, give them boys a heart attack? Seeing Jonathan's body like that with a knife in him would scare anyone." Cain said.

"Yeah, you shoulda' seen Dudley. He jest 'bout went off the deep end," Orson chuckled.

"Let's be careful not to spook them too much and have them take it out on Pa."

"Yeah, I was thinking the same thang after seeing how them boys acted."

"Since they think we're dead, it's best we don't show ourselves in case our plan backfires," said Hop.

"Let's jest be real careful," Orson quibbled.

"I don't want Pa placed in any danger."

"Son, ain't none of us want to see anything happen to yer Pa," Hop reassured him.

"What about Jonathan's body? It's not right leaving his body like this."

"Son, there ain't time if we want to catch up with yer Pa."

The trio left Jonathan tied to the tree, and continued trailing the James', with Orson in the lead.

As Vick led the men further into the forest, the unfettered golden rays of the sun took turns penetrating through the tall evergreens. All while Vick was leading the James', he was looking skyward at a lone hawk, which appeared to be leading him. He was no longer simply wandering aimlessly in order to bide time. He had taken the hawk's presence to be a sign, as the hawk led him into areas of the forest he had never seen before. Vick led them deeper into the forest, crossing over beautiful rolling streams and brooks, waiting for Orson and Hop to rescue him. When Vick was a boy, he never ventured that deep into the forest, so all the beautiful scenery was new to him. There were signs of former inhabitants, and he figured a Clan of mountain people once lived there.

Following the hawk, Vick led the James' up a cliff with a 20 ft. drop into a beautiful waterfall. Vick saw the waterfall as an opportunity to escape. He knew if he jumped for the fall to evade the brother's, that they would not follow. His main worry was, even if he survived the 20 ft. jump into the waterfall, he might not survive the waterfall's 30 ft. descent. But there was nothing more he could do, if he had any hope of surviving and rescuing Elizabeth from the James'. Vick was running out of options. To make matters worse, he was unaware that the waterfall emptied into a large, deep pool of raging whitewater.

Vick knew Orson and Hop were following him, but his concern was more for their welfare than his. Occasionally, his thoughts became negative, thinking of a multitude of things that could go wrong to prevent his rescue.

Everything appeared to be in slow motion as Cain watched Vick jump over the cliff and fall into the cold, churning water that immediately swept him into the waterfall. Cain saw Dudley fire his rifle at his father, and then watched his body float downstream. He had no idea that Vick would survive the fall.

"Orson, I gotta git to Pa. He's been shot."

Cain galloped his horse to the edge of the cliff and jumped from his horse into the water below that immediately swept him into the waterfall. When Cain jumped, Orson imagined two coffins that he would be burying after the recovery of their bodies.

"Hop, what the hell is he thinkin', goin' after his Pa like that?"

Lonnie and Dudley were caught completely off guard, as Orson and Hop opened fire on them. Being cornered, the brother's fired back, striking Orson, who fell from his saddle. They exchanged more gunfire, and realized they were trapped in that location. They decided to join Vick below, knowing it gave them better odds of living, than remaining there like sitting ducks, as by now, the bullets were zipping by their heads. Neither considered that falling into the waterfall was an extremely hazardous stunt. Their objective was to play dead and allow the whitewater to carry them as far down stream as possible in order to make their escape. As luck would have it, they both survived the jump. Once out of sight, Lonnie called out to Dudley.

"Try to swim ta shore!"

"Lonnie, I ain't gonna make it." Dudley was bobbing up and down, trying to swim to the edge of the stream, but the whitewater was still too strong.

The James' could see Vick's body floating face down atop the near-freezing water, and not too far behind was Cain bobbling up and down as he fought the raging water. They feared Vick had drowned, and their hopes of finding the treasure were gone.

Vick did as they did and played dead, although he had complications from the fall.

"We in a helluva mess now," Lonnie thought, as the rapids continued to carry them downstream.

By the time Cain oriented himself, after the free fall from the cliff and the tumble down the waterfall, the James brothers were out of sight.

Lonnie also presumed Vick was dead. He anguished, while fighting the water to stay alive thinking they lost their chance to find the treasure.

Dudley and Lonnie were helpless, as the rapids continued to carry them downstream only a short distance behind Vick and Cain. Although Vick was tired and confused from the waterfall he managed to swim to shore after the stream narrowed. Vick confused and bewildered found a grove of trees not too far from the edge of the stream. He was pretty banged up and was not at all coherent when he dropped to the ground. Even though he was at least a mile away from where he jumped he could still hear the waterfall plummeting into the whitewater below. Vick felt relieved that he survived but he was unaware that Cain and the James' were bobbing in the whitewater a distance behind him.

Cain finally found himself to safety but passed the location from where Vick exited the water. He had no idea the James' were alive, and fighting their way to freedom. Cain assumed they had drowned along with his Pa. His main concern was finding Vick's remains and burying him if need be.

The narrowed area in the stream contained large boulders that acted as water barriers. Lonnie struggled to swim close to one of them and managed to get behind it and slow his progress. Without the strong force of the whitewater pushing him downstream, he was able to lunge for the bank, grabbing onto some shoreline rocks. He managed to crawl onto the bank where he collapsed from exhaustion. They had no idea that only a short distance ahead they could have walked out of the water. Seeing his brother fight to keep from drowning, Dudley successfully attempted the same maneuvers. Freezing cold and stunned from the fall, they lay near the embankment until they could catch their breath. Then the reality of their situation began to sink in. Dudley thought if they didn't die from the rapids, they would surely die from the men they assumed was Orson and Hop.

"Lonnie, what we goanna do? I'm freezing."

"Whining ain't gonna help—so shut it up. Ain't no need ta show our face in Jonesboro and stand a chance of bein' hung," Lonnie explained to Dudley. "With Vick bein' dead, there ain't no treasure."

"I reckon all this was fer nothin'. Lonnie that shore looked like Cain and 'Ol' Eagle Eye shootin' at us. There ain't nare one 'em dead unless there's a special kinda ghost who can swim. Right now, I don't care 'bout no damn treasure, I just want ta git' warm around a fire."

"I know, but my matches got a little wet," Lonnie said, sarcastically. He looked at Dalton like he was crazy.

"How fer away do you think we are from that waterfall?"

"I'd say near a mile. What we gonna' have ta do is git back there and try to find our horses. Ain't no telling where they are."

"What if we run into them bastards that tried ta kill us? I 'spec they comin' this way looking fer Vick and we don't have no way ta defend ourselves," Dudley said.

"They wasting their time 'cause they ain't gonna find him," Lonnie replied.

Lonnie, how ya' know Vick's dead?"

"Are ya' dumb and stupid at the same time? You seen his body floatin' on top the water…so what's it gonna take ta prove it to ya'?"

"But, we need ta at least find a way to the other side of the stream and make certain."

"Ain't ya heared nothin' I've said? The man's dead! And I'm a freezin'."

Back at the site Orson was in bad shape after being shot. Blood was gushing everywhere. He slid out of the saddle on the ground when everything got blurry.

Hop, in total dismay, rushed to his side to care for him. "This ain't no time for you to take a bullet," he said. Orson smiled. "It's all up ta you ta take care of my boys."

"Orson, I can't go and leave you like this! You're hurt, and we need ta git you to a doctor."

"Don't worry 'bout me and no damn doctor. I ain't giving up, so do as I say and git yerself back."

"I ain't going nowhere until I help you with that shoulder of yours."

Hop examined the gunshot entry and then put some tobacco over the wound. After taking some bandages out of his saddlebags to dress the wound, Hop took Orson's saddle from his horse and propped him up the best he could.

"Ya shore ya ain't no doctor carryin' all them bandages with ya?"

Hop planned to stay with him but Orson insisted that Cain and Vick were in need of Hop more.

After the James' survived the waterfall they realized that all those they thought were dead, were either alive or some spirits coming back to haunt them.

"They're after us!" Dudley cried out.

"It ain't no time fer ya to start that whinin' again," Lonnie reprimanded.

"Well, if they're alive, where is Orson?"

"Ol' Eagle eye is probably someplace ahead of us."

"Lonnie, what we gonna do without horses?"

Battling his way through vines and deep brush Cain called for Vick just in case he was alive. He chose to remain in hiding as he looked for his Pa just in case the James' had survived.

"Pa, if you can hear me, say something," he cried out.

Vick thought he was dreaming again as a faint voice called out his name. "That sounds like Cain."

Once again he heard the cry of his son. "Pa, if you hear me, I'm coming for you."

"It's a trick," Vick believed. "There's no way that can be Cain. My son is dead."

Vick could hear the movement of bushes, and thought his mind was playing tricks on him since he was not quite lucid from the fall. "I must save Elizabeth," he thought. He was sure that hearing Cain's voice was just another one of his dreams. After all, he had just spoken with Hawk, who's dead. And no ordinary man speaks to the dead. Vick tried to move, but he was in a state of shock and overcome from hearing Cain's voice. "If it is Cain, I want to tell him I'm sorry I wasn't there for him when he was growing up."

Seconds later, Cain was looking down at his Pa.

"Pa, are you okay?"

"Cain, I hope you can forgive me for not being around when you were a boy."

"Where did that come from," Cain thought. It was evident that his Pa was not thinking clearly. He smiled and said, "Pa, don't worry about that. We're going to have plenty of time to catch up when we get you out of this place."

Vick felt Cain's hand.

"Son, is it really you?" Vick could not control his tears, believing God was allowing him to see his dead son one last time.

"Pa, it's me, and I'm here to take you home." Vick reached for him, sobbing as the two men embraced.

Vick had no concept of what was happening.

"You're taking me home? Son, I can't go without your mother."

It was too much for Cain, seeing the vulnerable side of his Pa so he bent down and held Vick as they cried in each other's arms. After a few minutes of weeping, they finally got control of themselves. "Pa, how do you feel?"

"I reckon I'm feeling better since you're here. Are you planning on staying with me?"

"Pa, we're not staying. You and me are leaving.

They're waiting for us up by the waterfall. When I saw you jump, I came in right behind you."

By this time, Vick was beginning to face reality and accept that he was alive.

"Cain, is it really you? I see you, but I'm afraid when I wake up you'll be gone."

"Pa, you're not asleep... you're going to be just fine. I finally found my way home, and I'm here to take you back with me."

"Son, I don't know what to say. I thought you were part of the dreams I've been having. If this ain't a dream how did you get here and where you been all this time?

Pa, we have to figure out how we're gonna get out of this mess. We're both freezing.

"What about Orson and Hop? Are they with you?"

"Pa, they're just fine but we're not so let's get out of here."

Vick was excited with the presence of Cain and began asking, one question after the other as they walked along the shoreline.

"Did you see them James boys? They shot at me when I jumped into the waterfall. I imagine they're still up there waiting to finish me off. Cain, we have to get back to the manor and rescue your Ma. Those boys said they kidnapped her."

"Don't worry about Mother…she's at home, held up in Orson's cabin until we get back. She's the one who sent us after you."

"Thank God, your Ma's okay."

Vick had no idea how Cain would find a way across the stream but he had to trust that they would make it back to Orson and Hop.

After they found their way across the stream they had no idea if the James boys were still alive.

Chapter 32

MAKING IT BACK TO THE WATERFALL VICK AND CAIN WERE WERE
stunned to learn Orson had been shot. The old fella was lying on
the ground with his head propped up on his saddle. He was very weak
from the loss of blood, but the tobacco had managed to stop most of
the bleeding. Hop also helped by using his hand as a compress.

When the men rode up, Hop walked over to fill them in on what
happened.

Cain jumped off his horse and rushed to Orson's side, assuming he
was dying. "How did you manage to get yourself shot?" Cain asked.

"I didn't even know I was hit until I looked down and saw the
blood. Cain, thank God ya found yer Pa. Watcha thank about our boy
coming home?" he asked Vick.

"Right now, it's you I'm worried about."

Vick could see the pain in the old gentleman's eyes, as he tried to
make a joke in order to hide his grave concern. Vick quickly thought
back to the time when he was a hunted man, and Orson let him ride
free instead of arresting him. "Orson has always been there for me
when I needed him, and I plan to do the same for him." Vick bent
down to talk with him.

"Orson, I figured y'all were looking for me, but I had no idea that
Cain was with you."

"I didn't have nothin' ta do with that crazy kid of yers jumpin' in
that waterfall ta go after ya'." Orson coughed while trying to laugh. I
reckon yer a good sight fer my sore eyes.

"Vick remembered the whiskey in the cabin. "We got to get something for Orson's pain," Vick thought.

"Hop we're going to be staying the night at Panther Holler. We have no choice, but the next morning we need to leave at first light so we can get Orson home. He's gonna need some looking after." Orson closed his eyes and nodded his approval.

Hop motioned Vick out of hearing range from Orson so he could discuss Orson's condition in private.

"Vick, he insists he can ride home on his own. What do you think?" asked Hop.

"If it was any other man except Orson, I'd say no way, but this ol' sidewinder is tough as nails. First thing we're gonna do is patch him up good, and then after a goodnight's rest come morning, we'll be heading home. He's gonna need a doctor, for sure."

Lonnie and Dudley spied on the men as they knelt around Orson however there was no way they could steal their horses and make it back to Panther Holler.

"Lonnie, ya thank we can make it all the way back ta that cabin without freezing ta death?"

"I reckon we ain't got no choice, since we ain't got no horse. We jest have ta do what we gotta' do. They gonna be movin' 'Ol Eagle Eyes and when they do we gonna be right behind 'em, jest in case we git a chance ta steal us a horse."

Dudley gave Lonnie a hint of a smile, while he shook from the cold and wet clothing that had not yet dried. Much to their surprise Vick and the men moved out leaving them eating dust.

Vick had done the best he could patching his old friend up. "Orson, I hope you can hold on long enough for us to get you to a doctor."

"There ain't no good doctors in Jonesboro, and I thank I'd be better off doctoring myself. They're all quacks if yer askin' me."

Ornery and tough was the only label one could pin on Orson with any degree of certainty.

He was cracking jokes, but no one was laughing because of the seriousness of his condition.

"You think you can ride with that wound?" Hop asked.

"Don'tcha worry 'bout me... what about them sidewinders ya' shot?"

"Last time we saw 'em, they were headed downstream. There will be no treasure where them boys are going. What ya' say, are you ready to ride?" asked Vick.

"I reckon so, if we take it kinda slow and easy."

"We're going to try to make it back to the cabin before nightfall," Cain spoke up, a little louder than usual.

"Lordy, I jest took a bullet and yer talkin' ta me like I'm deaf, or jest about dead."

Vick believed Orson's very last words on earth were probably going to be in the form of a joke.

It was rough going, but the old man hung in there, making it back to the cabin. Vick and Hop helped him to bed, and then Vick gave Orson strong whiskey to help his pain. He stayed lucid long enough to say, "That's my boy," and then passed out.

Vick felt giving Orson a shot of whiskey now and then would help keep him alive. He remembered using it for medicinal purposes when he was a kid. After a couple of sips from the jug, Orson would always perk up, initially that is.

On the afternoon of the third day, the foursome rode up to the manor in record time, with Orson still among the living, but very weak.

"I told y'all I wanted ta go ta my house," Orson said. It appeared the old codger was on his last leg. Had they been on the trail another day, Cain feared Orson would not have made it.

Elizabeth was watering her outside plants when the men rode up. She dropped her bucket when her eyes locked onto Vick.

She ran to Vick, embracing him before he had a chance to explain that Orson was injured. "Lizzie, it's Orson," Vick said. She paid no mind to what he said, turning her attention toward Cain who was now running over to Orson.

"Thank God you all made it in one piece. I've been so worried. Please tell me it's over."

After seeing her boy was okay, her eyes fell upon Orson, who was wavering in his saddle.

"Vick, is Orson hurt, or drunk?" Elizabeth asked. Of course, he was both, since he had been drinking to ease the pain.

"Howdy doody, Lizzie," Orson said. He hesitated, and then fell from his saddle onto the ground.

"Oh my, Orson's drunk."

"Lizzie, we got to get Orson to bed. He's been shot!"

"Shot? Oh no! We need to get a doctor. Vick, what on earth happened?"

"I'll explain later, but we need a doctor…and fast."

Orson's breathing was erratic, and everyone sensed he might not make it if they didn't find a doctor right away.

"Hop, why don't you run into town and see if there's a doctor."

"Vick, that's wasting precious time. There's a hospital in Trumann and if we hurry we can make it before nightfall. Hop stayed behind since there was not enough room in the car.

"Don't worry about me. You all jest go and take care of Orson. I hope he can hang on till ya' get there."

"Well, let's pray we make it in time."

On the way to Trumann, the conversation was light, since everyone was consumed with worry for Orson.

"Pa, Orson don't look like a man in his seventies, does he?"

"No, and he don't act like it neither," Vick chuckled.

Two and a half hours later, they were in the Trumann hospital looking for the doctor. Orson was totally out of it, rambling on about Lucy. "There's my girl, ain't she pretty?" Orson said. Hearing him talk as if Lucy was present bothered Cain.

"Pa, remember when you were wounded, and Orson took that bullet out of you and you started talking out of your head? Well,

Orson had a theory about that. He said, when a man starts talking to the dead, he's not long for this world. Do you think Orson is dying?"

"Son, I can't answer that question. Only the Good Lord knows when a man's time is up. You can't fight age or anything else when your number comes up, I believe that's when you die. I'm afraid Orson is getting close to his number. If I had to guess, I would say his chances of survival are slim, so we all need to prepare ourselves."

Cain walked away to keep Vick from seeing him tear up. He thought, "If I lose Orson, there won't be anything left that helps keep Lucy's memory alive."

Birdie was the only person on duty when Orson was brought in, but she was experienced and skilled enough to handle the emergency. Cain introduced himself and gave her a brief account on how and when Orson was shot.

"Nurse, can you tell if he's going to make it?" Elizabeth asked.

"I'll let you know as soon as I examine him." Birdie determined Orson needed immediate surgery.

"Ma'am, are you the doctor?" Vick asked.

"No, but I'm trained. Don't worry...I know what I'm doing. And please, call me Nurse Crumb. You folks are not from here, are you?"

"We're from Jonesboro, and the man you're about to examine was at one time our sheriff. Orson Cargill is his name."

Birdie felt like someone had thrown ice water in her face. *My goodness, this man could be Lucy's father, and he's alive, she thought. She needs to see her father before he dies.*" She knew how much Lucy had suffered when she got the news that her Pa, and the man she was engaged to, had been killed. *Cain could possibly be the man she had intended to marry.* All these thoughts were reeling inside her head. *I've got to keep him alive, at least long enough for Lucy to see her father,* Birdie feverishly determined. She then found herself ordering Cain to go to the church and fetch the doctor. "Tell Dr. Cohen I need him now!"

When Elizabeth heard Birdie say Dr. Cohen was at the church, she instantly thought of the article in the paper announcing the doctor's engagement to a woman named Lucy Cargill. Still, Elizabeth could not bring herself to believe the woman with the same name was Lucy. It's nothing more than a coincidence," she pondered.

"Pa, I reckon there's only one church, since Nurse Crumb didn't say where it was."

"Son, do you want me to go with you?"

"No, that's okay. I think you should stay with Ma."

As Cain drove into town, there, nestled among tall evergreens, was a beautiful white church. After seeing well-dressed people coming and going, he thought he might be interrupting a function of some sort, possibly a wedding, or funeral. He hated to break up whatever occasion it was, but he had to find the doctor.

Walking through the doorway, he spotted a man hunched over a table, signing papers, and surrounded by several other men. He imagined the man was Doctor Cohen. *Oh no, it is a wedding, and I'm barging in!*

One of the men, who thought Cain looked out of place, stepped over to ask if he needed help.

"Sir, are you lost? This happens to be a private affair for Doctor Cohen and his bride-to-be...Ms. Lucy Cargill."

Hearing Lucy's name startled Cain, and he thought he must have misunderstood the man. *This has to be a coincidence, or my mind's playing tricks on me*, he thought. *How can there be two Lucy Cargill's living a short distance apart? It doesn't make sense.*

"Sir, did you say Lucy Cargill?"

"Yes, soon to be Mrs. Mark Cohen, marrying the man talking to the gentlemen at the table. Is there something I can help you with?"

"I'm so sorry, but Dr. Cohen is needed at the hospital...it's a crisis."

"You wait here, I'll get Doctor Cohen, and tell him he's needed at the hospital right away."

"Thank you, I'm sorry to intrude."

Cain watched as the gentleman walked over to Dr. Cohen, and quietly spoke to him. The doctor looked at the stranger, and wondered who the tall handsome man might be.

Cain stood there with a thousand questions in his mind until the doctor approached him.

"I'm Dr. Cohen... you say I'm needed at the hospital?"

"Yes sir! An old gentleman friend of mine has a gunshot wound, and I'm afraid he's not going to make it through surgery. I was sent here by your nurse to fetch you."

"I'm on my way. Meet you at the hospital." The doctor paused briefly, then asked Cain if he would take time to find Lucy, and tell her to have one of the guests drive her to the hospital.

"Certainly...I'll be there shortly," Cain replied.

Cain convinced himself that this "Lucy Cargill" was not the same Lucy he was once engaged to.

He walked over to one of the guests and asked if he would find Lucy, and tell her she should have someone drive her to the hospital. "Sure, we'll get her there. You don't worry about anything."

Cain had almost reached his car, when he heard the sound of footsteps. *I'm afraid to look* he thought. He turned slowly and saw a beautiful woman who looked very much like Lucy. Cain was in the shadows watching her as she looked in every direction, as though she was searching for someone.

I can't believe the likeness of this beautiful woman who is either Lucy or her twin, and she's walking toward me.

All Lucy saw was a tall man standing by his car.

Cain felt a strangeness inside him as he was approached by this mysterious woman. It was dusk as they encountered one another. This man looked familiar to Lucy, even from afar, but now as she stood face to face, she thought, *Sureley this can't be..This is someone who looks like Cain, only a little older and mature. He's handsome like Cain, she thought.* Lucy assumed her mind was playing tricks on her.

"Sir, my fiancé just left for the hospital because of an emergency. Is this your emergency?" As soon as she spoke, Cain knew for certain who the mystery woman was. "Oh my God, it is Lucy!"

Cain was unable to speak, seeing that she was very much alive. Suddenly, the moon shone on Cain's face, and she got a better look. She began to tremble. "Do I know you?" She touched his arm. "You look like someone I used to know..." Cain was in as much dismay as Lucy, finding her alive and residing practically a stone's-throw from Jonesboro.

She walked closer to him and looked deeply into his eyes. "I do know you." She paused taking a better look. "Oh my God, it can't be. I'm not imagining this, Cain, it is you, and you've come back! He stood there with tears running down his cheeks trying to be composed. He was still unable to speak. Lucy touched his cheek with her fingertips, and ran her hand across his face, as though she was examining every new line. Her voice trembled as tears welled up in her eyes.

"Lucy, we thought you were dead. I've never stopped thinking about you, even though it's taken forever for me to find you," he said.

"Cain, I'm so sorry but someone told me you were dead."

Without hesitation, she threw her arms around him and kissed him with one long passionate kiss. Then she buried her face in his strong chest, and cried. "Cain, you've come back...but it's too late for us."

"Lucy, what do you mean, too late?"

He looked into her eyes, and he saw such sadness.

"Cain, I'm about to be married. I'm promised to Mark...Dr. Cohen, who just left for the hospital."

He pulled back from her. He still did not understand. "Lucy, I thought you died in the fire when the manor burned. We even had a funeral for you, and now, I see you're alive and about to be married. I'm afraid none of this makes sense to me."

"I'm here and I'm alive, but I heard that you were murdered, along with my father. You have to understand...when I learned that, I had no reason to return to Jonesboro. Had I known, I would have been there waiting for you. I also learned that Vick and Elizabeth had moved away to Texas. I went home once, but no one was at the cabin, so I put the place up for sale. There was nothing left for me, since daddy was dead, and Elizabeth and Vick had moved to Texas. That's when I made the decision to stay in Trumann, and work in the hospital. I wish I would have known.

"Lucy, I don't mean to shock you further, but your Pa is at the hospital now, and he's been shot. I'm afraid it's quite serious. That's why I came to fetch the doctor."

Lucy stood stunned for a moment, then spoke.

"Cain, you mean Daddy's alive?" she fervently exclaimed. "Please take me to him!"

"Of course, but we must hurry."

Cain ran around to the other side of the car and helped her in. Needing reassurance, she asked again, "You mean, he really is alive?" this time, more in the sense of a question.

"Yes, Lucy...but I don't know for how long."

For the first part of the trip, they rode in silence. He knew Lucy was still in shock, trying to absorb what all had happened since she had been away.

Finally, she broke the silence, "I can't lose him." She began to cry. "Cain, please pray that he survives, so I can explain to him what happened. I don't want him to think I deliberately stayed away." Cain rested his hand on hers as he drove. All the rest of the way to the hospital they kept glancing at one another, just like two young people first discovering love. It was as if the old feelings from the past had resurfaced, and they had fallen in love all over again.

When they arrived at the hospital, Lucy slung open the car door and ran into the waiting room, where Vick and Elizabeth were. Seeing Lucy alive was quite a surprise for them. Elizabeth ran to her, throwing her arms around her. "Oh Lucy, it is you! I saw the article in the paper about your upcoming marriage, but I had no idea it was you. I convinced myself that if it were you, you would have let us know."

"Elizabeth, I want to talk to you, and answer all your questions, but right now I have to go to surgery where Daddy is. I can't lose him."

"Lucy, wait! Orson is already out of surgery. We were told to wait a while before we see him."

"Well, I'm not waiting. I know where he is, and I have to see him." They acknowledged it was not the appropriate time to have a conversation with Lucy. They watched as she ran down the corridor to the room where Orson was wheeled.

Mark had no idea the man he was tending to was Lucy's father. He was puzzled whenever he saw her face. "Lucy, is there something the matter?"

"Mark, I can't explain now, but this man is my father, and for over two years I've thought he was dead." Birdie felt compassion for Lucy, seeing her eyes filled with tears. Recognizing her need for privacy with her father, she directed Mark out of the room.

"Why don't we leave, and let Lucy have a little time with her father?"

Lucy took a wet cloth and began bathing her daddy's face.

She was overcome with emotion and began to sob, seeing Orson fight for his life. She knew that he might not make it, and hoped, before he died, that he would open his eyes just one more time so he could see she was alive and okay.

She bent down and whispered into his ear, "Daddy, if you can hear me, I want you to know how much I love you. I know you tried to be tough on me when I was growing up, but now I know why. You were good and I knew deep down you loved me." Lucy was unaware that Cain was standing in the doorway listening to her as she spoke to her father.

"You've got to get better so I can tell you what a wonderful father you've been to me."

Although Orson was still unconscious, Lucy continued to pour out her heart to him. "Daddy, you need to know I had no choice after

I escaped the fire. My hands and hair were badly burned from trying to escape. After I found my way out of the flames, a Clan of people called the Jackson Whites kidnapped me. Had you not toughened me up as a child, I would never have been able to withstand their abuse. Many times, I thought I would die after what they did to me. And then my hands became infected."

Cain listened to Lucy as she continued her soul-bearing outpouring. *I pray to God he hears her*, he begged in thought. Cain imagined the worst of what possibly happened to Lucy. *My God, what she must have gone through. He couldn't help himself from listening, and feeling her pain.*

"Daddy, there was no way I could escape. I would have run away if I could, but they guarded me every second." Cain's heart went out to her. Again, he knew he had to have Lucy as his own, even though she was promised to another. He tried to resist, but his love for her was more than he could stand. He walked over and rested his hands on her shoulders. Lucy's beautiful blonde hair had grown back more beautiful than before, and the sweet scent of her fragrance captivated him, just as it did years earlier when he asked her to marry him.

Lucy stood and turned, then placed her arms around Cain's neck.

"Oh Cain, how has this happened?" He chose not to speak, but to just hold her close, as she sobbed her heart out to him.

It was during the embrace that Mark walked back into the room to check on Orson and Lucy. When he saw her and Cain together, there was no mistake that the two had a much deeper relationship than just friendship. He felt clumsy and awkward, as he searched for the right words to say. Nothing came out. Finally, with complete embarrassment, he walked out of the room. Lucy caught a glimpse of Mark as he turned and walked away.

She pulled away from Cain as soon as she realized that Mark had seen them embracing.

"Cain, I'm sorry, but I have to go to Mark. I'll be back before Daddy wakes up." He watched as she ran down the corridor after Mark.

"Mark, please wait…you don't understand." She continued to follow him down the path to the rose garden. "Please, you have to listen to me," Lucy pleaded.

Cain was afraid the two years of absence had changed Lucy, and she had created a new life for herself. *She's still the same girl, but something inside of her has changed.* He imagined it was too late for them. When Lucy ran after Mark, he sensed her loyalty was for the man she had promised her love to. Time had moved on without him. He was certain that Lucy would marry Doctor Cohen.

Chapter 33

Life is never easy, and Mark felt his world crumbling around him. This was supposed to be the happiest time of his life, yet in a minuscule moment in time, all the joy he felt with his upcoming marriage to Lucy, turned from unequivocal happiness, to pain.

It was a beautiful night in the rose garden, just beyond the rambling house that had been turned into a hospital. Mark felt like he had been hit with a ton of bricks upon seeing Lucy in the arms of a stranger, who was obviously no stranger to his wife-to-be. *There was something more than friendship going on between them, and I need to find out what it is before I can go through with this marriage,* Mark reasoned. Once confident of their relationship, he now no longer believed that things were as tight as before between himself and Lucy.

Lucy, who was trying to explain to Mark what he just witnessed, had no sooner caught up with him, when Elizabeth appeared, telling her that her father was regaining consciousness.

"Mark, please don't jump to conclusions. I need to talk to you, but for now, I need to be at my father's side before he awakes." Mark had a confused look, which she could do nothing about at the time. More importantly, was for her to be near her father when he awoke.

"Elizabeth, are you sure Daddy is coming around?"

"Nurse Birdie told me where you might be, and asked that I go find you and let you know that your daddy is regaining consciousness."

"I'm sorry Mark, but I must hurry. I don't want someone else to see him before I do."

Everyone was on pins and needles as Lucy approached Orson, who was still groggy from the ether. Although not quite lucid, her father was trying to focus his eyes.

"Daddy, I'm here now, so don't you worry about anything."

"Lizzie, is that you?"

"Orson, we're all here with Lucy," Elizabeth stated.

"I told y'all I didn't need no damn doctor." Orson's voice was weak, but there was something very much alive inside him, as he tried to open his eyes."

"It ain't right, y'all lyin' ta me 'bout Lucy."

"Daddy, I'm here, can't you see me?"

Orson ignored Lucy's voice.

"Lizzie, am I the only one who can hear Lucy?"

"Daddy, when you open your eyes, you'll be able to see that I'm right here by your side."

He squinted his eyes, as if he was afraid of what he might see. When he saw Lucy, he started crying. "Lucy, my little girl." He was so shaken by her presence that he began hyperventilating. "Birdie, can you do something for daddy? He can't catch his breath."

Birdie stepped over and told Orson to breathe slow and easy. "Try to settle down, Mr. Cargill," Birdie said.

Orson was looking at Lucy square in the eyes, unable to speak. She was sure that he was still feeling the effects of the ether. His eyes kept scanning the room, as if he was reconfirming that he was in the hospital. Then he saw Vick standing there with Lucy.

In no time, his erratic breathing settled down a bit. "Lucy, you're really here?" She held his hand as he tried to sit up. "I gotta git outta this bed, 'cause my little girl is gonna leave me. Vick, can you see Lucy?"

"I reckon I can, and I can promise you she's not going anywhere without her daddy." Having Vick's confirmation that Lucy was there in the flesh caused a tidal wave of emotion for Orson. He bawled like a baby. "Lucy, my little girl, I thought we lost ya' in that fire at the manor," he kept saying, as he continued to sob.

"Orson, I think you need to rest. Lucy will be right here when you wake up."

"Dang it, how can I sleep, now? I'm awake, and I need ta find out where Lucy's been. We all buried ya' and now yer alive. Where ya' been?" Orson demanded.

Lucy bent over and kissed her daddy, who began crying again. "I thought I lost ya'," he sobbed. "Where have ya' been?"

By now, there wasn't a dry eye in the room. Lucy turned to Cain, "Can you tell daddy what happened...I just can't."

"Tell me what? Jest tell me...I need ta know," Orson pleaded.

Cain walked to the bed and explained about the Clan that kidnapped Lucy after her escape from the fire.

"Ya' telling me them men that showed up that day at Lucy's funeral took my daughter after she escaped the fire?" Orson continued to wake more by the minute.

"Git me outta here, I'm goin' after 'em." Orson tried to get out of bed but the pain and grogginess was too much, and he fell back onto his pillow. "Well, I guess I can't go jest this minute, but I aim to as soon as I can git out of this God-forsaken place." Birdie came into the room just as Orson was going into his rampage.

"Daddy, you don't have to worry about those people. They've moved on, with a little help from the folks here in Trumann. You're not to worry, because they're not going to be hurting anyone else. Right now, I want you to relax and lay quietly so you can heal. You need to get well enough to make it home."

"Lucy, if I go back ta sleep, yer gonna be here when I wake up, ain't ya'?"

"I'm not going anywhere." She grabbed his hand as his eyes closed.

Orson drifted off as he whispered, "Lucy, I'm sure glad you've come home ta me. I shore missed ya'."

Lucy felt sorry for Elizabeth, who was crying. She knew how much Lizzie loved her father, because she had taken care of him while she was away.

After Orson fell asleep, Dr. Cohen walked back into the room. "Birdie, can I see you outside, please?" he asked.

They walked down the hall and privately discussed Orson's condition. "What do you think? You're the one who operated on him. Do you feel he's going to make it?" asked the doctor.

"I can't say for sure, but if he continues to make progress during the next few days, I believe he'll be fine in just a short time. In the meantime, you can get to know your father-in-law to be. I can tell you one thing; he's going to be a handful. Do you think you're prepared for that?"

"He's Lucy's father, and I'm sure he wants her happiness, but I'm not sure about Cain Porter. Can you tell me anything about this man?"

"Mark, I think Lucy is the only one who can answer your questions. Certainly not me."

After speaking with Birdie, Mark walked back to Orson's room where Cain and Lucy were holding vigil. Seeing the two together, he sensed Lucy and Cain might have been lovers. "That's got to be it," he thought. The more he looked at her, the more he wanted answers.

"Lucy, could I see you for a minute?"

"Mark, I promised Daddy I would be here when he wakes. Can't this wait?"

He had hoped she would step outside to speak with him privately, but her refusal made him feel rejected. And to make matters worse, she did it in front of Cain. Again, he was very embarrassed that she did not take his feelings into consideration. Mark's paranoia made him feel like an outsider, but what bothered him most was a father who had been brought back from the dead. *Who are these people I have to deal with when Lucy and I marry?* This really concerned him."

When Mark first met Lucy, she had no one. But now, instead of being dependent on him, she had family and friends in her life who were nothing more than strangers to him. He wasn't sure he could deal with that. *Somehow, I have to get this over to her that when we marry, we will have limited dealings with people she knew before we married.*

These feelings that surfaced made him loath the insecurity it brought out in him, and rather than face it, he chose to have Lucy all to himself. *Perhaps when she has time to get used to her father being alive, she will once again be the Lucy I fell in love with.* Without saying, Mark planned to keep a distance between himself and Lucy's father and friends, who were all hovering around her. *We have a lifetime together that will never include the Porters*, Mark promised himself. His main concern for the moment was getting her father well enough to be discharged, and send them all back to Jonesboro.

When Orson awakened from a deep sleep, he sat up in bed. "Lucy!" he screamed. She had just left his room when he suddenly awoke, thinking perhaps he had been dreaming. "Lucy!" he shouted again. Orson was just about out of bed when Lucy came running into his room.

He fell back onto his pillow and began to mumble. "I wasn't dreaming Lucy is really here. Lucy, come here beside me. She walked over and took his hand. "Ya' ain't goin' nowhere agin', are ya'?"

"No daddy, I'm going to be right here as long as you need me."

"Well, when am I gettin' outta this place?" She wanted to laugh, seeing her father back in rare form.

"I don't know, we'll have to make sure that wound of yours is healed enough for you to leave. Right now, I think the doctor would like for you to rest, so you can go home when it's time."

"Ya' know how I feel 'bout them doctors. Ain't nare one of 'em know what's wrong with ya'. I don't need no quack tellin' me when it's time fer me ta go home."

"Well...I can already tell you're better. You're still as ornery as ever. Daddy, you've got to get better so you can walk me down the aisle."

"Beg yer pardon. Did ya' jest say ya' was gettin' married? Hmmmm, well I'll be, yer gettin' married. Who to?" Orson asked.

"Let's talk about the wedding later. I should have waited until you're feeling a little better to bring it up. I can see you're going to worry, and that's the last thing I want. So forget about me getting married."

Orson's eyes were darting around, like he was thinking.

"Daddy, just try and rest."

"Well, can I at least ask who you're plannin' on marryin'? I don't reckon I know 'em, do I?"

"I don't know if you remember, 'cause you were pretty groggy when you met him. It's Dr. Cohen...Mark Cohen, the doctor here at the hospital."

Lucy could see Orson's blood pressure rising.

"Yer marryin' a damn quack doctor?" he all but shouted. "Ya' know how I feel 'bout 'em. Ain't a damn one knows what they're doin'."

"Daddy, please don't compare Dr. Cohen to a medicine man. That's all you've ever known; some man driving a wagon through town selling home remedies. Mark is educated, and he's a wonderful doctor."

"Well now, I didn't mean ta git ya' all upset, calling yer intended a quack. But it looks like ya' could have remembered how I feel about them quack doctors."

"You just won't stop, will you?" Lucy bent over and kissed Orson on the head. He lay there with his eyes darting and his nose twitching. All the while, Orson was making a plan.

"Lucy, I ain't feelin' so good. Do ya' mind pourin' me a glass of water?"

"Daddy, are you hurting? I knew I shouldn't have told you I was getting married. It's gone and made you sick."

"Child, I don't want ya' worryin' 'bout me. I jest need some water, and maybe I'll git ta feelin' better." Lucy stayed and pampered Orson until he closed his eyes. Unbeknownst to Lucy, Orson had decided to do anything he could to prolong his stay in the hospital. *I have ta put a stop ta this wedding, and I need time to figure out jest how I'm gonna do it, even if I have ta play near dead.*

Each day, Orson demanded all of Lucy's time, and she eagerly obliged. She felt it was her responsibility to nurse him until he was well enough to travel home. One afternoon, Dr. Cohen came into Orson's room to examine him. The wound was almost healed, yet Orson was still complaining about pains here and there. Being an experienced and astute doctor, it didn't take Mark long to figure out that Orson was faking his condition. He monitored Lucy and the care she was giving him, and decided he would speak with her about his suspicions regarding her father.

"Lucy, can I speak with you in private, please?"

Orson was also a man with keen intuition, and he had the feeling that Mark was on to his malingering, so in order to continue with his deception, he knew he had to "step it up".

"Lucy, ya' ain't gonna be gone long are ya'? I might need ya'."

"No daddy, I'll be just a minute, and then I'm coming right back."

As Lucy was walking out of the room with Mark, Cain walked in. They glanced at one another in a casual, but friendly manner. Cain was trying his best to give Lucy the impression he was not disturbed about her approaching marriage.

"Orson, you look like you're about ready to go home. Why, you look downright bright-eyed and bushy-tailed."

Orson sat up in bed, like the spry old man he was, and insisted that Cain come in and close the door behind him.

"Come here, I need ta talk ta ya'."

"What's wrong? Are you upset about something?"

"I reckon I am. I'm worried 'bout Lucy and that jackleg doctor she's planning on marryin'."

He could see the wheels turning, and knew that Orson was up to something."

"Ya' know that Lucy plans on marryin' that quack doctor, don't ya?"

"Did Lucy tell you that, or did the doctor?" Cain asked.

"She ain't marryin' him if I have any say about it. That's why I'm a puttin' on... makin' her thank I'm sick. I gotta git her back home where she can take care of me long enough to thank clearly. That girl of mine doesn't know her own mind."

"Orson, I won't say a word, but have you thought about how you are hurting Lucy by acting like you're sick when you're not?"

"I tell ya', he's got Lucy under his spell, and I ain't gonna stand fer it. She's comin' home with me so she can clear her head."

Cain didn't want any part of Orson's plan, but he wasn't going to break his confidence, since Orson was so passionately against his daughter marrying someone he did not think was right for her.

Finally, Mark had Lucy alone, to talk to her about Orson's antics. His intentions were to be carefully diplomatic how he told her, for he knew she was coddling her father, whom she assumed, was still in grave condition. "Lucy, I'm glad that we're alone so I can speak with you. I've thought about you every minute. I hope you're as excited about our wedding as I am. Finally, we can have a quiet time together without any distractions."

"What do you mean, distractions?"

"I didn't want to have to say anything to you about your father, but you do know he's faking, making you believe he's in pain when he's not?"

"Mark, I can't believe what I'm hearing. My daddy has been brought back to life right before my eyes, and you're accusing him of faking his condition."

"Lucy, I'm sorry, but your father is being deceptive with you, and it's time you know what he's up to."

"Up to, what are you talking about?"

"Your father wants you all to himself, and I think it is apparent he is trying to create a rift between me and you."

"That's absurd. My father would not stoop that low to come between me and the man I plan to marry."

"Well then, you don't know your father like you think you do. To tell you the truth, I would only be able to take him in small doses. I'm not going to stand for a father, or any other man, to come between me and the woman I love."

"Actually, I am very glad to have this conversation, because I feel just like you, in some respect."

"You do?" Mark asked, somewhat surprised.

"Yes, in my opinion, I will never stand for the man I marry, to come between me and my father. So we do have that in common."

Lucy was angry with herself for not sensing this about Mark. His paranoia was a side of him that she had not seen before, and it was totally unflattering to her. She realized she did not know him well enough to become his wife.

"Lucy, I didn't intend to upset you. I'm sorry I had to mention this to you about your father, but he's got you wrapped around his little finger. I couldn't handle another man having that much control over my wife. I can see you're unhappy with me now, but if you think about it, you'll know I'm right. Please, take your time and think about it," Mark suggested.

Lucy shook her head in disbelief. Finally she had come to her senses.

"Mark, I had no idea you were this insecure regarding my daddy. He's not just some man as you suggested... he's my father. I think it's you who plans to control me." She could see the handwriting on the wall, and knew it was time to end it with Mark. There was no way she would allow anyone to come between her and the man who had been both mother and father to her. She owed everything to her father, who loved and cared for her as a child, and who would give his life for her. She did not sense that type of love and devotion from Mark.

Instead, she sensed control and selfishness, something she could never live with.

"Mark, I've thought about it, and I cannot go forward with our marriage."

"You're not serious."

"Oh, but I am. My father and I will be checking out of the hospital tomorrow morning, and will be on our way back to Jonesboro. You're a good man, but not for me. I'm sorry, but this has to be goodbye."

Lucy had never known Mark to have a temper, but when he left the room he kicked over a cabinet that housed all of the medical supplies. Birdie heard the loud noise and ran out of a patient's room to see what was the matter. She knew it had to be something to do with Lucy and Mark.

After the supplies spilled, Lucy bent down, and was picking them up when Birdie came to her aid.

"Lucy, what on earth happened?"

"I'm afraid Mark was not himself today. I know this will be a shock to you, but I had to break our engagement."

"So, is this why the medical supply cabinet spilled on the floor?"

"I didn't realize he had a temper," said Lucy.

"Better to see it now than after marriage," Birdie offered. "You know, Lucy, I always felt you were settling after Jason's death. So, I'm not surprised."

"You're not? Why didn't you say something and save me from this."

"I'm sure you would have thought I was meddling, after all, I was Jason's sister— that's why I couldn't."

"He should have never kicked over the cabinet... that was it for me."

"A man with a temper, huh?"

"Yes, a side of him I did not know existed."

"Birdie, tomorrow morning I'm checking daddy out of the hospital. I think he's well enough to go home to finish his recovery. I'm afraid of what might happen if he stays here."

"Need I ask if you're leaving with him."

Lucy had tears in her eyes as she explained why she had to leave.

"I hope you understand. I can't allow daddy to be by himself. Birdie, I hope you know how much I care for you and the hospital, but my place is in Jonesboro. What would be nice is if you would come with me. We can use a good doctor."

"Lucy, my place is here, just like yours is in Jonesboro. But my dear, you have a future with someone else."

Lucy gave Birdie a long pensive look, as though she had peered into her soul.

Leaving Birdie, who was like her sister, was going to be very hard, and she wanted to make sure Birdie understood why she had to leave.

"Birdie, when I chose to stay here, it was because I was still grieving for the loss of my father. You'll have to come to Jonesboro for a visit from time to time."

"You remember…my sister lived there," she said.

"I hope you understand but if it wasn't for you I'm sure I wouldn't be alive today."

"Strong-willed Lucy…I've seen the compassion you've had with our patients, and I've seen the grit you have hanging out the side of a car shooting a rifle like a man. Had I not been there for you that day, you would have found another way. That's who you are, and I'm sure you learned that from your father. Don't you worry, the hospital will carry on, so go and be happy. I know your life is with your father, and I have a feeling, with someone else, also."

The two women embraced, and then Lucy walked back into Orson's room.

Chapter 34

LUCY THOUGHT IT BEST TO WAIT UNTIL THEY ARRIVED HOME IN JONES-
boro before breaking the news to Cain and Orson concerning
her broken engagement. She wanted to wait until the right time before springing it on her daddy that there was not going to be a wedding.

The next morning, after Orson's release from the hospital, he
continued his charade, complaining of pain, when there of course,
was none.

Lucy laughed inwardly, as did Cain; listening to Orson moan and
groan. He was such a bad actor, and it became apparent to Lucy that
Mark had been right all along about Orson's deception.

Ordinarily, Lucy would have chastised him for carrying on the
way he did, but she did not want to do or say anything that might
tarnish the miraculous reunion with her father. Besides, she knew and
understood his noble reason for doing it, and frankly, the whole thing
had become laughable.

Having a little fun at playing along, Lucy asked, "Daddy, do you
think if I stay home with you that you'll get better?"

"Yeah, I suppose, but it ain't gonna happen overnight," Orson
said, pitifully.

The old chap had finally overplayed his hand, Cain thought. Even
though Lucy had not confided in him that she knew of Orson's antics,
he knew she was on to him.

During the two hour drive to Jonesboro, Orson wondered if Lucy
still had a spark for Cain. Two years of being away could change a person and their feelings. He assumed that Lucy had changed, based on

her acceptance of Mark's marriage proposal. *I jest gotta give 'em time to rediscover each other*, Orson figured.

Once they rounded the bend past the manor, Lucy marveled seeing that it had been rebuilt.

"I can't believe the manor has been rebuilt. It looks the same."

Cain passed the manor and drove directly to the small place that Lucy and Orson called home. When she saw the small cabin that housed so many of her childhood memories she realized how much she had missed being back home. The little place was like heaven since Orson was back. For the first time she felt secure and safe. Being back in familiar surroundings was like old times. The only thing missing was the trail of dark smoke coming from the chimney. She remembered all the times she waited for her daddy to come home after rustling outlaws. Sometimes he was away for weeks at a time. *He's always been here for me*, she thought.

Orson was unable to stay in character during the three hours it took to get home, and it became annoyingly obvious that he was acting.

"Daddy, how does it feel to be back home?" Lucy asked.

"I'm glad fer one reason, and that's because I have you taking care of me."

"What about the pain you've been having?"

"Them pains let up ever now and then, but I could have another flare-up anytime." He said, wincing his brow and looking sheepish.

Cain saw Orson twitch his nose, and sensed he felt bad about lying.

Lucy was slowly working her Pa; baiting him a little at a time to see if she could trip him up. She wanted him to confess that he had been lying about his pains.

"Daddy, would it be safe to say that you'd feel much better if I wasn't marrying Mark?"

Orson's eyes began darting around, another indication that he had been lying.

"Funny ya' should ask about that. I got ta thanking that once ya' got home ya' might have a change of heart about marryin' that whippersnapper. Lucy girl, I don't want ta make ya' unhappy, but that man jest ain't right fer ya'."

"Would any man be right for me, or are you always going to try and interfere with whoever I choose to marry?"

"Now Lucy, that ain't a fair question."

Cain was listening, and was surprised to hear Lucy sternly confronting her father. "I think I should step outside while you and Orson have a chance to talk," Cain said. He walked outside before they had a chance to respond.

"Lucy, quit foolin' yerself 'bout this fancy pantsy doctor of yers. Cain is the one ya' should be marryin'. You've been so wrapped up with me gittin' well, and worryin' about that horse doctor friend of yers, that ya' ain't had time enough ta know what all Cain's been through."

"What do you mean, what Cain's been through?" Lucy asked.

"Me and him were shot, and lucky for me, I came home, but Cain didn't. We thought he was dead cause we were both ambushed."

"But obviously he wasn't killed. So, he had a choice, didn't he? I'm afraid I don't understand."

"The boy was purdy shot up and couldn't remember a thang. He jest now gained his memory back, and came home about a week ago.

"You mean he had amnesia?"

"I reckon that's what ya' call it. But fer two years, he didn't even know his name. We never gave up lookin', but finally, Vick and Lizzie had to face the fact that Cain was dead. The only thang was, he weren't dead. It was a surprise to everybody when the boy came ridin' up. Nobody knows anything 'bout what happened to 'em. I guess he'll tell us when he's ready."

Lucy gave deep thought to what her daddy told her.

"So that's why he never returned home. I had no idea. All I heard was you and Cain were shot and killed. I can't tell you what it did to me, knowing I would never see either of you again. I thought there was nothing left for me.

"Ya remember them James boys, Lonnie and Dudley? They the ones who ambushed me and Cain in Texas."

"Daddy they're the ones who burned down the manor and left me for dead. I managed to escape but not before I was badly burned. They left with something but I couldn't make out what it was."

"We're gonna be taking care of them boys. They'll be getting what's comin' ta 'em."

As bad as it was I recovered from my injuries and that's when I learned Elizabeth and Vick had moved to San Augustine." Lucy did not elaborate on what all happened to her after the manor burned. She felt Orson was not ready to hear how abused she was by the Clan, and especially, Munk. "Daddy, I need to tell you that I was married briefly to Birdie's brother, Jason, who died trying to protect me from the Clan. He was a good man, and he and Birdie were both responsible for my survival. They nursed me back to health, and took me in like family. After a while, I married Jason when I knew that I would never see you and Cain again.

"Daughter, if I'd known you survived that fire, I would have never stopped lookin' fer ya'. All this time you was jest a few miles away, and I didn't know." Lucy hugged Orson, as they wept in each other's arms. "Daddy, I'm so sorry." Orson pulled back, since he never liked showing the vulnerable side of himself. "I'm jest glad yer home now." His voice cracked as he tried to speak.

Orson wiped his tears and snorted into a handkerchief, trying to compose himself.

"I'm home now and I want you to know I'm not going anywhere."

"Ain't ya' going back to Trumann and marryin' that Mark feller?"

Lucy hesitated before she told Orson about her broken engagement.

"I broke things off with Mark before I left Trumann. You were right about him."

"You did? You ain't jest pullin' my leg, are ya'?"

"I don't want to go into it now, but things became very strained between us."

"I told ya' 'bout that quack doctor of yers. Ya' have ta listen ta me 'bout these things. Are ya plannin' on tellin' Cain 'bout whatcha did?"

"Why don't we keep this between me and you for a while. Do you think you can do that?"

"I'll try, but I ain't good at keepin' secrets, 'specially when I know ya' should be tellin' the boy that ya' ain't gettin' married and leavin' town."

"Please don't, Daddy. I'll tell him, but you have to give me time. I don't want him to get the idea that I broke off my engagement because of him. Do you understand? To tell you the truth, I don't think I will ever remarry."

Orson was surprised, hearing Lucy make such a strong statement about marriage.

In the days that followed, Orson recovered fully, and Lucy began thinking about going back to Chicago to re-establish herself at the boarding school. She had still not spoken to Cain about breaking her engagement to Mark.

There were several opportunities for him to learn the truth, but Lucy went on with her plans without confiding in him. He assumed she was making big plans to return to Trumann to marry her doctor.

One afternoon, there came a downpour while Lucy was in town. Cain saw her running toward her car, doing her best to escape the rain. She was carrying a bundle of clothing that she had planned to take to Chicago, but Cain assumed it was to be part of her wedding trousseau, after she married the successful, Doctor Mark Cohen.

Hurrying along, she was high-stepping, trying to dodge the water-filled potholes. Seeing her struggle, Cain pulled his car into her path, and offered her a ride.

"Lucy, get in before you're soaked."

She was still quite a distance from her own car, so she hurriedly jumped into his car to keep from getting her new clothes wet.

"Oh, thank you Cain…such a downpour we're having. I'm lucky you came along when you did."

"At least you're dry in here," he said, rather shyly. Lucy pointed to the leaky windows inside Cain's car. "I don't know if I'm going to stay dry with all the water coming in around your windows."

"Dang it, I should have had those windows fixed. I'm sorry, I've been meaning to get my windows repaired, but the weather was so good I kept putting it off. Tell you what, let's get you home and then we'll pick your car up later."

"Sure, as long as you can see to drive. I've never seen it rain this hard."

The sky had turned dark with a cold front coming in, and they could hardly hear for the rain clamoring down on the roof of the Model T.

"Lucy, I hope you don't make yourself sick in those wet clothes." Riding back to her house, Cain thought she was more beautiful than ever, with her long blonde hair dampened by the rain. He felt a rush of excitement, having her alone for the first time since he had been home. "Soon Lucy will be married to someone else, and if I don't make a move now, I'll never have another chance."

Once again, she became enamored with him, just as she had as a young girl. Having those feelings come back was a complete surprise, since she had forgotten how he captivated her heart as a teenager. She remembered him after he came home from college; dancing with the other girls, while she thought he was ignoring her. She studied Cain's profile as he faced the road, and thought how little he had changed since the time they became engaged. He was still the dashing heart-throb she remembered from over two years ago. "After all this time, and after all I've been through, the candle still burns in my heart for Cain."

Because of the circumstances in Lucy's life, she had changed, and she thought Cain might have changed also. Her reality was that she could not have children, since Munk and the others had made sure of that. To remain hopeful for a future with the man she loved could prove to be selfish, and Cain might end up hating her. Lucy was much too tenderhearted to stand another rejection. She remembered how they talked about having children.

Driving was becoming more of a task than Cain had bargained for. He was having great difficulty seeing the road, and steering the car at the same time.

"Lucy, I don't know about driving in this weather. It's not letting up." He could see the panic in her face as the car began slipping and sliding. The small tires on the Model T were not providing enough traction to keep from skidding off the road.

"I've got to find a place to park this thing before something bad happens," Cain said. Lucy was recalling the time Birdie was driving when their car slipped off the road, nearly killing them. Cain too had a traumatic experience when on that fateful day, he learned that Eileen and their unborn baby were murdered. *The storm was much like today*, he thought. "The first place I find, I'm going to stop and ride out this storm."

It seemed like forever, but finally Cain saw the carriage house that had been Elizabeth's painting studio as a child. "Lucy, there's the carriage house. What you say we try to make a run for it and sit the storm out. Don't worry about your belongings. They'll be drier here than if we take them out in the storm."

Cain steered the car toward the house, but got stuck in the process. They looked at each other and smiled. "Well that's that!" Lucy stated.

As soon as Cain said, "make a run for it", Lucy opened the car door and ran toward the front of the house, with the sweeping rain soaking her, with Cain following close behind. After they reached the porch, for a moment, they looked into each other's eyes, both dripping wet. *How beautiful she is*, he thought. For the first time since their return to Jonesboro, Cain saw a glimmer of hope.

When they walked into the cold house, Lucy noticed how dark it was. Since the curtains were drawn, she immediately went to the windows and opened the curtains. The storm clouds and rain darkened the sky, allowing very little light to pass through the windows, and there were only a few hours of daylight left. Even after a moment of being there, she noticed the musty air of disuse.

Cain went to the fireplace to make a fire, but there were no matches nearby. He turned to Lucy, who was shivering. "I'm sorry, but it looks like we may be out of luck with the fire. Would you want to change into something that belonged to mother? I remember her saying she had stored boxes of clothing here, and if there's something you can wear, it will be better than staying in wet clothes. I wouldn't want you sick before your wedding." Lucy felt a pang of disappointment, hearing him remind her of the wedding.

Why would Cain mention my wedding if he still cared for me? she thought. He walked into the bedroom and found a box of clothes, but instead of women's clothing, it was a box of blankets and bed sheets. *Well, this will have to do*, he thought. He brought a blanket for Lucy and apologized to her for not having clothing she could slip into.

"Lucy, this is all I have. Mother must have meant bed clothing instead of her own clothes." "I suppose I have no choice, do I." She took the blanket and went into the bedroom to change. She looked back at him as he walked into a small kitchenette. The bedroom was nice with only a neatly made bed and dresser. *How cozy the house would be if we had been able to make a fire*, she thought. She gazed into a mirror leaning against the wall, and after shedding her wet clothes, was pleased with the reflection of her naked body. Lucy was blessed with a figure any woman would envy. No one would ever suspect that she had been raped multiple times by members of a brutal scum-of-the-earth Clan. She wondered what Cain might think when he saw she had nothing but a blanket around her. She purposely draped one side of the blanket off her shoulder in order to get Cain's attention. When she walked from the bedroom, Cain was bent over, feeding logs to a glowing fire. He had not given up on his search for matches, and luckily found some in a kitchen drawer. He too had stripped from his wet clothing, and was wearing only a blanket wrapped around his waist. Cain's chiseled upper body and muscular shoulders aroused her. When Lucy walked toward him, he likened her to a princess. He was mesmerized with her beauty, and stammered a bit while explaining that he had found some matches. Lucy's blanket hung demurely over one shoulder. Seeing her in the shadows of the fleeting light, with only the glow of a warming fire, was very sensual, and Cain could hardly restrain himself from taking her in his arms. *I mustn't let her know that I'm still in love with her. It would be unfair to create confusion for her since she and the doctor are getting married*, Cain rationalized.

Lucy felt guilty about keeping her breakup from Mark a secret. *Cain has a right to know*, she thought. She was overcome with passion for him, and she could not continue to have him believe she was marrying.

"Cain, I've been waiting for the right time to tell you this, and now is as good as any. I'm sure it's of no consequence to you, but Mark and I broke off our engagement. Just so you know, I'm not getting married."

Cain was surprised, and wondered how long she had kept him in the dark.

"You're not getting married?" Cain thought she had chosen the perfect time to tell him, considering both of them were almost naked. He took this as meaning there was hope for the two of them. Following his natural impulses, he took her in his arms and kissed her. Not just a kiss, but a long passionate kiss that left her breathless. She finally pulled away from him. *How could I have read her so wrong*," he thought.

"Cain, I don't want to lead you on."

"I don't understand, when all I've thought about is you. Don't you feel the same?"

"I need to explain something to you. Two years is a long time, and people change."

Cain's love for Lucy prevented him from hearing what she was saying, and feeling another rush of passion, he took her in his arms and kissed her again.

"Can you tell me... that's changed? You kissed me back." He was still holding her as she looked into his eyes. She felt his warm body against hers, and it aroused the desire in her, but she could not allow his advances. Once again, she pushed him away. "Cain, you have to stop this. There's something more I need to tell you. He look perplexed, as she went into the full story of what Munk had done to her. Cain, I can never have children. I know how much you want a family, and I can't ever give you a son or daughter. Eventually, you would come to hate me. Mark never wanted children, and he understood. This is what drew me to him. That's the only reason I agreed to marry. It would be unfair to you, knowing how much you want children. It's not a problem now, but it would be in days to come. Cain, I would feel guilty that I married you, when I could never give you a child of your own."

Cain immediately thought about little Jared, but for some reason, he decided to wait to tell her. *This might be too much, and I don't want to spoil the mood with a detailed explanation. First, I have to convince her that I would be marrying her for herself, and not just to have children.*

Orson began to panic, thinking the worst of what might have happened to Lucy. It had been raining nonstop, and she had not returned home. *Lucy could bekidnapped again, or possibly been in a wreck,* he thought. He didn't know what to think, since she had not made it home. Finally, he stood it as long as he could. I have to find her. He slipped into his rain gear, ran to the barn to saddle his horse, and rode to the manor. There he would have Vick drive him to look for Lucy.

By the time Orson made it to the manor, he was soaked to the bone. Even his rain gear could not keep him from getting wet. He knocked on the door and waited, then called out for Vick. By the time Elizabeth and Vick heard him and came to the door, Orson had collapsed from the wet and cold.

"Oh my God! It's Orson, and he's fainted!" Elizabeth cried out. Vick, what was he thinking coming here in the rain?" It has to be something to do with Lucy. She would never consent for Orson riding here if something hadn't happened."

"What are we going to do?"

"First thing, we have to get Orson to bed, and then I'm taking the car to see if Lucy is in some kind of trouble."

They both wrestled with Orson's limp body, but managed to get him into bed. "Vick, you go, and I'll stay here and try to revive Orson."

When Vick arrived at Orson's, he ran to the door to see if Lucy was at home. He didn't see her car, so he assumed she was in town somewhere. *Perhaps she stayed in town to keep from driving in the rain.*

Vick slid back into his car and drove to town. There he found Lucy's car parked near the mercantile store. After checking some of the stores, he realized that Cain had not come home either. Perhaps they're together, he supposed. "If so, this could be the reason neither of them have made it home. He was sure that was the case.

Driving back to the manor, Vick spotted Cain's car stuck in the mud a short distance from the carriage house. He walked up to the front window of the house and peered in, only to see Lucy and Cain sitting near each other wrapped in blankets. *Under normal circumstances, this would be too embarrassing if I barged in,* he told himself. But he knew she would want to know about her father.

Vick rapped on the door to get Cain's attention. As soon as Lucy heard the knock, she ran into the bedroom.

Cain was surprised to see Vick out in the rain.

"Son, you and Lucy need to get dressed and come with me. I'll wait for you in the car. "Pa, don't jump to conclusions about this. It's not what you think."

"I'm not thinking anything. You and Lucy need to hurry. Orson's been out in the rain looking for Lucy. When he showed up at the house, he collapsed before Elizabeth and me could get to the door."

"Is he going to be okay?"

"I don't know, he was out cold when I left."

"What can we do for him? There's not a doctor around that can treat him," Cain pointed out.

"Son, we'll talk about this on the way home. You need to get yourself dressed."

Lucy was glad that Vick waited in the car so she would not have to look directly into his eyes.

"I think we need to take Orson back to Trumann in case he develops pneumonia," Lucy said. There's not a doctor around that can treat him if he's this sick."

Luckily for them, the rain stopped long enough for them to make it to the manor.

It was dusk when Cain and Lucy walked in on Elizabeth, who met them with that certain look. "Elizabeth, what is it? Daddy's okay, isn't he?"

"Where have you been? Orson came here looking for you and when we got to the door, he was laying on the porch, out cold."

Lucy looked at Cain as if they had done something wrong. "Mother, just a minute. I rescued Lucy from the rain, and it was impossible to get home without running off the road. We tried to make it home, but it was raining too hard. When I saw the carriage house, we stopped to wait it out."

"Well, I'm sorry you all got stranded, but poor Orson was so concerned for Lucy that he rode all the way here in the rain. I think we need to take him back to Trumann as soon as it stops raining."

"Elizabeth, where is daddy?"

"He's in the upstairs bedroom. I think he's awake now, but I'm not sure he's in very good condition."

Lucy was as pale as a sheet.

Elizabeth was ringing her hands with worry. "He's been through so much," she said. "We need to get him to a doctor."

Lucy ran upstairs to check on her father, while Cain spoke with Vick about driving to Trumann.

"Pa, my car's stuck at the carriage house. Do you think you can help me?

"Son, are you talking about right now?"

It's going to be a mess, but it's better to go now than wait. I don't know how long we're going to be in Trumann with Orson, and we'll need both cars. That's why I need my car, so we can go and come as needed."

"Well, let's go so we can hurry back and get on the road. I don't think we should wait until morning, since Orson is showing signs of pneumonia."

They feared he needed the hospital before he had a turn for the worse. "Lucy, I don't want you blaming yourself," Elizabeth said. "I would have done the same thing." Lucy's eyes welled up with tears as she thought about losing her father. "Elizabeth, I have a feeling daddy's not going to make it," she whispered.

"Don't y'all be talkin' like I ain't here," Orson muttered.

It took over an hour to free Cain's car from the mud. Once back at the manor, Elizabeth and Vick thought it best if they lay Orson in the back seat of their car, and have Cain and Lucy follow behind them in Cain's car. "Is that alright with you, Lucy," Cain asked. "All I want is to get daddy to the hospital. I don't care how we get there."

After beginning the three hour drive to Trumann, Cain reached for Lucy's hand. "Don't worry, your Pa's going to be just fine. You know Orson, he always bounces back," Cain said, in an attempt to be of some comfort to her.

"Not this time, Cain. I've seen that look before on patients in the hospital, and I doubt he makes it to Trumann." Lucy started to weep.

"You have to remain positive. Right now, Orson's fighting to stay alive, and he needs you to think he's going to make it," Cain instructed.

"I know you're right, but I'm so scared of losing my daddy."

As Lucy cried, Cain put his arm around her as he drove. "He's going to be just fine...you have to have faith, and I'm sure Mark will be right there by your side."

When they arrived at the hospital, Birdie was at the front desk to admit Orson. "Let's get our patient to a room and check him out!" She shouted to an attendant who was on duty. She briefly hugged Lucy, and then walked with the attendant to Orson's room. After the examination, Birdie suggested that she have Mark give his opinion before they decided if Orson had pneumonia.

"Birdie, can daddy recover from the pneumonia?"

"I hope so...if his body rejects the medication, then you might prepare yourself."

Lucy started to cry when Mark walked in. Seeing her for the first time since their separation gave him hope. *Perhaps God sent her back to me*, he thought. He walked over to Lucy and gave her a lingering hug. "Lucy, don't cry. You know we'll do all we can to help Orson get well." Cain had walked toward Orson's room and saw Lucy in Mark's arms. His immediate thought was they had made up, and were possibly going through with the wedding. After seeing them embrace, he decided to distance himself from Lucy.

Several days passed, and Orson was showing signs of recovery. Lucy was in his room when he opened his eyes for the first time. "Lucy, did ya' bring me back ta this horse doctor?" Birdie heard Orson speaking negatively about Mark. "Well sir, if it wasn't for this horse doctor, as you implied, you wouldn't be alive today. I would suggest you appreciate his skill, and respect him for the years he's trained to take care of ornery patients like yourself."

"Well, excuse me ma'am, but that's jest the way I am."

"If that's the case, I suggest you try and change a bit; if not for yourself, then for Lucy's sake."

Lucy had never heard Birdie come on so strong.

Orson grinned and turned to Lucy. "I reckon she got me told."

"Mr. Cargill, we're not here for your foolishness. We're here to get you well so you can go home and have a normal life."

"Well, Miss Birdie, ain't ya' figured out that there ain't nothin' normal 'bout me?"

Birdie started laughing, and then Lucy joined in. The cheerful noise echoed throughout the hospital.

Elizabeth and Vick heard the laughter coming from Orson's room.

"Well, I guess that means Orson's gonna live," Vick announced with a big smile.

"Thank God, now we can go home," Elizabeth said.

Chapter 35

ONCE AGAIN, ORSON HAD BEATEN THE ODDS, AND WAS ON THE ROAD **to regaining his health.** Birdie suggested that they keep him for another week before making the long trip back to Jonesboro. She explained to Lucy that he might have a relapse if they allowed him to leave the hospital too soon.

Cain stayed as long as he could, but his hope of changing Lucy's mind concerning marriage, was fading. Seeing her embrace Mark the day she arrived at the hospital was the catalyst for his pessimism. After Orson was admitted, all of Lucy's attention was directed to her father. The only exchanges Cain had with her were cordial, and it became very uncomfortable for him to stay on, when he assumed her feelings were for Mark Cohen. If she truly intended to marry the doctor, he did not want to interfere. As much as he wanted Lucy for himself, his first concern was her happiness.

Lucy had turned only 21, but hardship and diverse life experiences had made her wise beyond her years. She had convinced herself that marriage to Cain would not work because of her inability to have children. *Somehow, I have to get this across to him.* Lucy grappled with that thought.

That evening, Lucy walked into the hospital's rose garden, where she often went for solace. There she could clear her head and think. Cain was watching Lucy from a window up above. The night seemed magical as Lucy strolled through the garden. It was warmer than usual, especially for late November. Cain was longing to be alone with the woman he loved, but he did not know if she planned to meet Mark. That evening, as difficult as it might be, Cain planned to leave Trumann if Lucy did not respond favorably to him. *After I leave, Lucy will be free of me. I should have never interfered with two people who had committed themselves to each other,* Cain thought.

After a while, he decided to allow his presence be known.

Cain anticipated her reaction as he walked to the garden. *If she doesn't want me, then I must leave for her sake, as well as my own,* he nobly reasoned.

Lucy heard footsteps coming toward her. The walkway was made up of gravel and it was impossible to stroll quietly. She hoped it was Cain, and not Mark who was walking toward her. As the footsteps came closer, her heart began to dance, as she wishfully imagined how it would feel to know that she belonged with Cain and no other. On the other hand, she hoped to have his understanding when she explained why she could not marry him. She was a woman torn, and her ambivalence toward Cain was the result of a battle between her heart and her mind. No matter how hard she tried to make the "right" decision, she could not deny that she was madly in love with Cain. Suddenly, there she was, face to face with him. Her heart wanted to believe how wonderful it would feel to have a true safe place where she belonged. It should be worth fighting for, but she conceded that it would do more harm than good, since she could not condemn Cain to a childless marriage. *I must be strong and make him believe that his place is with someone else who can fulfill him as a father.*

"Lucy, I haven't had a moment alone with you since Orson's been sick. I saw you from the window. I hope you're not waiting for someone else."

"Cain, why would you think that?"

"I thought you might be waiting for Mark, and I wanted to tell you that tomorrow morning I will be leaving."

"You're leaving?" she asked.

"Yes, tonight is my last night. I have to go out of town for a while."
He paused, "I have business and there is someone I must see."

Lucy imagined that Cain had a secret life, since he had not discussed where he had been for the last two years. *A man as handsome as Cain is bound to have a love somewhere*, she supposed.

"Cain…I think I understand."

"You do?"

"Yes, who knows why things happen. You and I would have been very happy if my life had not taken a turn in a different direction.

"Lucy, we can change that right now if you want." She looked pensively into his eyes and told him she would always love him, but it was too late for them. "Cain, I'm sorry, but I love you too much to marry you."

"Are you saying a child is what's missing, and without a son or daughter you can't marry me?" Lucy had not heard it put so bluntly, but it was precisely what she meant.

"Cain, I know you. At some point you would want a child, and that would be selfish of me; knowing I had you, but unable to bare you a son or daughter. You have a right to have a family, and if I took that from you, I'm afraid it would destroy our happiness together."

"I see…I think I understand. Tomorrow morning I'm leaving town. I really don't know for how long, but I didn't want to leave without saying goodbye."

She was stunned that he was so forthright and candid, but deep down, she knew he needed to go in search of his life.

Cain gave Lucy a gentle kiss, and then walked away.

Lucy had underestimated how devastating that goodbye was going to be. *I had no idea it would hurt this much*, she lamented.

The next day, Cain drove back to Jonesboro. It was mid-morning by the time he reached the manor, and Elizabeth was there to welcome him home.

"Cain, you're back. How are Orson and Lucy?"

"They're both good. I think Orson will be well enough to travel home in about a week. Ma, I need to ask you a favor. I need to go out of town tomorrow morning, and I won't be back for about two weeks. I don't want you to worry about me, but there's something I have to tend to."

"Son, is everything alright?"

"Let's just put it this way…It'll be alright when I get back."

"You're very secretive about this. Is there something you want to share with me before you go?"

"I knew you were going to ask, but now is not the time."

"Ohhh, you! You're always so darn mysterious."

The next morning, Vick and Elizabeth bid Cain farewell, after helping him load the car for his trip.

"Cain, are you sure you want to go off by yourself?"

"Pa, you and Ma need to be here to pick up Orson and Lucy."

"You could have Hop go with you. At least he would be company."

"I'm fine, I'm fine! Don't be so concerned about me. I'll be home as soon as I take care of some business."

Vick embraced Elizabeth as they saw their son drive away.

It took that day, and the better part of the next, before Cain arrived on the outskirts of Beaumont. Martha was on the porch shelling peas when she saw a Model T coming her way. The dust was flying as the little car puttered closer and closer. She stood up, straining to see if it was someone she knew.

Cain saw Martha trying to make out who it was. Finally, he waved his arm.

"Oh my, that's Cain! He's come back! Martha picked up little Jared and started walking hurriedly towards the car. "Cain!" Martha hollered, as she approached the car. The moment he exited the car, she handed his son to him. "Jared, this is your daddy. He's come home."

Cain had a few packages to surprise Martha with, but his eyes were fixed on Jared. "The boy's grown," he said. "I imagine he has since you last saw him," Martha replied. Cain gave Martha a kiss, then went back to being mesmerized by Jared.

"Hi little man, I'm your Da Da," Cain whispered.

"Jared, this is Da Da. Can you say Da Da?" Jared took his hand and pushed on Cain's face. "Da Da,"Jared said, and then reached out for Martha.

Cain smiled. "Martha, you've taught my boy how to talk since I've been away." About that time little Jared said, "Mama."

"He understands."

"Sure he understands," Martha attested.

She was very happy to see Cain. As much as she loved Jared, she was glad that his Pa finally came to get him. *The boy rightfully belongs with his father*, she told herself, "and *I'm not getting any younger*." Taking care of a toddler at her age, was getting the best of her.

"How long will ya' be stayin?" asked Martha.

"Not long… I'm going to be busy helping out when I get back home. We have a big place to take care of."

"They must have been happy to see you. Did ya' tell 'em about Jared?"

"I guess I should have, but my mother's known to be a little pushy sometimes, and she would have insisted on coming with me. She has plenty of time to be a grandmother."

"Cain, while you were gone, a letter came for you. You stay here with Jared while I fetch it."

Cain couldn't imagine whom the letter was from. He saw the postmark was Woodville, Texas. Before he opened the letter, he remembered he had left Martha's address with the two men who were caretakers of Aggie's place. His hands started to shake as he opened it. Being a lawyer, he knew the feel of legal documents, and inside the envelope was a legal notice.

Martha was watching intently as Cain quietly read the letter. She saw his face change to concern.

"Martha, can you and Jared go inside while I read this? I'll be in as soon as I know what's going on with this letter." Cain walked to his car and got in, giving himself complete privacy.

It was a legal document relating to Aggie's death, and attached to it was her last Will and Testament. Cain could hardly believe what he was reading.

"How could she be sick enough to die, when I just saw her no more than a month ago?"

"My God, Aggie's dead, and Jared is the sole benefactor of her estate. "Aggie made sure Jared was well taken care of," Cain thought. There was also a letter addressed to Cain, to be delivered to him should something happen to her. He hurriedly opened the letter and read it to himself.

"Dear Cain and Jared:

Should you be reading this, you will know that I have died. Cain, I am so sorry that I kept this from you. I suppose I should have told you but the doctors said I had only a few months to live and I needed that time to see Seth and tell him his daddy's Will has provided well for him and he shouldn't interfere with Jared who is the heir to my property and holdings. Cain, my Will is among my things in safekeeping. You don't have to worry about Seth. He understands completely. My doctor who has been treating me said I had a rare disease, which cannot be identified. Thank God you found us when you did, for I would hate to have known what possibly could have happened to our son had you not come to Woodville when you did.. I pray you will protect him from Jonathan who will harm our son. Be happy Cain,

Aggie"

Reading the tender letter from Aggie upset Cain to tears. "What she must have gone through," he thought. "No wonder she allowed me to ride away with our son that day. Had she lived, she would have never given Jared to me."

Cain reconciled that he would always have a special place for Aggie in his heart.

"Of course, she had no idea that Jonathan was no longer a threat, since he was dead."

By the time Cain came into the house, Martha had rocked Jared to sleep. This gave her a chance to hear Cain out, since his face was an open book. She saw his sad eyes and knew something was wrong. It was obvious that he had been crying.

"Cain, has something happened?" He looked at her, but could not say a word. He handed her the letter and then walked out toward the barn.

Martha read the letter.

Oh my! I can't believe Jared's mama is dead. She felt sorry for Cain, knowing that he would be raising Jared without his mother. *Cain's heart must be breaking*, Martha imagined.

Later that evening, Cain came back into the house to discuss plans with Martha. "Are you sure you don't want to come to Jonesboro with me and Jared?"

"Cain, how 'bout I come fer a visit sometime later on. I got Wendell here and the rest of the hands that I have ta feed, and it wouldn't be right ta be leavin' 'em left to fend fer themselves. I hope ya' understand."

"I do understand, but you'll always have a home with me and Jared. If you ever have a mind to sell this place, you can come to Jonesboro so me and our boy can take care of you."

It was only that Cain cared so deeply for Martha that she knew he would always be in her life.

The next morning, as always, Martha had a big breakfast and a sack full of goodies for Cain and Jared for their trip back to Arkansas.

Vick hated to admit it, but he was getting a little worried, since Cain was undoubtably delayed. "What do you suppose happened to Cain?" Elizabeth asked. "I reckon the boy has a mind of his own. If I were you, I wouldn't worry," Vick answered. He tried not to show his concern.

Orson was home and getting around pretty good by now, and Lucy had begun to anguish over letting Cain get away from her. Her heart had finally won out. *Now I've ruined everything. I might as well go back to Chicago*, she contemplated. She had given up hope that Cain would ever come back; *I must have been absolutely stupid to let him go.*

After two weeks passed and the days came and went, Lucy wasn't the only one concerned; so were Vick and Elizabeth.

"Why didn't the boy tell ya' where he was going?" asked Vick.

"I don't know, you know Cain…he's so secretive. We don't know what kind of life he had during the two years he was gone. I didn't feel right asking him, and he didn't tell me."

"Well, let's hope he comes home soon, or I'm going after him."

"After him? We don't even know where he went."

"All I know is he headed out that way," as she pointed to the south.

Vick took Elizabeth in his arms and kissed her. "It ain't so bad being here alone is it?" Lizzie knew what he meant. "You're silly! Has anyone ever told you that?"

"Well, I'm just sayin," Vick laughed. Then he took her in his arms and whisked her upstairs.

"Vick Porter, you put me down this instant."

"What are you going to do if I don't?" Vick asked, as he continued to hold her.

He kicked the bedroom door shut and then dropped Elizabeth on the bed.

"Now, you're all mine," Vick whispered in her ear.

Several days later, Elizabeth brought Vick's lunch to him while he worked. The weather was cool, and it was approaching Christmas. "Vick, do you hear that? That may be Cain." Elizabeth thought she heard a car in the distance.

They both stood staring at the road until the little car came around the bend, then both said in unison.

"It's Cain!"

Vick dropped his tools and walked with Elizabeth to the front of the house.

When the car was in range, they saw a child standing near Cain.

Surprised they didn't have time to react, or even give thought to whom the child belonged too.

Cain pulled to a stop, got out of the car, and then reached in to retrieve Jared.

The scene of Cain holding a child was something their minds were not prepared to grasp.

Vick and Elizabeth stood silent, with their mouths agape.

Cain held Jared close to him.

"Pa and Ma, I want to introduce you to your grandson, Jared."

You could have knocked Elizabeth and Vick over with a feather.

"Grandson?" Elizabeth asked in shock.

Vick smiled, while Elizabeth's face turned to puzzlement. She reached for the child to hold him. "Da Da," Jared said, as he pulled back and reached for Cain.

"Cain, is there something you would like to tell us?" Elizabeth asked.

Vick stood there speechless.

"Let's go inside, and I'll tell you everything."

"Don't you think you could have told us about Jared? We had a right to know."

"I planned to tell you, but I had made a promise to Jared's mother. It had something to do with Jonathan and the James brothers. I had to protect Jared. Ma, I knew if I told you, you'd probably want to bring Jared home. I thought it best to keep my son a secret until I took care of the men who would want him dead."

"Where is Jared's mother? Why didn't she come with you?"

"It's a long story. Why don't we go into the library and I'll tell y'all what happened."

Vick took Jared from Cain. "I hope you don't mind if his grandfather holds him for a bit. Vick looked at his grandson, and then at Cain. "Boy, you're sure good with the surprises, aren't you," Vick said to Cain.

"No doubt he's a Porter," Elizabeth said. "He looks just like Cain's baby pictures."

Orson enjoyed Lucy doting over him for a while, but it really wasn't in Orson to stay cooped up in a cabin for any stretch of time. Days passed, and he grew more and more restless.

"I gotta git outta this place. I'm going stark raving mad jest a sittin' in this house. I need ta git on my horse and git me some fresh air," Orson told Lucy.

"Daddy, are you sure you're up to riding. I don't want you pushing it."

"Pushing it or not, I aim ta take me a little ride."

Orson knew that Lucy was having a bad time ever since she came back from Trumann. He guessed it had something to do with Cain, although she had not said a word to him about it. The more Orson thought of Lucy leaving, the more he wished that Cain and Lucy would come to their senses.

Orson walked to the barn and saddled up, then rode toward the manor. He planned to tell Cain that Lucy was not herself. He didn't care that his daughter would be furious about him speaking for her. It's about time them two put thangs aside and finish what they started two years ago, Orson decided.

When he rode up to the manor, he saw Elizabeth and Jared in the yard watering her plants. Orson thought, "Who's the child?"

Curious as all get-out, he rode up to the house and started quizzing Elizabeth.

"Well, who does this little feller belong to?"

"Orson, why don't you come in and have some of my pecan pie, and I'll tell you all about it."

Orson winced his eyes, and looked deeper into the boy's face.

"Ain't no need fer ya' to tell me a dang thang. That little feller is the spittin' image of Cain. Why ain't he told us 'bout his boy? I hope y'all ain't plannin' on lyin' ta me 'bout this little feller and who he belongs to cause he's Cain made over."

"Orson, would you like to know the story, or do you already know it?"

"Well, I guess I can come in fer a piece of pie, but don't ya start lyin 'bout that boy, 'cause he's Cain's...ain't he?"

Orson patted the boy on the head, unsure whether or not he should accept Jared, until he found out how Lucy was going to react to it.

"Well, where this boy's mama?" Orson quizzed.

"Orson, Jared's mother is deceased."

"You mean...died, as in dead?"

"That's a strange way to put it, but yes, Jared's mother died a few months ago. That's all I'm going to tell you right now. I'm sure Cain is waiting to tell you the entire story."

"Lizzie, I know this was a surprise ta ya', finding out ya' had a grandson."

"Yes, it was at the time, but now, I don't know how we ever got along without our Jared. He's a precious boy."

All Orson could think about was Lucy, and wondered how she would feel after hearing Cain had a son.

Chapter 36

AFTER GETTING OVER THE SHOCK OF BECOMING INSTANT GRAND-
parents, Vick and Elizabeth were thrilled at having Jared as a
new addition to their family. He was everything they had hoped
for in a grandson, and now the family was almost complete.

After retiring early to bed after a long day, Elizabeth laid thinking
of the time she first saw Vick. *That was so many years ago, yet it seems like
only yesterday*, she pondered. Elizabeth had loved him from the first
time she saw that huckleberry smile of his.

She was only 9 years old when she first caught a glimpse of Vick.
Although they were young, she never forgot how his eyes melted her
heart. She knew there was something very special about him.

Elizabeth, who was born of wealth, never believed that one day
she would marry this young poor boy. But life had taken many a fateful turn, and she had every reason to hate Vick, for he was responsible
for exposing her father's corruption; gaining his fortune by trickery
and theft. Vick, who brought her father and his dishonesty to a halt,
was also partly responsible for her father's suicide. There were many
reasons for her not to marry Vick, and yet, because of him, she was the
happiest woman in the world. Lying there beside him, she recalled
the heart-wrenching life he had, but this seemed to not have fazed
him. Many times he would tell her: "Lizzie, you have to live the hand
you're dealt." Vick was an exceptional person, husband and father, but
she never assumed he was destined to accomplish a great deed. All
she knew was he had completed her life. She rolled over and snuggled

close to him. As she looked into Vick's face, she noticed his eyelids fluttering, as if in a deep sleep. "He's dreaming," she thought. He was dreaming alright—dreaming and much more.

Once again, Vick was swept away by a higher power, and transported back in time. He and Sam were young boys running and playing with Hawk, their Indian friend. Armed with their ineffectual self-made spears, they were following Hawk further and further into the densest part of the woods near Panther Holler. They came upon the waterfall where Lonnie and Dudley James held him captive. Astonishingly, it had a likeness to the same waterfall that he and Sam played near when they were young boys. While watching these scenes unfold, an uncontrollable force invoked some vital memories of his past: when the panther almost took Hawk's life, and how he saved his young friend from a violent fall into the waterfall. Everything was beginning to come together; the mystery of the manifestations that for so long haunted his dreams were about to be revealed—he could feel it.

Suddenly, his thoughts gave way to a wondrous vision: a magnificent hawk came flying toward him through a resplendent sky. He watched the metamorphosing of the great bird as it magically turned into Chaytan, his protector and friend. As before, Vick found himself clothed in a stunning tribal robe, and witnessing a great number of Indian souls as they arose from their graves, and ascended high into the sky. Generation after generation of these spirits followed. Then, the beautifully bright day turned into darkness, except for a fire, around which danced a number of chanting Indians. Their chant was repetitive, and Vick did not know what they were saying. He was about to speak, when Chaytan communicated with him in thought. Anxious to understand the meaning of his recurring dreams, Vick asked once again why he was dressed in a robe, and why he was chosen.

"You were chosen because of your pure bloodline," Chaytan spoke. While still stunned by this enlightenment, he next saw a handsome Indian warrior who was heavily adorned with necklaces made of pure gold and jade. Vick noticed that the man riding toward him shared his same likeness and similarity. Vick felt the man was one of his ancestors who came to honor him. After a brief moment the man rode away and the magnificent hawk disappeared.

Vick was left with a final impression that filled his mind; after the last frost, and the first smell of spring, he would return to Panther Holler.

The next morning, Vick appeared to be shaken. He remembered each and every detail of his dreams, and accepted his responsibility to fulfill his destiny. There was also a notable change in Vick, for he was more subdued, and it made Elizabeth curious to know why. *He must be worried about the cotton business,* she thought, while noticing some gray hair around his temples. It was the very first time she noticed the graying. *It's as if it happened overnight.*

Elizabeth decided to speak to Vick about his restless slumber.

"Did you sleep well last night?"

"Why do you ask?" Vick countered.

"I don't know, you were restless in your sleep, and at one point I saw your eyelids fluttering. You seem tired today...as if you didn't sleep well."

"Elizabeth, don't worry about me, I feel fine," Vick assured her.

Nevertheless, she was concerned, for she had not seen such intensity of thought before in him. It was as if he was there in body, but his mind seemed miles away.

Cain also noticed Vick's change.

"Pa, you plan to work in the fields today?" Cain asked.

"I'm not sure Cain, I'm going to tell you like I did your Ma. I have some things I have to deal with. Don't worry about me!"

Cain was puzzled by his curtness, and remembered only one other time Vick responded to him in such a manner, and that was shortly after Vick was released from prison.

~

After meeting little Jared, Orson was itching to tell Lucy about him. He did not like keeping secrets from her, and this one was really gnawing at him. *She needs to know the truth about Cain's son,* Orson believed.

If Cain ain't gonna tell her—I am! He was unaware that Lucy had given up on wedding bliss, and decided to move back to Chicago and re-establish herself with the boarding school.

This is runnin' me slap-dang crazy, thankin' 'bout that boy of Cain's and him not tellin' Lucy. I'm giving 'em one more day and if he ain't told her, then I'm gonna' tell her myself, Orson vehemently contemplated. The next day, he decided to go and speak with Cain himself.

"Daddy, where you going?" asked Lucy

"I'm going ta see a man 'bout a dog," Orson stated.

Lucy had heard that phrase many times before when Orson did not want her to quiz him. "Daddy's up to something," she was convinced.

Vick and Cain were working in the fields when they saw Orson ride up. He reined his horse in their direction and started right in on Cain.

"Boy, ya owe it ta my girl ta tell her 'bout Jared. I came ta tell ya' she's gotta hear it from yer lips today or I'm tellin' her myself."

"Orson, I don't know what you expect. I've told Lucy how I feel about her, and she told me she couldn't marry me. I can't change her mind if it's already made up!"

"It ain't my business ta tell ya' if ya' gonna marry or not, but it seems ta me y'all are friends and she has a right to know about Jared from you."

"Cain, Orson's right," Vick agreed.

Standing on one foot and then the other Cain agreed to go and talk to Lucy.

"Okay, perhaps you're right. Let me finish up here and then I'll take a ride to talk to her. I hope you'll both be satisfied."

"I jest don't want my girl leavin' fer parts unknown a'fore learnin' the truth.

"Do you think hearing that I've had a son with another woman is going to make Lucy want me? I don't know how much more rejection I can take. But Orson, I'm going to do it in order to satisfy you."

"Well, I'd appreciate it!" Orson replied.

It was bitter cold and snowing that evening, but being a man of his word, Cain went about fulfilling his promise to Orson. The entire countryside was blanketed with a good mixture of ice and snow. After an early supper, Cain bundled Jared up and headed for Orson's. "What better way to tell Lucy than to let her meet Jared in person."

Elizabeth tried talking Cain out of taking little Jared, but since they were going in the Model T, she agreed. The closer Cain got to Orson's, the more he realized going out into a winter storm was probably foolish. He felt he should have waited for a break in the weather, but he was committed by his word to Orson. As the small car plowed through the snow, old feelings for Lucy began to stir, and the excitement of seeing her again was overwhelming. His heart beat faster the closer he got to their house, and he wondered if meeting Jared would destroy his chances of ever marrying her.

December was an unusually cold month, and there were snowdrifts and icicles hanging everywhere. The visibility was getting worse by the minute. Elizabeth had wrapped the boy in a beautiful heavy coat and matching cap. She made sure young Jared would be warm. Cain thought he was such a handsome boy.

When they arrived at Orson's, Cain took Jared from the car and headed for the door. Each step was a crunch of ice beneath the new-fallen snow. *It's treacherous, but beautiful,* he thought. *I can't stay long. We must get back before it gets worse.*

Cain noticed the frost build up around the windows, and the only thing showing was the soft glow from the kerosene lamp burning inside the cabin.

He regretted his decision to come out in the snow, since he knew he had to drive back.

Lucy was startled when she heard a knock at the door. Orson jumped up before she had a chance to stand. *It's probably someone for Daddy,* she thought.

Cain was sure Orson had already spilled the beans to Lucy about Jared. *I know 'em too well,* Cain thought.

The door opened and Lucy was surprised to see Cain holding a young boy. The idea that the boy might be his, did not cross her mind.

"Come on in here and git yerself and little Jared outta the cold," Orson said.

Lucy thought, *It appears that Daddy knows this child.* She wondered what the connection was with Cain and the boy.

"Hello Lucy," Cain said.

Seeing her expression he knew he had been wrong about Orson... *he hasn't told her.*

Lucy rose from her chair and walked toward the child. She thought Jared and Cain favored, but she was still not prepared to jump to any conclusions regarding the child. *They favor,* she thought, *It may be just a coincidence.* Somehow the shock of seeing the boy with Cain didn't allow it to register.

When Lucy came closer, she said, "Who do we have here?"

"Lucy, this is Jared...my son."

"Your son?" she asked. Her eyes fell on the boy and then back to Cain.

"Yes, when I left Trumann I told you I had to leave to take care of business."

"So, this is the business you were speaking of? Elizabeth's heart sank seeing Cain with his son that she was unable to give him. She managed to hide her emotions. "Well, he's sure a cute little business," Lucy said, and then looked at Cain for an explanation.

"Why don't you take the boy's coat off and stay a while," she suggested.

Slowly it began sinking in that Cain was married and had a child.

"Cain, I don't undertand. Why didn't you tell me you were married with a son."

Little Jared began squirming as Cain started to talk. "Lucy, do you mind if I let him down?"

"No, not at all." She kept looking at Jared as he walked toward her. *He's such a beautiful little boy*, she thought. *Now Cain can go on with his life and I won't have to worry about making the right decision.*

Orson felt the tension growing, and decided the best thing to do was make himself scarce. "Lucy, I'm gonna' leave y'all ta catch up. If y'all need me I'll be at the barn. I have a little filly that I need to look in on." Cain knew it was only an excuse Orson was making in order to give him and Lucy time to talk it out.

"Orson, it's pretty grim out there. Why don't you stay and keep us company."

Orson had his coat on and out the door before Cain could stop him.

The snow was quite heavy, as Orson trudged towards the barn. *Cain ain't goin' no place at the rate this snow is comin' down*, he told himself.

Lucy and Cain talked for what seemed hours, while he told the long story about how Aggie found him after he was shot.

"So this is when you and Aggie got together, and Jared's the result." Lucy pieced the story together.

"I suppose you can say that, but it's not like you imagine."

"Cain, you can't regret what happened between you and Aggie, since that relationship created little Jared."

"Lucy, you have to remember that I had no one, and neither did Aggie. I didn't have a name or know of my past. Everything was a blank. I thought it would soon come to me, but it didn't. After a while, Aggie and I became close. When she left, I had no idea she was carrying my child.

Cain told her the entire story, even about Martha and Glen Cormack, and how Glen concealed Cain's true identity.

"Lucy, if I had any knowledge of my past or you, I would have come home immediately. When Glen showed me a poster he picked up in town, that's when my memory started coming back. But it didn't happen overnight. There are things in my past that I still don't remember. But I remember you, and what we had together. I've thought of nothing else since then."

"Cain, what about Aggie, surely you want to marry the mother of your child." He explained that Aggie ran away. "After she left, I didn't have anyone. I was completely alone."

Lucy saw the sorrow in Cain's eyes, and wondered if he was still in love with her. "Cain, where is Aggie now?"

"After Aggie left Henderson, she met and married a man who killed his father. It was an accident, but her husband got a sentence of 20 years in the Huntsville Prison. Shortly after that, Aggie died of some mysterious illness. I only found out when I went to Martha's to bring Jared home."

The time had gotten away from them, and Lucy began to worry about Orson.

"Cain, Daddy should have been back by now. I hate to ask you, but would you go to the barn and see about him. Do you mind? I'll stay here and get better acquainted with Jared."

Cain put his hat and heavy coat on, and then walked out into the night. The snow had slacked up a bit, and it was quite beautiful with the moon glowing through the mist. Before he got halfway to the barn, he saw what looked like a body lying in the snow. Apparently Orson never made it to the barn. Cain fell to his knees and rolled Orson over, brushing the snow off his face and clothing. He bent down to hear if he was breathing. "Oh no! Not Orson!" Cain was shocked beyond belief, seeing his old friend Orson dead in the snow. There was no time to grieve. *Somehow, I have to get him out of the snow.*

Cain lifted him from under his arms and dragged him into the barn. The jolt of finding an old friend dead in the snow subsided, and grief had taken its place. Cain wiped the frozen snow from Orson's face, and then cried. "Orson, you old sidewinder…why did you have to leave us?" Cain said aloud. "How we gonna make it without you?" Cain tried to compose himself, but Orson was like another father to him, and he just let his emotions flow. He knew that he would have his hands full when he went back to the cabin to tell Lucy. *She's gonna be devastated when I tell her how I found Orson.*

Keeping Lucy contained was going to be another problem, and he knew it. Cain tried to appear brave, but it was apparent that he had been crying. *I can't let her see me like this*, Cain thought.

The snow made it difficult walking, but Cain plodded his way back to the cabin. When he arrived, he was clearly upset. If he had tears on his face, they were frozen by now. He brushed the snow off him and then turned to Lucy.

"Where is Daddy?" she asked softly.

Cain just stood there with a look that implied something had gone terribly wrong. "Cain, why don't you answer me…where is Daddy?"

Cain quickly looked around and saw Jared sleeping on a little bed in the other room.

Lucy's name was all he got out before she lost it.

She ran to Cain and began pounding on his chest. He tried to hold her, but she kept fighting. "Cain, tell me Daddy is okay…please!"

"Lucy, I'm sorry, but I found Orson in the snow. He didn't even make it to the barn. He's gone."

"Noooo!" Lucy screamed. Noooo! Tell me this isn't so." She looked at Cain as he held her. "Cain, I can't lose my Daddy, when I just found him."

"I'm so sorry Lucy, you know how I felt about Orson; he was like a father."

"Where is he now? Is he in the barn?"

"Yes, I moved him out of the snow and covered him with some blankets." Lucy continued to sob.

"Cain, I need to go to him."

"No, I'm not letting you see your Pa like this. Orson wouldn't like it, and besides, there's nothing either of us can do until morning."

"I know, but I can't let him be out there by himself."

"Lucy, Orson's gone. It's just his body that's left. Tomorrow, after it's daylight, we can do something, but right now we can't. Please try and understand."

Lucy continued to cry until she was interrupted by a knock on the door. Cain knew it had to be Vick, who, as always, was concerned about him. Both Vick and Elizabeth were standing at the door, all bundled up in the freezing cold."

"Cain, I'm sorry, but we were afraid for you and the boy. Is everything alright?" No one answered until Elizabeth saw Lucy. She thought she and Vick had interrupted a private conversation.

"Lucy, are you alright?" Elizabeth asked.

Seeing that Lucy was distraught, she walked toward her. "You're crying, what's wrong?" Elizabeth finally noticed that Orson was not among them. "Lizzie, Daddy is dead. He was on the way to the barn and died in the snow."

"He died in the snow?" Elizabeth asked.

Elizabeth found a chair and sat down. She was in total shock. Vick was standing by, observing the scene and thinking about Orson and how he would like to have been with him. *My old friend rode on without saying goodbye*, Vick thought.

"I reckon Daddy had a heart attack. He had been complaining of indigestion, but I had no idea it was his heart."

Vick walked over to Lucy and took her in his arms, then spoke to Cain.

"Where is Orson now," Vick asked.

"He's in the barn. I did the best I could, and pulled him in from the snow."

Vick was visibly upset. His voice cracked. "You all stay here. I'll be back in just a minute."

Lucy tried to follow, but Elizabeth cautioned her about the snow. Reluctantly, Lucy turned and ran into her bedroom.

Vick walked slowly through the snow, trying to comprehend what happened. *Anyone could get confused and become lost in this mess*, he thought.

Vick saw the glow of a lantern that Cain had lit. He walked reverently toward Orson's body, which was covered with several blankets. Only Orson's boots were showing. Vick recognized the boots that

Orson had worn over the years, all covered with snow. *I can't believe Orson's gone.* Vick knelt by Orson and pulled back the blanket, and then broke down, crying like a baby. Afterwards, Vick wiped his eyes and looked around to find something to place Orson's body on. He found an old door, and pulled Orson onto it to keep him off the frozen ground. He knelt by his body once again. "Ol' buddy, we had some good times, you and me, and I want to thank you for releasing me that time instead of lettin' that posse hang me." Vick expected to hear Orson make a joke, as usual. But there was no joke this time, nothing but silence from a man who always had to have the last word.

This time, he really is dead, Vick thought, *and there ain't a damn thing I can do to bring him back.*

Vick thought about how unfair life could be, to take someone you love. He remembered how he felt when Sam died way before his time.

Sam, I'd be mighty obliged if you would show Orson around. He's an ornery old cuss, but you'll learn to love him just like I did.

Vick's pain was reserved for someone special, and Orson was that.

Chapter 37

THE AIR SEEMED TO SPARKLE THAT MORNING, AND THERE WAS THE most dazzling blue sky overhead, with just a hint of a white cloud when Orson was laid to rest. Bunky Willams, who worked in the bank, joined his friend Rufus Ward, who as a Deputy once rode with Orson, were in town to pay their respects. Those two, along with Charlie B and Vick, agreed to be pallbearers. When they carried Orson to the gravesite, he was buried next to his beloved wife who had died many years before him.

My old friend has a good day to make his journey home, Vick contemplated.

All those who came to pay their respects to Orson felt a great loss, as though a small part of their life was gone forever.

It was blistering cold, but no one could complain that the day wasn't specially made for a man who had touched so many lives. A rascal of a man, he was: a friend, father and one you would never want to test if you were on the opposite side of the law. Orson was stern, full of laughter at times, but mean as a snake if anyone broke the law. This is how Orson developed his good name, being a "what you see is what you get," kind of a man. He was respected for his straight arrow approach to life. And to many of his peers he will live on in memory as being one of the orneriest old coots known to man, or at least to the people of Jonesboro, Arkansas.

Cain stood with Lucy during the burial ceremony as she wiped her tears. All others close to Orson had none left to give. It was just a solemn group who had grown up knowing Orson as "The Man".

When they left the burial site, the guests had only a short distance to walk to the cabin. People brought mostly food, but some brought trinkets of a sort that Orson had whittled for them, such as a slingshot or a little play truck that he had made for them when they were children. It was a day of celebration, all for a great man of the law.

Chapter 38

WHEN THE FIRST HINT OF SPRING FINALLY APPEARED, CAIN FELT IT **was time for new beginnings, and during the months following Orson's death, he went daily to check on Lucy.** Many times she would be busy quilting, just to have something to do. Her life had become unraveled when Orson died, and she was living day-by-day trying not to think about her last days with her father.

Slowly, Lucy began to heal, and the only thing she looked forward to was visiting with Cain and little Jared. The boy had come to know Lucy, and was more attached to her than anyone knew.

One evening Cain had planned to take a drive with Jared when, surprisingly, the boy blurted out, "Mama!" Cain thought he was talking about Elizabeth and tried to pull Jared from the car, but instead he bowed up and said, "No... Mama."

At that point, Cain realized that he had to ask Lucy to marry him. There was too much time that had passed and not only did he want her to be his wife, but apparently his son already considered Lucy his mother. There was no one better than Lucy who could fulfill Aggie's wishes as a mother for Jared. Cain knew Lucy would love Jared as her own.

As the days passed, Cain planned how he would ask for Lucy's hand. Elizabeth was spending more time with her since Elizabeth needed help in the gardens. "Lucy needs to keep busy," Elizabeth imagined. While the women worked around the house, the men worked in the fields. Of course, it went without saying that Elizabeth was creating reasons for Cain and Lucy to be together.

Spring was in the air and all the mixed fragrances from the garden seemed to be wheedling romance. For the first time since Orson's death, Lucy felt alive. She began taking another look at Cain, although he had refrained from pressuring her about a relationship with him, since it had been only a few months since Orson's death. He refused to prey on her vulnerability and make her feel forced to make a decision as important as marriage. He wanted Lucy to come to him on her own time, and not because she was sad and lonely.

~

The Gardenia Ball was a yearly event, and Elizabeth was busy planning for the special night. She had deliberated for weeks to make sure the event would be perfect.

The gala was once again held at the manor, and, as always, Elizabeth had outdone herself with the decorations. She had strategically placed gardenias all around the house, making it fragrantly opulent and festive. Then there was the aroma of other fragrances that permeated throughout the house, which would take her guest's breath away. After Elizabeth and Lucy finished decorating, the ballroom looked stunning enough to impress a foreign dignitary.

During the process of decorating, Elizabeth who needed Lucy's help arranged for her to stay in the carriage house near by.

The date of the Ball had finally arrived, and Elizabeth was scooting around making sure that every last detail was completed. Just before the guests arrived, she lit the candles and arranged the food in such a fashion that everyone would feel welcomed and valued.

Before the first guest appeared, Elizabeth stepped back and acknowledged Lucy for her exceptional good taste and expressed gratitude for all her help, suggestions and hard work.

Cain had arrived early to carry out his own plan to pop the question to Lucy. *This is the night*, he nervously anticipated.

There were out-of-town people invited to the gala, which included Birdie and even Dr. Cohen who accepted the invitation to attend. It had been sometime since Mark Cohen had seen Lucy, and he was looking forward to being with her since he heard that Orson died. *Lucy might be more encouraged to marry me since her father's death*, he thought. *After all, months had passed and Lucy was still single. Apparently, Cain is not the one*, Mark resolved.

Cain was standing there waiting for Lucy to arrive when Birdie Crumb and Mark Cohen made their appearance. *Oh no*, Cain thought. He should have been aware that Mark was coming, but Elizabeth was much too busy to tell him. *Thanks Ma*, Cain thought.

"The one thing missing was our dear old friend Orson who always spiked the punch," Vick said, under his breath after he sampled the drink.

Just as the clock chimed the bewitching hour, the guests began trickling in, and mingling about. The people of Jonesboro and surrounding areas were always impressed with the festivity of the manor. They knew how hard Elizabeth worked to make everything beautiful. It had always been THE party. Years ago, when the first Ball originated, the brick driveway had only contained horse and carriages but now that it was well into the twentieth century, most people had cars. Many of them were different makes, rather than just the Model T, which was still Elizabeth's favorite.

Vick had his own opinion of the crowd that evening, and thought they were rather stiff. *It's a shame Orson's not here*, he thought. Vick quickly left the room and came back with a big jug of liquor, good and strong that he brought back from Panther Holler after Orson was shot. "This one's for you Orson." Vick poured every last drop into the punch bowl and then tested it himself. "Oh yeah!" he said. He felt sure he could hear Orson laugh, and then say as he always did, *It's strong enough to burn the hair off yer tongue.*

When Lucy walked into the manor, every eye in the room was on her. She wore a beautiful pink taffeta dress with a scarlet ribbon around her waist. Her hair was long and flowing, with a single barrette that pulled her hair to one side, just over her ear. When Cain saw her, she took his breath away. Mark Cohen was determined to ask Lucy to marry him. Elizabeth rescued Lucy from the crowd that was offering their condolences for Orson's passing, and insisted that Lucy come meet some people she did not know.

Vick was watching the crowd when the punch was served. Men were beating their chest after they took their first drink, and the women were looking at their husbands as if to say save me. He was sure the folks were looking for Orson, even though they knew he was dead. One thing for sure, the party livened up after one drink of punch. At one point, Elizabeth walked over to Vick, " I know what you did" she said. About that time, Birdie came over and jokingly said, "We serve this to our patients just before we operate." She giggled and walked away.

"Vick, how could you?" Elizabeth scolded.

"Do what?" he asked, and then smiled as he walked away.

"Oh you!" was Elizabeth's only response.

Like father, like son. Cain took a drink of the punch and thought about Lucy. *She needs a drink of this*, he thought. "Yup, that's how I'm gonna do it, and this is the perfect time." He poured himself and Lucy a drink and felt a new confidence; a new resolve. *What the heck have I been doin', waitin' so long?*' he thought. He knew he had been right to give her some space over the last few months, but at some point he should have gathered enough nerve to ask her. *I should have told her, 'we're getting married, and that's all there is to it', and maybe that's exactly what I'll say right now*, he thought. Suddenly filled with energy, he sought her out in the crowd, but she wasn't there. *Maybe she's outside*, he guessed. *In fact, that's the perfect setting for a proposal! Under the night sky, big ol' moon, stars all around…yes sir!* Only now did he realize how long he'd been waiting for this moment, and the fact that it was almost here was overwhelming. Eager to find her, with his two punch glasses in hand, he hurried out onto the veranda and stopped short. There in the center of the huge veranda, under the full moon and domed by the night sky bursting with stars, was Mark, down on one knee proposing to Lucy.

The two punch glasses tumbled silently into the grass.

Cain quickly slipped around the corner so he wouldn't be seen. He slumped against the wall, no strength in his legs, no air in his lungs, and his eyes as cold and empty as the pit of his heart. A whirlwind of thoughts stormed through his head: loss, regret, and the most profound heartache that felt like his life was draining rapidly out of his body.

Cain rushed around the side of the manor. He needed to get as far away as he could. His insecurities had hold of him now, and they ran rampant. He knew Lucy missed working at the hospital, missed the good she was doing there, maybe what he had assumed was her tentativeness toward him was really disinterest. Maybe she had already decided months ago to go back to Trumann and start a new life with Mark.

Cain ran from the party, jerking the tie from his neck, and reeling from the rejection that was just too much to bear. Without thinking, he ran to the stables, threw a bridle on his horse, and without changing out of his party clothes, jumped bareback onboard, dug his heals into the gelding's ribs and shot out into the night. Sometimes a fella just needs to ride. Besides the heartache of losing the love of his life, he was also deeply upset with himself for not "manning-up" when he had the chance.

Vick had seen his son through the window rushing toward the stables and went outside to find him. Before Vick got to the barn, Cain's horse sped off into the night. Vick shouted, "Son, wait up," but it was too late. Cain had galloped out of the corral as though he was riding on the wind.

Vick thought, *something's goin' on.*

Vick turned and headed back to the party. As he approached the manor, he saw Lucy walking inside from the veranda followed by Mark.

"Oh, well, that ain't good," Vick acknowledged.

It was a perfect moonlit night, but now the moon and stars seemed to be mocking Cain. He rode hard through several creeks until the voices and music from the party faded to silence. He saw all manner of brush, mostly grapevines coiled around trees as he rode. Several times he spotted white tail deer as he made his way into the denser part of the forest, disturbing the birds and creatures in the bush. He paid it no mind. It meant nothing. Most everything meant nothing to him right now.

He stopped abruptly when he realized he was at the same lake where he had brought Lucy when he proposed to her the first time. Funny how when you think things couldn't hurt any worse, something comes along and makes it sting even more. *How in the world did I end up here?* he thought. Thinking back to that time, it seemed like a lifetime ago. He remembered it was here by the lake that she refused his advances when he tried to make love to her. It suddenly occurred to him, *There's no going back, it's really over. I've lost the only woman I've ever loved. How can life be so unfair?* He sat quietly for a moment, at the depths of despair. But then he thought of the injustices his father had born, and those his mother had lived through as well. And then he remembered that he had a son to raise, and that was more important than anything. Life had to go on—pain and all. He took his time returning to the stable. He found solace in the rocking of the slow lope and the full, rhythmic breaths beneath him. Something about riding "hide to hide" with no saddle brings a man closer to what's real, what's important. It makes one connect with life in a more basic, primal way. After arriving at the stable, he got off his horse and led the gelding back into the front of its stall. Cain brushed his horse as the breathing gradually slowed. Still rich and deep its rhythm made him realize every moment in life is important, every second means something. That's when he heard someone behind him. It was the voice he both yearned for and dreaded.

"Cain, I need to talk to you."

He knew Lucy was here to tell him that she was marrying Dr. Cohen. *I might as well face the music,* he thought, *and try to be a man about it. But just how happy for her am I supposed to pretend to be?* he wondered.

"Cain, I looked for you and couldn't find you. Why did you leave?"

He couldn't face her just yet. He kept his back to her and kept brushing.

"I'm sorry, but when I saw Mark proposing to you, I knew I had to get out of there." Cain knew he had to do the right thing, and here and now was the time, so he turned around to face her.

"Lucy, I wish you all the best, I do...I know that—"

And that's when he noticed her tear-stained cheeks, and a look in her eyes that said there was no strength in her legs, no air in her lungs, no blood in her heart; as if she was desperately trying to keep the life from draining out of her body.

And all because he was acting like he really didn't want her.

"Why are men so stupid sometimes?"

Without knowing she'd just said that, and without realizing what she was about to do, she lunged into his arms and kissed him; the kind of kiss that'll change a man's life...forever.

"I want to marry you. How could I want anyone else?" she whispered soulfully. Cain was struck with a moment of confusion, "Lucy, did you just propose to me?" Cain asked wryly.

Lucy was suddenly embarrassed. "Um, yeah, I guess I did," she giggled.

Cain took her in his arms and whispered in her ear, "in that case, Lucy, I accept your proposal," They could both feel the passion building between them, passion that had been building for far too long.

Lucy, I want to do this right, I think we should wait till we're married."

"She shook her head and kissed him again.

"Lucy, you just can't kiss me like that until then."

She took her hands and held each side of his face as she looked deeply into Cain's eyes.

"Well mister, then you better hurry up and marry me," she teased.

With the sound of the horse's rhythmic breathing behind them, they held each other as if they were one person, and always would be.

One week to the day there was another Gala, but this time everything was decorated in white.

Everyone close to the family was in attendance, of course, except Orson, who was sorely missed. But if you were there that day, you felt his presence.

Cain's heart was beating a mile a minute as he waited to see his bride. When she walked down the stairs toward him, he thought she looked stunning in Elizabeth's wedding gown and veil that Lucy had chosen to wear. Cain was the typical groom, worrying about whether he was going to make a good husband and father. *She's ravishing*, he thought, as he met Lucy at the end of the stairs, from where they would be escorted through the seated crowd to the minister. Elizabeth carried the trailing part of the gown until they reached Vick, who was holding little Jared. There they all stood together as one beautiful family.

After the happy couple exchanged their vows, the Church bells rang and it turned out to be the most beautiful wedding Jonesboro had ever seen.

"I only wish my Daddy could have been here to see me and Cain married. Perhaps he is watching over us today. Yes, I'm pretty sure he is."

Chapter 39

As the days grew longer, and spring had come to an end, Vick **had another vision as he lay beside Elizabeth sleeping.** *This time he saw the same ancient warrior riding a chestnut gelding toward him. The warrior was dressed in jade and gold. It was explained to him that now was the time to return to Panther Holler to find the "road that roars." There he would fulfill his destiny.*

A road that roars, what does that mean? he questioned.

Although he was caught up in the apparition, he understood how difficult it would be to leave Elizabeth without telling her the truth and why he would soon be leaving. His concern was not to cause her unnecessary worry.

The warrior communed with Vick that he should tell Elizabeth he was returning to Panther Holler but spare her the details.

Vick still had questions, but this time the visitation was short and very vague. How will I know where to go? Was this his last thought? As the warrior rode away, it was conveyed to him that he must look toward the sky.

Vick was relieved to know that Cain would be returning soon, and that Elizabeth would not be left alone. There was small talk among them as Vick waited for the right time to tell Elizabeth he was leaving.

At breakfast that morning, Elizabeth looked into Jared's eyes and thought how those deep brown eyes looked so much like Vick's. She sat there wondering when Cain and Lucy would return from their honeymoon, since Jared was getting to be a bit of a handful.

Taking Jared from her, Vick finally approached the subject. Seeming unconcerned, he walked over to the window to look out.

"See... daddy's coming soon," he said.

"I think Jared has really taken to his grandpa," Elizabeth said.

Vick turned and smiled.

Now is as good a time as any if I'm gonna tell her, he thought.

"Elizabeth, I need you to sit down and let me explain something to you. She looked at him with complete surprise.

"I need to do something. I'm going back to Panther Holler—today."

"Did I hear you right? You're leaving for Panther Holler?" She asked.

"Yes, I have to go, but I want you to understand that I'll be back."

"Vick, I'm afraid I don't understand. Did something happen?"

Vick thought, *How am I going to get into this. She's gonna' think I'm crazy if I tell her the truth.*

"Elizabeth, I need you to trust me."

"Can't you tell me why?" Elizabeth assumed it had something to do with the James boys and Vick wanted to protect her. Perhaps Lonnie and Dalton survived and Vick knows about it.

Vick kissed her and then left for the bedroom to pack.

He's not himself, she thought. She picked up Jared and walked outside onto the porch, as if to will Cain and Lucy's return before Vick left. Walking back into the house, she could hear him rummaging around upstairs, packing his things. She knew it was no use to try and persuade him for he was going.

He's going to need food. Despite her disappointment she wanted to make sure he had enough food to get by for a few days.

"Vick, is there anything I can do to make you change your mind?" she asked.

He took her in his arms and whispered in her ear.

"Lizzie, don't worry... I'm coming back."

It was heartbreaking seeing the man she loved ride away when she had no idea why and for how long. For the first time, Elizabeth felt insecure with Vick and their future together. *Did I ever really have him?* she asked herself.

Hearing the rattling sound of the Model T, Elizabeth knew the new-lyweds were returning home. Why couldn't they have been here earlier, before Vick left?

Anxious to see Cain and explain to him that Vick had left, she ran out the door with Jared to meet them. Although Elizabeth was panicked, in contrast she saw a happy couple. Concerned that she would be spoiling their homecoming she tried to shield her sadness, watching as little Jared ran into Lucy's arms.

"Mommy, Daddy," Jared called out.

Vick should have been here to witness this, she thought.

"We're home now," Lucy said. Cain sensed something was seriously wrong with his mother.. He knew her well and had no problem reading her.

"Ma, where's Pa? Did something happen while we were gone?"

"Cain, I don't know how to tell you this, but your Pa left this morning for Panther Holler."

Cain thought she was teasing him, but she was much too serious. "When did he leave?"

"He left early this morning. He packed his saddlebags and rode off. I didn't know what to think. I had no idea he was going until he sprung it on me."

"Did he say anything else? He's bound to have said something besides 'I'm leaving'."

"Cain, he was very secretive."

"Ma, I spec' Pa might need me."

Cain turned to Lucy and explained that he had to go fetch his Pa. "I hope you understand," he said.

Although Lucy hated to see Cain leave, she agreed that he must go.

Within the hour, Cain was packed and ready to leave. He kissed Lucy and Jared goodbye, then saddled his horse and rode away.

Lucy comforted Elizabeth. "Don't worry about Vick— "Cain will bring him home," Lucy assured.

Chapter 40

Vᴄᴋ ʜᴀᴅ ɴᴏ ɪᴅᴇᴀ ᴛʜᴀᴛ Cᴀɪɴ ᴡᴀs ᴏɴʟʏ ᴀ ᴄᴏᴜᴘʟᴇ ᴏғ ʜᴏᴜʀs ʙᴇʜɪɴᴅ **him.** There were shortcuts that only Cain knew about that saved him time.

Pa will take the safest route, going around streams instead of through them, Vick figured. The spring rains had melted much of the snow, making the creeks cold as ice.

The first creek Cain came to was swift and full of swirling currents, but it did not stop him. The gelding swam to the other side as Cain guided him around boulders and on top of rocks. Afterwards, they were on the trail again, crossing several other creeks that Cain guessed Vick would not go through. This greatly saved time in Cain's efforts to catch up with his Pa.

When Vick arrived at the entryway to Panther Holler, his horse stepped off the main road into the rich green thicket. Once again he was returning to Panther Holler, a place that held so many mixed emotions. The good ones were of his brother who was buried there. With pride and a sense of rending loss, Vick imagined being back in the Holler with Sam, who had died so awfully long before his time.

It was a beautiful spring day, and memories of his past flooded his mind. Vick felt calmness as he rode deeper into the woods. It was as though Sam was calling for him. His journey was peaceful and fulfilling as he thought of his brother and the day he died. Even though Vick knew he was not to blame, deep down he wondered if Sam would still be alive if they hadn't run away. For some unknown reason he began to understand things more clearly, and understood that his life was part of a master plan, much bigger than he could imagine.

Cain was now only a short distance behind Vick after leading his horse into the thicket. He dismounted and examined the ground for fresh tracks. *Pa can't be far ahead*, Cain calculated. *Soon I'll be caught up and then I'll try to talk some sense into him.* This was Cain's mission, to bring Vick back home where he belonged.

Under normal circumstances the first stop would have been the old scout house, but Vick kept going.

He rode until darkness deepened. The twisting trail became difficult to follow when Vick finally stopped to feed his horse. *This is plenty good to make camp*, he thought. He settled around the campfire, sipping a cup of coffee and thinking about Orson. *If Orson was here the old feller would be talking my ear off.* Vick smiled as he felt the presence of Orson. "I couldn't make the ride without you," Vick said out loud.

The next morning, after a good night's rest, Vick awoke invigorated as he set out again. He felt an urgency to get where he was going. When he arrived at the blue lake where he and Sam camped as kids, Vick looked across the body of water. There perched on a large limb was the same beautiful hawk he had seen so many years before. It stretched its wings as if to say hello. Vick wondered if the hawk was Chaytan. If ever he doubted that Hawk was his protector, he certainly did no longer. He remembered the words of Orson when Vick told him about Chaytan vowing to always be Vick's protector:

"Well, ya still here ain't ya'. And you've endured more than yer' share," Orson would always say.

Vick saddled up again and continued his journey. He remembered the instructions he received from his dream; that he should look to the sky. As promised, the hawk flew from tree to tree, each time waiting for Vick to follow.

It was still morning when Vick caught sight of Panther Holler, the cabin where he had spent much of his youth. This could never be home, with all the blood that was spilled here. He wanted to hate the place, but something deep inside shielded him from what would normally be abhorrence. How could he hate the place where Sam was laid to rest?

Vick had a desire to stop and look around the place, but something encouraged him to keep riding. Little did he know, the James' had taken up residence there since they could not risk returning to Jonesboro where they could be caught and sent to prison.

If Vick had stopped at the cabin he would have seen all the holes dug as Lonnie and Dudley searched for the "buried treasure." They were convinced Vick had buried it someplace around the cabin or in back of the storm shelter.

Riding past the cabin, Dudley caught a glimpse of a man on a horse.

"Lonnie, I thank we got company. That was Vick Porter that jest rode past our cabin."

"Ya' shore it was Vick?"

"Yup, I bet he's here fer' the treasure. What ya' thank?"

Totally consumed with another chance to find the treasure, they saddled their horses to ride.

By coincidence, Cain caught sight of the tail end of Vick's horse as it ran past the cabin. He was eager to catch up with his Pa and find out what was going on. It never entered Cain's mind that the James boys might be hiding out in the cabin.

Lonnie and Dudley were behind the storm shelter saddling up when they saw Cain ride by.

Once again, Dudley thought Cain was a ghost who had returned from the dead.

"I ain't goin' nowhere," said Dudley. Lonnie looked at his brother with contempt.

"We're goin' alright, so shut yer mouth and stop whining. Ain't no such thang as a damn ghost."

"Well, tell me how a man that's suppose ta be dead jest rode his horse by us."

"Ther's only one reason I can thank of— cause he ain't dead," Lonnie yelled.

"Now come on brother, and git ahold of yerself. Times a wastin."

"What we gonna do?" asked Dudley.

"We gonna kill 'em both jest after we find the treasure. Let's give 'em a little time ta do the diggin' and then we'll surprise 'em."

Vick continued to follow the hawk who apparently was directing him to the waterfall. He imagined the streams were more treacherous this time of the year due to the winter snows, and hoped he wasn't going to be taking another bath.

By the time Vick reached the waterfall, Cain had Vick in his sight. He shouted to him, but his Pa could not hear for the noise of the churning water as it plummeted over the fall down onto the rocks. Vick reined his horse to a stop while reliving the earlier incident when he jumped into the waterfall to escape the James brothers who had kidnapped him. It was a miracle that he and Cain survived after Cain risked his life to save him.

Vick continued to look to the sky when he saw the mighty hawk glide down to a tree branch that extended over the waterfall. Vick thought, *How am I going to conquer the stream which is too turbulent and dangerous to cross?*

As Vick studied his next move, he saw a shadow appear behind him. He drew his gun with lightning speed before he realized the rider was Cain.

"Son, where in the hell did you come from?"

"Pa, are you alright? Ma told me I should try and find ya'." Cain felt he should not elaborate on his concerns at this point.

"I reckon I should have told her why I had to leave."

"Perhaps, but I think it's something you should tell me now. I need to hear from you why you're here."

Vick knew his son wouldn't believe him, so he decided to show him instead.

"Look there," he said, as he pointed across the river.

A panther sat on the opposite bank staring at them. Cain was startled to see an extremely large cat that was, in his opinion, eyeing them for his next meal.

"Well, the first thing we need to do is shoot that thing before he gets us," said Cain, as he unholstered his pistol.

"No." Vick stopped him before Cain had a chance to shoot.

"He's waitin' for us."

"He sure is Pa, for his supper!"

Vick just shook his head and pointed to the treetops high above the panther's head, where a hawk sat patiently.

"They're both waitin' for us."

Cain did not understand, and was looking at his father with deep concern.

"Son, I know this sounds crazy; you're gonna think I'm off my rocker, but that hawk has been leading me this whole way, and right now we need to find a way across this stream."

Cain could see there was no safe way to get across that rushing, swollen water.

"While we're waiting, why don't you tell me why you're really here," Cain insisted.

'Cain, I'll explain everything, but first I can't even hear myself talk here. Let's move away from the roar of these falls."

And that one word "roar" triggered something within Cain.

"Pa, do the words, 'the road that roars' mean anything to you?"

Vick was puzzled and stopped his horse dead in its tracks.

Vick slid out of his saddle, and Cain followed him a short distance from the waterfall to where they found a short downed tree trunk upon which to sit. Cain began telling his Pa about his vague and hazy dreams of an Indian on horseback, and that the only thing he could remember was the phrase, 'the road that roars.' Vick then recounted his dreams, including mention of the same phrase, and his instructions to look to the sky for guidance. Vick reiterated that he felt the hawk wanted him to cross the river. He wasn't sure how the panther fit in to all this, but he felt certain the cat meant them no harm.

Cain listened intently to his father who tried to explain about the mysterious dreams. However, the tale was far too complicated to be believed, he thought. Even though the explanation had a ring of truth to it, Cain could never believe such an extraordinary story.

"Pa, we can't ford that river. The water's runnin' way too fast."

"Right, but 'the road that roars' has got to be a road alongside this "roaring" river. So there must be a way across, either upstream or downstream, and we have to find it."

Cain was still not convinced.

"I can't imagine there's a way across downstream, as fast as this water is and as swollen as the banks are. We can try upstream, but it looks like just cliffs. I don't see how there could be a road anywhere along here."

"Well, we have to look", said Vick as he stood. When he turned back toward Cain, he suddenly froze.

"Cain, real slow now, stand up and step over here," Vick spoke calmly and quietly as he gradually moved his hand toward his holstered pistol. His voice was soft, but toned with authority.

"Now, Cain."

Seeing Vick's concerned manner, Cain rose cautiously and a bit confused. As he stood, he looked back over his shoulder and saw the reason for Vick's trepidation.

There, lying just inches from where they had been sitting, was a massive panther.

Cain instinctively reached for his gun, just as Vick raised his hand to stop him. "Wait! He won't attack. Look at his ears."

The huge animal lay docile and unaggressive in the grass; his ears fully forward and attentive, not plastered back against his head like and animal that's angry, frightened or aggressive.

"I didn't hear a thing. How the hell did he sneak up on us?"

"I have no idea, but if he wanted us, he coulda' had us. He ain't gonna do nothing."

The panther just watched them, as if he was waiting.

"More importantly, how the hell did he get across that river?! A few minutes ago he was on the other side. He's not wet, not even his paws. There's gotta be another way to the other side."

Cain hadn't taken his eyes off the cat, nor his hand off his pistol.

"Pa, this panther is really old. And he doesn't look too healthy."

Vick moved closer to the cat to get a better look. The animal, completely unthreatened, didn't respond at all.

"You know what, you're right, he is old. And he looks tired."

Only then did Cain notice the weariness in the old panther's eyes. "And he's huge! My gosh, his tail is almost six feet long."

"Cain, I think this is the same panther I shot when I saved Hawk. Look at those scars. You remember me telling you about the young Indian boy who vowed to always be my protector, don't you? Cain saw the long-healed bullet wounds on the panther's side and belly. He also noticed its rather labored breathing.

"Pa, you ain't tryin' ta tell me this cat is the same one you shot when you were a kid—are you?"

"I reckon I am son." Vick moved closer.

"You are old, aren't ya' fella." Vick couldn't help feeling some sort of kinship with the old creature, as he bent down to look into his eyes. "You been roamin' this holler just about as long as I have...survivin', fightin' the fight. I gotta hand it to you...you're still here. Well so am I. And we gotta find out how you got across that river."

Cain couldn't believe what he was seeing. His Pa and this animal definitely had a connection.

Vick stood, looked around, and then started back toward where he figured the panther had come from. As he did, the old panther slowly rose and followed him.

"Pa, watch yourself!"

Vick turned and stopped just as the massive cat slowly and gracefully grazed past him. Only then was Vick able to appreciate the sheer size and power of this magnificent animal. As old and weary as he may have been, there was no denying his potency. The cat walked toward a dense thicket at the side of the waterfall. He stopped and looked back at the men for a moment, and then pushed into the bushes and disappeared.

"He wants us to follow him," Vick stated, as he followed the cat to the edge of the brush. "C'mon Cain, we don't want to lose him."

Slightly less enthusiastic than his father, Cain caught up to Vick. As they got closer to the waterfall, the familiar roar of the water increased. Vick and Cain left their horses tied to follow the cat that was leading them into what seemed to be a heavy thicket. Once they parted the thick bushes and took a few steps in, "Son of a…there is a cave in here!" Vick had to shout to drive out the deafening sound of the waterfall. As Cain moved into the brush, he saw what Vick saw. There was a cave opening large enough for man and animal to pass through.

Pa, I hope you're not suggesting we go through this cave without a light of some kind.

The cave was a passageway directly under the river to the other side. As they looked into the cave, although completely dark inside, they could see light coming in from the opposite opening. They also saw a very large panther waiting patiently on the other side.

"Not to worry," Vick said. He made a point of bringing his container of coal oil and fashioned a torch from a stick and his bandana dipped in the oil.

Having light, they proceeded on.

Once in the cave, Cain was bracing himself with both hands, feeling along the wall when he felt something that could be carvings.

"Pa, wait! Look at the wall," Cain said, pointing at symbols, pictures and characters that had been carved into the rock walls of the cave.

"We'll come back to those drawings in a bit," Vick said. The men moved swiftly through the cave.

Since the cave was so close to the crest of the waterfall, the thundering noise of the falling water was deafening. Cain and Vick had to yell to be heard. The power of the rushing water also caused an intense vibration throughout the stonewalls.

"The road that roars, huh? I guess we know what that means now," Vick remarked.

The cave was only about 40 ft. long, slightly more than the width of the river itself, so it wasn't long before they emerged on the other side. As they exited, Vick could see more carvings on the walls at this end as well. The images on this side were more elaborate and plentiful, as if a story was coming to an end, Vick surmised.

Cain looked cautiously around them, "Where's that panther? I don't much like not knowing where he is."

"The hawk's gone too," Vick responded.

"So now what?"

Vick considered their options.

"Cain, I think those pictures in that cave may mean something. It's gettin' late in the day, I say we bed down here tonight. It looks like there's a clearing just beyond these trees, and that'll give us a chance to figure out the drawings."

Cain was a bit uneasy about the plan, but could tell Vick was determined to do what he felt was right.

They both returned through the cave, tended their horses, and brought what they'd need for the night back through the cave. The clearing just beyond the trees was small and well isolated from the elements by the tall, dense forest all around. They were about to enter the cave when there appeared Lonnie and Dudley.

"Cain…easy Cain, easy."

"Keep your eye on him, Lonnie. This one is fast, but I believe that one's faster."

"What the hell do you boys want?" groaned Vick.

"Shut yer' mouth and drop yer' guns … and I mean now!"

There was a hunger in Dudley's eyes that Vick had not seen before, and he knew they meant business.

"Do as they say, Cain!" The men unbuckled their holsters and let them drop to the ground. Vick and Cain were thinking the same, "*how in the hell are we gonna' git outta this one?*"

"We saw yer' horses and found you're little secret passageway, and we know ya' buried that treasure right around here somewher'. Now the only question is, just how much do you wanna be dead?" Lonnie prided himself with the threat.

"There's no treasure, boys. There never was."

Vick knew they weren't going to believe a hawk and panther story.

Dudley looked over at his brother and then back. It was clear to both Vick and Cain that these two unpredictable scumbags had a plan all worked out.

Dudley's calm and ruthless demeanor was unsettling to Vick, who saw him kill Jonathan "jest because he wanted to."

Cain noticed how nervous Lonnie was when he spoke.

"Now here's how this is gonna work. If you don't tell me what I want to know, Dudley here is gonna shoot your young'un— in the face. And then you get to watch him die. And then if you don't talk, I'm gonna start shootin' you. First in the knees, then the thighs, and then the belly. And I'm gonna just keep shootin' till you hand me that treasure. You'll talk eventually...you know you will. But then you'll die—screamin'!

Vick, who was a master of manipulation, was desperately searching for a play. But every possible option put his son's life at risk.

"Now, if you fess up right now—well then, you two can just run along home— empty handed of course. Ya' got three seconds."

Both Cain and Vick knew they would never leave alive under these circumstances.

Lonnie looked at Dudley holding his gun on Cain.

"Guess we know ya ain't dead. Ya been alive all along, ain'tcha boy. Now we git to do it all over agin and snuff the life outta' ya'."

Vick figured this was finally it. This was the one hand he couldn't win.

Then, as if out of the ether, from over Vick's head, like a flash of black lightning, something happened. But it was so fast and so quiet, it was incomprehensible. All Vick could tell was that the James brothers suddenly disappeared. It was as if they were instantly thrust backwards into the blackness of the night.

If it hadn't been for the sound of crushing bone and the ripping of human flesh, there would have been no clue as to what had just occurred. That is, until that blood-chilling, hissing snarl echoed through the forest.

It seems that the old and weary panther had one more ass-whuppin' left in him.

Cain quickly tossed the dry leaves onto the fire, and in seconds there were flickers of light; just enough to see the flash of two bright yellow eyes as the panther glanced back at them.

Then, with a little more light from the fire, they could see that magnificent animal, radiating lethal brutality, take one of the bodies by the forearm and drag it to the other body, laying one arm over the arm of the other body and crossed at the wrist. The cat then opened its massive jaw, grabbed both bodies by the wrist in one bite, and briskly dragged Lonnie and Dudley out of the clearing towards the river. The sounds of feeding continued at the water's edge.

"Well I reckon I'm done sleepin' for the night," Cain heard himself say shakily.

"I think its fittin' that those two boys go where they're going together."

Vick lay back down and closed his eyes.

"You're goin' back to sleep?" blurted Cain.

With closed eyes and a relaxed brow, Vick said, "I reckon so. I've never felt safer."

The next morning Vick's mind was at peace, but like an old dog with a bone, he wasn't about to let loose of something till he was good and ready. Cain had resolved to wait patiently till his father had finished wrestling with the frustration he felt from not being able to complete the final task he had been charged with: to find where the great secret treasure was buried.

"It's here," Vick whispered almost mournfully.

"I know it is, Pa, and we'll find it. Just not on this trip. We're short of supplies, and we got weather coming. We'll have to come back another time."

Vick didn't budge. "Sometimes you're just not ready to fold," he said.

Then, for some unknown reason, Vick turned and went back into the cave.

"There's something missing and it's here."

With daylight and a lantern, they walked the cave, studying the carvings on the wall until they saw a small offshoot cave they had overlooked in the middle of the tunnel.

"Well, well, look what we have here."

"Pa, how did we miss this? You're not going in are you? What about the Panther? He might be in there."

"No son, the Panther is gone. No one's ever gonna see him again. He was here for one purpose and he's fulfilled it. He's free now, and I'm going in."

Vick could see it was an opening just about his size.

He slowly kicked away the debris and small stones around the opening, then quickly wiggled into the cave and disappeared. After a moment Cain heard a massively resonant echo from a very soft spoken voice say, "Oh my God..."

Cain didn't wait. Being younger and thinner, he slipped through the narrow passageway with ease and emerged on the other side. As soon as he saw his surroundings, his jaw dropped and his breath was taken away.

They found themselves standing on a ledge inside a massive cavern at least three stories high. Vick immediately began to descend a bending carved pathway leading to the cavern's floor.

The walls, from ground level to the tip of the ceiling, are carved in glyphs, (pictures that tell a story).

Cain marveled at the carvings on the ceiling that reached more than 30ft. up from the floor. "How did they make those carvings on the ceiling...I mean, how'd they get up there?" Vick, still gazing at the walls as though in a trance said, "They'll tell us."

Cain sensed something different in Vick: a focus, an authority.

"Son, this is their history. All of it...from the beginning." Vick read the walls as if he'd always known how, yet in reality, it was being revealed to him for the first time.

It's where the Original People came from, how they got here—they walked all the way—from the other side of the world."

Vick turned to the opposite wall and absorbed the signs and messages for a moment. "And this is their future...no...it's more of a guide—of how they should reach their destiny...the abundance that's awaiting them. It's all here Cain, the whole story."

Vick stared at the far lower corner of the wall for a long time. "And there's me—with a bunch of rocks."

In the lower corner, both observed the large symbol of a man with a line through his head, signifying a hat, the same symbol Vick interpreted as himself when he saw it in the cave that crossed the water. The figure is holding a number of stones in his hand. There appeared to be omnidirectional rays around the stones, as if representing shining or glowing.

Vick suddenly looked about the cavern for something else of significance. Moving to the center, he noticed a large flat stone resting on the ground. He brushed away the dust with his hand and uncovered another carved figure of a man with the line through his head. Without hesitation, Vick knelt down and flipped the stone over. "It's a pit!" he exclaimed.

Cain rushed to him with the lantern, but not before Vick reached down into the darkness and pulled out a stone. It was larger than a man's fist, almost potato shaped. One end was jagged and almost pointed. None of this immediately registered with Vick or Cain.

They both, however, did take notice that it was sparkily and as clear as glass. Vick stared at the stone as light from the lantern reflected through it. The multicolored light was bouncing all around them, and onto the walls and ceiling of the cave shedding more light. They had never seen anything so brilliant as the stone Vick held in his hand. They were pure and blinding.

"This is how they did it," said Vick. "This is what they used to carve into these stone walls...wait a minute!"

Vick set the stone on the ground and picked up a nearby rock, a hunk of granite the size of a large watermelon, and raised it over his head.

"Pa, what are you doing? Don't!"

Never flinching Vick hurled it down with all his might onto the clear stone beneath. As the stones collided, the echo was deafening. The granite stone burst into pieces and fell away, leaving the clear stone from the pit virtually unscathed.

"Son, I knew it. Bring the lantern here." With the light from the lantern they could clearly see the pit was filled with at least 50 other luminating stones; none of them smaller than a man's fist.

Pa, is this their treasure?

"Cain. These are tools. This was their greatest treasure...their tools...they did not value the diamonds for what they were, but what they could do."

"I've never seen or heard tell of a diamond this big. It must be worth a fortune, and there are about 50 of them," Cain remarked.

"Son, these are the tools of communication to pass on knowledge to future generations. There's only one stone hard enough to carve into these granite walls, and that's a diamond.

Vick knelt and pulled one stone after another from the pit. Some were more sharply pointed than others. Some were more flat and broad, as if to be used as a hammer or axe. All were uncut, but there was no hiding their refracted gleam when the light hit them.

"This is their legacy, the tools with which to teach their descendants all their knowledge and wisdom." Vick pointed at different places on the wall. "Where to plant...where to hunt...how to raise a boy. There are many generations of knowledge on these walls. And it's all these diamonds that made it possible. This is what that panther has been guarding...until now. Now it's up to us."

"Well, what are we supposed to do?" asked Cain.

"Good question, replied Vick, as he moved back to the wall with the symbols he knew represented him. He began reading again; trying to unveil answers to their questions.

"After many years of bondage the great Chief's will come together...and they will build great cities..." Vick stopped and looked around the cave. He then spoke slowly, "Cain this is very interesting, but before this destiny can come to be, all these guidelines have to be followed. And all this bloodline will be empowered...with enlightenment."

"Pa, you can see all this in these carvings?"

No one is more surprised than me. "Like I read a hand of cards. It's their language, their written language, and don't ask me how, but I know it...I surely do."

Vick looked back to the wall, then returned the diamonds to the pit. "For now, we leave it all here. Somehow, someway, we'll know when and what to do next." Vick then flipped the large flat stone back over the opening and kicked dirt over it.

"How do we know it'll be safe here? What if someone finds it?" asked Cain.

"Oh, that ain't gonna happen. Look there." Vick pointed to a carving right above the tiny cave opening where they entered. It was a carving of a panther sitting, sphinx-like, watchful, and on guard.

"I was wrong about the panther being gone, I know it sounds crazy, but I'm guessing he knows when he needs to be here. And I have a feeling he will be around for a long time."

The implication gave Cain an eerie feeling. "Pa, how long ago do you think these carvings were done?"

"No tellin'… hundreds, maybe thousands of years ago."

Cain pointed at the panther carving.

"There's no way that panther could have been—

Vick cut him off. "We both know that's no ordinary panther, Son. Let's just leave it at that."

"Let's git on outta here."

As they mounted their horses, Cain heard his father's voice, gentle and friendly.

"Well, there you are," he seemed to say with a sense of accomplishment and contentment.

Cain eyed his father looking up into the sky as the lonesome hawk circled high above them.

"I wondered where you had gotten to," he continued.

"Look Pa", pointing to the top of the waterfall. Vick looked and saw the magnificent panther sitting stoically over the crest of the falls, watching them.

Vick hollerred out, as if to an old friend, "We'll be back! Not sure when! You watch over things! Thank you!"

"So you're talking to animals now, Pa?"

Vick chuckled warmly, "Am I?"

That night, Vick and Cain bedded down at the old scout camp. After a quick supper and Cain's many questions, (all of which Vick answered with, "I don't know" or "we'll know soon," or even "we'll know when we need to know".) Vick nodded off immediately and slept better than he had for years.

As he slept,

Once again, Vick saw the hawk waft down through the midst and settle on the ground before him; the same hawk he'd come to know so well. Slowly the hawk began to change into his childhood friend, Chaytan.

He commanded Vick to listen to the Great Ancestral Spirit. At last, Vick was about to understand why his dreams were beleaguered with so many manifestations.

"Vick, my son, the Spirits of Old have summoned you here." Hawk stood before him with the reverence and dignity of a brave warrior. Vick stood frozen, and in complete awe at Hawk's resplendent countenance. But one thing puzzled him. Why did Hawk refer to him as "son"?

"Come, and do not be afraid." Hawk beckoned him with outstretched arms. Out of respect, Vick walked toward him, and listened to the Spirit explain:

"Many years ago, you were chosen because of your devotion and respect for our people and our customs. "We once had great trade with the white man, but after many moons, white man killed our buffalo and seized our land. People of our villages were murdered, and our women and children had no one to care for them. We did what we could to protect ourselves, taking what we could to survive. Our enemies tricked our people, robbed us, and after many deaths, we knew we could no longer trust them."

Vick was trying to digest what he was hearing. As the thoughts filled his mind, he was reassured that he was the chosen one to deliver the great treasure.

"You have proven yourself. When you fought against the Great Panther, we knew you were the chosen one to help us. You share the blood of your mother and our people."

Vick wondered why his Pa never told him of his mother's heritage, and that he and his brother Sam were half Indian. He continued to listen as the Spirit answered more questions.

"Your mother was one of us, and this is why Hawk rescued you and Sam as children, so you would become a great warrior".

As Vick tried to understand, a huge panorama of events flashed before his eyes.

In one scene, he saw himself and Sam as young boys tied to a twenty-foot rope, with their father walking away and leaving them. There were scenes showing his father mistreating them, depicting the hunger, pain and sadness they suffered. He watched his entire life, from a boy to his present age, unfold before him over the watchful eye of Hawk.

It was then that the miracle occurred. As Hawk stepped forward, another metamorphous took place. Vick could hardly believe what he was seeing for the boy who was known as Hawk became taller, his hair longer, as he transformed into a beautiful Indian woman; a squaw with a gentle and tender nature, yet strong of spirit and will. Vick was bewildered as his memories of his mother resurfaced. This Indian woman is my mother, came Vick's epiphany. He did not quite understand, but somehow it didn't matter. All he knew that Hawk had been his mother and he was very happy to see her.

"It was you all the time," Vick said with such tenderness. You were Hawk my friend when Sam and me were boys.

"Yes, my son, I have always been with you. You boys needed me to care for you. It was I, and not Hawk, who loosened the ropes that bound you boys. It was I who took you into the forest and played with you and your brother. Vick was privileged to see the many times his mother saved them from a life of loneliness. It was not Hawk, a young Indian boy, but his mother that would run and play with them, who loved them when they needed love, brought them food when they were hungry, and quilts to cover them when they were cold. His mother had always been there watching over them.

Vick then witnessed his greatest test of all—the twenty years in a harsh and evil prison. He watched in horror as he saw the beatings administered to him as a prisoner that severely tested his mental strength. He marveled at his shrewdness when he was forced to gamble. Many times, he had to win just to stay alive. All these events established Vick as a warrior in the eyes of his ancestors.

As Vick's dream continued, he understood that in mortality, it was meant for him to suffer hardship, disappointment, death of loved ones, and finally, to become the warrior in his ancestors' eyes. All these misfortunes, and his responses, enabled Vick's personal growth, which would lead him to achieve greatness.

His ancestors knew that Vick was chosen to discover the great treasure, but it was made known to him that this cannot happen until all the great tribes of the original people come together in thought and deed. Vick wondered if it would happen in his lifetime.

Once again, Vick was miraculously standing on top of a mountain, but this time he was dressed in a multi-colored robe, which signified royalty of his people.

"I will always be with you," his mother said.

Vick watched as his mother slowly transformed back into a hawk. From the campfire below billows of smoke appeared, and quickly took on the faces many Indians whom had died by the hands of their enemies. He watched as these souls were carried upward on a breeze, higher in the sky, as if Vick was called upon to free them. Many of these souls were those who died on the "trial of tears". He knew these were the ghosts of valiant Indians who had lived before his time and who had suffered many hardships.

Vick continued to watch the great warriors dance to the rhythmic chants and drumbeats that were celebrating him. Once again the great hawk circled above and around him. He sensed it would be the last time.

The next morning when Vick awoke, Cain was already dressed and saddled, sitting by the fire watching his father.

"Pa I didn't have the heart to wake you."

Vick nodded then rose from his bedroll. "I understand this now. All of it, even the parts that don't make sense." Quickly changing the subject, Vick said, "Son I'm ready to go home. I miss my wife."

"Pa, do you think you'll ever return to Panther Holler?"

"I really don't know. I suppose we'll have to wait and see."

The secret of the knowledge of the original people may be still waiting until the time comes to deliver the treasure of their ancient knowledge to the original people for their resurgence of glory.

There are legends in the hills of Arkansas; legends of boys becoming hawks and of panthers bearing the souls of great warriors. Some say black panthers don't exist, that they're the stuff of legends and lore. But some say the veil that lies between the world we see and a world we choose not to understand, is far thinner than we could ever imagine.

There is a legend of a great secret that is being held far beneath the deep running waters of the Ozarks. There the secret of completion and redemption is being held till the time has come, when the wisdom of the ages will be returned to the original people, the givers and guardians of a place called Panther Holler.

"Seek not this place. Seek not disturbance of the Ghost of Panther Holler."

Pre-Cherokee Legend

About the Author

Annie Clark Cole lives north of Houston Texas, with her husband, Jim Cole a retired Military pilot, American Airlines Captain and FAA Training Center Program Manager.

Prior to discovering her love for writing, Annie had a successful career in wholesale/retail clothing. She was also a Flight Attendant with American Airlines and the owner of a popular Antique and Gift store in Montgomery, Texas.

Annie and her husband Jim have 3 children between them. They also have 3 grand daughters and soon to be three great-grand children. Annie and Jim's two poodles are a writer and pilot's greatest companions.

Coming Attractions

CAJUN FIRE 2016

RETURN FROM PANTHER HOLLER 2017or 2018
Part of the Panther Holler series
.

Check website— Annieclarkcole.com for updates.
To contact Annie Clark Cole by email Annieclarkcole@gmail.com
To purchase Ghost of Panther Holler contact Amazon.com
If you are looking for an autograph copy contact her by email.
Annieclarkcole@gmail.com

Made in the USA
Charleston, SC
06 October 2015